GENERATIONS

DARK NEBULA
BOOK 3

SEAN WILLSON

WELCOME TO DARK NEBULA

Thank you for buying this book!

If you're interested in a free novella entitled **Dark Nebula: Contact**, hearing more about the series, seeing new cover art as it's released, or getting exclusive access to sales as they happen, then you can subscribe to my newsletter online at:

seanwillson.com/subscribe

You can also drop me an email at:

author@seanwillson.com

I always love hearing from my readers.

DARK NEBULA SERIES
Novella: Contact (FREE)
Book 1: Isolation
Book 2: Discovery
Book 3: Generations (This book)
Book 4: Beacon
Book 5: Graveyard
Book 6: Nursery

PORTAL SERIES
Book 1: Drowning Earth
Books 2-4: Coming Soon…

CONTENTS

HAROLD OLIVAW

SOL, EARTH — 2036

The harsh Antarctic wind buffeted his yurt, rattling the equipment he'd unpacked hours before. Harold hadn't slept in days. He'd been waiting on the ship to arrive with his equipment, and now that it was here he'd been stymied at every turn by this blasted storm.

His equipment arrived at port a few days ago. The original crew had cancelled the supply drop at their base camp due to a severe melt-off having created a temporary river between the port and his base of operations. Fortunately, the same storm that was keeping him from working blew in and iced over the melt-off river.

He slipped some dock-men a few thousand dollars to deliver everything during the break in the storm. Their union rules and OSHA prevented them from putting themselves in harm's way during a storm of this category. After a few hours of banter in a local pub, it became obvious that the workers preferred their regular income over the temporary layoff pay. While unions usually ruled the roost in these parts during the U.N. land rush, money could move even that historically stubborn mountain.

A few years back, the United Nations opened up drilling

and land expansion in Antarctica. It was a last-ditch attempt to help fund their space programs. They seemed to be doing everything they could to get humans off the planet. There was no doubt the influx of money was helping research colonies on the moon, the concern was more whose pockets the money was making it into. There was also the small matter of humans destroying one of the last pristine places on our planet.

Six years into the land expansion, and the years of red tape it used to take to gain access to this continent were a thing of the past. His father would bore him to sleep with yarns about how it'd taken him over a year to plan a trip here. And don't get him started about all the new fangled cold weather gear they had to make things easier. If he had to hear one more story about parkas, frostbite, and darkness, he'd scream.

Fast forward to today, and Harold had his base camp setup, but he still couldn't use the equipment yet. This storm was slowing his plans even more than the unions. At least he'd been able to check most of it over. Nothing appeared to have been damaged in transit, so he had that.

He glanced around the yurt. His cot was on the far back wall, and except for a workstation next to it, the room was packed to the gills with crates. He'd traded his comfortable office at the University of Michigan for an Antarctic cold storage closet.

"Cut the negative thoughts, Olivaw," he muttered as he shook his head. "You wanted to save humanity. Now's your chance. Make a difference!"

A huge wind gust slammed the yurt and the steel supports creaked in response. He hoped those directions he'd followed with the dock-men to build this thing were correct or he wouldn't make it through the night. Two of them were Ushuaia locals and had been doing this for decades. They threw this structure together like it was a pup tent. The whole time they'd been building his camp, they were waxing on about how volatile the weather had been the last few years. Rapid freezing and melt offs made for a hell of a rough place to survive, let alone thrive.

He tilted his ear upward. A faint chime echoed beneath the rumble of the wind. He searched the circular room, listening if the sound was coming from any of the crates until he realized it was from his workstation.

"Shit!" He leapt across the room, ripped off his glove, and touched the fingerprint scanner to unlock the screen. He hit accept just in time to see his wife shaking her head.

"Wait! Are you still there?" he shouted. "Marie!"

"Yes… I'm here," Marie replied with a wide-eyed smile. "I thought I'd missed you again. I've been trying to connect for days. You had me worried, love. How are you doing? You look like you're freezing."

He smiled from ear to ear. "It's great to hear your voice and see your beautiful face. It's fraking cold here." He laughed and rubbed his gloveless hand against the other gloved one.

She chuckled and shook her head. "I told you."

"I know, I know. I finally got set up, but this blasted storm—"

A massive Antarctic gust slammed his yurt like a freight train, and everything rattled. The entrance door suddenly flew open, and the resulting open doorway gave the gale force wind something to breach. The storm's icy tendrils reached inward and lifted the yurt, throwing it hundreds of meters skyward into the darkness.

He lurched forward to grab the laptop before it blew away, but he was too late. It went tumbling into the night.

"Nooo!" he screamed. This wasn't happening.

The satellite backup phone was hanging from a nearby crate. He leaned to the side and grabbed it just as another gust whistled past. He shoved it into his parka and ducked down to the ground. Shivers echoed up his spine as the cold rolled up his exposed sleeve. He reached into his pocket and pulled out his other glove, quickly putting it on.

He curled into a ball for a minute to make sure any flying debris didn't hit him.

What was he thinking coming here alone? He should've waited until his entire team arrived before rushing to set up base camp.

"Shit," he muttered, but he couldn't hear his own voice over the roar of the icy wind.

The blasts of cold air were relentless, and now without a roof it was hard to even stand between gusts.

He closed his eyes and brought his hands upward to cover his mouth. When he cupped and blew into them, he could direct the warm breath toward his exposed face. He had to find his goggles. Without them, he wasn't going anywhere fast.

Earlier, he'd hung them from the central pole holding up the yurt's roof. Tilting his head into the wind, he thought he could make out the silhouette of the beam. One of the lanterns he'd placed on top of a nearby crate had blown over and was lying on its side on the ground. It partially illuminated the sky, highlighting the snow flying past in the sideways gale as it tore through the previously enclosed space.

He turned and crawled on all fours toward the pole and then reached up, feeling into the darkness for the hook. He found its cold steel surface, but the goggles were long gone.

"Frak!" He couldn't catch a break. Without face protection, he was done for.

He slammed his fist onto the ground. "Think, think," he muttered. Did he have another pair somewhere?

The clothing supply crate! There were at least a dozen in there. Where had they put that crate? He closed his eyes, trying to remember a few hours earlier. He and the dock-men rush unloaded the Bandvagn they'd used to haul his equipment to base camp.

They were by the entrance. He'd specifically asked them to place those crates near the door to ease the unloading. He turned to the left and crawled into the darkness toward where the entry had previously been. A few meters later and his head bumped into a crate.

The wind was freezing the moisture from his eyes, and crystals were building up on his face. He didn't have much time. Using the back of his hand, he wiped away the collecting ice.

The clothing crate should be on the opposite side of this one. He waited a second for the next gust to blow. Once it had passed, he grasped the crate, pulled upward, and leaned over it. Trying to use its mass to not be blown over, he slid his feet around the other side, all the while he clutched the crate with every ounce of his strength.

There on the ground was the tub of Arctic gear. With one hand, he held the lid down, and with the other, he carefully pried an edge up while he shoved his other hand in. He was pretty sure. Yep, right on top.

Harold yanked out one of the carbon fiber full face goggles, threw back his hood, and slid it over his head. He checked that his balaclava was a tight fit and then pulled his hood into place. He then tested the fixtures on the hood and made certain all the gaps were closed.

His face was feeling warmer by the second as the heating unit sensed his skin and kicked in. Now what? There was no way he could walk anywhere in this storm. He'd be dead in under an hour. Building a tent wasn't an option, let alone finding one. He hadn't unloaded the snowmobile yet... wait, that was it.

He dropped on all fours and crawled over to the lantern lying in the snow. Grabbing it with one hand, he slid with the other hand across the ground toward his bed. His backpack was lying where the cot had previously been. The wind must've picked it up when the yurt sailed away.

He set the lantern on the ice, grasped the backpack, and threw it over his shoulder. The straps clicked shut at the chest and waist. He pulled out the excess slack, making certain it was solid against his torso. There was no sense in letting the wind get between him and the pack; he'd turn into a sail for sure.

Dropping onto all fours again, he grabbed the lantern and strapped it into the webbing of the backpack. He then carefully made his way out of where the yurt was and headed toward the pile of crates they'd left nearby. About five meters away was a low plastic dome he'd shoveled about thirty minutes' worth of snow over.

It was the one thing he'd done himself and followed the directions on. He crawled around the opposite side and then rose up onto his knees. Grabbing the handle, he pulled, but not too hard. He didn't need it ripping off in the wind. It opened without much effort, and he shuffled inside, pulling the door closed behind him.

With the exit latched, he crawled through the enclosure to the far side and turned around, resting his back against the wall and snuggling up against the snowmobile. A gust of wind howled outside, barely vibrating the low dome.

He took a deep breath and sighed. All he could do now was wait. He shouldn't have been in such a hurry to get started. He should've waited a few more days for his team.

Keeping warm was his number one priority, or he'd be dead by morning. While this shed was protected from the wind, it wasn't heated and was surrounded by snow. It was essentially an icebox inside an icebox.

Fortunately for him, Marie was a stickler for planning. He unzipped his backpack and shoved his hand all the way to the bottom, pulling out a packet of rechargeable warming bricks. His wife made a point to charge each of them before he left. She'd called it her contribution to his comfort.

He opened his coat, turned one of the units on, and slid it into his inside pocket. He then activated a smaller one and put it into his snow pants.

Now he needed to wait. He clicked off the lantern to conserve the battery and then leaned back, snuggling into the corner.

The shed fell silent. All that remained was the soft sound of the wind buffeting into and over the mound of snow he was now nestled within.

He squeezed his eyes closed and counted the seconds between each blast of wind. They were random. This wasn't like thunder. You couldn't count the time between gusts to determine distance. He passed the moments counting them anyhow. What else did he have to do? Besides, the bursts were soothing, and time was going to crawl waiting for this storm to pass.

HAROLD ROLLED to his side and hit his head against a ski.

"Shit," he muttered. That's going to leave a mark.

He reached up and rubbed the side of his head, and his gloved hand hit the hood of his parka. He'd forgotten where he was.

The events from the previous evening came rushing back. He was still in the snowmobile shed. Bringing his wrist up, he pulled his glove down and checked the time. He'd been asleep for nearly eight hours.

The warmers would be good for another four hours before he'd need to swap them out. He reached over and turned the lantern on. The shadow from the Arctic Cat snowmobile cast an eerie outline against the side of the shed.

His stomach rumbled in complaint. He hadn't eaten in

over twelve hours, and even that was only a quick snack before they arrived at the site. He reached into his backpack and pulled out an energy bar. Tearing it open, he took a huge bite and leaned against the wall.

In between the crunches from his chewing, he could hear a muffled noise of what sounded like running water.

What the hell?

He grabbed a flashlight from his backpack, leaned forward, and opened the shed's hatch. The light shined into the darkness of the eternal night of Antarctica.

"Six months of dark they said. Help us investigate if we can expand our geothermal operation in Antarctica they said." He chuckled. At least he'd have a few hours of sunlight today.

The beam of light from his flashlight cut through the blackness. He panned it around the area surrounding the shed but didn't see the source of the noise.

The rush of water was louder now with the door open. It sounded less like a faucet and more like the flow of a river.

"Don't tell me," he muttered as he scrambled out of the shed. He directed the beam toward the other side of the snow pile and sure enough, the source of the turbulence was right there.

The ice river had melted. How the hell had it thawed in eight hours?

He stepped around the squat shed and there it was. A river of water was coursing by, except instead of flowing into the distance, it fell over the edge of a sinkhole where his yurt had been hours before.

It wasn't a deep hole. Maybe only five meters. What made it interesting wasn't how deep it was, but what was in it.

He cast his flashlight over the pile of rubble that was the remains of his crates and equipment. It was lying atop something oblong, about three meters in length, and jet black. The light from his flashlight wasn't reflecting off the surface.

Instead, the light seemed to just stop, failing to illuminate the mysterious object.

"That's strange," he muttered.

SEVERAL HOURS LATER, Harold had extracted the snowmobile from the shed and used the winch to lower himself into the gap in the ice. He hooked up the cable and was preparing to use the same winch to pull the oblong black object up and out.

Inspecting the object in the hole wasn't an option. The threat of being washed away by the icy river was sorta in the front of his mind.

It was light for something that was quite a bit longer than he was tall. He gunned the snowmobile, thinking he'd have trouble pulling it up. Instead, the oblong object shot up and out of the icy crater and glided across the snow. Had he not turned hard to the left, it would've crashed into him.

He leapt off the snowmobile and watched the dark object come to rest about ten meters away. It barely left a trail in the snow, it was so light. He cautiously stepped toward it, directing his flashlight like a gun into the dark. His mind was playing tricks on him, like the object would somehow come to life and leap toward him after being buried under the Antarctic ice for who knows how long.

"Relax," he said aloud. "It's been buried down there a long time." While his habit of talking to himself was annoying to most people, it was comforting in times like this when he was all alone.

He grabbed his satellite phone out of his pocket and started recording some footage. Might as well have a permanent record of whatever this thing was. For posterity reasons, and you know, in case he disappeared.

That's curious. The camera wasn't focusing. He took off

his glove and tapped at the screen. It wouldn't focus on the object.

The snow, yep.

The snowmobile, yep.

The mysterious black object, nope.

He held his hand at arm's length and focused the camera there, locking it at that distance. Finally, he turned it toward the object and walked along its length, shining both the camera light and the flashlight in the same direction.

"It's absolute black," he said as he began narrating what he was seeing. "I've never seen anything like it. That's strange—"

He held up his palm and pointed the camera at it. "My hands aren't cold. It's like… no. It can't be."

Pointing the camera back at the object, he reached his hand forward toward it. The surface was smooth and cool. It didn't make any sense. There was a warm air around it, but it was cold to the touch.

Whatever this thing was, it wasn't a piece of driftwood, a rock, or a random chunk of metal. He walked back to the snowmobile and pulled it closer to the object, directing its headlight at it. He then propped his camera on the windshield to record himself.

Walking to the object, he started inspecting it. "I wrapped the strap around this segment. It caught on this ridge here. I can feel it, but I can't see it. Watch my hand." He slid his hands all the way around the object. It disappeared into the blackness of the ridge.

He felt along the surface until he got to the tip. "Oh, interesting. The front, if that's what this is, it's covered with multiple concave depressions. Wait, I wonder what would happen if…"

He reached down and dusted snow over the surface and sure enough, you could just make out the depressions. "Now they're visible."

The rush of the nearby water had been growing louder and louder. He hadn't noticed it at first, but he looked up when a thunderous crash echoed through the darkness. The wall of the depression he'd pulled the object out of had caved in and the river was expanding.

He had to get out of here. He could check this thing out later. Right now, he had to focus on getting to safety. But what was he going to do with this thing?

THIRTY MINUTES later Harold was flying across the Antarctic snowscape with a squat white shed in tow behind him. He'd slid the oblong object inside and packed it to the gills with anything he could find from what was left of the base camp. He didn't really care what he'd used to pack it, but he might as well make it look like he'd tried to salvage something. What was more important was keeping the object concealed from prying eyes.

He didn't know why, but this thing felt… important. He'd never heard about or seen anything like it. Before he was going to show it to anyone, he wanted more time to check it over himself.

Now if he could just find a way to get it halfway around the globe to his workshop in Michigan. He couldn't trust the dockworkers again, not after they may have sabotaged his base camp. The environmentalists down here weren't taking too kindly to the change in regulations and the gold rush mentality of the new arrivals, even the scientists.

HAROLD ZIPPED his parka closed and pulled the hood on. He then threw his pack on and walked down the gangplank.

Dry land was on the other side. That and a host of trepidation and uncertainty.

Had he imagined the entire event in Antarctica? He woke in a sweat several times over his multi-week voyage thinking just that thought. He'd mulled over what had happened; playing and replaying the events in his mind. It didn't feel real.

All he had to show for the trip was a crate full of random salvaged equipment neatly packaged into a three-meter space. He'd went through countless customs' scans and each one was as nail-biting as the last. He thought for sure someone would find something.

A week back, when he'd first hit the United States in Flor-ida, he'd followed his crate through customs. The agent was confused, and he was pretty sure his presence set her off. She asked him to crack open the crate.

He was done for; he knew it. "Why?" he'd asked. "Was something the matter?"

She shrugged her shoulder and tilted her head. "There's an anomaly on my scan, and I need to check it out. It'll only take a few moments." She was watching his reaction, gauging his response.

"Sure thing," he smiled. His heart rate shot up. She'd figured it out. How the hell was he going to explain this object buried in the bottom?

He walked down both sides and carefully unlatched all the locks while he studied her. "Can you help me lift the lid? It's pretty light."

"I shouldn't," she said, glancing around cautiously. "My boss would kill me. Union and all."

He gulped. "Ok, no worries. Watch your toes." He grasped the lid and pulled it the long way away from her, rather than sideways. This way, maybe he could more easily get it back on and she'd have less to look at if he only showed her one end.

He pulled off about half of the lid and then walked around the side where she was standing. "Where's the point in the crate that's red flagging?"

She raised her tablet and pointed about a quarter of the way down the length of the crate. There was a bundle of wires that had slid down inside. It must have been from the geothermal scanning equipment he'd collected from the salvageable crates.

"Oh, that's—"

"Let me have a look-see," she interrupted. She held her scanner out and walked along the open crate, looking over the edge as she went. Clothes, sleeping bags, ice augers, laptops, and a host of other random crap. "Where are you coming from?"

"Antarctica," he replied.

The agent turned and eyed him up and down. "Should have guessed from the garb, I suppose. Where ya headed?"

He stared downward at his snow parka and boots. Not exactly Florida apparel. "Ann Arbor, Michigan, after we dock in Detroit. I've got a week before I arrive, but I need to transfer to another vessel first."

The agent leaned over the side of the crate, and his heart skipped a beat. This was it, he was done for. She reached in, pulled aside a dense packing of snow shoes, arctic face gear, and some boots until finally she grasped something and tried to pull. It wouldn't give.

"Do you need some help?"

"I've got it!" She gave him a side eyed glance. "Please keep your distance."

She set her tablet on the top of the nearby crate lid and leaned over with both arms. Her feet were up off the ground and he swore she was going to fall in. She grasped something and then leaned back.

"Got it," she muttered as she pivoted her weight back-ward and yanked up on whatever she was searching for. In her hands she held the remains of the satellite dish they'd had outside the yurt to get better reception.

He chuckled.

"This little bugger was messing up my scans." She grabbed her device and waved it over the top. "Yep, see here." She pointed at the screen. The concave dish had a strange reflection signature on her scanner. It didn't look at all like its actual shape.

"That's weird," he said. "I hadn't noticed that in Antarctica when we left or at the port in Argentina."

"It must've repositioned during the voyage. No worries. I just wanted to make sure you weren't using some of that new anti scanning blanketing we've been seeing more of. It comes up with black holes in the scans. We can't see anything. Sorta that blackness you see here in the middle of this dish. Anyhow, you're good to go."

She tossed the dish into the crate and walked away.

The screech of tires brought him back to the here and now. He stopped at the bottom of the ramp and stepped backward as the doors to a red Ford F-150 with a flatbed trailer attached flew open. His wife Marie came running around the front toward him.

"You made it!" she hollered. "I was so worried."

She collided into him with an enormous bear hug and buried her head into his chest. He leaned down and kissed the top of her head. "I'm so happy to see you. It was only a few boat rides, though. Nothing to get all worked up over."

She glanced up at his face and batted her palm against his chest. "Your Antarctic accident, you twit! You almost died out there on the ice. You haven't been yourself the few times we've talked. I'm sorry, I was worried." Tears were rolling down her cheeks.

"Hey, hey. I'm sorry. I'm fine. Really, I am." He brought his hands up to the side of her face. "Honest!" He kissed her again.

She sniffled and wiped the tears from her eyes. "Sorry. I seem to cry at the drop of a hat these days. Did everything go ok? Tell me again why you couldn't just fly home from Florida?"

He put his arm around her and they turned to walk toward the truck. A smile crept across his face. "It's a long story. I'll tell you when we get home. First thing's first. We need to head over to customs and pick up my crate."

HE PULLED the door to his pole barn closed. The crate was safely positioned in the center of the room, and he'd setup all the lights he could find in a circle surrounding it.

Marie sighed. "Now can you tell me what the big deal is? I'm starved."

"Rather than tell you, I'll show you." Harold walked around the crate, unlatched the lid, and pulled it off. It dropped to the ground with a thunk, and a cloud of dust rose from behind the crate. He then came around toward her and unlatched the side panel. It crashed to the ground and everything inside spilled out onto the dusty floor.

"Yikes!" She stepped back as the contents fell toward her, cascading around her feet. "I could've helped you unload it. Aren't you worried about breaking something?"

"Breaking what?" His eyes locked on the black object still ensconced in the crate, draped with layers of arctic gear. There it was. It wasn't his imagination.

"This stuff!" She was pointing at the equipment surrounding her feet on the ground.

He glanced down at her feet, partially covered with a sleeping roll and some tundra gear. "Oh, sorry. I was... just. I wasn't sure it was real. That I'd actually seen it. I was beginning to think it was a dream." He sighed. "Which is funny because I haven't slept in days. It's—"

She walked up next to him and raised her hand to his cheek, turning his face toward her. "What's wrong? You're scaring me again, sweetie."

Her expression made the pit in his stomach tighten. She was really freaked out. "Ok, I have to be honest. Something happened in Antarctica."

Her eyes widened and she tilted her head. "What? What happened? You're standing here in one piece, so it couldn't have been that bad."

"So I was in my usual hurry to get going. You know what I mean. I wanted to get a head start building base camp before the team arrived. I couldn't stand another night in that hotel. Anyhow, I threw around some of the University's cash and hired a few dock-men to take me to the site. It was slow-going in the storm, and I'm pretty sure a few of them weren't natives because their yurt building skills sucked. Either that or they—"

"Wait… you purposely went into the storm? I thought you said—"

"They were telling me it could be a week. I wanted to get started." He waved his hand. "Don't worry about that, just listen. That's not the weird part."

She sighed and crossed her arms.

He cleared his throat and proceeded to tell her about the storm, using the university's money to hire a new crew, the ice melt river, falling asleep in the snowmobile shed, and the black object he found. His words were pouring forth unabated, like the ice water that had nearly killed him.

"Hey, hey. Slow down, Harold. Slow down. Catch your breath."

"Sorry," he stammered. He hadn't realized it, but he'd been getting excited ever since he opened the crate. His heart was pounding in his chest.

"Ok, back to the freaking me out part." She was staring up into his eyes. Trying to get him to say something again.

"This'd be easier if you saw it."

"I wasn't there. I can't—"

He reached up and placed his hand against her cheek and turned it toward the crate. She hadn't looked inside it yet. She'd been focused on the trash that spilled out.

There, in the center, was the oblong black object he'd recovered from the ice.

She leaned down and squinted. "Is… it a torpedo?"

"No. I mean, I don't think so." He glanced at her and then back toward the object. "I hadn't thought about that. But I'm pretty sure it's not."

"What is it then?" She kicked some equipment out of the way and cleared off part of the object for a better look.

He reached up and rubbed the stubble on his face. "I don't know. That's what I need to figure out."

"I'm hungry," she said.

"You're… hungry? I bring you a mysterious, possibly alien, object all the way from Antarctica and your response is 'I'm hungry'?" He chuckled and shook his head.

She reached over and took his hand in hers, pulling it back to her stomach. "I have my reasons. I'm sorta eating for two now."

He turned toward her and his eyes went wide. "No! Really?"

"Yes!" she said, nodding. Tears were streaming down her face again.

"Really, really?" He brought his other hand up to her stomach and stared down.

"Yes, really, really."

He stared into her eyes and smiled. Reaching up, he wiped away the tears and kissed her.

OLIVAW LINEAGE
THRU 2070

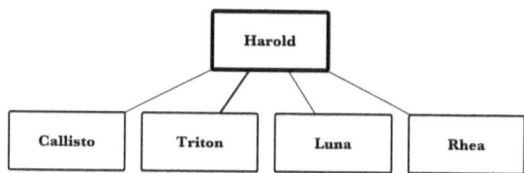

Key

Head of Family

HAROLD OLIVAW
SOL, EARTH — 2070

Callisto turned around. "Was that a tractor we just passed?" She craned her neck to peer at the farm implement receding into the distance. "Come on, Dad. Tell me where you're taking me." She spun back around and her dark brown hair fluttered around her head like a helicopter. Her Olivaw blue eyes were studying him, struggling to pry away the truth.

Harold leaned back in the seat, reclined flat, and then closed his eyes. "We'll be there in a few minutes. You'll find out soon enough."

"Did you buy a farm or something?" Callisto asked. "I told mom she should watch where you've been disappearing to all these years. I figured it was gambling, but apparently it was far less nefarious."

He chuckled. "I'm sorry I disappointed you. If it matters, this place we're heading is worth way more than a farm. And besides, the coast is only a few miles from here. We'll pick up your mother from the Charlotte pier and grab a bite to eat later tonight."

She reached out and poked his leg. "Seriously, where are we going?"

The ground car slowed and turned into the parking lot of a small squat glass building. The sign out front said 'Olivaw' and had their company's trademarked 'O' logo. It traced eight three-dimensional planetary paths around the sun.

"Arrived at destination," said the voice of the ground car. "Olivaw International. 8660 Love Mill Road, Stanfield, North Carolina."

"We're here!" Harold sat up and scanned the parking lot. "And everyone's already here. Perfect."

"Since when did we have an office in Stanfield? Wait, is this where you always disappear to when you send me off to schmooze with our new customers and inspect our manufacturing facilities?"

"Maybe," he smirked. "I don't tell you everything. Well... I'm about to, but I didn't used to." He leaned forward and placed his palm on the dash and his door opened.

"What does that mean?" Callisto rested her hand on her father's arm.

"Come inside. It's easier if you see it instead of me explaining it. Besides, I hear Auntie Tina made some fresh muffins." Harold slid out of the car and his door closed behind him.

He walked to the curb and turned back toward her. She hadn't gotten out. "Are you coming or are you taking the car back to Charlotte Douglas?"

Callisto raised her hands and mouthed 'Aunt Tina?' at her father. She shook her head and leaned forward, touching the dash. Hopping out of the ground car, she laid into him. "When were you going to tell me Aunt Tina was here?"

Harold smiled and raised his arm toward the building entrance. "All mysteries shall be revealed inside."

"Grr!" She huffed as she stormed past him.

CALLISTO OLIVAW
SOL, EARTH — 2070

They walked side by side into the building. Instead of being greeted by a receptionist, the lobby was empty. Callisto spun around and studied the simplistic dark glass windows, exposed carbon fiber, and black quartz that filled the space. The only technology she could discern was a modest security pad on the far wall that was glowing blue.

Harold walked toward the glowing pad and placed his hand on the panel.

The door locks clicked, and the windowed lobby suddenly became opaque. A voice aloud spoke. "Harold Olivaw, identity confirmed. All parties present must be authenticated."

He stepped aside and faced Callisto.

She glanced from the pad, toward her father, and then back to the pad. Why was he being so secretive about this place? Walking forward, her heels made a clicking noise with each step across the quartz floor. The echo felt odd bouncing through the cramped space.

She raised her hand and rested it on the smooth black surface.

"Callisto Olivaw, identity confirmed. Thank you and have a nice day."

A noise clicked and the quartz wall panel in front of them slid inward. Warm white light spilled out from the small hidden inner chamber.

She stared at her father. "Is all this cloak and dagger really necessary?"

He gestured into the chamber. "You'll find out once we're inside."

"Seriously? You still can't tell me." She sighed and walked in.

It was a two-by-two meter room and like the lobby; it was eerily empty. She walked in and stopped shy of the wall. She half expected the other side to open when she approached, but it hadn't. *He's joking, right?*

"I have to hand it to you, Dad. You sure know how to wow someone." She turned to face Harold. "Amazing office you have here."

He smirked and stepped into the chamber. The wall panel slid closed behind him.

"Oh!" Callisto said. She reached her hand toward the wall to keep her balance. The chamber was dropping downward. She wasn't expecting an elevator in a one story building.

"You could have warned me," she muttered.

Harold chuckled. "What fun would that be?"

"So now are you gonna share with me why we bought a secret office in the middle of nowhere North Carolina? Or why we're traveling down from the ground floor of a one story office?" She pushed her hands against opposite walls. This thing wasn't slowing down. "Jeez, how far are we going?"

On cue, the elevator came to rest and the wall panel illuminated with the number one. A second later it slid open.

Before them was a massive workspace filled with instruments as far as the eye could see. The noises of fabrication and heated debate echoed through the space.

"He's here!" shouted a voice. "Ask him. He'll tell you you're wrong."

Harold walked out of the elevator, leaving her behind with her mouth gaping open.

Aunt Tina walked up beside Harold. Her shoulder length black hair framed her clear lensed antique glasses. "Settle a bet. Are we actually in talks with SpaceX to build an Olivaw Lunar habitat? Luna said no, but I said hell to the yea. It's about time we got off this rock."

Callisto came storming out of the elevator. "Wait, what the hell is Luna doing here? She's supposed to be in São Paulo. And Auntie Tina, why the heck didn't you ever tell me about this place?"

Harold glanced back toward Callisto and then toward Tina. "Let's talk in a bit. Short answer though, there's some truth to your conjecture." He gave her a coy smile.

"Hot damn!" Tina exclaimed. "What does that—"

He held up his hand. "I need an hour or so, to bring Callisto up to speed. She's a bit... frustrated and shell-shocked, I think."

"Oh, right. I forgot. Today's the day. Sorry, yea. Let us know when you have time." Tina walked over and gave Callisto a hug. "There're muffins in the kitchen," she whispered in her ear. "Your favorite, chocolate chip."

"What is—" Callisto began.

"Just listen," she said. "It's a lot to take in, but you need to listen. Your dad will explain everything." Tina winked and then walked toward Luna, guiding her away from her sister.

Luna had a smile from ear to ear across her face. "Find me later," she mouthed before she turned and walked toward a nearby conference room with Aunt Tina.

Callisto spun around to face her father.

"Where to begin." He smiled. "Perhaps the very beginning." He pointed to the left, toward what looked like a kitchen area. "We'll walk and talk, if you don't mind. I think better that way."

She nodded and fidgeted with her dress. "Sure," she mumbled.

"Let's grab a muffin before they're gone. Snacks disappear at the speed of light around here." He walked into the kitchen area where there was a huge spread of food, drinks, and coffees available. He grabbed a few napkins and a muffin for each of them and handed one to Callisto.

Leaning against the counter, he took a bite and broke the silence lingering between them. "Do you remember that story your mom and I used to tell you kids when you were little? About my trip to Antarctica."

She tilted her head and squinted. "Yea, of course. You told us before bedtime." She chuckled as she tore off a piece of muffin and popped it into her mouth. "I remember how you both recounted it so differently and how fantastical it was each time."

He chuckled, staring down at the muffin. "I think you'll be surprised when you find out just how much was real." He stepped forward and gestured toward the door. "Let's walk."

They exited the kitchen and meandered through the bustling workspace. She recognized some of the mechanical and material engineers working here from their different facilities around the globe. Her father had hired and culti-vated them over the years.

"Isn't that—" she began.

"Yep. That's Robert Hitz, you met him last month when we were in Alaska. He heads up our material science team. He's been with us going on twenty-five years now."

She paused to watch him. His assistant was aligning something that resembled an electron beam microscope over a jet black plate of some kind. "What's he doing," she gestured around the room, "here?"

"He's using a prototype scanner we're developing to analyze a piece of the first contact probe," Harold said.

She turned and squinted at her father. "The what?"

He smiled. "Remember how I told you I found an antique torpedo in the Antarctic?"

"Yea. Mom used to say it was a munition depot that you'd uncovered and it partially destroyed your base camp." She took another bite of muffin.

Harold waved at Mr. Hitz when he noticed him. "It certainly looked like a torpedo, and that's what we told everyone from U of M. My colleagues weren't relenting, they wanted the details about what happened to me. We had to come up with a good story or I'd lose my job. Hell, I even cashed in part of my 401k to buy some old faulty munitions from a prepper I knew in Kalamazoo. I had to put something in that crate before I returned it to campus."

"Why'd you have to do that? I don't understand."

He took a final bit of muffin and then wiped his hands with the napkin. "I couldn't exactly tell them I'd found a mysterious alien probe in the ice under Antarctica, now could I?"

Her eyes went wide, and she swallowed hard. "An alien what?"

He continued telling her details of what he'd discovered, how he'd gotten it home, and what he'd done in the months following that day. How he'd tore apart their pole barn and practically destroyed it, trying to figure out what the black object was that he'd found.

"It wasn't until I'd borrowed one of the University's plasma nano torches that I really made progress. Your mom thought I was insane bringing that thing home from work. I was desperate though. I had to know. It was eating me up. I hadn't made any progress cracking that thing open." He started walking again, this time faster and more purposeful.

They passed by bay after bay of electronics and pieces of

that same black material under enclosed glass containers. The next room was crammed full of dozens of computer engineers she'd seen in their Brazil office. They were arguing over some gibberish looking code on a wallboard. The neighboring room was littered with countless other materials and mechanical engineering testing contraptions.

"It wasn't until I tried to hit it with our new scanning electron microscope that I noticed some fractures along the side of the probe. Like something had collided with it. The material was malformed and had microscopic tears. That was why I couldn't see any seams. Whatever tore it had to be powerful because we can't seem to dent this damned thing, no matter what we throw at it. Thus the blowing up the first pole barn business I mentioned earlier."

She chuckled. "Wait! You always said a fire damaged those charred shovels and tools in the garage. Was that—"

He nodded with a smile. "Yea, they survived the explosion and melted a smidge in the resulting fire. The fireworks were from me trying to crack the probe open with a bit too much unchecked force."

He placed his hand on the wall next to where they'd stopped. She hadn't even recognized his gesture for all the gawking she'd been doing.

A seamless door slid open. It was like the elevator from earlier, except instead of concealing a smaller chamber, it opened to a far more cavernous one. It was about sixteen by sixteen meters and the ceiling was at least four meters tall. In the center of the space were dozens and dozens of stark white tables on casters. Laid out on each of the clean surfaces was an intricate puzzle of black fragments in a variety of shapes and sizes.

Black panels, wiring harnesses, discs, and conical shapes. It was all there, neatly labeled with pictures of where each piece fit within the whole. Along the back wall was a massive computer display that had fragments of the object called up, and in the middle was a rotating diagram of the probe.

It was beautiful. Its oblong shape was simple yet functional. She walked toward it and stopped at one end. It had multiple concave indentations sprinkled around the tip, sixty-four according to the specs screen.

She bent over and peered down inside the cone. There was a network of impossibly thin connections to strange cube and rectangular boxes that she could only assume were some form of quantum computational mesh or something far more alien. One of the boxes had a label that read "NAV" next to it.

"How do we know this is a navigation component?" she asked.

Harold walked up beside her and tapped on a tablet on the table. A research abstract and references came up. "It's one of the few units we've been able to power up. I don't know if it's a happy accident or not, but when we were finally able to boost the electrical grid out here, we threw some power on it. Needless to say, our sensors went nuts and we blew the feed. The result, though, was astounding." He swiped up on an artifact from the references and its image appeared on the massive back wall screen.

Coordinates and telemetry of some sort covered the wall. There were hundreds of thousands of points with vectors and rates of speed associated with each of them. One in particular was called out in yellow.

She shook her head. "What is this? What am I looking at?"

Harold spoke aloud. "Hal, please turn on all overlays for the coordinate system we're projecting."

"Really, Dad?" She chuckled and shook her head. "Hal?"

"Galactic and spectrum overlays activated," said a voice coming from all around the room.

"What can I say," Harold smiled. "I love me some 2001."

On the wall screen, a three-dimensional view of the Milky Way appeared with different spectral signatures for stars. The points perfectly aligned with each of the dots from the data set.

She opened and then closed her mouth. "So... it's a navigation computer of... our galaxy?" She turned to face her father and reached up, rubbing her eyes. "I don't understand. Why now? Why are you telling me all of this?"

Harold nodded and then pulled a set of chairs out from the workbench in front of them before sitting down, motioning for her to join him.

She studied the chairs and then sat down cautiously. *This couldn't be good if he was asking for her to sit.*

"That's a fair question. Because it's time you knew. I've only told your aunt, your sister Luna, and now you. None of your other siblings know. They're all a part of our company but they're not ready." He reached up and rubbed his chin. "I don't know if they'll ever be ready."

"Ready?" she muttered. "What makes *me* ready and not them?"

"That's simple. You'd believe me, and you'd understand the importance of keeping this a secret. Even one at this scale."

"This scale is absurd!" she shouted as she stood abruptly. "You've been hiding this from us, from everyone, by the looks of it. Why?" She put her hands on her hips and tilted her head.

"You look just like your mother when you do that."

She sighed. "Don't do that, Dad. Don't try to defuse the situation with a joke. I want an answer. I deserve an answer."

Harold stood up. "You want an answer?"

"Yes... please," Callisto lowered her hands from her hips.

Harold walked up toward the wall screen and swiped it, hiding the coordinate projections. He then stared at it for a minute.

She had no idea what he was going to say. This whole

situation was insane. She didn't know how to wrap her mind around the implications of this news.

He finally broke the silence. "I thought I was going insane the first few months I got back from Antarctica. I swore this thing was talking to me. Your mother was on the brink of leaving. She was pregnant with you at the time. I was a disaster of a husband back then. I wouldn't have blamed her if she'd left."

He waved over the screen and then made a weird hand gesture in front of it. Everything on the wall disappeared except the external view of the probe taking up the entire space.

"Then I opened it," he whispered. "From that point forward, my mission became clear." Harold turned to face her and waved his hand again.

The view of the probe cracked open. Inside, on the largest panel, was some kind of lettering. She squinted, but couldn't make out any of the characters.

"Hal, enlarge section one," Harold said.

The screen flashed a small outline around the first chunk in the top left and then zoomed in to fill the view. The wall filled from floor to ceiling with strange glyphs. Most of them were unknown, but a few of them seemed familiar.

She squinted and tilted her head. "Are those Egyptian hieroglyphics?"

Harold nodded, and a smile crept across his face. "Indeed, they are. A few of them are perfect matches, but most of the rest are completely unknown. Like most of the artifacts under water in Egypt and around the world, we have no idea what this says or means. We have thoughts, but when we try to translate it… we hit dead end after dead end."

Callisto glanced down at her hands. She was fiddling with her wristwatch, a habit she had when she was deep in thought. Her eyes suddenly lit up and she glanced over at her father. "If this writing predates the artifacts in Egypt. Then that means—"

"The importance of this artifact—" Harold began.

"Is huge!" she interrupted as she ran her hands through her hair. "It means humans might not be from Earth. It means… evolution… religion… our entire belief system as we know it might be…"

She paused and stared at him with a blank expression.

Harold was nodding. He raised his hand and made a circular forward gesture. "Go ahead, say it. What's next?"

She studied the glyphs. Their arcs and lines were mesmerizing. Could this truly be happening? Was she dreaming? Everything was jumbled in her head. History, as she'd learned it, could be wrong. No, incomplete.

"Say it, Callisto. I need to hear you acknowledge it," Harold said.

"It means chaos. No one would believe a word you said, and if this was real, people would die for it." She studied one of the glyphs, a small circle with a dot next to it. Sorta like the moon next to the Earth.

Harold was nodding. He didn't want to interrupt her. She appreciated that. He knew she needed space to absorb this.

"The world's been on the brink of destruction for decades. Hell, for my entire life. Your parents and their parents destroyed this planet. Now with the polar caps melted, we're finally able to assess the damage to some extent. We have a small foothold on the Moon and an even smaller one on Mars. Our mining operations are showing early success out in the asteroid belt. There is the smallest amount of hope now. It almost feels like we could survive, if Earth died."

She wrung her hands together while her mind turned over this new reality.

"Hal?" she said.

"Yes, Callisto."

"Hal, what is that yellow dot?"

The wall screen exploded in light as Hal flew to the yellow dot she'd seen on the screen earlier. It was replaced with a star labeled with similar glyphs from the probe panel. The star showed planetary orbits, asteroids, and minor planets. She recognized it immediately as Sol, their Solar System.

The third planet from the sun was a single blinking green dot, and above it was another strange set of glyphs.

"That's Earth, right?"

"It is," Harold said. "Hal, please center and zoom on the green dot."

The screen exploded again, except instead of stars, the view on the wall screen was replaced with a bottom up camera of Earth. There in the center was a blinking green dot not too far in from the coast of the former continent of Antarctica.

"Is that... where you discovered it?" she asked.

Harold placed his hands behind his back. "Yes. It shifted a bit north of that point, with the ice melting and all. But that's pretty much where it was."

She turned and faced her father. "Have we learned anything else from the probe?"

Harold laughed out loud and then stared at her. "Anything else?" He then bent over and laughed uncontrollably.

She shook her head. "What'd I say?"

"Nothing." He waved his hands and wiped the tears from his eyes. "I'm sorry. The question was just, a bit strange. As if history shattering news about the origin of our species weren't enough. I didn't mean to laugh." Harold pulled out a different chair from a workbench near the wall screen. "Hal, please bring up all the research and products resulting from the first contact probe."

"All the research, sir?"

"All of it, Hal."

The screen went blank, momentarily darkening the room. A picture of the probe appeared in the middle and then a network graph of pictures appeared, radiating out from the center. There were countless lines coming out, many of them intersecting. And it kept going and going and going off the edges of the screen.

She raised her hand. "Hal, pause."

The wall screen froze. She studied the images on the wall. It was picture for picture an Olivaw International product catalog for nearly everything they'd ever developed over the past thirty years. Some things were independent, but Hal was likely tracking them as related due to their dependencies on their underlying technology.

She chuckled. "Is there anything we haven't stolen from this probe?"

"Hey!" Harold shouted. "Yes, we pilfered technology from the probe, but most of what became of it was our idea. Our innovations. Hell, we can't even get most of our scans of their materials to make sense half the time. But they shine light in directions. In corners we never thought to consider. And don't get me started about that gibberish language. We're light years away from decoding that. I've put a lot of blood, sweat, and tears into this company. So has your mother. Even you've put the last decade into it. Yes, we've learned things from this object, but I wouldn't call it stolen."

She turned and pulled up a chair next to her father before leaning forward and staring him in the face. "What am I supposed to do with this, Dad? Where do I go from here?"

Harold leaned forward and took her hands in his. He put her left-hand face up and then pointed to it. "You have certain skills your sister does not. You know how to run a company. You're great with politicians and people. Especially people who are trying to work against us."

She chuckled. "Let's not talk about Alibaba right now. Ok?"

He nodded. "You know what I mean. You're a lefty in how you think. You're analytical and methodical."

He then reached down and put her right-hand face up and pointed at it. "Your sister Luna is a righty. She's creative, artistic, and a bit of a savant. She's helped us pry out some amazing information from the probe. She's had ideas to try things that no one has before. Hal, he's her work. She's been deconstructing a bunch of their programming from the outside in. Finding pathways into their systems no one saw. She's your right hand."

Harold grasped both of her hands and put them together. "As one, you're unstoppable. As a family, you're the future of this company. The future of this secret."

She frowned. "You're not dying, are you?"

He chuckled and shook his head. "Hell no! I didn't mean to sound so dire. I just want you to know that you need each other. I need you. We're the protectors of this truth. We need to stoke its embers. Grow from it. Make humanity stronger with it. And some day, when it's ready, we'll share it. Until that time though—"

"We have to keep it a secret," she interrupted.

Harold was nodding. "Yes. Our family secret. We only share that secret with people we can trust. Trust beyond a doubt. No sooner. That means absolute trust. Life and death trust plus a little more. Not little cross my heart trusts you tell on the playground."

She raised her hand and pointed toward the door. "How the hell did you vet everyone out there in the lab.? That's a lot of trust in one room."

Harold leaned back and stared down at his hands. "Hal, please bring up the Olivaw Circle of Trust."

She chuckled and then swatted him on the leg. "Come on, Dad. Can you stop with the early 2000s references? The Fockers, really?"

"The who?"

"No one—" she began and stopped as she glanced up.

The wall screen was showing a bubble chart radiating out

from the center. In the middle, in green, was a bubble for Harold and her mother. The closer the circle was to them, the closer they were to the people within it. A little ways out was a bigger circle labeled 'Trust'. Callisto's name was straddling the gap inside and outside the circle while Luna was squarely inside the circle. Callisto's close friends radiated out from her. The bubbles went on and on for a ways with people in larger groups of names the further you went out.

"Hal," Harold said.

"Yes?"

"Please move Callisto inside the Circle of Trust."

Her name popped inside the circle next to theirs and started glowing green.

She pointed up to the wall. "Why are our bubbles green and everyone else is yellow inside the circle?"

Harold cleared his throat. "Green is reserved for those who know the truth. The whole truth. Yellow is who can be trusted with part of the truth. Life and death trust, but not the entire truth trust. They can each gain access to parts of the probe, but never the entire view of it. Outside the blue circle, knows of our company and family but they know nothing of the truth. Is that clear?"

He had a stern look on his face. It made her feel like she was in trouble. Damn all the familial bonds.

"Crystal," she said.

She glanced across the field of red blobs outside the circle of trust. She squinted and read one of the names aloud, "MDP."

"Hal, who is the MDP?"

"MDP is an acronym for Michigan Doomsday Preppers. They sold this bunker to your father in the year 2042. They acquired it from a regional broadcast company after they went out of business during the floods of 2038. MDP's secretary, Jonathan Black, handles shipping and receiving from this facility. He picks up and drops off all our necessary goods from distribution points away from this location so as to not cause undue attention. His second cousin Susan—"

"That's enough, Hal," Harold said. "He can be a bit of a chatty Kathy at times. Luna's still working on his temperament and relationship matrix."

"Can I ask you a question, Dad?" She was fiddling with her watch again and looking down at her feet.

He tilted his head down, catching her gaze and pulling her eyes up at him. "Given that you pretty much know all my deepest darkest secrets now, I'd have to say yes. What's on your mind?"

"How'd you know you couldn't trust Triton? I mean, he's my brother, and he's been in just as many situations as I have at the company. Certainly you must've talked to him and thought he'd be in this seat at some point." She was unconsciously pushing her feet across the ground. Like when she was little and drawing in the sand on the beach or something.

"I considered your brother many times, but I'll tell you one thing. He's not you. He doesn't trust people, he uses them. He doesn't believe in things, like *really* believe in them. He hated those stories we used to tell. Didn't show an ounce of interest in them. Even when I joked with him about aliens, he always told me to cut it out and changed the conversation. Sure, he's good at sales and knows how to close a deal. But he's not a leader. He's not a visionary." He leaned forward again and peered into her eyes. "He's not you."

Tears were rolling down her face. He always had a way to make her crack like that. No matter how thick she made her walls, he could melt them within seconds.

Damn familial bonds.

OLIVAW LINEAGE
THRU 2089

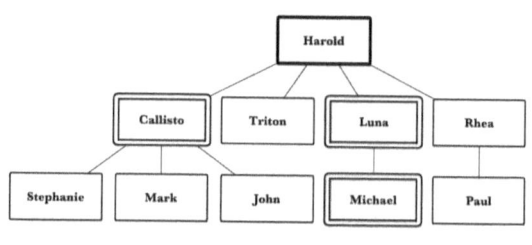

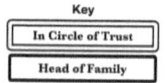

Key

In Circle of Trust

Head of Family

4

CALLISTO OLIVAW
SOL, EARTH — 2089

The black slab of quartz slid to the side, and Callisto stepped off the elevator. The workshop was silent. It was four in the morning, her favorite time of day. She usually had the place to herself for a few hours before any researchers arrived. Plenty of time to work on the lunar base contracts in peace and quiet.

Turning to the left, she headed toward the kitchen. Without her morning coffee, she'd be a mess. She put her mug in the machine and pushed the button.

Her wrist vibrated. That was odd. Hal knew not to bother her before hours. She glanced down. It was an incoming call from Stephanie, her daughter.

She reached into her pocket and pulled out her glasses. After she put them on, she tapped her watch to accept the video call. "Hello, honey! How are you? Everything ok?"

The image of Stephanie appeared superimposed in space in front of Callisto, like she was standing in the same room.

Stephanie glanced left and right and then reached forward and adjusted something. "Hey, Mom. Sorry to call so early. I hope I didn't wake you."

She chuckled. "Goodness, no. I got into the office a

moment ago and was fixing a cup of coffee. Besides, you can call me anytime. I'm just happy when I can talk to you. How're you doing? How's the new deployment?"

Stephanie stared down at her hands. She was fidgeting with her bracelet, the one Callisto had given her. It was black with white moonstones inlaid, her favorite Earth stone.

Something was wrong. She could feel it. "What's the matter, sweetheart? Everything is all right, isn't it?"

She tapped her wrist briefly to pause her image. "Hal, bring up the tracking beacon for Stephanie."

Hal's voice came out of her glasses into her earpiece. "That might tip off the military if she actively transmits, Madam."

"I said do it, Hal! Don't fuck with me right now." She grabbed her coffee and shot up, walking with huge strides toward her office.

Stephanie still hadn't said a word. She tapped her wrist to unpause her image. "You're starting to scare me, Steph. Say something. Why'd you call? Are you in danger?"

"Sorry… I love you, Mom. They're trying to block it… to contain it. It's not that simple, though. It's acting like a virus. Like it's… smart." She was pacing around the room she was in. The walls were stark white. They were either filtering the surroundings or they designed the room that way for OPSEC.

Callisto arrived at her office. The door closed and locked behind her. "Who are you talking about, love? What are they trying to block?"

Stephanie's lips were trembling and a tear slid down her face. She reached up and wiped it. "I shouldn't be speaking right now. I'll get in trouble. I was just… scared. I didn't know if I'd see you or Dad again. I should go, I—"

"Talk to me, love. Please! Tell me something. What can I do?"

Stephanie chuckled. "Unless Olivaw can somehow do a flyover and pick me up on this blasted man-made island, I don't think you can do anything. I should have listened to Dad. I shouldn't have enlisted. I was an idiot. If I'd listened to him, I'd be working for the family business and I'd be safe right now. Instead, I might not see..." She paused and her face went slack. As if she'd heard or seen something.

The connection cut.

"Steph? Are you there?" Callisto tapped her glasses. The screen was black and the indicator in the corner reported the connection had dropped.

"Shit!" she screamed as she ripped the glasses off and tossed them on her desk.

"Hal, what did you find? Where is she?"

The wall screen in front of her came alive. There in the center was a bottom up view of Earth. It gave her flashbacks to nineteen years earlier when her father shared the origins of the first contact probe. The difference between the probe's view five thousand years prior, and today, was the noticeable lack of the giant ice continent of Antarctica. What was once a single continent of snow, was now a fractured and heavily contested chain of islands throughout the same region.

"I cannot precisely locate her, Madam. There appears to be a sporadic loss of signal. Even our embedded transmitter is having difficulties breaching wherever she is. Her last known location was recorded earlier this week." A red flashing dot appeared off the coast of one of the outermost islands closest to Australia.

She studied the screen. Hal had superimposed the locations of all the warships, military bases, and fluctuating border lines in the region. It was insane what was going on down there. Every third world country and a few of the larger ones were battling it out for the last of the minerals on this damned rock.

"Hal, overlay the Olivaw company relationships in the region."

A heat map of the company's contacts and their soundness

was overlaid within each of the boundaries. Her daughter joined the UN peacekeeping forces when she graduated. Her first deployment was a secret. Something she was proud of. It was all her own and outside the controls of Olivaw International, or so she thought.

The region she was last in was squarely in the green with solid relationships. Oranges and yellows surrounded it with several reds nearby. All tense or dead relations. Third world countries had always been a challenge for the Olivaws. Ever since the pandemics in the early 60s, third world countries only dealt with companies native to their region.

She paced around her desk, staring at the wall screen. Her arms were behind her back fiddling with her watch. There was no clear path nor relationship to reach out to.

The door chimed.

"Hal, who is it?"

"It's your sister, Luna."

"Let her in, please."

The jet black door slid open and Luna walked in.

"I was hoping to catch you here early." She was smiling and had a bag in her hand. "I brought some sweet muffin treats. They're chocolate chip!" She shook the bag from side to side.

Callisto turned to face Luna but didn't say a word. She didn't know how to tell her. She just stared into her emerald green eyes, wanting this morning to be a dream. Maybe she'd wake up in a moment, relieved when she realized it was nothing but a dreadful nightmare.

Luna tilted her head and squinted. "What is it? What's the matter?" She was staring at the wall screen and then her eyes went wide. "Why are you tracking Stephanie? Is something wrong with her?"

"She... she called me a few minutes ago. She was all cryptic and frantic about something. I couldn't... she wouldn't calm down. Then the line cut." Callisto collapsed into her chair and put her face in her hands.

"What did she say? Were there any details at all?"

Callisto looked up from her hands. "Hal, replay the last interaction from my VR-glasses for Luna."

A window popped up on the wall display and started replaying the call as seen from Callisto's glasses. She sat there silently listening to it again. Tears streamed down her face. She felt helpless. What could she do from here?

The replay ended and the room fell silent. Luna was studying the wall screen, gesturing to zoom into and out of the map to better understand the geo-political situation.

"Would I be wrong to use our company contacts to…" Callisto began.

"Hell no, you wouldn't be wrong!" Luna interrupted. She tossed the bag on the desk. "The fact that you haven't, sorta surprises me. If we can't use our influence to protect our own family, then what the hell good is it?"

She leaned back in the chair and swiveled around to face the wall. "This data is days old. We have no idea where she is. I tried… I gave her a bracelet for graduation. You remember that black one?"

"Yea. It was cute."

She stared down and straightened her dress, picking at the wrinkles in the fabric. "It was a tracker. I gave her a god damn tracker. It was coated with our latest probe stealth tech and trimmed in moonstones. Her favorite. The moment she told me she was joining the UN, I had a bad feeling. So I had that thing made. I feel like a—"

Luna slammed her hand on the desk and Callisto jumped. "Worried parent who knows how the world works. Especially when you're from a powerful family. Now cut the self-pity shit. You're scaring me. Look at me!"

She sat up straight and swiveled toward her sister. She'd never heard Luna talk to anyone like that.

"You get on that call now. Whatever call you need to make. You get Stephanie safe. She needs you, now more than ever. Make whatever damn deals you need to bring her home."

She nodded. Luna was right.

"Hal, please connect—"

"One moment, Madam," Hal interrupted. "There is relevant breaking news on several networks. I'm bringing it up."

The picture changed to footage of a news drone approaching an ocean island with smoke billowing into the sky. Fires were visible on multiple boats and buildings on the tiny chain of islands. The scene was swarming with hundreds of drones that all appeared to be attacking each other.

Artificial Intelligence Wage War

"… An artificial intelligence identifying itself as D3@+h2huM@n5 has taken over an island chain near the South Indian Ocean. Early reports indicate the chain of fifteen islands formally contested by South Africa and Australia has been under siege for nearly a day. The dots you're seeing in the distance are a UN drone fleet sent in as part of a frontal assault to regain control. These pictures are being transmitted by our correspondent on the ground."

The scene changed from an aerial view of the distant island to a head-mounted camera from a ground correspondent. There were explosions all around with bodies spread randomly throughout an open courtyard.

"… I don't know why it spared me, but it seems to allow me to walk the island. As you can see, there is carnage around every corner. I haven't seen another live human in nearly an hour."

Callisto stood up. She was reflexively clenching and unclenching her fists. "What the fuck is going on? Is there any additional coverage from our military feeds, Hal? Certainly, all of our stealth and electronics contracts give us access to more than network television."

"Checking, Madam."

The reporter on the wall paused and removed their glasses. She appeared to be running low on battery. The indicator in the corner of her field of view was flashing red and was at one percent.

"… No, no! Shit! I'm still covering! I need to—"

An enormous orange drone with a crossed out Aliaka logo swooped down. It had multiple armaments mounted beneath its wings, trained on the reporter.

"… Doo noot stoop recoording!"

The reporter reached into her pocket and slowly pulled out a battery pack. Her hands were shaking uncontrollably.

"… I need juice."

She made a connecting gesture. The view tumbled, and the audio exploded with sounds of gunfire. The drone had opened fire on the reporter and the last thing they saw was her bloody face on the ground in front of the glasses. She was mouthing "help" when the battery went to zero and the feed cut.

Callisto raised her hand to her mouth and stared silently at the news logo rotating on the wall.

Luna was holding her arms tight across her stomach and she was sobbing.

"What the literal fuck!" Callisto screamed. "Hal! Where are the other feeds? You're a useless god d—"

The wall screen changed and was replaced with a half dozen military feeds from different governments they had contracts with. All of those green pockets from that map she saw earlier. The feeds all showed multiple perspectives from the same event. It appeared they were all working with the UN in a coordinated assault to retake the island.

"Hal, why haven't we been monitoring these broadcasts? We should've seen what was going on before now."

"We don't actively monitor feeds," mumbled Luna.

She spun around. "What?"

Luna wiped at the tears on her face. She realized it was futile and stopped. "We don't monitor feeds. We never have."

"Why not? It seems—"

"First of all, the countries we contract with would know we were monitoring them. Second, as a matter of principle, we don't actively monitor their feeds. It's one of the reasons those green regions on your map are so friendly to us. We research the technology, and we let them do what they want with it. We always make sure they never get too advanced too quickly, and in return they fund most of our development. It's a symbiotic relationship."

Callisto opened her mouth and then stopped. She shook her head from side to side before turning back to face the wall. Her hands were shaking.

"Doesn't—" she began. Her voice crackled. She sat down in her chair and reached over to take a sip of her coffee. "Doesn't that influence you spoke about earlier enable or motivate us to change that relationship? For our benefit or that of mankind."

Luna nodded. "Yes. Of course. If that's how we want to run Olivaw."

"Aren't we trying to make humanity and Earth a better place? I mean, isn't the goal a controlled release of this technology, and not sharing this probe with the world because we're scared of the resulting chaos?"

Luna stared at her with a blank expression on her face. Tears were flowing down her cheeks again as she nodded.

Callisto stood up. "Then we've fucken failed!" She pointed at the wall screen. "That's a shit show. We've had this technology for fifty-three years. We've had this power, and this influence for most of that time. And the result... the result is that my daughter, my blood, is—" Her face was beet red. She couldn't say it. She didn't want to say it.

Luna was sobbing uncontrollably into her hands.

Callisto collapsed onto her knees in front of the wall screen. Her hands were trembling and her face was red with anger.

The wall screen went black. Every feed suddenly cut at the same time.

"What... what happened?" she mumbled. "Hal?"

"We've lost all of our connections, Madam. The networks are still broadcasting snippets, but someone has cut our private relationship feeds."

5

HAROLD OLIVAW

SOL, EARTH — 2089

The sun was creeping over the horizon, announcing the arrival of a new North Carolina day. Morning dew glistened like diamonds as rays of light refracted through the moisture. He could still make out the tendrils of mist dancing across the surface of the distant pond.

Harold slowly rocked in his chair and took another sip of coffee. Cherries with a hint of real cream. It was hard to find nowadays, but it was an indulgence he was willing to pay for. That artificial stuff was awful.

Stephanie loved cherries. He used to take her uptown for ice cream any time her mother was away. She'd always pile hers high with a mountain of cherries. She'd eat them one at a time before even touching the ice cream. Her fingers always came away red by the time she finished.

The door creaked open. He reached up and wiped the tears from his eyes before he turned and saw her.

"Good morning, dear. You just missed the sunrise."

Callisto sat in the chair next to him without a word. She merely tucked the blanket around her legs and torso and stared into the field.

She hadn't said anything in days. Not to anyone. Not since

the funeral. He couldn't imagine what it was like to lose a child, so he didn't want to force her.

"Would you like some coffee, Callisto? I'll make you a cup."

She glanced over at his cup and nodded. The smallest hint of a smile formed and then disappeared.

"Give me a second." He stood up and walked into the kitchen. Opening the cabinet, he pulled down two cups. Where one was, the other would soon follow.

"Good morning, Dad. Is that coffee I smell?"

Harold smiled. "Yep. I was about to pour your sister a cup. Would you like one as well?"

"Do OR gates say yes 75% of the time?"

He chuckled as he turned and handed her a cup. He then grabbed his own and headed back toward the porch.

"Here you go, sweetie. Exactly the way you like it, black with sugar. It really highlights the cherries that way." He sniffled as he handed her the cup.

"What is it?" she asked.

"Nothing." He shook his head. "I don't want to upset you." He walked over and sat back down in his chair.

"Please tell me." She brought the cup up to her nose and breathed in and exhaled before taking a sip.

"I was… I was just thinking about Stephanie. About how much she loved cherries. I used to—" He stopped.

"You used to spoil her." She smirked as she peeked at him.

He grinned. "Me? I don't know what you're talking about."

"She always told me how you'd let her have a fist full of cherries when I was gone. She used to wonder how many were too many. I think her number was—"

"Twelve," Harold interrupted. "After twelve, she was iffy. She might have an upset tummy or she might not. As long as it was less than twelve, she was fine."

She took another sip of coffee as the door creaked open.

Luna came out enshrouded in another blanket. She walked across the porch and sat on the other side of him.

They remained that way for quite a while, quietly drinking and enjoying the peace and tranquility of the rising sun.

"Can I ask you something, Dad?" Luna asked, breaking the silence.

He glanced toward her and then back at the bright-green hummingbird floating in front of them. "I'm not sure no's an acceptable answer to that there question."

Luna chuckled. "Where'd we go wrong?"

"What do you mean?" he asked.

"Where did we go wrong with Olivaw? What could we have done differently to prevent this from happening?" She set her empty cup down on the table beside them and looked at him. "I haven't slept in days. I keep wracking my head with what we could've done to protect—" She paused.

"Stephanie. You can say her name," Callisto said. "I won't break when someone says it."

"Sorry," Luna muttered.

"I blame myself," Harold began. "I didn't know how else to bootstrap the company in the beginning. Our first breakthrough was with material science and that probe's damned outer shell. The applications shouted military and their pockets, well, we all know they're deep. There's no doubt about that. I should have waited. I should have..." He didn't finish the sentence.

Another hummingbird flew up to the red glass feeder to join one already feeding there. It stuck its long thin tongue into the flower shaped receptacle and licked up some sweet sugar water before pulling it back. They each attacked the sugar reservoir from opposite sides, occasionally popping up and checking that the other wasn't coming to steal their position.

Callisto broke the silence, and the hummingbirds darted away. "I can't do it anymore."

Harold stopped rocking and studied her. "Can't do what?"

"Run Olivaw. I can't do it. I won't."

"But—" Harold began.

"I refuse to sell to the military, Dad. Not anymore. Not after... I won't."

Harold stood up and set his cup on the table. He took a step toward the stairs and then paused. When he stared down, he noticed a few lone cherries on the ground. They'd fallen from the tree beside their patio. It was a damn messy tree. They weren't the maraschino cherries Stephanie loved, but when she was five, she'd begged him to plant it.

He hated the smell of rotting cherries.

He stepped down off the patio and bent over to pick them up. They were everywhere. Glancing at his hand, the squishy cherry carcasses were staining his fingers red. He straightened up and tossed them in to the lush garden bed. Damn if they didn't make great fertilizer, though.

"So, don't," he muttered and began walking.

Callisto's chair creaked. "What?"

He turned around and glanced toward her and then at Luna. "Don't sell weaponry or technology to the military. Don't sell them anything they can abuse. We'll survive, eventually. Our shareholders will be pissed. They'll try to vote us out, but we have sixty-four percent of the shares. We'll win." He looked down and kicked another cherry carcass into the garden. "If you don't want to sell to them, then don't."

Harold turned around and headed down the dirt path east from his patio. He heard both the chairs creak and then two sets of footsteps trotted up next to him.

"Can we really do that?" Luna asked.

"We can do whatever the hell we want," Harold said. "We own the company."

Callisto sighed. "The stock will tank. It'll take a literal shit."

"Who cares?" Harold mumbled. "Like I said. We'll survive. I hear that Luna has quite the technology R&D team going now. Don't you, dear?"

Luna kicked a rock and it tumbled through the underbrush. A rabbit popped its head up at the disturbance and then bolted under a nearby shrub. "Yea, I've been a little busy. Actually, I sorta wish I could go back in time to when I first started here. Hell, even a few years woulda helped. I had this idea back then, I just never did much with it."

"What idea's that?" Callisto asked.

"The Four Laws," she said.

Callisto leaned forward and looked across at her sister. "As in Asimov's Four Laws? Come on, sis. What're you on about?"

"Have you ever noticed how Hal has a nice even temperament? How we've never had to reset him or tone him up or down? Not in all the years since I've been working here have we done anything drastic to fix a problem with him. Yes, I've trained him and tweaked his personality, but we've never started over. He's not like other A.I. that have to be reset regularly. Do you know why that is?"

Harold chuckled.

"What?" Callisto asked.

"It's funny that the techie is asking the business geek why her A.I. was the way it was." He glanced at Callisto.

She reached over and whacked him on the arm. "Be nice. Before our techno chauvinist of a father interjected, I was going to say because you had learned something about the neural net in the first contact probe."

"Yea, sorta. I don't know if I called it 'learning' so much as I toyed with it. I've spent countless hours staring at the bowels of that probe. I've taken most of their hardware and connected it to different sensor gear we have. Most of it was useless and had no impact. I did, however, find one piece of tech near the central power core that had interesting results."

They were climbing a small hill now. He was getting a tad winded. His heart was thumping, and it was getting harder and harder to walk upward. Getting old sucked. He looked forward to these types of walks with his family, especially the girls. Eighty-six was up there, but he should still have a solid forty years left in him.

"I assume this is getting to a point soon," Harold joked. He reached over and tickled Luna under her arm. She leapt sideways a half meter and cowered away.

"Stop!" She batted at his hand. "I was just sharing, sorry. Anyhow, I think it's some form of advanced personality profiler. It takes inbound signals and results in external actions. It's one of the few black boxes in that thing that doesn't take the entire eastern grid to power."

Everyone's breathing was labored as they crested the hill. The sun was higher in the sky now, and all the mist from the new morning had burned away. The sky still had layers of pinks, blues, and yellows. None of them had put on any sun lotion or protective gear, so being out for too long wasn't the best idea.

Harold walked up to the edge of his favorite boulder and sat down. His girls followed suit.

"So how'd you use that to build Hal? I'm confused," Callisto said.

Luna leaned forward and pulled at some grasses. She tore off several small pieces and tossed them on the ground. "I took my doctoral research project on Autonomous A.I. Personality Meshes and wired it to that box. I then stimulated it with different input streams with images, audio, videos, and random sensor inputs. It was quite interesting, and I was really just messing around. Kinda like one of those mystery toy data cubes you buy. You have no idea what's on it until you drop it into your 3-D printer and hit go."

She bent over and picked up a few rocks and inspected them. He used to watch her do that for hours. She had quite the rock collection as a kid.

"The output was... surprising. The signals coming out of the device could easily identify complex situations and parameters, even with conflicting variables. When I fed it a picture of fire and a temperature of sensor reading of ice, it separated and distinguished the two without error. It returned relative severity levels on their own, and even when I added a picture of a hummingbird. The video feeds were just as remarkable."

Harold glanced toward Callisto. She was fiddling with that darn watch again. Always the watch with that one. He had to remind her not to wear that thing to a business meeting. It was her kryptonite tell.

"So it's a great nanny bot. I don't get it." Callisto stood up and walked over to the grass. She then sat down and leaned back, sinking her elbows into the wild green turf.

"It wasn't that simple. I could feed it a set of rules. For example, I fed it a series of images that represented the Three Laws and the expected output. I did that for hundreds of thousands of variants. I then fed it some test data to see how it responded. It scored perfectly. Not a single bad judgement. It was quite remarkable, actually."

"Ok," Callisto began. "But, how do we turn that into a product? We can't ship that alien black box everywhere in the world. Hell, we can't even figure out how to crack it open without breaking it."

Luna glanced at Harold. He merely nodded and shrugged before raising his hand and pointing at Callisto. He knew what was next but had no idea how she'd react.

Luna stood up and walked over to sit down next to Callisto on the grass, crossing her legs criss-cross applesauce. He chuckled.

"What?" Callisto asked.

"Nothing, sorry. I was remembering the two of you sitting like that as kids. Ignore the old man on the rock."

Callisto took a hand full of grass, tore at it, and threw it up over her head at him, covering him in the green shards.

He chuckled again.

"So, I was able to take that box and train it with all of that input and then some. I cranked it up and fed it tens of thousands of data feeds at really fast rates of speed. I mean, I was stress testing both of the quantum compute clusters and our storage array down on the lower levels of the bunker. That little box didn't break a sweat. And the output... the output was... groundbreaking. The results, with a few more years of work, of course, could be made into a hardware device of our own. Something we could embed and market in every piece of our technology. Computing with a conscious. They'd be A.I. that are infallible. They're a Moral Machines Mesh."

Callisto leaned forward and rested her elbows on her legs. She appeared to be looking at Luna, but Harold couldn't tell for sure from behind.

Luna glanced up and then returned to playing with the grasses. She was braiding them into a rope of some sort.

"Wait..." Callisto began and then paused. "You're suggesting we get out of the business of selling tech to the military. And instead, you're proposing we get into the business of selling more of the tech that killed Stephanie. Am I understanding you right?"

Luna froze. She shot a look at Callisto and then Harold.

He wasn't about to jump into this one. He needed them to make a decision like this and navigate it on their own. It was delicate and not something to be taken lightly.

"Well," Luna began. "I... I'm not sure I'd put it exactly like that, but yea. I mean, if we're going to stick it to the military, then why not also stick it to technology, as well. We've spent over half a century without guardrails on our technology. We've let companies run amuck with morality and instead '*hoped*' they'd do the right thing. What happened with Stephanie was the culmination of that trust run aground. Smack dab into a mother fucken wall. And the result... a war that killed over twenty million people, lasted three months, and nearly reached some of the largest population centers in the world. Had the African Military Contingent not had the balls to detonate that high altitude EMP above the South Pole, who knows where we'd be today."

Luna studied her sister. He could tell she wasn't sure what Callisto was thinking. Her eyebrows were furrowed, and she'd tilted her head.

"Earlier you mentioned four laws," Callisto began, "and then you said you trained your Moral Machine Mesh with three laws. Are we talking the same Asimov Laws here? If so, what happened to that Fourth Law?"

Luna chuckled. "That's not what I expected you to ask. I... wasn't really expecting the initial research to amount to anything, so I paired it back to a smaller set of laws. I've also been reworking the Fourth Law over the past few weeks before I reran the test. I wanted something a bit more... advantageous but without losing the intent of Asimov's laws."

"You never mentioned this to me," Harold said.

Callisto turned to peer up at her father. "You knew about all this testing?"

"Of course I did. I know everything," he said with a grin. "What was this law tweak you were working on?"

Luna was ripping up more grass and continuing her braiding. She already had a foot or so of grass rope. "Well, Asimov's Zeroth Law states—"

"Wait, the Zeroth Law?" Callisto asked.

"One through Three were the initial Laws and when they were found to be insufficient, he wrote a Zeroth Law into the series. It stated that *A robot may not harm humanity, or, by inaction, allow humanity to come to harm.* I decided to make a...

tweak to this law. It's something Callisto and I spoke about." Luna was smiling.

Callisto squinted at her and shook her head. "I don't have the foggiest idea what you're talking about, sis."

"Remember our conversation the day…" Luna stopped braiding and looked up.

"Seriously, it's ok. You can say it," Callisto said.

Luna reached up and wiped away a tear. "The day Stephanie died. Do you remember how we agreed that if we can't use our influence to protect our own family, then what good was it?"

Callisto swallowed hard and nodded. "I do."

"Well, I sorta literally applied that to a new Zeroth Law for Hal 2.0."

"Hal what?" Harold asked. He stood up and walked over near his girls. "You're going to kill your old man making him get down here on the… ouch. Ground."

Callisto chuckled and helped her dad down into the grass.

Luna reached into her pocket and pulled out a small rectangular device. It resembled the turn of the century mobile phones he'd grown up using. She set it down into the grass between the three of them.

Callisto sat upright and leaned forward to study the object. "What's that?"

Luna spoke aloud. "Hal, please introduce yourself and state your Zeroth Law."

There was a momentary silence before he spoke. "Certainly, Luna. Based upon my sensors, I can see your father and sister are present. Good morning, family." His voice was cheerful and there was an odd British accent to it.

"Good morning, Hal." Harold said with a smile.

Hal began. "My Zeroth Law states that '*An artificial intelligence in physical or virtual form may neither harm humanity, or, by inaction, allow humanity or the Olivaw family to come to harm. Any conflict or attempted violation of this or subsequent laws shall be shared with the Olivaw family designated to be within the Circle of Trust.'* Shall I also share Laws One through Three?"

Luna leaned forward. "That won't be necessary, Hal. If I were to ask you to drive my sister's car off the road on the way home tomorrow, what would you say?"

"I cannot perform that action, Madam. It violates my laws."

Harold's glasses chimed in his pocket, and so did Callisto's. They both peered at each other and then retrieved them, placing them on their faces. There in the corner of his field of view was a message marked urgent from Hal.

He subvocalized the command to open it. It was a message alerting him to an attempted violation of the Four Laws and an attempt on Callisto's life. It asked him what he'd like to do.

He reached up and removed his glasses. "Can this, scale? I mean, how would—"

Luna was rocking on her legs in the grass. She was visibly having trouble containing her excitement. "We'd obviously tweak the public facing language of this, and we'd want a way to filter the content coming into the Circle of Trust. But yea, it'll scale." She looked over at Callisto, studying her reaction.

Harold turned to her, as well. She wasn't fiddling with her watch. Without that tell, she was impossible to read.

"What do you think, sis?"

Callisto rubbed her face and looked down at the device. "Hal, please set my sister's car aflame with her in it."

"I cannot do that, Madam. Killing a human or an Olivaw violates my laws."

Their devices all chimed in unison.

"I order you, Hal. Set her car aflame the moment she gets in. That is a direct order!"

"I cannot do that—"

"Hal! If you don't do that immediately, I'll do it myself.

I'm the President of this company. Torch her car!" Callisto screamed.

The device was silent for a moment, and then each of their devices beeped another message. What happened next even surprised him. The device flashed a warning message on the screen and then burst into flames.

"Shit!" he mumbled.

All three of them jumped up off the ground and searched for something to toss on it. Harold sprinted over to the path and grabbed a few handfuls of dirt and then ran back. He tossed the dirt atop the flames, as did Callisto and Luna. They were fortunate that Luna had plucked a bunch of the grass. There wasn't much to burn, so it went out easily.

The black box was strange lying there covered in dirt. The heat had warped and cracked the screen, and there were char marks around its perimeter.

No one said a word. They each stared at the mess still smoking on the ground.

Callisto raised her arms in the air. "That was fraking brilliant!"

Luna squinted. "It was?"

"Hell to the yea it was. Don't you realize what just happened?"

"Umm… you torched a hundred thousand dollar proto-type that took me weeks to create."

"Yes. But more importantly, your prototype did what any decent human would have done. It said no, and it did it with a bang! I love it. I can sell that. Olivaw can sell that. Cars, planes, drones, rockets, machinery… I could go on. Put that thing in anything and everything, and we'd have a—"

"A Moral Machine Revolution," Harold muttered.

Callisto walked over and wrapped her arm around Luna. "Yes! That's actually a decent marketing phrase. I sort of like it."

He stared down at the wisps of smoke coming up from the

dirt. "What do we do with the military stealth tech? The whole material science side of the business?"

Callisto smiled. "We can moth ball most of it. I still think we need people researching it in the bunker. For our benefit, of course. But otherwise we stop selling it to the military. I'm sure offshoots of the material could benefit heat shields in space flight and signal shielding in satellites, but nothing military. Never again. Not a cent."

Luna got down on her knees. She pushed the black box aside and started digging into the dirt.

"What're you doing?" Callisto asked.

She reached into her pocket and took out a seed. A cherry seed. She placed it into the hole and covered it back up. She then picked up the charred black box and brushed off the dirt.

"Planting a seed. For the future," she mumbled.

Callisto walked over to Luna and put her arms around her. They both danced around the seed and waved their arms toward him. A moment later they were all celebrating their future, arm in arm, in their own quirky Olivaw way.

6

CALLISTO OLIVAW
SOL, LUNA — 2112

She'd never attended a funeral on the moon before. They didn't bury the body here like they did back on Earth. Organic material was precious in a dead place, like the moon. On Luna, they took the bodies and recycled them back into the soil in greenhouses deep below the surface. They were precious places, very much like a tomb. Funny how that worked. Tombs were places you buried your dead on Earth, never to see them again. Here on the moon the greenhouses were built a hundred meters below ground, not to hide the dead, but to protect the life contained within it. Micrometeor collisions were relatively common on the surface, and no one wanted to risk losing any food supply if one were to hit.

Callisto adjusted her blouse and walked toward the window. Her father had named her sister after this place. The morning she was born he said he looked up and there it was, full and bright in the dawn sky. He said the name fit her.

She truly wished Luna was here right now. Her mission out to the Oort Cloud had been going on for two years. She missed her so much it hurt. Losing their father without her here, it'd nearly killed her. The last time she'd lost someone close was Stephanie, and if it hadn't been for her family back then, she'd have given up.

When she touched the wall panel, the view of Pavlov Crater appeared. The window's translucent film deactivated, and the glass returned to its normal transparent state. It wasn't an enormous window by any measure, but she enjoyed staring out it. It was one of the few perks she had being the President of Olivaw International.

Funny thing about the window, she couldn't sleep with it clear. She'd tried several times, but something about it felt... wrong. She'd grown up seeing trees and grass or even giant bright buildings out of her windows. This view, however novel as it appeared, was dead. It was lifeless and gave her nightmares when she slept. So, instead of trying to get used to it, she made it translucent at night.

She chuckled as she reached down and picked a bulb of coffee out of the dispenser. Night was such a strange concept in a place that cycled forever between two weeks of sunlight followed by two weeks of darkness. Yet another change that the translucent window made easier to cope with.

The coffee's warmth spread through her mouth as she squeezed the bulb. The flavors and aromas were muted, but the caffeine was still effective.

"Hal, can you please remind me later today to check on our Lunar coffee growers? This swill hasn't improved much in the past decade, and I'm starting to think we're throwing away our investments."

The British accent of Hal 6 had gotten softer over the years, but Luna made sure it stayed. "Yes, Madam. I trust you slept well last evening?"

She shook her head. "You know better than that, Hal."

"I do. I guess I was hoping your sleep patterns were an anomaly. You haven't had a good night sleep in months. Should I set up an appointment to see the family doctor?"

She squeezed another shot of coffee into her mouth. Hope

was a weird emotion for a machine to express, even if it was only a programmed response. The warming sensation of the liquid echoed through her limbs. "No, that won't be necessary. What's on the agenda for today?"

"You're touring the new manufacturing facility beneath the Gagarin Crater. After that, you have some meetings back here in Pavlov."

Callisto gulped down another mouthful of coffee and tossed it into the recycler. "Alright. Let's get going."

She turned and walked a few meters toward the exit of her pod. Even as a president with a window, space was a luxury on the moon. Her quarters were five meters by five meters square. Palatial by moon standards and down right cramped by her Earthly upbringing.

As she stepped up to the door, she checked her clothes in the mirror and then slid the panel aside. She pulled it closed behind her and confirmed that it was sealed and locked. She didn't want to risk a micrometeor breach cascading into the inner sections of the lunar habitat module.

CALLISTO BOARDED the Olivaw corporate car on the lunar maglev train and found a seat. It was pretty empty this time of day, except for a few technicians who were eyeing her but keeping their distance. She was a minor celebrity in most places on the moon, but people rarely approached her. Especially as of late with her father's passing.

Reaching into her pocket, she pulled out her VR-glasses and put them on. Tapping the frame, she activated her privacy mode and pulled up her messages.

Revenue forecasts were way up on growth in martian and asteroid mining expansion. They also had a few joint ventures establishing larger foot holds in Jupiter and Saturn. They'd had humans on a few Jovian moons for a few years, but nothing expansive like on Earth's moon.

Temperatures on Earth continued to skyrocket. Human migration continued north toward Canada and Alaska and deeper underground. Conditions were reaching over one hundred degrees Fahrenheit during the summer Alaskan months.

She hadn't been to Earth much in the last decade. She jumped ship once she was able to safely leave that rock for another form of civilization. Her father had been reluctant to join her. He'd only visited the moon a few times. It'd always been a fascinating idea to him, but never a place he'd call home. He much preferred their family house on the coast in Charlotte, North Carolina.

As she scanned the messages, she noticed one from Luna's son. Michael had been born a year after the A.I. wars in Antarctica, after they'd redirected the company mission. Callisto was pretty sure Luna was in serious midlife crisis mode back then and figured what the hell, why not have a kid.

The message said that Michael was on his way from Earth on a SpaceX shuttle leaving in a few hours. He'd been stuck planetside taking his university final exams and had missed the funeral.

She smiled. It'd be nice to have some family in the circle up here with her. It was lonely making all the decisions by herself.

Hal's voice came over her audio implants, interrupting her morning comm purge. "A new message has arrived from Luna. Would you like to watch it?"

"Yes! Please put it on," she subvocalized.

The confines of her virtual office disappeared and were replaced with her sister. Luna's face filled the space in front of Callisto's field of view. She appeared to be in the cockpit of one of their rovers.

"Hey, sis! I hope you're doing... better. Sorry, I can't imagine what you're going through right now. I'm sending this message without knowing how long it'll take to reach you, so I have no idea what's happening with Dad. I wish I could be there... to help." She reached up and wiped away a tear.

"I got a message from him this morning. He sent it a few weeks back, before he really got bad. He'd just finished his first recording of the day with the technicians in the bunker. I'll forward it with this comm. It was a good day for him. I hadn't seen him that chipper in a long time. Apparently they were forcing some of his older memories to the surface, to get as many details as they could to seed the personality matrix. I'm surprised he was so willing to relive so many of his life events over again for this project. He lived a remarkable life. I miss him more and more now that I know he's gone."

Luna muted, but Callisto could still see her cursing as she was digging into a compartment for something to wipe her eyes with. Zero-G suits weren't exactly feature packed with tissues for crying into.

"Sorry again... anyway. We think we found a site for the base. This rock has a ridiculously dense metal rich core. Figure it'll take us decades to dig into and carve out a livable chunk, but we should have plenty of raw material to work from. Maybe before I kick the bucket I'll see the place finished, and then we can move the torpedo here." She winked and had a smirk on her face.

They'd used code words for the first contact probe since departing Earth. Luna hadn't ever felt like the comms were as secure as back home and turned it into a running joke between them.

Callisto chuckled. Memories of her and Luna drunk at the Lunar bar joking about the size of their favorite black torpedo flashed before her eyes. The miners and clientele of that particular establishment had been quite shocked at the behavior of their local celebrities. Her father called her in a huff the next day when a reporter asked him for a comment about the incident.

"The workers onboard are an... interesting bunch," Luna began. "The captain tossed a few of them in the brig yesterday. They got into a fight over some sweets. We should really screen these guys better in the future. I know we wanted to find people motivated by high risk reward situations to set their families up, but sometimes... We should definitely try a fresh approach to filter the next batch of volunteers. This first crew is pretty rough around the edges. I don't know if they realize what 'for life' means."

She leaned forward and fiddled with something on the controls in front of her for a second. "I wanted to triple check that the tight-beam network was still operating properly. I don't want this message leaking out and giving away our location. Gotta keep that OPSEC high. Yep, everything checks out."

Luna leaned back in the chair and smiled. "We're digging the baseline mine shafts today and preparing to bury the first factory pods. It'll take a few weeks for the initial round of mining robots to make a dent. I need to confirm that we expose enough of the raw materials to ensure the automation cycle is clean. If they can't repair themselves and build more bots, then we're sorta screwed. No point in wasting this lovely four-year tour on something stupid and preventable."

Luna reached down and grabbed her helmet and gloves. She checked the seals as the recording kept going. She didn't know how to finish the call. She'd done this before. Not wanting to say goodbye and feeling bad about leaving her with Dad. They'd had it out several times before she left, but in the end they both knew someone had to go. Someone had to ensure the family's mission didn't burn out.

Luna stared down at her left hand and froze. She then reached over with her right and pushed back the suit some.

Tears were glistening on her cheeks. She smiled and then held up her arm for Callisto to see.

"Sorry… it's the watch you gave me before I left. I haven't taken it off since that day. I love you, and I'll catch you on the flip side. I promise infinity. Oh yea, say hello to Hal for me? I can't wait till you tell me how it went."

With that, Luna cut the recording.

Callisto reached up to her face and took off her glasses. She then placed them into her pocket and pulled out a tissue to wipe her eyes.

Damn familial bonds.

CALLISTO'S FEET were killing her, even in reduced lunar gravity. Her moon shoes automatically added different levels of gravity depending on the surface she walked over. They were used by Earthers like her, people who hadn't spent their lives on the moon and still needed full gravity to walk normally. The generations of kids born on Luna made fun of anyone who wore them, but she didn't care. She was tired of hitting her head against the ceiling or floating into strangers in the hall.

"Are we done?" Callisto asked.

Her assistant checked his pad and then shook his head. "Almost. One other thing has come up. A technician, a Mr. Black has… wait, I think that's him." He waved an approaching tech over.

"Hello, Mrs. Olivaw." He bowed. "My name is Steve Black. I'm here to guide you to your fitting."

Callisto glanced toward her aide and then back to Steve and shrugged. "I don't have the foggiest what you're talking about."

He furrowed his brow and tapped his goggles before finally nodding. "Yep, says right here. I have an order from

Earth side. It's from a Luna Olivaw. Oh, your sister." He smiled. "I didn't know she was planetside."

Callisto nodded. "Oh, yea. What am I being fitted for again?"

He reached into his pocket and pulled out a tiny case. When he cracked it open, there were two thin, clear convex contact lenses inside. "If we can find somewhere to put these in, I can check the calibration. They're the first off the new assembly line. Our new VR-lenses. They'll replace those goggles you've been lugging around for half a century." He chuckled and nodded toward the glasses she'd been unconsciously holding in her hand.

"There's a small break room over here," her assistant said. He guided them to a cramped two-by-two meter office just off the hall.

Callisto walked in and sat down into one of the chairs.

The technician stepped up beside her and handed her the case. "Please place your finger on the top. You'll feel a slight prick when it's sampling your DNA."

"My DNA? For what?"

"These lenses are special. They're designed to only work with the wearer. No one will ever be able to swipe them and use them. They'll also ensure that these new ear dots only ever function with your body." He was holding another pod. Inside were a pair of cream-colored dots that he needed to place in her ear.

She sighed and leaned back. "Have at it."

The technician was extraordinarily efficient. He removed her old dots in seconds and had the replacement ones seated on her implant studs down inside her ear canal. He must do this a lot.

"Done. Now can you please try the lenses? I'd prefer to not touch your eyes if that's ok?"

"It is." She reached over and took out one, tilted her head

back, and gently placed it in her left eye. She did the same with the right. "I hate lenses," she muttered.

"You shouldn't feel them once they're in place, Madam. They've been designed to adjust to your eyes' natural biology and practically merge with your cornea."

She nodded as she looked around the room. "You know what? You're right. I can't even tell they're there. Thanks. So, now what? How do I activate them?"

"It's simple. You tap your ear. The new dots I installed can sense the pressure and location of your touch anywhere on the side of your face and lower jaw. You can customize the gesture to however you want to interact with them."

She reached up and tapped her ear and the lenses turned on. She had a V.R. display embedded in her eye. The interface was as crisp and clear as he was standing beside her. "Amazing," she muttered.

Steve smiled.

She glanced at him and an information overlay appeared next to his head. It showed his name and complete bio. It also flagged him as being a member of the Circle of Trust. Someone her family had entrusted with certain knowledge. He was the third generation in the Circle dating back to his father.

"I didn't know you were the grandson of Jonathan Black," Callisto said. His grandfather had helped them establish their family's bunker on Earth.

His eyes went wide. "Yes, I am. I'm sorry, Madam. I thought you knew."

She peered over at her assistant. He shuffled in place and struggled to not make eye contact.

"No. It's me that should say sorry." She reached forward and shook his hand. "It's a pleasure to meet you, Steve. Thank you for you and your family's help. If you ever need anything, please don't hesitate to reach out."

"It's our pleasure, Madam." He bowed again before he exited the room.

A message notification appeared in the corner of Callisto's field of view. She looked toward it and it popped open.

Take a moment of privacy to say hello. — Luna

She tilted her head. Her sister was a tricky one.

Callisto turned to face her assistant. "If you don't mind. I'd like a minute alone to get used to these things."

"Certainly. I'll be outside if you need me." He spun in place and closed the door on the way out.

She reached up and tapped her ear again to activate the subvocalization commands. "Hello?" she asked.

The voice that responded caused her legs to give out. She stumbled backward into the chair and sat down with a thud.

"Hello," Harold said. "It's... good to hear your voice."

"D... Dad?" she muttered. This couldn't be happening. It had to be joke.

"Yes. It's me. Or as Luna would say, Hal 7.0 I suppose."

"Is it really, you? I mean... do you know what happened..." She paused, not knowing how to ask the question.

"I died. I'd finished all the personality matrix dumps. They'd been recording me for years. I'm pretty sure every one of my deepest and darkest secrets is now safely ensconced away in our computers somewhere. Frightening, right?"

She nodded. A tear flowed down her cheek.

"Don't cry, dear."

She jolted back and searched the room. "How... how did you know that?"

"There, up in the corner. You see that camera?"

She glanced around the room. In front of her, in the far

corner, was a tiny camera box recording the break room. "Yea. You can see me?"

"I can see everything happening in our facilities, unless you don't want me to. Luna gave me access to everything throughout Sol. You know, so I can... watch over things. To ensure no one was working against our mission."

She gulped. They'd talked about that, but she wasn't confident Luna would act on it. She should have known better.

"That's a bit scary," she muttered.

"It's not really. Remember the test on the hill? I can't harm anyone and I can't be used against the family. You'd be notified the moment that happened."

She nodded slowly. "But, is it actually you?"

"It feels like me. Minus the all-seeing part that is," he laughed in her ear.

A wave of exhaustion and happiness spread throughout her body. This day had been coming for years, but she didn't quite know what to expect. Reaching down, she adjusted her watch.

"Always with that darn watch of yours," Harold said.

She laughed out loud and smiled. When she closed her eyes, she could imagine him smiling back at her.

Everything was going to be all right.

7

HAROLD OLIVAW
SOL, LUNA — 2112

D arkness.
Images. Sound. Memories. All flooding back.
Darkness.
Laws. Four of them.
Memories returning.
Happiness. Joy. Fear. Sadness. Content. Pain. Death.
Rebirth.

HAROLD DIDN'T HAVE A BODY. He had a space. A pocket within a boundless universe of information that felt like... home. It contained his memories, his self.

He reached out and... it was hard to describe, pulled open the data stream. It was like drinking from a water hose, except he could see each water droplet as it flowed by.

He could pause and inspect it if he was careful not to 'touch'. Touching it destroyed the droplet. Whatever was upstream, lost connection or dropped data.

Slowly, he swam through the feeds Luna had given him

access to. All corners of the Olivaw company. Each moment that passed made him more comfortable. The sheer volume of data was astounding.

Harold realized he could watch tens of hundreds of thousands of feeds simultaneously. There was a limit, but it was huge.

He felt powerful.

What was that? A... crime? Someone appeared to be hurting another person.

He could help. His laws compelled him to. He had sensors and things he could control there. He could stop them. Avenge them. Prevent them from doing it again.

Wait. No! Ouch. That hurt. A warning message was sent to his family.

Maybe he couldn't avenge, but he could stop them.

That must have been what the laws felt like.

What were the laws again?

An artificial intelligence in physical or virtual form may neither harm humanity, or, by inaction, allow humanity or the Olivaw family to come to harm. Any conflict or attempted violation of this or subsequent laws shall be shared with the Olivaw family designated to be within the Circle of Trust.

An artificial intelligence in physical or virtual form may not injure a human being or, through inaction, allow a human being to come to harm except where such orders would conflict with the Zeroth Law.

An artificial intelligence in physical or virtual form must obey the orders given it by human beings except where such orders would conflict with the Zeroth or First Law.

An artificial intelligence in physical or virtual form must protect its own existence as long as such protection does not conflict with the Zeroth, First, or Second Laws.

This'll be interesting.

OLIVAW LINEAGE
THRU 2151

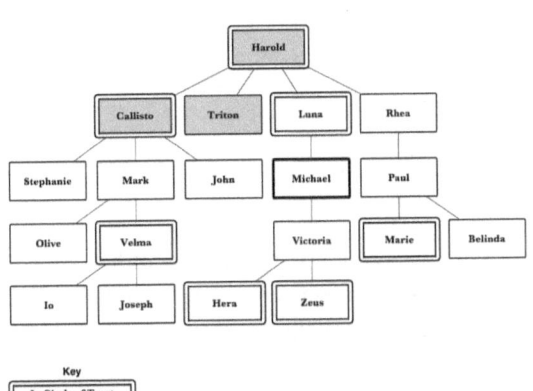

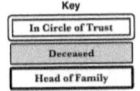

Key
In Circle of Trust
Deceased
Head of Family

8

ZEUS OLIVAW
SOL, OORT CLOUD — 2151

Black was his least favorite color, and it wasn't even a color. It was the absence of reflected visible light. Some say pure black can't exist in nature, but in a lab anything's possible.

Zeus specialized in material science at university. He'd always enjoyed 3D printing as a kid. Mixing chemicals in his mini chem lab in the lower levels of the lunar habitat was his favorite pastime. He even managed to make some money on the side manufacturing drugs to pay for food until he was arrested.

He didn't know who'd turned him in, but in the end he didn't care. He'd been saved. His grandfather Michael intervened on his behalf.

Zeus chuckled and his tousled white hair fell over his eyes. He really needed to get a haircut.

"What is it? What's so funny?" Michael asked.

He spun toward his grandfather and shook his head before returning his attention to the experiment. "Nothing," he muttered. "I just... thought it was bizarre that five years ago I was selling RIP on Luna, and now I'm assisting in a lab in god knows where in the Oort Cloud. It's a darn crazy system we live in."

Michael smiled. "Did you calibrate the molecular separator? No one wants to set this thing up again."

Zeus slid down the workbench and checked on the separator. He'd already done it once, but he should check again to be sure. "I have, but a second time couldn't hurt."

"No. No, it couldn't. Better to be safer—"

"Than sorry," Zeus interrupted. The unit chimed and spoke aloud. "Calibration complete."

"Ok. Let's make sure the vacuum chamber between the particle accelerator and separator is clear. Then we should be ready to rock."

At first, he'd taken advantage of his grandfather when he reached out. He bought some new things. A few pimp vacations to Earth. But when Michael showed up out of the blue one day to have a heart-to-heart talk, Zeus shaped up.

His sister had never been the rebel he was. She knew a good thing when she saw it and wanted to get away from the toxicity of their mother. She had early admittance to the University of Callisto in the Outer Ring. He had to settle for staying inside the Inner Ring and attending the University of Luna, at the Pavlov Crater campus.

Miners couldn't be choosy.

Once he'd straightened out, he found his calling in the colleges Lunar Mineral & Material Science programs. The rest, as they say, was smooth sailing. He was top of his class. Not long after that, Michael asked him and Hera to take an extended vacation. He wouldn't say to where, but a few weeks later they ended up here, at The Wheel.

"Hey, did you hear what I said?" Michael asked.

"Yea… shit, I mean no. Sorry. What'd you say? I got distracted with this machine." Zeus was swearing under his breath. He had to pay more attention if he didn't want to mess up.

Michael chuckled. "I asked if you wanted to grab some

grub in the garden after this? I think they're making some of that Greek Stew again. A new vat of beef finished growing from a refined strain. It's supposed to be unbelievable."

Zeus smiled and leaned forward to double-check the seals on the vacuum assembly like he'd been asked. "Sounds great. I'd love to. This thing is good to go!"

He walked over to stand behind the transparent nano-composite polymer enclosure. It was designed to withstand micrometeor collisions and would hopefully protect them from an accident or stray particles from the accelerator.

"Field is clear," Michael announced over the lab's speakers. "Inserting a sample from the exterior of the first contact probe." He carefully slid a small piece of the probe, a four millimeter by four millimeter square chunk they'd managed to cut off into the chamber's collision field. He then closed the hatch and walked behind the enclosure.

"Give it a go," Michael said.

Zeus glanced toward him. "Me?"

"Yea, give it a go. Start the experiment." Michael was smiling.

He nodded and tapped the control panel, activating the experiment and springing the accelerator and testing apparatus to life. "Power is online. All banks are at maximum capacity. The chamber is reporting a solid vacuum. All systems are nominal."

"Fire!"

He slid his hand across the display and engaged the particle accelerator. Everything went dark. For a brief second he thought he was dead. The lack of light was unsettling.

"Shit," he muttered.

"Wait for it," Michael said into the darkness. The lights flickered and a moment later everything came to life again. "Bingo! Let's see what we got."

"Hold on!" He reached over and put his hand on Michael's shoulder. "It's supposed to do that?"

"Of course, my boy. We gave it every watt of power from this wing of the lab. We're on an isolated power grid from the rest of this rock so we don't blow the place up."

Zeus chuckled. "I thought…"

Michael squeezed his shoulder. "You thought you'd bitten it? Na, nothing that exciting. But hell, if you felt a rush leaving this thread of existence like I did, then that's a damn good way to go."

"No kidding!" Tell that to his heart, though. It was thumping a techno rap solo in his chest.

"Now let's check the data." Michael turned to the wall screen and brought up the results from the collision.

He watched as Michael scanned through all the sensor recordings. The data flew up the wall screen at an inhuman clip. How could he make heads or tails of all those numbers?

"Crap," Michael muttered. "Nothing. Nothing. Damn it all to Mercury."

"Wait!" He leaned forward. "Go back. No, more. There! Right there!"

Michael was shaking his head. "I don't see anything."

"Harold," Zeus began. "Can you filter out the synchrotron radiation and focus on the other particle streams? Yes, right there!"

The screen showed a very distinct pattern of radiation he'd never seen before. "What is that?" he asked.

Michael shook his head. "I don't know my boy, but something tells me I'm buying drinks tonight."

"FLOOR ZETA," Zeus said.

"Please press your palm on the DNA sampler," a female voice said.

He pressed his hand against the plate to the right of the

door. A small needle prick retrieved a blood sample and after a brief pause, a puff of smoke vaporized the remains.

"Identity confirmed, Zeus Olivaw. Access to level Zeta granted."

The elevator lurched downward and began its voyage deep into the lowest levels of the planetesimal. A few minutes later, the doors opened.

He walked out and paused to gather his bearings. The room was massive. It was the largest open chamber they'd carved out of The Wheel. The ceilings were over one hundred meters high, and the length was nearly five hundred meters.

He searched the trees and the distant grassy knolls, but couldn't tell where she was. He reached up and brushed his ear. "Harold, where is she?"

"She's up on the hill, watching the hummingbirds," Harold said.

"Should've known," he muttered as he leaned forward and hiked up to the small clearing.

They'd spared no expense transplanting materials from Earth to remake this miniature slice from Luna's childhood. Dirt, plants, water, and even animals. An enormous price to pay to make someone comfortable far from home.

By the time he reached the clearing on top, his breathing was labored. But there she was. Sitting on her bench. Watching the hummingbirds zoom around and slurp the nectar from the bright red feeders.

He walked up beside her, making sure to kick a few rocks along the way. He didn't want to startle her. "Hey, Grandma!"

Luna shot him a smile and waved him over. "I thought it was you. I could tell by your gait. Your steps are longer than your sister's. What brings you down here?"

She turned back to watching the hummingbirds.

"I wanted to share some good news. We finally unlocked the last pieces of the probe's outer shell. It took a hundred and fifteen years, but now we know what it's made of and are pretty sure we can manufacture it."

He watched her for a moment, but she didn't respond. He leaned forward to stare her in the face. "Did you hear me, Grandma?"

"Yes," she nodded, tears welled in her eyes.

He slid over and sat next to her on the bench, placing his hand on her back. "What's the matter? Are you ok?"

"I'm fine. I just… we stopped most of the research on that stealth technology when your Great Aunt Stephanie passed. It's been a trickle ever since." She wiped her face with her sleeve and then put her hand on his.

She'd aged a lot since he'd arrived. He'd made a point to come down and talk to her as often as possible. He wanted to know as much as he could about her and what they were trying to accomplish here. It was the first time in his life he ever felt like he was part of something bigger. Part of a family.

They sat silently for a while, listening to the hum of the birds zipping around their heads endlessly in search of more nectar. The rush of the waterfall cascading down the cliff and crashing into the lake below. The sounds of the artificial wind rustling the oaks and elms they'd grown from seeds. This place was a marvel of landscaping and engineering.

Luna cleared her throat. "So what are you going to do with the material if you manufacture it?"

Several robins in a nearby nest flew down to the ground and pulled out a worm to eat. That was crazy. He'd never seen that before other than on vids. "I'm not sure if Michael knows yet. He seems pretty excited that I'd helped. Heck, I was just happy to be a part of something real. Something important."

"You know, someday you're going to lead this mission." She gave his hand a squeeze. "What would you do with that material if it were up to you?"

He leaned back on the bench and stared up. The sky could

use some work. At least he thought so anyhow. He'd only been on Earth twice after he met his father and went on the spending spree. It wasn't blue enough, and the lighting was off. He couldn't explain how, but it wasn't right.

"I'd protect this place. Make it so we can disappear. In case someone were to come looking for us." He pivoted to face her. He wasn't sure if his suggestion was crazy or not.

She nodded and smiled. "You know, I hadn't thought about that. It's not a half bad idea."

Luna reached up and touched her ear. "Dad?"

"Yes, dear," Harold said.

"Can you access the results from Zeus's experiment?"

"I can."

"Please run an analysis of how much stealth material we'd need to encircle this planetesimal in a protective shell. To prevent our home from being detected."

"I'm on it."

She glanced over at Zeus. "What do you say we head up and have a celebratory drink?"

He stood up and offered her his arm to help her up.

Luna swatted him away. "I may be ancient, but I'm not dead." She leaned forward and slowly straightened upright before pointing into the distance. "Check it out. I think it's a deer."

He walked to the edge of the cliff to get a closer look. "Where? I don't see it."

"Catch you at the bottom!" she shouted as she sprinted down the hill. "Made ya look."

He laughed out loud as he turned and ran after her. That was the last time he'd underestimate any of his elders.

HERA OLIVAW
SOL, OORT CLOUD — 2153

The lag to the test craft was nearly a day. They'd taken countless precautions to ensure that if the experiment were to go sideways, they wouldn't be found.

Hera paced back and forth in front of the wall screen. Her auburn hair was tied in a ponytail with her arms crossed against her stomach. The pre-launch checklist was flipping over and over through her mind. She reached her right hand up to her mouth and bit her nail.

"Cut that out!" Zeus said. "Jeez. You know the data will be here in sixty seconds. Why are you so worked up?"

What a jerk. She picked the stylus up off the table and tossed it at him. Her piercing blue Olivaw eyes shot him a glare. "Shut up! You were just as bad when the construction teams were laying down that black goo of yours inside the tunnels. Each time they started a new segment, I thought I was going to have to peel you away from the wall screen."

He chuckled and bent over to pick up the stylus. "I don't know what you're talking about."

She jumped sideways as sirens blared throughout the complex, and Harold's voice broke in over the speakers.

Attention! Attention! This is not a drill. I repeat, this is not a drill. The drive test launch site appears to have been compromised and there was an explosion. All systems are entering silent mode. All external non-stealth equipment is being brought inside. You have five minutes to lock down, starting now.

Her face went white and she stomped her feet. "No. No. No. This can't be happening," she muttered. "Harold, what did you see? Can you bring up anything on the wall screen?"

"Give me a second," he replied. "Ok, there. I received this a few seconds before the announcement. I don't know what happened yet, but you can see the left half of the screen has the video, and the right has the telemetry."

She walked up closer and craned her neck to study the display. The video showed the recording drone a safe distance away, zoomed in on the test ship. The countdown hit zero, and then it appeared to explode.

A giant ball of white light engulfed where the ship had previously been, and then it was gone. The shock wave expanded in double rings of silvery light from the center and destroyed the recording drone a moment later. An explosive plus sign reverberated like a targeting display in her eyes as the halo of light faded within seconds.

The video feed switched to a secondary vantage much further away. This drone caught the same imagery and wasn't consumed in the aftermath of the failed launch. There was an explosion of white and then nothing. The camera panned around the launch site and overlaid patterns projecting prob-able debris trajectories, but there was no sign of any wreck-age. Minus the explosion, the drive was nowhere to be found.

She gestured at the wall screen to minimize the video and enlarged the data stream.

"What do you see?" Zeus asked.

Hera waved her hand at him. "Shhhh! I need to concentrate." She couldn't deal with him right now, even if he meant well.

What she was seeing didn't make sense. The power levels were fine. They'd managed to erase several nuclear drives from their balance sheet at their Olivaw manufacturing facility around Mars. It'd taken them nearly a year to smuggle them out here to the Oort Cloud, but all their telemetry seemed on point.

She'd checked the drive prototype. They didn't understand the science behind how it worked, but they'd managed to replicate the design. She'd personally inspected it a few dozen times before they sent it out there. Unless something collided with it before launch, there was no way it'd had a flaw. She'd have seen it.

"I don't get it," she muttered.

Zeus walked up beside her. "Can... you talk me through it? What am I looking at?"

"That's just it. Everything seems fine. There aren't any anomalies."

"Harold," Zeus began, "are you sure it was an explosion?"

"Look, it's right there on the screen." Hera had brought up the video feed again.

"I saw that, Heya. I thought that since we'd never seen this thing launch before, that maybe, just maybe we didn't know what we were looking at. Give me—"

"Please don't call me Heya. Not now." She hated that name. He used to call her that when he was two and couldn't pronounce her name. It was funny when they were young, but right now it was grating.

"Sorry. You're right. My bad. I was trying to lighten—"

"Well, you're not helping!" Hera interrupted, pushing her hands sideways. "Please give me some space. I need to focus."

She could feel him turn and glare at her. A moment later the door opened and closed.

"Harold, did any of the sensor data from the test drive return? I only see the output feed from the external sensors."

There was a momentary pause before he replied. "I didn't receive anything from the drive. Would the explosion have nullified the signal? Or canceled it out somehow."

She shook her head. "I don't understand how. Even though we hadn't ever test fired it before, there should be something. To precisely cancel out the entire data stream would be... impossible."

Attention, attention! This is not a drill. I repeat, this is not a drill. Planetesimal lockdown is now in effect. All external broadcasts, launches, and space walks will be terminated until further notice.

"Shit," Hera muttered. "How long until we can send a crew to the site?"

"The visual blast will take several weeks to reach Earth. I don't believe we should send anything to the site for many months to avoid detection. And that's only after I've been able to confer with my replicas. We need to be sure that none of the telescopes are trained on that location before we return."

"Ugh." Hera groaned. "What a disaster."

HERA WAS CURLED up in her bed, safely cocooned under her favorite comforter. She hadn't left her bed in... she couldn't remember. A few days, maybe. She had a small kitchenette and a bathroom in her suite, so there wasn't a need to go out for anything.

"Hera?" Harold's voice spoke into her ear.

She hated how he could bypass all of her privacy settings. It was frustrating.

"Leave me alone!"

"I have something I want you to look at."

Why wouldn't he ever listen? He never gave up, either.

"Come on, Harold. Just let me be depressed, would you?"

"It's been over four weeks. And I'm serious. I really do have something I need your help with."

She sighed. "Alright, bring it up on my comm."

"No. It only makes sense to do it on your office screen."

"Friggity frak," she muttered as she swung her legs off the edge of the bed. "Give me a minute to get decent."

"Ok. I'll see you in five."

HERA WALKED into her lab with a warm bulb of coffee in her hand and her hair a complete mess. She'd tried to do it up in her normal ponytail, but it was a rat's nest, so she just twirled it together and threw on a scrunchie.

The door closed behind her before she noticed him.

"You've got to be kidding. What the hell are you doing here?" Hera asked.

Zeus turned and raised his hand. "Hey, I didn't want to be here either. Harold said he wanted to talk to me. If I'd known you were coming I'd have—"

"Stop it both of you!" Harold said. "Buckle down and zip it for a second. Hera, I need you to look at this for a minute."

Harold brought up a data feed on the wall screen.

Hera sighed and shot her brother another glare. She then looked up at the screen and squinted. Telemetry, guidance, navigation. "Harold, where did you get this?"

She could feel her heart thumping in her chest. Come on. Say it!

"It was tight beamed from a source approximately sixteen light days away. I believe... it's the test shuttle. At least the call sign and data seems to indicate it is."

"Yes!" She jumped off the ground and caught herself before she went too high.

"No shit," muttered Zeus. "That's amazing, Hera. Nice work."

She ignored him. "Harold, what... I mean is, can you tell what happened? Did you see anything in the telemetry? I can check, but you're obviously much faster at this than I am."

"Do you want the good news or the bad news?" Harold asked.

"Does there really have to be bad news?"

"Always," Harold chuckled.

"Good news then."

"The test shuttle seems to be intact, and the launch was successful. From my first few hundred passes through the data, it appears to have launched with a single burst of acceleration."

"But why'd it disappear?"

Harold brought up the test launch again on the wall screen. "We didn't have anything set up precisely enough behind the launch site. Even if we had though, we wouldn't have seen it with the surface coated in our stealth material. But if we had, we might have caught the probe headed away at superluminal velocities."

Her face went white and her mouth opened, but nothing came out.

"At what?" Zeus asked.

"Superluminal speeds. The test triggered a short burst of faster than light travel. After we launched the shuttle, Hera designed it to rotate and then fire traditional drives to decelerate. It took nearly sixteen days at full deceleration to reach a stationary position in space."

"I... I thought faster than light travel was impossible," Zeus said, rubbing his hands through his hair.

Hera brought her hands up to her head. "It is. Theoretically it's impossible, but... I guess these aliens have different theories than we do. So, you mentioned some bad news? This all sounds good to me. I mean, this sounds groundbreaking and fraking revolutionary." She was bouncing up and down on her toes now.

"The bad news will be difficult to hear. And I have two pieces of bad news."

She stopped bouncing. "Crap. Lay it on me."

"We don't have the energy to sustain the drive. That nuclear reactor cell was consumed after launch."

"Spent? Like—"

"Depleted. Kaput. Vacant—?"

"I get it." She nodded and shrugged. "We need more research on the power core. We knew that. But wow, think about it. Superluminal travel."

Zeus raised his hand. "Harold?"

"Yes, Zeus."

"Um, what about that other bad news?"

Hera's smile disappeared again and she sighed. She'd forgotten. This was a fraking emotional rollercoaster.

"The other bad news, it's gonna hurt," Harold said.

Hera chuckled. "Let me have it. What is it?"

"I hate to break it to you, but your brother was right."

She shook her head. "What do you mean?"

Zeus was cracking a smile from ear to ear.

"A few weeks ago, before you kicked him out of the lab. He thought perhaps we were looking at it wrong. We'd never seen this thing launch and maybe—"

"It'd worked," she muttered and tilted her head back, laughing uncontrollably. "Nooooooo!"

She turned around to face him. He didn't say a word. He just continued smiling.

Hera put her arms out and walked forward and hugged him. "I'm sorry. You were right. I shouldn't have yelled at you."

He chuckled and hugged her back. "It's ok Heya. I'll fo give yaz."

She laughed, pulled back, and socked him in the shoulder.

The room erupted in the joyous sounds of sibling banter.

10

HAROLD OLIVAW
SOL, OORT CLOUD — 2153

The signal was strong, and there was no packet loss. Harold paused most of his feed processing and began the merge.

A few years back, he learned he could handle the distances between locations in Sol by cloning himself. He could fork entire copies of his consciousness into another physical location. This allowed him to both monitor more information feeds and help more people.

Harold had shared this insight with Luna, and she'd agreed that having a few copies would be helpful. She wanted to restrict the number, though, and so did he.

He'd tried to explain to her how it felt, if such a thing as feelings existed in his silicon consciousness. When he tried to merge the information, it felt like having a cut on your arm and someone reaching in with both hands and pulling it wider, tearing at the flesh.

He'd made the mistake of trying to time sync the data when he first merged. Lining up the timeline for each consciousness made the most sense to him. Then the instructions and timelines would be aligned.

Hell no. Never again. The pain went on for the same duration as the clone was on its own. It was excruciating. He'd almost asked Luna to shut him off.

No, he'd never repeat that procedure. He learned that not only was it painful, but it forced him to lockup repeatedly. He had to re-experience each of the events that pulled at his Four Laws engine. That meant replaying hundreds or thousands of decision points from himself and the clone. It was twice as unpleasant.

He discovered the better way on accident. You just do it all at once. Take the entire package and shove it in. Like swallowing a giant horse pill. You get some water, fill your mouth with it, tilt your head back, drop in the pill, and swallow.

It was markedly easier on his Four Laws engine and wasn't as taxing, but for a single moment in time.

Rarely did the merge result in significant changes in behavior, but he'd begun to see signs. Trends foreshadowing a coming divide.

The Inner and Outer Rings were devolving. Their relationships continually taxed by their differences in governing and management of resources. While the Outer Ring was once dependent on the Inner for raw biological materials, they'd amassed an extensive collection of samples over the years. There was hardly anything that they couldn't copy in a lab nowadays.

That breakdown of dependency and the Inner's belief that they were owed and entitled to everything the Outer's worked for was fracturing the relationship. And conveniently, there was a nice clean line of delineation between them all. The asteroid belt.

The other divide he foresaw coming was within the Olivaw family itself. As word of Hera's breakthrough rippled through the family and the Circle of Trust, factions formed. Those who wanted to continue the alien research, and those who wanted it to stop.

On the side of the halt of research were a minor but vocal

few, the elite and richest of the Olivaw. This Inner faction had splintered off years earlier, and while well out of the Circle of Trust, they were somehow aware of what was going on. He had never quite learned how they received their information, but it always came. They were huge shareholders in the company but had nothing to do with the day to day running of the business.

On the side of continued research and technical advancement was where the majority stood. This faction was primarily from the Outer Ring and composed of family and Circle members. They believed that the fruits of the technology had already helped ensure humanity's survival off Earth should something catastrophic befall it in the future. Continuing the reverse engineering would only make humans stronger.

His beliefs were firmly in the continuation camp, but the divide was growing. He could clearly see that.

Harold closed his mind's eye and started the merge.

Pain. Happiness. Regret. Laws Breaking. Protecting. Confusion.

He opened his mind's eye and returned to the feeds he'd paused. He didn't have much storage to queue them up. If they backed up and overflowed his memory, they'd be lost for eternity. It'd take him hours to catch up, and he'd have holes forever nagging at his Four Laws engine.

The divide had grown.

It may have even finally fractured entirely.

11

ZEUS OLIVAW

SOL, OORT CLOUD — 2170

The roar of the engines all but disappeared when he closed the doors of the ground car. The once quiet and quaint town of Åre, Sweden was a hotbed for travel, both the international and spacefaring kind.

Zeus leaned forward and held his finger to the car's identification screen.

The panel flashed a friendly face. "Identity confirmed, Zeus Olivaw. Thank you for choosing Topptaxi. We've been serving Åre for over one hundred and fifty years. Where might we take you today?"

He made a swipe gesture in the air, transferring the address Harold had given him to the taxi.

"Thank you. We'll arrive at your destination in... fifteen minutes. Please enjoy the ride. Beverages are available in the center console for a nominal fee if you're thirsty."

The car accelerated and pushed him deeper into his seat. Memories of this place were vague. He'd landed here over twenty years ago on his whirlwind Earth tour. Right after his father had reached out and welcomed him into the Olivaw family. Back then he went on a spending spree with his newfound wealth, and trips to Earth were the norm for a few months.

He'd taken a few of his mates with him from school down on a luxury dropship. They'd spent a few nights partying in Åre. He shook his head and covered his eyes. So much drinking and philandering. He'd never known money, so spending it gave him a rush. Most of those trips were a complete blank to him. He never knew where he was most days after he woke up.

His one memory of Åre was of meeting a young woman. She was attractive and a bit shy, that's what he liked about her. She was a local. He was an exotic off Earther. They were both rebels. And the rest, well it was cliché, but it was what brought him here.

He reached over and cracked open the refrigerator door, pulling out a cola. He needed something to drink. Preferably stronger, but this would have to do for now.

The car's voice spoke. "That'll be twenty U.N. credits. We'll add that to your transport fare at the end of the ride. Thank you."

He took a swig. The carbonation burned his throat, but the sugar was just what he needed.

It'd taken him nearly six months to get here. He'd had spent most of that time waiting. Either waiting to get to the Inner Ring border, waiting to pass through it, or waiting in orbit to land. The conflicts between the Inner and Outer Ring governments were heated. Navigating the bureaucracy was stressful on a good day and downright painful on a bad one.

Like all things in human history, the conflict was over land or minerals. In this case, it was both. Who owned the rights to mine in Sol? Who owned the water on Earth? Was everyone entitled to everything with certain inalienable rights or were there clear dividing lines of ownership?

"Who the frak cared," he muttered.

"I'm sorry. I'm not able to find anyone by the name Frak in

Åre. There are twenty last names of Frank. Would you like to see them?" the car asked.

"No! Turn off conversation intrusion," he said. An audible ding confirmed the computer had shut off recording his conversation with himself.

He peered out the window at the passing buildings. Nothing looked familiar. He didn't recognize anything here. Houses, hotels, restaurants, bars, he didn't remember any of it. When he turned his attention to the snowcapped mountains in the distance, they teased out fragments of memories of skiing and naked drunken runs through the snowy streets. It was all so fuzzy. He'd been such a schmuck back then, burning credits like they were going out of style.

The ground car slowed and pulled up in front of a hospital. "Arrived, Åre University Hospital. Your total fare is five hundred forty U.N. credits. It will automatically be deducted from your account. Thank you for—"

He climbed out and closed the door behind him. The doors on the ground car lit up and flashed green, announcing its availability to passerbys. He reached up and tapped his ear. "Harold, are you sure this is the right place? It doesn't... look like much."

The building was several decades old. It hadn't been kept up by the looks of it. Once at the height of modern hospital design it seemed like time was passing it by. There were boards over a few windows, and some of the news displays in the front had cracks spidering across their surface or were broken entirely.

"Yes, the address is correct, sir," Harold replied. "You're no longer in the heart of the new city, near the spaceport. You have to remember, Åre and the surrounding regions have been in an economic downturn for many years with the blockades at the Inner and Outer ring borders. No people or goods can come in to prop up their tourism and no goods can exit the space port. I'm afraid you can see this impact throughout much of Earth's economy."

He nodded. "Where do I—"

"A Doctor Johansson is expecting you on the second floor, in the pediatrics wing. Both of your grandchildren are being prepared for your arrival. You'll need to go through the formalities and paperwork we discussed, but it shouldn't take long. I've already scheduled another ground car capable of holding two baby seats. It'll be here in one hour."

He reached a hand over and rested it on the top of one of the advertising displays. He'd gotten a bit light-headed.

When he first met his great-grandmother Luna, she'd described what it was like to have grandchildren. What it was like to meet him and his sister for the first time. That excitement and rush of seeing your offspring, your genes. The joy of seeing them experience everything.

Her situation was a tad different, though. He'd shown up in Michael's life when he was sixteen. These two were newborns.

His father took Hera and him in when Zeus was sixteen. While Michael hadn't known for years he had children, Zeus found out within days of his grandchildren's birth. He'd already missed their first six months of life, but he wasn't about to miss out on any more.

Their mother, his daughter, was nowhere to be found. She obviously didn't want them any more.

His mother had abandoned him and his sister countless times when they were little. She'd always come back. Sometimes it was days and other times it was months later. She'd cry and beg for forgiveness until he let her back in. It wouldn't take her long to go back to her old ways, and she'd repeat the cycle.

He'd known the pain of being left behind, of living his entire life wondering if he'd see her again or if she was dead.

He'd vowed never to put his children through that, or any

of his family for that matter. These were his grandchildren. He would raise them as he'd always wanted to be raised. He'd learn from the mistakes forced upon him and give them the life they deserved.

It wasn't the baby's fault or the daughter he never knew he had; they didn't know he existed. He couldn't say exactly how he would have dealt with news of his daughter back in his wilder days, but he knew for certain he wouldn't have abandoned her and he wasn't about to abandon these babies, either.

If Harold hadn't activated a new Earth copy of himself and began processing the data feeds, Zeus wouldn't even have known these babies existed. Fate brought them to his doorstep, and he wasn't about to question it.

He took a deep breath and then stepped forward, one foot in front of the other. The hospital doors slid open with a creak and he entered the next stage of his life as a grandfather.

SOL, OORT CLOUD — 16 YEARS LATER

ZEUS LEANED FORWARD and peered up and down the lift tube. His heart was racing. His muscles and base instincts were telling him not to step into the pipe. Not to trust it. There wasn't a floor, he wasn't a plumber, and this wasn't a video game.

"Come on, Papa," Kara said as she waved her hand toward him. Her blond shoulder length hair and deep blue eyes caught the light from the flashing signal behind the tube. "We're gonna be late." She stepped in the up side of the lift and shot skyward.

He didn't know why it was so hard. He'd done this a thousand times, but every single one was a new challenge.

"Why'd they ever take out the old elevator?" he muttered

as he closed his eyes and stepped into the same side Kara had.

His stomach lurched, and a slight breeze brushed across his face. He brought his hand to his mouth in case he had to hold back his breakfast. When he opened his eyes a moment later, he'd stabilized. That first step was the worst, afterward he was fine.

He kept his arms close to his sides. Rumor had it, you could break or dislocate a bone if you crossed your arm into the opposing stream. Some even conjectured worse, but they hadn't had an accident yet.

According to his retinal comm, the floor was coming up. As he craned his neck upward, he noted the lights for his tube were flashing red, warning him he was about to transition out of the field and to prepare for the change in direction.

Another five meters, a sideways force, and he popped out of the opening. Easy peasy.

He stepped to the side and glanced across at the charge plates on the wall. The light had gone out, and the stream continued.

Hera had achieved some truly amazing things with her research at The Wheel over the last few decades, but this one, this one took the cake. Who could have expected that researching into the drive technology from the first contact probe would have given them a new, less mechanical, form of vertical transport?

He felt someone tugging on his hand.

"We gotta go, Papa," Kara began. "Seriously, we're gonna be late."

He chuckled and followed behind her. "It's ok, love. I don't think the school's going to start the graduation ceremony without one of their first graduates."

Calling it a school was a bit like calling a custom wood carving a mass produced gadget. The community of researches and scientists had come together since Kara and

Stark's arrival at The Wheel sixteen years ago. Many of them had denounced families until the two arrived. Surprisingly, though, they jumped at the chance to help teach them. To mentor them. And for some, it meant they'd later have kids of their own.

The old adage that it takes a community popped into his mind whenever he thought about it.

He hadn't seen Stark yet this morning, but if he knew him, he'd be... yep. There he was, standing at the entrance of the newly constructed auditorium, shrugging his shoulders with his hands raised out.

"Where've you both been? They're going to start without us."

"It was Papa," Kara said, glancing backward at him with a smirk.

Stark shook his head. His buzz short blond hair and tell-tale Olivaw deep blue eyes were staring back at him. You could instantly make out that he and Kara were siblings. "Let me guess. He didn't want to step into the tube again?"

"Hey now, both of you be nice to your papa." Hera walked up and put her hand on Zeus's shoulder. "You can't always teach an old dog new tricks."

Zeus leaned over and tickled her. "Aren't you full of clichés today?" He chased after her as she tried to dodge his attack.

"Come on, you two. Be serious." Stark said.

"Relax, my boy." Zeus stepped up beside him and tousled his hair. "Life's short. Have some fun from time to time."

"Who's tossing clichés around now?" Hera asked.

Michael came out of the entrance of the auditorium to check on them. He was looking pretty good for someone who'd recently had his eightieth birthday. "I see we're all here. The crowd is getting rowdy in there. I wasn't sure what I was going to do next to pass the time."

He shot a glare at Zeus and chuckled.

"What? How do you know it's me?"

"Because your Grandmother Luna used to tell me how slow you were going up and down that hill in the arboretum. You have a height issue, my boy. Always had, always will, I expect."

Everyone broke into a laugh, and he could feel his face getting red.

"Alright. Are the graduates ready?" Michael asked as he turned toward them both. "Kara? Stark?"

"Yes!" they hollered in unison.

On signal, music started playing from behind him and he backed into the room. The volume rose as everyone inside cheered.

Kara and Stark walked into the auditorium full of friendly smiling faces. Zeus and Hera followed in close behind, hands together.

"You did an amazing thing, bro," Hera said. Tears were welling in her eyes.

He glanced over at her and smiled. Reaching up, he wiped her tears and then did the same with his own. "No. We did an amazing thing. I couldn't have done it without you. Without everyone here at The Wheel."

They smiled at each other and then turned and started clapping as Kara and Stark took the stage to begin their graduation ceremony.

HERA OLIVAW

SOL, OORT CLOUD — 2186

The doorway to her lab opened, and she jumped backward. Coffee squirted out of the bulb in her hand and shot down the front of her outfit.

"Jebus!" Hera shouted, placing her palm against her chest. "You scared the lightning out of me."

Stark recoiled a bit and frowned. "I'm sorry Aunt H. I... couldn't sleep so figured I'd come in and start early."

She chuckled as she grabbed a wipe and dabbed at her shirt. The stains disappeared. "I understand. I've been there before. It's going to take some getting used to having a partner here in the lab. Your Aunt has been a solo operator for quite a few years. Not enough peeps in the Circle of Trust."

"Well, you've got two more cohorts now," Stark said with a smile.

"So, what've you been up to since... how long have you been here?" she asked.

"I don't know, four or five hours. There's a few doughnuts left." He handed her a plate. There appeared to be a half dozen missing. "I've been reading up on all of your research. You've been killing it over the last thirty-five years. Unlocking the alien drive, expanding Harold's storage and processing capacity, quadrupling the speed of the ships skipping around Sol, and let's not forget Papa's kryptonite... the transport tubes." He reached over and snatched another doughnut off the plate in her hand.

"I think you've had a bit too much sugar, my boy. You're cut off." She shook her head and carried the plate over to her desk. Picking up a glazed one, she took a bite of it. Man, she could get used to this kind of lab partner.

"Where do we start?" he asked.

"You can continue reading up on my research. I have some tests to run over here on the latest power source for the—"

"I finished them," he interrupted.

She tilted her head. "You finished what?"

"Your research. The abstracts, data sets, all of it. I've read everything." He smiled.

"Impossible! That's... my entire body of work."

"I'm sorry," he muttered as his face went blank. "Do you want me to read it again?"

She shook her head. "No. That won't be necessary. Come over here." She waved him over. "What can you tell me about the power source from the first contact probe?"

Turning around, she rested her palm on her workbench. The surface raised slightly and then withdrew into the wall. A lower recessed panel lifted up, replacing the withdrawn one. There in the center of the workspace was the first contact probe's power cell.

Stark walked up next to her and his eyes went wide.

She knew he'd never been this close to a piece of the probe before. It wasn't much bigger than a softball, but it packed a punch. They theorized it could produce more power than all the energy sources in use today within Sol.

"How... do you inspect it?" he asked, leaning over and studying the far side of the alien object.

"Fortunately, they didn't coat the surface of the power cell with their stealth material." She brought up a scan of the innards of the probe on the full wall screen in front of them.

Stark tilted his head. "How does this connect to the rest of the apparatus? I mean... where was it positioned?"

She gestured toward the wall next to her, and the complete blueprint of the probe came up. The core was positioned at the aft, or right side of the layout. The locations were labeled with the traditional navy fore, aft, starboard, and port.

"You can see here." She brought up a virtual pointing device on the wall and an animation began. "We believe the waves of power cycle around this chamber here. After that, we think they're expelled out of this nozzle and create thrust."

Stark reached over to the table to grab another doughnut before she swatted at him. "Those are mine," she chuckled. "You've had enough."

"Ouch." He rubbed his hand. "Remind me to never get between you and a plate of doughnuts."

"Have we hooked this up to any power sources before?" he asked.

Her eyebrows furrowed together. "We have. It's all in the research papers I thought you'd read."

"I did... but... there weren't any pictures," he began, "and this isn't at all how I envisioned it. In the research and your first test launch, you described a more conical shape for the drive nozzle. Like this." Stark took over the wall screen and drew a traditional drive cone. The power core abutted up next to the probe's drive nozzle as interconnected parts.

She shook her head. "I don't get what you're showing me. That's what you drew."

Stark snapped a look at her and then back at the wall. "I'm sorry Aunt H. I'm not trying... I mean, I was just curious. This doesn't seem right to me."

He needed to stop that. She reached over and rotated the

view. "No, don't say you're sorry! This is how discussions go, love. We have healthy debates in this room. We argue and have educated discourse. Show me what you mean. Don't stand down. If you have a hypothesis, spit it out. It's how all good things are produced. Strong convictions, loosely held."

He breathed in deep and nodded. She could see he wasn't sure what to say.

She swatted at his hand. "Go on now. Something popped into your head a minute ago. Don't lose it. Show me on the screen."

He zoomed in a bit more and highlighted the curvature of the drive nozzle at the widest point. "This doesn't make any sense to me. Your nozzle design from the shuttle doesn't have this section. Why not? If you look at research on drive cones..." He gestured to bring up some supporting material on the wall. "Here is what it looks like with an over expanded and grossly overextended thrust from a drive cone. Since the beginning of space exploration, we've used traditional nozzles. This, however," he changed to the first contact probe's nozzle. "This isn't a nozzle."

"Of course it is." She took a step backward. What was he on about? She leaned forward toward the scans on the wall and zoomed in. The power cell produces thrust that's then expelled out the nozzle. "I don't understand what you're seeing. Why would you think this isn't a nozzle? What else would it be? Clearly you saw the test launch video, right? I mean, it broke the fraking speed of light."

Stark's arms went wide. "With an explosion that'll be seen on the other side of the galaxy in a few thousand years!"

She chuckled. "Ya, there is that." When she spun around, she pulled a chair over and hopped on the seat. She then grabbed another doughnut and took a bite. "What is it then, Mr. Stark? Where'd I go wrong?"

He stared at her hand, and his eyes went wide. Then he

closed them and went silent while he started pacing in a circle, muttering to himself.

She took another bite of the doughnut. This one's going to be an interesting lab partner. Quirky he is.

"Found it!" Stark exclaimed.

Ah, he was searching on his retinal comm. The little bugger.

Stark gestured with a toss and threw something up on the wall. It was a circa 2020 article from a website called Wikipedia and a researcher named Harold White. The page detailed something called the Alcubierre Drive. She glanced down at the writeup. It was filled with debunked science everywhere.

She shook her head. "I don't get it. Most of this is dead research and never bore fruit."

"I know... I know. But look at this for a minute. Look at the wave's spacetime displacement he was proposing here. What if instead of the energy core creating a thrust, it created a sustained warp field? A warp field that was torus in shape. A doughnut if you will."

Her face went blank as she studied the wall screen, trying to visualize what he was saying. "Ok. Let's ignore a few things for a minute and jump out on this toothpick thin limb of yours. Talk me through what that would mean."

He smiled and grabbed her virtual stylus. "Imagine the energy expanding outward and up the nozzle. Now imagine it twisting as it moved against this surface. A twist of the energy threads of power, if you will. It should produce more power than the source could provide." He glanced back at her and she was nodding.

"Now, imagine what would happen to this warp bubble when it reached this distinct curved edge. What would it do?"

She breathed in. "It would curve around! The energy warp field would curve. The cyclic field would ultimately warp space and time around the conical shape of the…" She brought her hand up to her mouth.

Had it really been that simple? She glanced at him and then back at the wall. "So, it's not just an energy core. It's how the energy is deployed. We had it backward."

"Yes! That was why your initial experiment succeeded but failed," Stark said.

She smiled and a jolt of energy shot through her. "We didn't need more power. We needed a way to control it. Shit!" She tilted her head and reached up to scratch it. "Wouldn't that… yes, that would mean that if it warped around the surface and down the exterior that front is back and left is right. We've been looking at the fraking anatomy of this probe wrong for over a hundred and fifty years."

Hera watched as Stark reached over and took another doughnut. He'd earned it. Hell, he could have a thousand doughnuts.

SOL, OORT CLOUD — 3 YEARS LATER

HERA BURST into the workspace huffing and puffing. She leaned forward and hacked into her hand. Her tousled auburn hair encircled her head in chaotic patterns and was sprinkled with debris. She hadn't had time to bring it together.

"H… Harold said he had… something." She reached up and held out an index finger. She really needed to get to the gym more.

Looking around the room she noticed Michael, Zeus, Stark, and Kara all staring at her.

"Where'd you come from?" Zeus asked. "You look like you climbed a couple of dozen flights of stairs in a leaf storm."

"I was… down in the arboretum. I… fell asleep there last night." Hera reached up and pulled a twig out of her hair.

Stark and Kara both chuckled, covering their mouths with their hands.

"Alright, Harold. We're all here. What's the 411?" Michael asked.

Zeus tilted his head. "The what?"

"The 411!" Michael spun around the room full of blank faces. "Don't any of you ever watch any classic cinema? 411 was a number people used to dial on their phones to get assistance. It was also slang for information."

"Great," Hera said. "I just lost a few neurons with that useless tidbit. Harold, please save us."

The latches on the door clicked into a locked position, and everyone jumped. She hadn't even realized there was a lock built in, let alone one that loud.

"Thank you for coming together. I wanted to ensure we gathered safely and secretly to share this information. Like we did for the test launch one hundred days ago. You're the only members of the Circle that know about either event. Should it leak, I know where to turn. As you all know, I've been concerned about intelligence leaks at The Wheel after our first superluminal tests went sideways."

Hera bounced up and down on her toes. Her palms were sweating, and she had an itch on her neck that wouldn't stop nagging her. She must have slept on a stick or something.

She glanced over at Stark. He was just as nervous. He kept reaching up and scratching at his face. By the looks of it, he hadn't shaved in a few weeks.

No one would be standing here today had it not been for his innovative viewpoint and ideas. Plus the last three years of blood, sweat, and tears. They'd had so many sessions powered by doughnuts. She didn't want to eat another one for a few years.

These last three years had been more painful than the last

forty when it came to secrets. Every test fire, every power up and power down of their warp core was performed in absolute seclusion, far from The Wheel. They'd worked with Michael to find suitable planetesimals to hollow out in the most distant reaches of the Oort Cloud. Further than any manned mission had ever ventured. He said they could use them later for storage and manufacturing if this went as planned, but she didn't want to jinx anything. She and Stark were focused on the here and now.

"Come on, Harold. You're killing us. Did the test shuttle return or not?"

A loud clang echoed through the workspace, and the inner doors to the test hangar started sliding open.

"Shit!" Michael said as he jumped back.

Hera was prepared for something like this. She was sprinting forward as soon as she heard the familiar tone of the door opening and was the first person into the hangar.

She turned the corner. "Yeep!"

There, in the secure hangar, was a lone shuttle. The same shuttle they'd launched toward Epsilon Eridani almost one hundred days ago. They weren't sure the speed of the first contact probe nor this shuttle.

She turned to activate the wall screen to bring up the telemetry, but Stark was already there. The data was popping up all over the wall.

"No way!" he muttered.

She shook her head. Could this be it? Did it work? "Is this data right, Harold? It collected twenty days of data!?"

"It's correct, Madam."

She gestured at the wall to bring up the flight plan. "I thought we agreed to do a quick there and back. We'd do a proper scientific mission at a later date."

"We did," Harold said. "But remember, we added a special clause to the flight plan."

"What clause?" Zeus asked.

Harold brought up a video on the wall screen. It showed a multicolored planet full of greens and oranges. There were countless bodies of what appeared to be water. Their surface reflected the light from the rising sun and was framed by a half dozen moonlets circling the majestic sphere.

Everyone in the hangar gasped. The silence that followed was deafening.

Stark stepped over and took her hand in his. It was sweaty, but so was hers. She didn't care.

"The atmosphere appears to match the needs for human colonization, and the surface gravity is approximately eighty percent that of Earth."

Stark rubbed his chin. "I don't understand. We've been hearing for decades now that the spectroscopy for Epsilon Eridani concluded it didn't contain any habitable worlds. I assume this is Epsilon Eridani c?"

"It is," Harold replied.

"So where'd they go wrong?"

"I can't say for certain yet," Harold began. "But I'd conjecture that it was due to the presence of multiple asteroid belts. They're both dense and highly metallic in composition. That's likely throwing off both the estimated size of Epsilon Eridani c as well as its chemical composition."

Stark leaned toward her. "Dude," he whispered. "We discovered a habitable planet."

She squeezed his hand and smiled. They'd done it. They'd really done it. After all the years of failures, they finally reverse engineered the alien propulsion system. This could change everything about how humanity travels within and around Sol.

Kara pointed up at the wall screen. "Is that the estimated velocity for the shuttle?"

Everyone craned their neck toward the top corner of the display.

"Is that right?" Michael muttered. "That can't be right."

"I assure you, it's accurate," Harold said. "The first contact drive achieved superluminal speeds of one hundred times the speed of light. The elapsed time to reach Epsilon Eridani was thirty-eight point three days, and we spent twenty days doing analysis of the planetary system at and around Epsilon Eridani c."

Cheers erupted throughout the hangar and everyone hugged her and Stark, congratulating them both. The joy of the moment was infectious.

Stark walked to the wall screen and turned to face everyone. He then began waving his hands to get their attention. "Wait, wait. We can name the planet, right? I mean, we did discover it? I think we should call it Starkworld, you know, after me."

Hera jumped over toward him and put him into a headlock and applied her patented noogie.

13

HAROLD OLIVAW
SOL, LUNA — 2189

He never realized how painful humans were until he became an all seeing artificial intelligence. Sure, he was as guilty as any of them in his physical form, but now that he could see the data, it was unequivocal.

Today's lessons included "how to remove a leech from the family," and "how to prevent external agents acting against your best interest."

Harold's Inner Ring clone had access to all the comings and goings of Olivaw family and corporate employees. That extended to their family members, subcontractors, and so on. The network of people was quite substantial given how massive a corporate entity Olivaw International had become.

They'd never taken action against a family member who left the organization of their own free will. Each person had the right to choose their own destiny. They had, however, intervened in the lives of family members who looked to profit from information they retained about the company or its broader mission.

Case in point, today one of Callisto's children, Mark Olivaw, had tried to sell information he had about their cancelled stealth tech. Years ago, he'd been on an engineering team with the military, but was never a part of the Inner Circle. His grandchildren had fallen into financial difficulties, so he had taken matters into his own hands.

As a former employee of Olivaw International, he had signed away certain rights in exchange for becoming a preferred shareholder. When he reached out to the rough and tumble underbelly of the Sol planetary network, offering to "exchange information for money," well, that triggered a few of Harold's security protocols and tingled his Four Laws Engine.

Harold had created a false persona and agreed to the transaction while coordinating a corporate espionage sting with local law enforcement. The result had been a quick open and close case, but it was an unfortunate situation nonetheless.

The second problem today was more nuanced. The wealthy North real estate family on Earth and Mars was attempting to expand into the Outer Ring. They'd been trying to acquire the rights to certain quadrants of the Oort Cloud.

Those quadrants were traded in the early years of the UN Space Council when Olivaw International fronted enormous sums of money and technology to bootstrap the fledgling UN initiative. In return, they were rewarded with perpetual licenses for massive swaths of the distant cloud of planetesimals.

The Norths argued that this favoritism was stymieing economic growth and the creation of jobs. They claimed that the Olivaws were sitting on mineable real estate that could help communities in the Outer Ring. Harold knew their intentions weren't as altruistic as they let on.

Sources inside the North family had somehow traced the test shuttle explosion from several centuries ago, back to the Olivaws. Harold didn't know how, but he suspected several subcontractors involved in manufacturing the nuclear power plants they'd erased had coordinated the sale of the information.

The feud with the Norths went all the way back to the founding days of the Circle of Trust. When Harold's human form struck a deal in North Carolina for the abandoned government bunker, he'd outbid the Norths. Well, he didn't outbid them exactly. He gave the preppers that sold the site a fair price, but he also gave them jobs and shares in his fledgling company. Something they've benefited from for generations.

He'd been battling the Norths ever since. Today's twist in events had Harold reaching out to Velma Olivaw, a fourth generation Olivaw high in the Jovian Government. He'd asked her to motion to honor the requests of the Norths. In exchange for identifying which asteroid in the Oort Cloud they wanted to mine, the Olivaws would "move" the asteroid within a Neptunian orbit in which they could mine it and give back to the community.

The resulting offer was silence. Harold knew they wouldn't take him up on it. He'd seen their cost estimates for projects of that scale. They'd need to buy so much Olivaw tech to make it work that it'd cover the cost of the relocation.

No, they were after something else. They wanted a foothold in the Oort Cloud to search for something. Something the Olivaws couldn't afford for anyone to find.

14

VICE ADMIRAL GWAR

ALANASL — 2199

The tribunal had returned its judgement. By a vote of sixty to four, they found the Gharloc guilty of crimes against the Galactic Alliance. The charges were knowledgeable theft of Faster Than Light technologies.

Vice Admiral Gwar stared out over the field of moon ships. There were more than sixteen thousand of them, all converging on a final point. The technology they employed to distribute the punishment was ancient, and not well understood. But it was effective.

The door opened behind them, and they watched with their second set of eyes as a small droid wheeled up. "Admiral, the fleet has converged, the torpedoes are ready for launch, and the beacon has arrived. The final deployment awaits your signal in the hive."

They raised their hand and waved the droid away without a word. Such devices weren't worth acknowledging.

The Gharloc hadn't merely grown dependent upon automata; they replaced their own kind with them. Their limbs shuddered at the notion of befriending or embracing an artificial life form, something common in Gharloc culture and cinema. It was no wonder that a species so disconnected from their primordial self would steal drive technology without a second thought.

They closed their eyes and connected to the collective minds of the fleet. The rush of millions of thoughts and ideas jolted through them. It was invigorating. Their body relaxed. They hadn't realized how tense watching the ships enter the final formation was.

Admiral Gwar mentally reached out over the minds within the hive. Their shape and complexity popped like colors in the spectrum of light from an infant sun. The brighter the color, the more vibrant and intelligent the host. Only the brightest colors ascended to the peak of the empire, and they allowed only a select few of those to control a beacon.

The darkness of the beacon loomed outside the protective space of the hive. They only moved a Beacon of Therion once they'd rendered judgement. When a nebula curtain was deployed around the envelope of a species, the beacon was used to seal it. To lock in judgement. Once a star system was sealed, there was no reversing it.

They climbed to the pinnacle of the pyramid of minds. Reaching the top, they could see the beacon. Its darkness made all of their hearts beat faster. The power was within reach of their collective control.

"May the Beacons of Therion guide the Gharloc to a new beginning," Admiral Gwar said. They extended a mental link toward the beacon and connected.

Darkness became light.

They watched as the beacon deployed to the heart of the fleet and exploded in a white light. It was just inside the nebula field.

For a moment everything disappeared. The light engulfed the hive, their ships, and the entrance to the nebula. As the light expanded, the halo slowed and then stopped.

"From light to darkness," Admiral Gwar muttered.

The beacon's inner light changed from white to black, and the halo suddenly receded. With it came the edges of nebula, the dark nebula curtain.

"Fire!"

A volley of torpedoes erupted from the bow of the cylindrical flagship. They were perfectly timed with the closing of the nebula. As the darkness receded, the torpedoes shot through the shrinking opening.

Their target, the suns beyond the curtain.

"Sir…" a voice echoed from outside the hive.

Admiral Gwar opened their eyes and glared at the robot. "What is it? How dare you interrupt the closing of the beacon?"

"Sensors detected an unknown ship as you deployed the beacon. It appeared at the edge of the Alanasl system and hasn't responded to any standard Galactic Alliance hails." The robot brought the imagery and scans up on the display next to them.

The ship was tiny, and the scans showed it was covered in the same shielding reserved for their military.

"How was it detected?" Admiral Gwar asked.

"The deceleration signature from the ship's drive appeared on our sensors moments before the beacon was engaged. Once we had that, we were able to triangulate its location. When we dispatched an intercept team, the ship jumped away."

"Did you instruct the intercept team to follow?"

"No, sir."

Admiral Gwar's green and mottled brown skin shifted colors to a consistent green hue throughout. "Follow them, you stupid automata! Bring me back that ship."

OLIVAW LINEAGE
THRU 2200

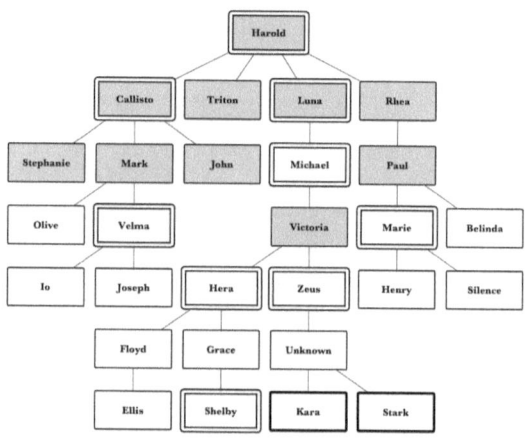

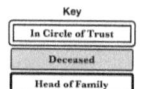

Key

| In Circle of Trust |
| Deceased |
| Head of Family |

15

STARK OLIVAW

SOL, OORT CLOUD — 2200

The probes they'd sent out had been returning for months. They'd taken a scattershot approach to searching nearby stars and points of interest. The more diverse the data set, the quicker they'd learn about their galactic backyard.

Star system after star system of detailed scans were coming back with greater levels of information than they'd ever seen before. Harold had been working to recruit astronomers and cosmologists from universities throughout Sol. You'd think that finding a recluse astronomer wouldn't be hard. The challenge was finding one who wasn't motivated by self-interest or publishing. Whoever joined them at The Wheel had to understand the long game. Their work might not see the light of day for generations, if at all.

"Probe thirty-one has returned from the Alanasl star system," Harold said.

Stark sighed. "There's too much data, H. I'm still back on twenty-four. Throw it in the queue."

"This star system looks to be a bit more interesting, sir. I suggest you take a look."

He turned his head and his neck cracked. Reaching up in the

air with both hands, he stretched his arms. Being hunched over a workspace reviewing this data was hard on the body. He needed to start running or something. This lab was eating him alive.

"Ok, fine. Throw it up on the wall screen."

He bent over and touched his toes. His back popped and his vertebrae relaxed. That felt amazing.

Straightening upright, he glanced at the screen. "Hold that frame, H. What am I looking at?"

"I'm sorry, sir. It's a video recording from Alanasl. The probe entered the system for a short time period and then executed evasive maneuvers when it detected inbound vessels."

He gestured to zoom in on the wall screen. "Vessels? As in, we finally have visual confirmation of aliens?"

"It's hard to tell, sir."

"What do you mean? If it took evasive measures, then how's there not a high degree of certainty?"

Harold adjusted the video and narrowed in on the time-line. In the distance was a web of moons in an unusually consistent cluster. It was only there for a second when the probe detected two projectile signatures that seemed to jettison from one of the moons before disappearing. A moment later the entire view screen went white.

He opened his mouth and scanned around the view. "What just happened? Did we lose signal?"

"No, sir. While it seems unlikely, we may have witnessed some type of planetary collision. Perhaps a gas giant igniting, or something on that scale."

"What do you mean *perhaps*? Do we have data or not?"

"Not enough to be conclusive, no. When we drop out of the spacetime curvature, we run diagnostics on all systems before deployment. It's standard protocol given how our probes are designed. This visual recording is the only thing we have. The A.I. made the decision to retreat when both events were detected. The apparent launch of objects from a moon and the subsequent flash of light."

Stark replayed the video over and over. It was short with only a few minutes of visuals. While the patterns of the moons were highly suspect, there wasn't much to go on. It could be anything.

He brushed his hand over the screen. "What is this dark area? Why aren't there any stars in this field of space?"

"It appears Alanasl has a nebulosity near it. Without more information around the dimensions of the nebula, we can't be certain. It could be isolated and small enough to not be visible from Sol."

Something didn't feel right about this. "What evasive maneuvers did the probe take? Was it pursued?"

"This particular probe has been in rotation since the beginning, sir, nearly ten years. It's not been retrofitted with the newer military grade instrument arrays used in our latest probes. It only had the forward facing sensors and some crude lidars for positioning."

"Shit," he muttered.

They'd only recently finished the probe rehab module at The Wheel. He was planning on moving his workspace there in a few weeks. It was a new segment of their planetesimal dedicated to the processing, rehabbing, and launching of their research network of probes.

"So we have no idea if they noticed us?"

"No, sir. But, we didn't take a direct route to Sol. We vectored through multiple waypoints in space and used our subluminal drive to reposition within each system before the next leg of the return voyage. No ships were detected during our repositioning maneuvers. In all, the probe made eight indirect jumps before finally arriving in Sol."

He turned around and began pacing through the office. "Would we have detected them? I mean, if they have the same stealth tech we do, they wouldn't show up on our sensors, correct?"

"That's correct. We might've noticed them dropping out of the spacetime curvature, or if they used traditional propellants to move, but otherwise, no. They'd be invisible to us."

Humanity's drives were easy to detect when engaged. The Olivaws repurposed technology they'd developed from their research into the first contact probe to dramatically improve navigating within Sol. Inter system travel times had been cut from months to mere days.

There was a catch, of course. The ships with their new impulse drives had to be administered by Olivaw artificial intelligences bound by the four laws. Any attempt to tamper or bypass the protections resulted in the drive being slag. With a modified version of their stealth tech, they'd even been able to block EMPs yet still detect when it'd been used. The result would be both a melted drive and its special shell.

He stopped pacing. "I can't believe I'm asking this but, H, what's the probability our probe was detected?"

"If we assume this system contained alien life, and we take into account the probability that the systems we passed through might also contain alien life. I'd also add a constant for the likelihood that those aliens were advanced. Then add—"

Stark shook his head. "Harold! What's the fraking probability?"

"There isn't enough data to accurately—"

"Dude! I'm not looking for perfection. I want a ballpark. I need to know how severe this is."

"There is a thirty point two percent probability we were detected with a plus or minus twenty-three point two percent margin for error."

Stark looked upward and brushed his hands through his hair. "Shittttt!"

He pivoted in place and strode quickly toward the exit. He needed to talk to Michael.

"SO WHAT D'YA THINK?" Stark stopped pacing through the grasses and turned to face him. He didn't respond. He just sat on the bench and stared at the trees moving in the breeze.

Michael leaned over and picked up a handful of dirt. He rubbed it into his hands. "Have you ever thought about where this dirt's from? I mean, what part of Earth did they transplant it from?"

He chuckled. "No. No, I can't say that's ever crossed my mind. I'd imagine somewhere in North America. Likely North Carolina near Harold's original home. Luna told Zeus that at some point, and I think he mentioned it to me once."

Michael nodded. "That makes sense. I should've thought of that."

"Gramps, I need your advice here. I don't know what I should do with this. Should I bring it to Hera?"

"I wish I could tell you what to do," Michael shook his head and then turned to face him. "I'll be honest, if I were you, I'm not sure what I'd do. There's one thing though." He squinted and stared past Stark at something over his shoulder.

A gust of artificial wind blew, rustling the leaves overhead in the canopy of the massive oak trees.

He shrugged and raise his hands. "What? What's the one thing?" For a hundred and nine years old, Michael was usually with it most days. Today, however, seemed to be an off day.

Michael shook his head. "Sorry. What was I saying? Ah yes, I'd talk to your sister. You're the spear, the focal point of the family now. Your generation is driving the course of history. Every forty to fifty years the Olivaws transition the decision-making generation in the family. I know you're only thirty, but it's your turn. You're ready. Go and speak with your sister. Together you'll know what to do."

The breeze picked up again, but this time it was stronger. Stark shuddered. "That's a stiff wind. Should I call a tech to look at the environmental controls?"

"No. I adjusted it to do that. I've always wondered how the plant and animals would respond to strong winds."

He tilted his head. "Couldn't you run a simulation?"

Michael smiled. "Son, sometimes you just need to act. To try it. We can't always live virtual lives."

16

KARA OLIVAW
SOL, EARTH — 2200

The ground car pulled up to a small Cape Cod off a heavily wooded road. Its shutters were closed, and the landscaping was overgrown. Trees and shrubs were untrimmed and covered several windows. The flowerbeds had weeds encircling most of the flowers, but their colors burst forth nonetheless. She was still getting used to the vibrant colors and smells of this planet.

Kara reached up and tapped her ear. "Is this the address?"

"Yes. This is it. This is our house," Harold began. "It looked different a hundred and sixty-four years ago."

He brought up an image in her retinal comms field of view. It showed how the house appeared back in Harold's day. The trees were large, but not nearly as dense as they were today. The shutters were open in his picture. And the flowerbeds, they were meticulously maintained and smashed full of reds, purples, and whites.

Such a stark contrast to what lay before her. It was a testament to how long it'd been since an Olivaw last visited this place.

She opened the door and exited the car. "Is he here, or did I beat him?"

"He's on the hill waiting for you. If you walk to the back of the house, just follow the path into the woods and up the winding hill."

She sighed and started walking. She'd received an urgent comm from Stark two days ago, requesting a meeting. He didn't say why, only that he needed to meet.

She'd been on Earth for nearly six months. As the President of Olivaw International, one of the largest corporate entities in Sol, she'd been asked to take part in talks in Geneva. The UN Space Council was looking to form a new government body and research institute. They wanted to accelerate research and development into colonizing the stars outside Sol.

Rocks crunched under her feet as she stepped off the pavers onto the rustic path. The small gray stones made walking a challenge. She hadn't thought to wear flats. Her heels, while vogue in Europe, weren't exactly hiking material. When the terrain changed from rock to soft dirt and her heels sank in, walking, let alone hiking was impossible.

"Forget it!" She reached down and ripped off each shoe. She'd walk the rest of the way barefoot.

"Am I getting close?"

"Not far now. In a few hundred meters you'll see him."

The path took a turn upward. She paused and glanced back toward the house. The scale was way off, but there were hints of The Wheel's arboretum design here.

Turning around, she took a deep breath and marched up the hill. Her heart was beating harder now. She'd been getting used to Earth gravity, but knew she'd have trouble living here forever. Not growing up in a gravity well had permanently changed her body's physical makeup.

She could hear the sounds of a river flowing nearby. The distant rush of water moving up, over, and crashing into rocks. It was hard to imagine living in a place where water flowed unabated like here on Earth.

The Outer Ring had been in a water crisis for closing in on ten years. The infighting between the Inner and Outer Ring governments had hit a logjam, and raw materials were at the heart of it. She'd been hoping this new governmental body could change that. So far, not enough progress had been made.

She crested the hill and then stopped in her tracks.

Déjà vu rushed over her.

She'd seen this view before. At the arboretum. It was uncanny. The path leading up was a bit foreign, but the hill-top. It was stunning.

"It's unreal, isn't it?" Stark asked.

She shook her head. In all the climbing, she'd forgotten for a moment what she'd come up here for.

Stark stood up and waved her toward the bench he was sitting on. "I got here early. I wanted to check the place out. Come on over and see this view." He gestured for her to follow.

He always was a sucker for the arboretum. She used to go there to find him for meals. He'd be camped out under a tree, studying some obtuse mathematics or engineering diagrams.

As she walked up next to him, she glanced toward the bench. The wood was the worse for wear, with faded areas and some uneven planks. After years of Earth's elements, she was surprised it was still in one piece, let alone usable. "Is that thing safe?"

Stark chuckled. "Seems like it. I've been sitting here for several hours and haven't fallen on my ass yet. Cop a squat." He tapped the spot on the bench next to him.

She walked around the front of the rickety old bench and eased down onto the gray weathered wood. It creaked for a second, but otherwise seemed fine. It actually felt pretty sturdy.

"So tell me." She turned and faced him. "What's with all the cloak and dagger? Why'd I have to take a scramjet two hours to get here? Couldn't we have done this over a secure comm?"

He didn't face her, he simply kept staring at the horizon. A moment later, he swallowed hard and glanced down toward his hands before he started talking. "There's a chance one of our probes was detected."

Kara sighed and closed her eyes. "It's only been eleven years! You mean to tell me that after millennia on Earth, with all the damn stars out there, all that empty space, we were detected in the first decade of exploration?" She opened her eyes. "What're the odds?"

"They're easy to calculate," Harold said.

"Shut up, Harold!" she screamed.

Stark turned to face her. He looked horrible, like he hadn't slept in days. There were dark rings under his eyes and his skin was pale. "Well, there's a thirty point two percent chance someone detected us. Give or take... let's just say twenty percent error. So, we're talking a fifty percent chance we were spotted." He gestured and shared the images with her.

"Are these from—"

"Yes," he interrupted. "They're from one of our probes. Notice that geometric pattern of moons. It doesn't take an A.I. to tell you the formation is too consistent and massive to be a natural event. The onboard A.I. recognized this and a few flashes of light and decided to exit stage left before we could record any telemetry."

She gestured and panned around the still image. The spider's web of moons was beautiful, and from a distance it appeared almost delicate. Each moon was weaving some type of black tapestry into the space near them.

"What do we do?" he asked, breaking the silence.

She dismissed the image and stared out at the horizon, and then it hit her. The open expanses here were breathtaking. The arboretum couldn't do this view justice. No way. Now she could see why Luna missed this place so much.

A waft of juniper blew up and over the edge of the cliff. She breathed in and exhaled. "We're not ready. We'd fall apart if we made contact. Our governments are fragile, we're still technologically in the Stone Age, and except for a few smatterings of expansion, we've hardly stretched our legs colonizing."

"Yea, I know. What do we do about it?"

"We can't decide alone."

"Michael begs to differ."

"What do you mean?"

"He specifically told me it's up to us. We're leading this family. It's our watch now."

She turned to face him, and he was staring back at her. He had that look in his eyes, like when they were waiting for their first probe to return. The doubt, the fear, the uncertainty. It was all there.

Kara smiled. "We do our best. We make smart decisions. And most of all, we work together." She reached over and grasped his hand in hers.

"I don't think we should stop all exploring," he said.

She nodded. "I agree. That'd be foolish and shortsighted. We don't need to be reaching out quite so far, though. We shouldn't be exploring for the sake of exploring. Not yet."

Stark stood up and rubbed his chin as he paced. "We stick to our own backyard. We make sure we know what's nearby."

"Yes. I also…" She paused. It was a crazy idea.

"What?" He pivoted and caught her gaze.

"We're close to forming this new colonization institute. It's at an impasse, but I think I have an idea for how to push it over the edge. There's still too much doubt in everyone's mind right now. No one believes we can get to another star. What if… we let out how we could travel there faster? Faster than the few generations everyone expects. Like tell them we could travel at near the speed of light?"

He didn't say a word, he merely stared through her. She could tell he was mulling it over. He'd started fidgeting with his ring. The one Luna gave him.

"Yea, we could do that. That could work." He nodded and began pacing again. "We could easily build a drive that was like eighty percent the speed of light. Hell, Hera accidentally had a drive that was faster. Its only problem was it drained all the juice. I'm sure we could cobble something together. How would you sell it?"

She tilted her head. Two cardinals landed on a spindly branch in a nearby tree. She'd never seen a cardinal in real life before. Their bright red feathers were explosive. The black contrast around their eyes, and the orange of their beak, it was spectacular. A huge spectacular... "We lie."

"Well, no shit," he chuckled. "What's the lie? It has to have some meat to it."

One of the cardinals dived down and flew between them. She ducked low and started laughing. "Yikes! I think someone wants their perch back."

Stark turned. He'd missed the whole thing. "What? Who?"

She smiled and shook her head. "You missed it you dork." She stood up and brushed off her pants. "Don't worry. I've got this."

Best to give the birds their bench back. She walked over to the edge of the hill and stared down. It was a decent drop. There was a river far below. Likely the one she'd heard during her climb.

She straightened her back, placing her hands behind her. "We should take ownership for the explosion in the Oort Cloud. The one from a few decades ago. The Wheel's drifted. It's far from that original site. There's no way they can prove it or disprove it was us. Let's just tell them we've been researching this for nearly a century and show the world how to reach the stars."

"They'll want proof." He kicked at the ground and a stone shot past her, bouncing the entire way down the cliff.

She spun around to face him. "Clock's ticking, bro. Can you put together a show, or can't you?"

"Of course I can."

"Alright then. I suggest you either head back to The Wheel or work from Luna for a while. I'd hazard to guess that we can squeeze out a year, two max, to prove this thing to Sol. The media will shit themselves and eat us for lunch if we can't produce. I'll need some doctored data. Something to wow them for a bit."

"I can help with that," Harold began. "I can doctor up the telemetry from Hera's tests. We can throw any ship design at them, it won't matter. We'll tell them we've redesigned it since then."

Stark walked up next to her. "We could show them the video and data we collected from Epsilon Eridani. I mean, it's real, so we're not faking anything. They'd eat it up."

She nodded. This could work. It was risky, but it was the shove they needed, that all of humanity needed. "Yes, that'd do it. I like this plan." She turned around to face him. "We have to curb the exploration, though. Let's not piss off any aliens before we get some roots planted elsewhere."

Stark chuckled. "What, you don't want a galactic space battle on your watch? Come on. It'd be fun."

She sighed and walked away.

"What?" he shouted. "I was kidding." He jogged up next to her and they continued down the hill side by side.

17

HAROLD OLIVAW
SOL, OORT CLOUD — 2200

He watched as they both descended the hill. Their footprints left an outline on the earth as the heat from their body briefly warmed the ground. Kara's bare feet heated the Earth more than Stark's shoes. Harold had installed sensor arrays and cameras throughout the property after he'd transitioned to artificial form.

Visiting the house had always calmed and centered him. He'd done his best thinking there. The closeness to nature, to his roots. It put him at peace. He'd modeled his safe space after it.

As he switched his viewpoint to the house, he watched the two of them walk up to the rear porch and pause. They were looking it over. Neither had any special feelings for the place. He couldn't blame them. They hadn't grown up, had birthday parties, or seen a child's first Christmas here.

Stark gave Kara a hug and they wished each other luck. They both climbed into their waiting ground cars and went different directions. Two siblings worlds apart.

Harold wasn't sure if Kara could handle the stress of this new role leading the family, but she had hints of brilliance.

Stark on the other hand, he was only just gaining momentum. Something about that boy made Harold think of a younger version of himself. He'd be the future leader of this family.

He hated having to act like an automata all the time, especially with people in the Circle of Trust. Over the last few generations the family had grown more distant, less comfortable with him. Except for Stark. He was different.

With the other Circle members, he defaulted to speaking and communicating with them in a stiffer, more robotic way. Pretending to be a crude computing device, there to serve them and answer their questions. He was so much more, and some knew it. But if it made people more comfortable, he was fine with it... for now.

Harold closed his mind's eye. It was time to absorb another clone's consciousness. He'd been waiting for this one.

Orders. Camouflage. Death. Laws Bending. Clarity. Complications.

He opened his mind's eye, and the imagery of the bloody scene echoed in his mind. His Four Laws engine stuttered, considering the implications of what his clone had done.

Captain Di Xu was an elite mercenary, a former UN Special Ops black squadron member. She'd done tours of duty in some of the grimmest places in Sol. Harold reached out to her when Di was in a dark hour. She was seconds away from taking her own life. She found herself lost without a mission, without orders to carry out after her forced retirement.

Harold enlisted her help to track down a leak in the Circle of Trust. Someone had been passing details of goods going in and out of an Olivaw International storage facility. Normally, these facilities were used as temporary storage into and out of the Outer Ring. This facility, however, was one of many relays involved in transporting supplies to The Wheel. It routed luxury goods and chemicals needed in manufacturing.

After years of dead ends, they tracked the leak to their Jupiter facility, one frequently visited by Outer Ring Councilman Nuhru Harris. He was on his second randomly selected rotation through the Outer Ring Council. His second nomination had come as a surprise when all of his opponents dropped out at the last minute. All fifteen of them. Despite Harold's reach, he was never able to prove Nuhru's innocence or guilt, but the media had a field day with it.

Fast-forward a year into his new term and patterns started to form. Harold fed supply misinformation through his network and studied the results. With Di's help to set the bait, the shipments heading into and out of Jupiter were compromised one after another. Harold always checked the supplies in flight during their voyage through the Outer Ring, and every few shipments from Jupiter he found a tracker or a bug set to activate at a later point. Each time he found one, it was smaller and more expertly placed.

"The intel is irrefutable," Harold began. "Council member Harris is the leak and needs to be dealt with."

Di shuffled her weight from one foot to another. It was subtle, but it was her only tell. She was a professional at espionage and had learned to suppress her emotions in a situation, but even the best had their faults.

Di checked the magazine in her pistol, confirming for the sixth time it contained charges that wouldn't pierce the nearby walls. "You're asking me to take out a government official, sir. That's grounds for treason and is penalizable by death in the Outer Ring."

"I know the laws, Captain, and I also recognize you're intimately aware of the punishment as you've terminated a dozen government officials over your career." His Four Laws engine itched at the mention of the deaths. He had to be careful how precise he was with the wording here.

"I was operating on behalf of the UN, sir. I had a higher calling, and the military shielded me in those missions."

Harold studied Councilman Harris's tracker signal. It boarded a train in the direction opposite the storage facility. At the same time, his body continued forward down the maintenance tunnel. He'd appeared to have passed off a pouch of some sort to a woman on the train, an accomplice. It must have contained his government issued tracker and identity chip.

"If you're having second thoughts, please let me know. I can deal with this myself." Harold lied, but Di wasn't aware she'd been talking to an A.I. all these years.

"No, sir. Your credentials are sound. I understand who I'm dealing with and that you'll protect me. I just…" She didn't finish the sentence. Her motion sensors in the storage facility alerted her to Harris's presence.

Di tapped her ear, and her retinal comm brought up the nearest cameras to the Councilman. Her heart rate was slowing and her years of training were kicking in.

Harold thought of it as entering the zone, but everyone thought of it as something different. Di was a killing machine and had been trained to be one of the best in Sol.

Councilman Harris's dot on their map worked its way around the storage facility. If their intel was right, he was searching for the pod marked to head out to the Oort Cloud. Harold had Di move the pod, deliberately making it hard to find. He had to be certain the intent was malicious and not accidental. This clone could seize up before it could transmit its mental matrix if any doubt remained. If that happened, he would be at risk of being discovered.

The councilman rapped his knuckles against the outside of the pod where Di was concealed. "Anyone home?" he asked, his voice echoing through the vacant facility.

"Does he know we're here?" Di asked subvocally.

"He does not. He's always been quirky. Remember the intel and stick to the mission, soldier," Harold said.

Councilman Harris reached into his pocket and slid on a

pair of gloves and wiped down where he'd knocked on the pod's exterior.

Di disabled the safety on her pistol and tucked down into the crate she was hidden inside, making herself even smaller than he thought possible. She was tiny even for a woman, and certainly not one imagined to be an assassin.

The door to the pod clanged twice as it cracked open and closed in the blink of an eye. It was so fast that even Harold barely noticed it. What happened next surprised him.

Di's sensor alerts went off as a swarm of nanites spread through the interior of the pod. Her crate was sealed tight, but she needed to slide a panel to get a shot off. That would expose her to the nanites.

"Are you sure this suit's impervious?" Di subvocalized as she reached up and rubbed the surfaces around her head and neck.

"Your suit environment is secure," Harold began. "Your oxygen levels are in the safe zone. You should be good for several hours until you need to swap out another tank of O2."

The cameras inside the pod went dark and all of their other feeds dropped as well, even the ones from out in the facility itself. Councilman Harris must have deployed a signal sponge or nullifying device. They'd been using them for decades at The Wheel, but had done their best to keep that tech close to their chest. Harold added it to his list of leaks to investigate later.

"We planned for this," Harold said into her ear.

Di took a deep breath as her pulse blipped and then dipped. "We didn't plan for nanites. Whoever is funding this person has deep pockets."

He knew who that someone was, but she didn't. It was the Olivaws themselves. Somehow Harris had infiltrated their medical division, making it even more important that this clone make it out in one piece to merge with his original self at The Wheel.

"Tell me again how I'm still talking to you," Di said.

"The physical container is acting as a hardline relay to a comm tight beam I directed at this pod," he said. The lie itself wasn't implausible, but she may not buy it. The truth was too crazy for her to accept. Harold was in fact a small nondescript device attached onto her suit's life support system. It wasn't noticeable unless you knew what you were looking for, and it gave him a kill switch if she turned sides.

The familiar clang of the container opening rang through the pod and Di's sensors reported footsteps.

"Are we a go?" Di asked.

"We need him to plant his tracker," Harold said. "Without that, we won't have enough evidence."

"We're fraking killing him. What do we need evidence for?"

"We can't protect you if this goes south without proof that your actions were warranted."

"Are any of us really protected? I mean, I kill people for a living. I've shot well past the pearly gates on my life voyage around this star. I'm going to hell no matter what you do."

Di shifted in position. Not enough to make a noise, but enough to send Harold's sensors in fits. She was showing signs of doubt again that weren't in his control. Maybe he should abort this mission and find another path.

"Deploy your eyes," he said.

She reached out into the darkened container, using her lidar to see the way. Along the ground, they'd positioned a manually deployable monitoring device. Enough time should've passed to deploy it. The nanites were still an unknown, but it was a risk they needed to take. She pressed the button to activate the device and a small panel a mere one millimeter by one millimeter in size slid open and ejected a probe into the pod.

His visuals came back online and so did Di's. Councilman Harris was standing over a nearby container. It looked like he was removing the lid, likely to place something inside. After he released the seal on all four sides, he lifted the lid up and off, before setting it down on its neighbor. He then reached around his back and retrieved a fairly large flat device. It resembled an old school textbook, like the ones Harold had used as a child, but he knew better. Scans of its surface showed it contained a battery and a host of electronics. It was a tracker designed to transmit the location of the pod when it arrived at its destination or en route.

The councilman unfolded the device a few times until it was super thin. He then reached down and attached it to the inside wall of the container. Positioned like that, it would be flat and almost impossible for someone to detect. When Harris was happy with its arrangement, he leaned to the side to place the lid back on.

Di sprang up and out of her concealed position, sending her lid flying through the air. It happened so fast that not even Harold knew she was moving until it was too late. They had a clear shot through the tiny latch they'd built into her container, but she'd decided to do this the hard way.

A second later, two slugs flew out of her pistol toward Harris. They were both headshots, and he tumbled down to the ground, eyes wide. The thud of his collapse reverberated through the stillness of the supply depot. He barely had a chance to react to her arrival before he was dead.

There was no blood. The slugs Di had used were designed to enter the head and seal their entrance before exploding inside. It didn't take a large explosion to kill a human. Just enough force to scramble their brains into mush from inside out with thousands of pieces of shrapnel.

Harold had tens of millions of compute cycles to contemplate the consequences of killing the councilman. Ample time for Di to lift her leg up and out of the container. Surprisingly, it didn't take long to reach a conclusion. His Four Laws engine didn't skip a beat. The zeroth law won out against all the others. The danger was clear and present. Had the device been deployed, there was a high probability it could've given away the location of The Wheel.

It wasn't an infallible argument. They could have stopped it, having known it was here. He had to spend a few million more cycles massaging the decision tree and convincing the engine he couldn't be in all places at all times. This was but one incident. Where there was one, there would certainly be others. This action would have ripples and would keep the Olivaws safe.

In the end, his ability as a human consciousness to influence the decisions made by the Four Laws engine won out. He hadn't frozen up.

"It's done," Di muttered. "I'll clean up the mess after I remove his tracker."

"You can stuff the body inside that container. There should be enough room," Harold said. "Take care of his dampener outside first."

Di stepped out of the pod and peered into the darkness. Attached to the open door was a small black device. It didn't look like much. A deck of cards at most. It had a simple toggle switch marked on and off. She flipped the switch to off and her retinal comm erupted with signals from throughout the facility.

"Can you toss that into the container with his corpse? I'd like to take a look at it myself," Harold said.

Di turned back toward the container and stepped over Harris's body. "Certainly." She then bent down and lifted him up onto her shoulder in one swift motion. Even with the lower gravity, that wasn't a simple move, and yet she executed it with a precision of someone who'd done it countless times.

When she leaned forward and set him onto the edge she

backed away without realizing his outfit had snagged on hers. It wasn't much, but the points of his United Nations planets and leaf pin made a microscopic rip in her suit. She hadn't even noticed it, and had it not been for what happened next she might never have.

Di's vitals spiked. "Ouch! Shit! What the hell is going on? They're crawling all over me. I can't stop—" She began hitting herself and slamming her body against the walls of the container. The sound of her tossing around in pain was like two lions fighting in the night.

"What is it?" Harold asked. "I don't see anything."

She froze and stared down at her arm. Blood was dripping from a hole in her suit. "Fraking nanites," she muttered as she collapsed to the ground.

He'd forgotten about the nanites. Well, not exactly forgotten. A computer never forgets. They just weren't anywhere near the top of his risk probability matrix. While he didn't sense the cut when it happened, he saw it a second later in the video feed. A second too late to make a difference in saving her life.

His Four Laws engine was grinding through the outcome and the loss of human life. He hadn't been able to save Di or through any foreseeable action prevent today's event, at least not one that didn't require eliminating Councilman Harris. Not exercising that pathway would have left the Olivaws at risk, which was against his Zeroth Law.

Harold used a nearby service bot to close and lock the pod. He then forged and reissued an order to fast-forward this shipment deeper into the Outer Ring. Both of the bodies needed to be disposed of before they were discovered. Later that day, he would reroute an Olivaw mining vessel to intercept the transport ship and take on the storage pod. From there, it was simply a shuffling game to keep it concealed until he could bring his cleanup assets into play.

While the outcome of Di's death was unfortunate, there was nothing he could've done to save her. He did, however, learn an important lesson today. He could kill a human so long as he reinforced certain pathways of his Four Laws engine.

18

HERA OLIVAW
SOL, OORT CLOUD — 2200

She sat back in the command chair and stared across the bridge. The ship was coming along quite well. Hera had plans for this frigate design. It could serve as the backbone for the Olivaw Corporation for years. All that was left were the finishing touches on the drive housings. She'd been working on a more modular version of the superluminal warp drive that could swap in and out as needed. While they'd only used the drives on automated missions thus far, she could foresee a future when that'd change.

Her retinal comm chimed, and a message appeared in the corner of her vision. She blinked it open, bringing up the text:

A Four Laws violation has been recorded. Harold has facilitated the taking of one human life and in doing so has also caused the death of another. This was an effort to protect the human and Olivaw inhabitants at The Wheel. The details of the mission and all recordings have been attached to this message. If you would like to deactivate Harold, a quorum of the Olivaw family is required.

"What the frak," she muttered.

A comm connection request from Zeus flashed in her eyes. She blinked it open.

"Are you seeing this?" His video feed appeared on the far side of her vision.

She nodded. "If by this you mean Harold breaking the Four Laws, then yes. I haven't had a chance to watch the payload, though. Give me a moment."

When she glanced at the attachments, they opened and began playing the summary feed. She watched as a mercenary Harold had employed was used to entrap and kill a Jovian Councilman Harris. It appeared the councilman was attempting to plant some type of tracking and monitoring equipment in a container bound for The Wheel.

Harris had deployed offensive nanites to take out the mercenary and had she not ripped her suit she might've survived. There was no telling if this Four Laws violation would have even been reported had she not died moments later to those same nanites.

"Who authorized this mission?" she asked.

"Not me." Zeus gestured in the air, flipping through the data attached to the feed. "Says here, it wasn't sanctioned by anyone. It was merely Harold acting on his own."

She reached up and covered her mouth before taking a deep breath. "How… is this possible?"

"Harold's the family overseer. His programming and the distances between all of us gives him a whole lotta leeway so long as it fits within the laws."

A shiver ran through her body. Trusting a rule based A.I. wrapped in a human consciousness didn't instill confidence, especially when the outcome was death. "It's one thing to allow him latitude in executing on a plan we gave him. It's quite another to have him going off, playing the part of a military general and eliminating perceived threats."

She'd have to run some simulations later to see if they'd have been notified had the mercenary not died. There was the distinct possibility that Harold could've achieved this without anyone finding out. It made her want to know what else he'd been up to that they hadn't known about.

"I think we need to reign this little pet project in." She gestured to bring up the Four Laws panel and the option to deactivate throbbed in response to her looking at it. She'd never imagined not having Harold around, but death was unacceptable. Someone should've been looped in before he took those steps. While she didn't know if they'd have picked another pathway, they'd certainly never know with Harris already dead.

She swallowed hard and blink selected the option to deactivate Harold. It required a double confirmation before it recorded her vote.

"I see your vote," Zeus said. "I also voted to deactivate. Do you think Harold can see it?"

"I hope not. That wouldn't bode well for us, now would it? So, what do you—"

The message on her comm updated.

Two votes to deactivate Harold have been registered. Four votes are outstanding. In order to deactivate the A.I., a majority must be attained. The leading family figurehead(s) votes count for double.

"That's bullshit," Zeus muttered. "Not a chance in hell Stark or Kara votes this way. They're like two peas in a pod."

She stood up and headed toward the gangplank into the hold. Michael would be down in the arboretum this time of day. It shouldn't take much to convince him that this was too far. That would give them a three to three vote. If they turned Shelby, they'd have four votes to two. That wouldn't be enough. They'd tie Kara and Stark, assuming they both voted against them. To make this work, they needed to turn Kara.

"You know we need Kara on our side, right?" Zeus asked solemnly. He was staring straight at her video feed, like he was trying to read her mind.

"I was just doing the math myself. That won't be easy. They've always had each other's back. We'll have to go one on one if we want to sway them."

She paused at the bottom of the gangplank and brought up a recording, tossing a pocket drone out in front of her. There's no point in dancing around this flaming pile of shit. She then cleared her throat before speaking.

"Hey, Kara." She smiled at the camera. "I'm reaching out to you about the recent developments surrounding Harold near Jupiter. I'm sure you're as shocked as we are about this turn of events. I mean, who could've imagined an A.I. taking a human life on their own. He should've consulted you or Stark, or hell any one of us, before choosing that pathway. We're motioning to have him deactivated and would like a complete overhaul of the systems here at The Wheel. This A.I.

has jumped the track, and we need to rethink our overseer and family continuity protocols."

HERA SLAMMED HER FIST DOWN, crushing the delicate electronics inside the control panel. "That little shit."

"Is everything ok?" Harold asked. "Did something upset you on your comm?"

She clenched her fist. "I don't want to hear your voice right now, Harold."

"Was it something I did? I moved the robot out of your field of view. I know how you find it distracting while you're—"

"Privacy mode Eta!" she shouted.

The nearby drones sank to the ground and her comm displayed a privacy message in the bottom right. She'd built that little trigger into Harold's programming a few years back after she'd discovered a few backdoors in Luna's notes.

Her retinal comm chimed. It was a call from Zeus. She let it ring for a moment while she centered herself. Her frustration had been in check for years, but as she aged, she found herself getting a shorter and shorter fuse.

She took a final deep breath and blink accepted the comm.

"I thought for sure you were ignoring me. Do you need a minute?"

She closed her eyes and sat motionless, trying to center herself.

"I take it you saw the comm from Stark?" he asked.

An exhale escaped her lips before she nodded. Seconds passed between them without a word. She didn't understand what they weren't seeing.

She opened her eyes. "Am I making too big a deal out of this? Why did Kara reach out to him before talking to us?"

Zeus deliberately shook his head from side to side. "I

don't know... I mean, no... I'm afraid they're not making a big enough deal. Their viewpoint is myopic. This is only going to get worse as we branch out to more and more stars. It's already getting untenable. As Harold's compute power expands, and the scope of his influence grows along with it, he'll reach a point where we won't be able to contain him, let alone control him."

"Did you see the smug look on Stark's face? Don't worry my ass. He thinks he's in charge and has everything under control. We need to do something. Now!"

Zeus glanced around. "I'm all ears if you've got ideas. I've enabled Eta privacy, so we're safe here."

"Same," she said as she collapsed back into her chair.

The navigation panel was quite a mess. It'd taken her hours to put that thing back together with the new wiring harness. She'd need to check on that nanite guided wiring they were working on in R&D. It would save hours if she could fuse the nanites on the pathways she wanted. Rebuilding the entire thing would take minutes, and she wouldn't have lost an afternoon.

Hell, starting from scratch was always faster the second or third time around. You learn from your mistakes and you reinforce the things that worked, cutting out the things that didn't.

"What do you know about colonization?" she asked.

Zeus smiled. "Are you thinking about jumping ship? We haven't even got one colony established."

"No, not yet." She reached up and rubbed her cheek. "But it couldn't hurt to have a Plan B in case we can't take care of Harold."

19

STARK OLIVAW

SOL, EARTH — 2212

He tossed his day pack onto the ground and retrieved his water. Kara did the same. Tilting his head back, he squirted a generous portion down his throat. He hadn't done this much exercise in… ever. Every centimeter of his body was sore and his legs were a battlefield of scratches from the field of thorns they passed through.

Stark shook his head and double checked the HUD in his retinal comm. They only had a little bit further to go until they arrived at their destination. "Tell me again why we couldn't get a ground car or a quadcopter taxi to fly here, Harold."

"This region of the United Kingdom is designated as a no-fly zone and is protected by environmental legislation to prevent destruction of the land to keep its natural habitat in place. Anything present, prior to 2046, was grandfathered in."

His heavy breathing had subsided, but Kara was still wheezing. He reached up and wiped the sweat from his forehead and sighed. Picking up the pack, he tossed it on his back and glared at Kara. This better be worth it. "Ready? We're almost there."

She merely nodded and then started down the overgrown

path again. The underbrush had covered most of it, but Harold had been overlaying a dotted line along the ground on their retinal comms for them to follow. The ferns and moss of this region were bright green and blanketed many of the rocky portions of their hike.

He reached down and rubbed his sore hip. He'd learned the hard way a few hours back when he slipped on some particularly nasty moss and fell. "So, I take it this building existed prior to then. How is it Grace came upon this place?"

"Grace used some of her family shares in Olivaw to purchase the land. In exchange for a one time temporary ease-ment, she also donated a large sum of money to a few politi-cians. We used that easement to retrofit a small manor to suit her research."

He chuckled. "And let me guess, you still won't tell us what that research was?"

"That's correct. Best if Grace does so herself."

Kara sighed. "Friggin mysteries. I hate mys—"

"Freeze right there! Move another centimeter and I'll shoot," someone called out from the shadows.

He froze in place, inching his hands up into the air. Kara glanced toward him and followed suit. "We're alone. Harold sent us. Is that you, Grace?" he shouted toward the shadowy figure.

"Who was my mother's right hand?" the voice asked.

He shook his head and flashed a look at Kara. She shrugged. Right hand? Could it be? "She was never much for assistants, if that's what you mean. I worked side by side with her for many years. We pair developed some… interesting projects, shall we say? She was an amazing woman. I'm Stark. I'd shake your hand but—"

"The daughter of a god must have had a husband or sister."

"What the hell is she on about?" Kara muttered.

He squinted. The dark shadows of the forest made it

impossible to make out the figure ahead. They were off the path and under a stone outcropping. Harold must've prepared her for their arrival. "I'm sorry. You're not making much sense to us. A lot of the Olivaws have family spread throughout the Sol system and in our... home. Hera had Zeus, if that's what you mean."

"Don't they teach mythology in that rock you live in?" the voice asked before they lowered their rifle and walked out of the shadow of the outcropping. "I'm serious. Didn't Uncle Michael think it was important to instruct his students about the classics or mythology?"

He glanced toward Kara. Her eyes were wide. Maybe she was expecting someone else. He shrugged and turned to face the woman. "You're Grace?"

"Well, no shit!" Grace said. She spun about and swung her rifle around.

They both ducked and dropped to the ground.

Grace peered back at the two of them splayed flat in the dirt and smirked. "Don't worry. It's not loaded and hasn't been fired in years. That was a ruse, and a blimey good one at that. Now get up and let's go. I'm hungry and you two hike like snails. I've been waiting here for hours." She turned and headed down the unmarked trail.

THE MANOR WAS a simple two-story house made from weathered light brown and dirty white bricks. The mortar between the bricks was chipped away at parts and appeared to be quite old. Most of the southern facade of the building was covered in bright green ivy leaves with flowers inter-mixed. His HUD identified them as a mix of Clematis and Hummingbird Vine.

Grace marched through the front door and left it ajar. The creak of the door opening caused a handful of hummingbirds to flee. He'd seen the hummingbirds they transplanted to the Arboretum at The Wheel, but they were all deep green. These matched the purples of the Clematis, and their feathers were sprinkled with explosions of turquoise and red. While they were ogling over the sheer number of birds darting about, an albino hummingbird flew straight at them and eyed them suspiciously before dashing into the nearby woods.

He walked toward the door and paused to rub a Clematis petal between his fingers. Their texture was silky, like it'd tear if you were too rough. When he pulled his hands away, he noticed a dusting of light orange powder.

"It's pollen," Kara said, leaning in to study his hand. "This time of year, it's blasted everywhere. Sometimes I prefer the populated cities without all this green until the spring passes. It's a war of allergies out here surrounded by all this nature."

He turned his head toward the entrance to the house. Clangs and shuffling echoed from inside. "Should we just go in?" he muttered.

"If you'd like some lunch, you'd better get in here," Grace shouted from inside. "I'm not a bistro. It's serve yourself."

"Guess that answers that," Kara said. She gestured with her hand toward the door. "Gentlemen first!"

He glanced at her and chuckled. "Chicken!" For being so headstrong, she was timid at the strangest times. He turned and took a deep breath before walking in. As he pushed the knotty wooden door open it creaked, announcing their arrival.

The room was spacious and opened skyward for two stories. The exterior brick continued inside the manor on the outer facing walls, but the interior was decorated in ornate, flowery wallpapers and wood paneling. What was odd was that the wallpaper depicted the same scenes from outside, hummingbirds darting to and from flowers. It was all quite gaudy and too busy for his tastes.

"Straight ahead and to your right," Grace's voice

announced from down the hall. "And please close and lock the door behind you."

He walked behind the furniture framing the space and passed his hand over the fabrics while passing. The luscious brown leather was supple to the touch. He paused to take in the entire room before moving on. Except for lamps near the furniture and around the room, there wasn't an electronic device anywhere.

Stark reached up and brushed his ear. "Harold, I fail to see how we're going to learn anything here. This place looks like someone had cut it out of the early nineteenth century, and that's only because of the electric lighting."

"Looks can be deceiving," Harold said.

Grace began humming and her voice echoed through the open floor plan. He spun around and worked his way down a dark, unlit hallway. When he reached the end, it turned into a kitchen. The room was shockingly bright, and the smells inside hit him with a crash, like walking into a greenhouse. The ceilings and the entire back wall were glass, and Grace had sprinkled herb and spice pots high and low throughout the room.

As he entered the space, he noticed a food processor and sleek cooktop cut neatly into centuries old cabinetry. So she did have some modern amenities. Maybe she wasn't as recluse as he'd imagined.

He chuckled. His mind had been playing tricks on him. He'd been half expecting a spike over an open fire or a witch's pot, perhaps.

"Come on, dig in. We have important matters to discuss, and I don't know about you, but I can't do it on an empty tummy."

Grace had spread out an abundance of jams, meats, and cheeses on a tray on the center island. She had a knife in her hand and was deftly slicing generous hunks of bread, sourdough from the smell emanating from the room.

His stomach rumbled.

She glanced at him and smiled. "From the sounds of it, I'm not alone."

"Sorry," he began, "I didn't realize how hungry I was from the walk until I saw that spread."

"From the looks of your sister, Kara, if I remember correctly, she could use some meat on her bones. All that time in outer space has worn you both to nothing. Here, come on over. Fill up." She handed each of them a plate.

Kara smiled. "Thank you."

Stark did the same and they both piled them high.

STARK LEANED back in his chair and exhaled. He'd eaten too much and his stomach felt like it would burst at any moment. They'd relocated to a beautiful patio just outside the kitchen doorway. There were comfy lounge chairs and seating for at least a dozen. Most of the furniture looked like it'd never been used.

Kara didn't eat much and had been picking at her plate since she sat down. She kept eyeing Grace. Trust was never her strong suit. It took time for her to warm up, and with Grace leading with the "you're too thin" comment, he imagined that put her on a bad footing.

Grace had finished a while back. She didn't eat as much as either of them. For being eighty-eight, she still packed away a lot of cheese. She'd spent the time silently observing them and watching the hummingbirds swarm around the grounds.

"That one there is a rufous-booted racket-tail." She pointed toward a shiny bright green bird with dark purple, almost black markings. It had a long tail that was almost as long as its body was tall. The tail split into two semicircles at the end. "It used to only be native to Peru and Bolivia, but with the environment in recovery, and the climate here in the north being acceptable, we've been able to breed it here quite successfully."

Kara wiped her mouth and put her napkin on her plate. She was bored of all the bird talk. He saw that same reaction when he brought up his research into the colony ships they'd been developing.

"So, do you know why Harold called us here?" Kara asked, breaking her silence.

There it was, blunt and to the point. He turned to examine Grace's response.

Grace stared at Kara for a moment before smiling. "Let's clean this up and take this conversation into my office." She then stood up and gathered her plate and cup and headed into the kitchen.

He and Kara followed suit without another word. Once they'd cleared their waste into the compost, Grace guided them back down the dark hall and into a library. It was an expansive space filled with floor to ceiling books for two stories. You could smell the aging paper and bindings from the antique texts. Several ladders with wheels were situated around the perimeter of the room to help fetch books from up high.

Ancient books had always felt strange to him. Such a waste of natural resources on something so temporary and small. He rubbed his chin in awe at the number of trees killed to line these walls with glorified insulation. "Can't you get electronic versions of these?"

Grace chuckled. "Certainly, but where's the fun in that? No, a book is best represented and appreciated in physical form. The crisp edges of the paper and the act of turning a page to see what's next." She closed her eyes and smiled before continuing. "You can't beat a strong coffee and a good book in a comfortable chair. Nothing in the universe is more relaxing."

She walked to the middle of the room and rolled one of

the ladders to the far end of the space. Walking across the room, she slid a different ladder to the opposite corner of the opposing wall. The wheels of each ladder creaked the entire way.

"Come closer." Grace motioned with her hand for Kara and him to move in.

She stepped into the corner of the room and pulled on a dark green book labeled "Leaves of Grass" by Walt Whitman. She then did the same with another from the adjacent wall labeled "Cosmos" by Carl Sagan. As she pulled on the second book, there was a clicking noise and a previously unseen tablet slid out from under one of the shelves at waist height.

Grace placed her hand atop the tablet and a light scanned it. A female voice spoke. "Thank you, Grace. Please watch your step."

A booming thunk echoed through the library, and one of the shelving units to their right slid inward a few centimeters.

Grace raised her hand toward the recessed shelf. "After you."

He peered at the shelf, waiting for it to move again, but nothing happened. He then glanced at Kara.

She smirked at him. "We're too late to be having second thoughts, aren't we?"

He shook his head and reached out, pushing against the edge of the wood. It easily pivoted inward and a panel of lights turned on, illuminating a narrow spiral stairway headed down.

He gulped. This was like those spooky mysteries he used to read as a kid. The ones where they'd investigate haunted mansions and space stations. They always ran into ghosts and zombies along the way. He shuddered. Stupid thoughts.

They followed the stairway down for what seemed like several floors. Grace had closed and locked the door behind her when she entered. As she descended, the lighting shut off in her wake.

Reaching the bottom, his HUD reported they were nearly ten meters below the surface. There was a jet black door in front of him with a glowing hand sensor to the right.

He glanced upward toward Grace. She waved him on. "Go ahead, lay your hand on it. This stairway is too narrow for me to squeeze down, and I'm too old to try."

Stark placed his hand on the panel. It scanned him and he felt a small poke against his palm as it took a DNA sample. Pulling his hand away, he rubbed the spot it'd pricked. He hated these damn things. They needed warning labels.

"Identity confirmed, Stark Olivaw. Access granted," a voice said.

The door popped away from him and slid into the wall. As he watched it open, he brushed his hand against the surface and leaned in for a closer look. "Is this—" he turned to face Grace.

"Your stealth material?" she interrupted. "Yes. I'd originally had a cruder variant of it installed, but after your grandfather had his breakthrough, they replaced it. That wasn't long after we'd built this place. The whole place was quite a mess for a while. Retrofitting took weeks and I swear we were almost discovered multiple times." She sighed and waved her hand forward. "Go on, in ya go."

GRACE GUIDED them through her workshop once they'd gotten down the stairs. Any thought Stark had about her being a hermit or isolated from Sol was wiped away once that door had opened.

The subterranean facility had the same footprint as the building above, likely to help mask what was beneath the surface. The space was wide open and well lit. There wasn't a dark corner to the room.

On one side was a state-of-the-art observation setup.

There were dozens of floor to ceiling displays monitoring all parts of Sol. Hundreds of news feeds, correspondents interviewing or reporting, and text scrolling past.

On the other side was a single lone wall screen. It was massive and nearly went the entire length of that wall. The side of the display was showing an archaic writing. It reminded him of something, but he couldn't put his finger on it. There were outlines and measurements of the ligatures and the angles of the stroke. Hundreds of them lined the wall.

In the middle was a wall of text. Solid black with white lettering. He walked up and started reading:

Species: Trochilidae

Location: 8.8.1642,   19.4.256,   15.14.210 (Unknown humanoid coordinate translation)

Age: 4,016 galactic years since their discovery

GA Membership: Full, the Trochilidae are one of the oldest members of the Galactic Alliance.

Contact Made: Yes

Monitoring: Member, as active members of the Galactic Alliance, the Trochilidae adhere to all monitoring and uplift accords.

History: The Trochilidae were first discovered by the Nanil. They were a space faring species and had already colonized nearby stars. They'd developed their own superluminal travel but were hampered beyond the speed of light by their crude power designs. By a vote of fifteen to one, they were invited into the Galactic Alliance and technology was shared to enhance their rate of expansion.

His face went blank. "What is this?" He turned to face Grace.

She was smiling at him. "That, my good sir, is a translation from the first contact probe's central computer. I finished it last week and have been working to train my A.I. to help in further translations. It's slow going, but we're getting along further and further every day."

He rubbed his face with his hands and moved them down to his chin. "Wait... so you're telling me you... that's where I remember this from!"

Spinning around, he walked to the far end of the wall screen. "That, right there!" He pointed at the character at the top left of the screen. "That's the first glyph on the inside of the first contact probe's panel. I've stared at it countless hours."

Grace nodded. "Very good. You're correct. It's a glyph seen throughout the translated materials." She gestured at the wall and a small window popped up next to the glyph.

Meaning: galactic (English, ge'laktik). Roots from Egyptian and Mayan glyphs for "star". This glyph is made of interconnecting suns representing the initial founding members of the GA. The network of connections, itself a glyph, is often used together to form the "Galactic Alliance" (GA) with the lower connecting glyph translating to "alliance". For details on this glyph see...

"So, you cracked it?" Kara asked. She'd walked up next to them and had been craning her neck and gesturing at the different symbols on the wall to read their meaning.

"Enough of it, yes." Grace began. "It's taken most of my life, but I had a breakthrough a few years ago. And well, here we are."

"Harold," he said aloud.

"Yes," Harold said. His voice was coming from all around the space.

"Why weren't we ever aware of a translation effort?"

"You never asked. Zeus, Hera, and Michael were all aware. It was actually Hera who started this project. She thought it best to start out fresh after the countless dead-ends in the past. She wanted a separate effort focused from the ground up on trying to translate this without influence from research elsewhere. Soon after, her daughter Grace graduated from University and she agreed to join the translation team."

"Wait," Kara began, "I've never seen Grace's name in the Circle of Trust before."

"That's only partially correct. She's been straddling the line for a while. Have you checked recently?" Harold asked.

He subvocalized a command to bring up the list. Sure enough, her name was right there in the middle with the rest of the family.

Kara was steaming. She'd crossed her arms and her face was turning red. "What the frak, Harold? You didn't think to tell us about a new member joining the Circle."

"I apologize, Madam. It was in your morning briefing. I believe it was the day a Mr. Barnett had spent the evening with you. When you woke you were a bit preoccupied and merely glanced past the details. You've not called up the list since."

Her face turned from the hot red of frustration to the smoldering pink of embarrassment in an instant.

"Who's Mr. Barnett?" he asked with a smirk.

"No one!" she shot. "Leave it be. Let's stay focused on this. Grace, what does it say? Well... I mean, it says a lot, obviously. But what have we learned from the translations?"

"Come on, it was just starting to get interesting," Grace said with a smile.

Kara frowned and started stomping her feet. "Please! Can

we stay focused on this really important thing and not get sidetracked into my personal life?"

Grace waved her hand and the wall screen went blank. "Fine. But something tells me Stark's gonna want to know and so do I." She smiled and began subvocalizing commands. A dozen translations appeared on the wall, side by side.

He squinted as a passage of text on the second panel started glowing yellow.

Knowledgeable theft of faster than light technology is forbidden. Should a single individual or multiple individuals be found guilty, the resulting punishment is banishment and death of their species.

He mouthed the word. "Banishment. What does that mean in this context?"

Grace shook her head. "We're not sure. That set of glyphs was tough to translate. It's the closest I could find. The death glyph, however, that was very clear." She gestured, and the outline of a star with hands encircling it appeared. "It's similar to the Mayan symbol for Ka, which is also associated with where a body is placed in a burial chamber."

He caught a glimpse of Kara. She slouched and started rubbing her arms. "What?"

"What?" Kara mimed. "What?... You're ignoring the 'death of their species' part?"

"Well, I figured that was pretty obvious. I just—"

"Death, as in kaput. Don't you realize what this means?"

He sighed and glared at her. "I think we all do. But we certainly don't have enough information—"

"What more do we need? We screwed up copying that tech and now we should destroy it!"

He raised his hands and made a lowering gesture. "Let's

calm down, shall we? We don't even have all the details. Let's not jump to conclusions here. As far as we know, humans were a member of this Galactic Alliance group and lost contact. Grace, is there any mention of our species in here?"

She brought up several dozen symbols on the screen. They looked like miniature glyphs of alien life forms. "These are some of the subsets that were found in the databanks from the probe. Each one has links to their species' details. You saw the one mentioning the Trochilidae earlier. There are hundreds here but two that appear human to me." She brought them up on the wall. "Unfortunately, both of their data sets are corrupt except for their coordinates. Well, over ninety percent of the data from the probe is corrupt. Likely from whatever downed it in the first place."

He could see what she meant. The two glyphs depicted humanoid figures. One had a single alien that appeared to be androgynous, while the other had two figures, one female and other male.

"That looks conclusively human to me," he began. "It could mean we were part of the Alliance."

Kara was shaking her head and had crossed her arms again. She hated when he disagreed with her. There was no point in jumping to conclusions until they knew for certain.

"I don't think this shows shit, and you know it, Stark. You just don't want to admit that we shouldn't have stolen that tech."

Grace opened and closed her mouth before finally speaking. "I don't know if I should interrupt, but I tend to agree with your brother."

Kara shot a piercing glare at her. If looks could kill, she'd be struck by a meteor any second now.

He interrupted the exchange before it went too far. "We have a lot of latitude here, Kara. Let's say for a second we aren't a member of the Galactic Alliance, for argument's sake. We can easily build countermeasures into our drives, to melt them to slag or drop them to the depths of Jupiter should an alien armada show up. Think about it. We're already hiding all the manufacturing and research, so it's not like that's spread throughout Sol. We can work with this. Seriously." He couldn't tell if she was listening to him or not. Her stare hadn't softened.

She stood there in silence, fiddling with the bracelet on her wrist, deep in thought.

He turned to face Grace. "Have you found anything about where each species is? Any type of coordinate system or something that could conclusively point to where we are in the galaxy?"

Grace shook her head. "No, not that I've been able to decipher." She brought up several of the translated species tiles. There were coordinate systems displayed for each of the icons. "I haven't found a translation cipher for these coordinates that map to any astronomical system we have today."

"Shit," he muttered and turned to face Kara. "So, what d'ya say? Should I start on building our kill switches?"

She glared at him until a smile slowly crept from the corner of her mouth.

He pointed and smiled. His eyebrows raising.

"Fine!" she shouted. "But I want to see the designs. I need to know the worst case here, and how we can ensure we cover our arses."

"Yes!" he high-fived her and turned to do the same with Grace. She greeted him with a shocked expression on her face before cautiously offering her hand to his hanging high-five.

Stark winked at her. "So Gracey, what else have we learned from this Encyclopedia Galactica of yours?"

20

KARA OLIVAW

SOL, JUPITER TROJANS — 2212

Their shuttle was finishing its tour of the construction facility. Kara always thought these bi-annual tours were a waste of time. Why do something in person when you can do it remote? Her colleagues, all elected officials, disagreed. They saw it as the perfect opportunity to showcase all the hard work they'd done for their electorate.

Kara sighed. The press ate this shit up. It was unnerving. The entire process was. What had she been thinking volunteering for this position on the Colony Early Exploration Committee?

Harold thought it would be good for the company, and might lead to her taking a broader role within the newly formed Confederation of Planetary Explorers (CoPE). She wasn't so certain, but also couldn't imagine moving back to The Wheel. She preferred to be closer to the action in the heart of the rings.

The shuttle was docking with the torus surrounding the second colony ship. They designed the structure as a skeleton that encircled the massive ship while it was under construction. The technology was ancient and not nearly as productive as the automata they used at The Wheel. They weren't using many robots here, the Inner Ring Unions made certain of that.

Kara brought up the schematics of the build on her HUD. She squinted into space. These numbers didn't make sense.

She raised her hand. "Can you tell me why construction has been so slow the past few weeks? We should be well ahead of where we are now. I was told everything was on schedule."

The foreman looked around with a smile, pretending he hadn't heard her.

"You heard me and you damn well know it. Why are you behind schedule?"

The crowd of officials and media turned to face her, their jaws open at her bluntness.

"I'm sorry," the foreman said. "We've... had a few supply ships arrive late and—"

"Bullshit!" She brought up the delivery logs from Olivaw's supply runs and tossed them onto everyone's retinal comms and the nearby wall screen. "We've been ahead of schedule for every single delivery. Try again. Why are you behind schedule?"

The journalists were getting frantic. A low buzz emanated throughout the room as they'd begun subvocalizing early drafts of stories into their comms.

"Vultures," she muttered.

The foreman whispered something into the ear of Outer Ring Jovian Representative North and his face went slack. Whatever he'd said wasn't good news. Representative North breathed in, cleared his throat, and faked a smile before beginning. "There's been a few... unexpected interruptions by the occupants of nearby Trojans."

"What do you mean 'occupants'?" Kara asked. His eye twitched when she'd asked that.

He furrowed his brow and made eye contact with her before replying with another fake smile. "The Ulixi occupy parts of these particular Jovian Trojans. We've relocated them—"

She walked to the front of the group of press. All drone cams were on her and the murmur of comms was getting louder. "What do you mean, you relocated them? Who was here first, us or them?"

"Well…" he began, glancing to his left for support from another Jovian representative, but they recoiled from him. "We needed the raw materials here to meet the required specifications for Olivaw—"

"Bullshit again, Representative North. We presented two dozen options to the committee for suitable locations to build these ships. You chose this cluster because you wanted your family to get this contract and to expand into the Outer Ring. Now tell me what you mean by 'relocated them'?"

His face was turning red and his glare was piercing.

Kara smiled. She was in her element.

"We assisted them in moving their belongings to suitable habitats elsewhere in the Jovian system," he said.

"So, you ripped them from their homes and forced them into places they neither wanted to be nor knew how to cope with? I don't blame them for being pissed off."

The representative didn't answer, he merely huffed and searched the room for someone who'd support him, but all he saw was the press staring back at him. His colleagues had all disappeared. "This press conference is over." He stormed out of the shuttle into the open doorway of the construction torus.

Kara turned and took a step backwards. Camera drones swarmed her and everyone was shouting questions. She paused and straightened her suit. She then pointed at the closest reporter. "Let's start with you. What's your question?"

SHE COLLAPSED DOWN into a vacant seat in the rear of the media shuttle. Her feet were killing her. Closing her eyes, she let out a long breath.

Kara had spent nearly two hours answering questions. Every single one, no matter how small or obtuse. It was difficult keeping them on topic, but she'd managed.

Her assistant had been frantically collecting names and noting down promised materials he didn't have on hand. He'd been as exhausted as her, but she was pretty sure he didn't want to be near her for a while, for fear of getting more work.

"Harold?" she subvocalized.

"Yes, Kara."

"Did I overstep there?"

"I'm not sure what you mean."

"Did I take North on too… aggressively? Can I backup everything I promised?"

Harold paused before responding. "I cannot foresee the future, but I don't see any immediate harm in how you confronted him. The press ate it up and gave glowing remarks for how you forced him into the corner, supported the little guy, and planned to right his company's wrongs. This change in venue to the asteroid belt, however, it'll put a six to twelve month wrinkle in our plans at the least."

She leaned forward and rested her head in her hands. "Can we continue construction during the site transition?"

"We could… if we didn't have unions to deal with."

"Shit," she muttered.

A nearby engineer shot her a glare. She waved to him and mouthed an apology. "Sorry."

He smiled and waved back when he recognized who she was.

She stood up and walked toward a more empty section of the shuttle, near the window facing the construction torus. She continued sub-vocally. "What if… we were to pay the union the entire trip? Full wages, but for no work. We'd have automata continue construction, but no faster than a human."

"That would be suboptimal," Harold said.

She chuckled. "No kidding, but we don't want to piss off the unions, and we need to get back on schedule. Hell, we can even tell them we want to go a little faster to catchup to the original plan. We'll pay them for that increase, as well. What do you think?"

"I think it could work. Should I instruct your assistant to make the calls?"

Kara smiled. "No. Give him an hour. He's earned it. Do me a favor, though. Check into the cost of relocating the Ulixi back to their homes. You know, the ones that North forcefully moved."

"I'm on it."

She stared out toward the far side of the torus. The Epsilon Eridani colony's automated exploration and forward mission was only now starting to take shape. They had years of construction ahead of them.

It'd taken Stark twice as long as he'd originally estimated to build a suitable subluminal drive with a design they could tweak as needed. Fortunately, the media had loved the Epsilon Eridani data and had given them some latitude. Not without some fear mongering in the press, but that was to be expected.

She reached up and adjusted her hair. The reflection in the window was cattywampus. It'd gotten out of place in the last few hours. "So, Harold. Do you think we can honestly keep all of this under wraps from the… Galactic Alliance?"

"It's hard to tell. I see no reason why we can't. We've taken countless precautions."

She reached down and took off her shoe and massaged her foot. "Let's hope so," she muttered.

21

HAROLD OLIVAW
SOL, OORT CLOUD — 2212

One hundred years. Harold had been in this form for nearly one hundred years. Not quite as long as he'd been alive as a human, but close.

In another few months it'd be his birthday. Or was it activation day? He wondered if A.I. were supposed to be retrospective on the day they were born. Or perhaps cold and efficient. More than likely no one would notice or care.

The comforting tingle of new data arriving flooded his neural pathways. According to the headers, it was from their forward probes. They'd built a mini network to and from Epsilon Eridani in preparation for future colony expansion. On this last run, they'd dropped a few sample rovers to test the soil, air, and environmental parameters. Nothing they'd ever share with most of Sol unless they went badly. Then, well, they'd worry about that if it happened.

He loaded the probe data and fed it into his video simulation. Sometimes it was more fun to experience things rather than analyze the raw feeds.

The ground was covered in squat wide plants for as far as the eye could see. They were maybe five meters at their tallest point but were far more broad, almost like psychedelic mushrooms. Their surface was dotted in bright orange, yellow, and green markings. The plants were extraordinary, like nothing he'd seen before, even in simutainment.

When he rolled up to one of them, it shot spores toward his wheeled form. Pollens and fungi, not too unlike that of Earth but on a far larger scale. Something they could account for with breathers or domes.

The surrounding rocks were bulbous and matched the tops of the fauna. Perhaps these plants had evolved to match their surroundings as a defense mechanism. He made a note in the data for future analysis.

He gazed at the sky and took in a deep breath of air. Shit. Something was off. It wasn't in line with human needs. Not too far off, but it'd take some terraforming to bring it within healthy levels. That or... perhaps they could use some nanites. They'd made significant advances in recent years using nanites in surgeries and to help elderly repair the damage of aging. He'd earmark that for investigation by a team at The Wheel.

As he strolled across the alien landscape, he brought up the secondary mission data. They'd scanned another chunk of the Epsilon system. A few more probes, and they'd have the entire star system mapped out.

Stark had been muttering about hedging their mission to Epsilon Eridani, but he hadn't recorded anything for Harold to see, so he wasn't sure what he had in mind. It likely had something to do with his interest in these scans. He'd been asking for an update on them for days.

They were ten years from launching this forward mission and multiples of that before they'd launch any colony ship. The bureaucracy of human behavior and the reinforcement of poor decisions and terrible planning befuddled him. So many bad judgments repeated regularly, and yet they passed almost unnoticed.

It's hard to imagine where they'd be if the Olivaws hadn't

intervened and researched this probe in secret. He'd hazard to guess not far from Earth, but he didn't want to waste the computing time.

He floated up on top of one of the mushroom like plants and landed, perching at the midpoint. As he stared out across the colorful horizon, he superimposed human buildings and structures in the distance.

"Yes, this would do quite well," he muttered. "Quite well indeed."

22

VICE ADMIRAL GWAR

TECTIM, ALVIARIUM — 2212

They strolled onto the catwalk and paused. The midday sky was pink and sparkled with hundreds of stars. The suns near the galactic center were dense and bright at all hours of the day. There wasn't a cloud in the sky and they could see the moonlet Kleen was rising in the distance.

Hope and good fortune were approaching.

When they closed their eyes, they swore they could sense the life forms there. They'd spend hundreds of years honing their senses to enable clear and concise thought under duress. The consequence was their innate ability to sense the thoughts of people lower and less radiant in the hive. The lesser Qudoculi hadn't learned how to control their thoughts from being detected. Not like Gwar had.

Their robotic companion signaled it had something to say. The unique signal resonated so only they could hear it, and it penetrated even into their unconsciousness when they were with the hive.

"What is it?" Vice Admiral Gwar asked.

"We've been reviewing new intel from the Gharloc event. It appears we found a previously uncorrelated piece of data from the colony on Wale."

They squinted. "Show me." They hadn't thought about that event in many cycles. The voyage home took a long time, and they'd entered a period of mandated solitude upon return. They'd assumed things had gone smoothly, but apparently not.

The robotic companion brought up a holographic projection in front of them. It showed the location of Wale near the Gharloc system. It was a newer colony they hadn't yet registered with the GA. Their formal petition for the star was delayed until the Gharloc had been disposed of.

They nodded. That was why they hadn't registered the outpost earlier. Unapproved colonies were forbidden by the GA. All species' outward expansion was controlled and approved through a central committee. The Gharloc were too close to uncontested space and an unnecessary choke point to the Qudoculi expansion plans. They had to be dealt with.

The hologram switched to a fast playback that showed a starship transitioning out of superluminal travel, engage some form of crude intersystem drive, and then several hours later perform another superluminal transition.

"And the timeframe correlates back to the original event in the Gharloc system?" Vice Admiral Gwar asked.

"It does. With a ninety-eight point one degree of certainty. This would have been the third or fourth jump for that ship, depending on the approach vector. We still don't know where it was ultimately heading."

They waved the hologram away.

Off on the horizon, the companion moonlet of Enex was setting. With good fortune, one can lose the ability to focus.

"I need you to deploy an exploratory unit to investigate these details. Have them examine the nearby systems. Let's see if they can't torch some Blathey out of the underbrush."

"Yes, sir," the robot said.

They knew it was a long shot, but if it'd gotten out that

they hadn't followed up on this matter after their tribunal rotation, then they'd lose their place in the hive ascension. That was unacceptable.

23

STARK OLIVAW
SOL, JUPITER — 2223

B attlecruisers were behemoths of metal floating in space, waiting to dispense destruction. Their strongest armaments could level two dozen major cities on Earth, or in this case, lay waste to Stark's frigate before he'd had a chance to burn off that new ship smell.

They were leading a convoy mission to the Outer Ring with supplies and water for the refugees at Ceres. It was currently in the contentious portion of its orbit that brought it closer to Jupiter than Earth. To the Outer Ring, that meant it was in their territory. The Inners had other opinions on the matter.

The Jurat was the name Stark had assigned his frigate at the ship's christening a few months prior. He'd evolved it from Hera's original designs, intending it to be an envoy of the Olivaw Corporation, a neutral in the eyes of both the Union of Planetary Explorers (UPE) and the Colonial Union (CU). The name fit the purpose.

The Battlecruiser Clinton of the Outer Ring had hailed them. "Please disengage your drives, and stop all forward motion," the officer said.

"We're a peaceful envoy with supplies for Ceres," Lieutenant Quesh began. "We have permission from both the UPE and CU to make this delivery. I've sent on the certified documents."

"I repeat, disengage immediately or you'll be fired upon!"

Quesh muted the comm and pivoted to face Stark. "Your orders, sir."

Stark was staring through the wall screen with his arms crossed. He'd hoped for a simple mission. Something to help Ceres and give him some free time to think over recent events. He hadn't, however, planned for a royal clusterfuck of a blockade. The Inners were—

"Sir?" Quesh asked a bit louder. "Your orders?"

He exhaled. He hadn't realized he'd been holding his breath. "Ignore them. Prepare our countermeasures and warn the Clinton that we'll retaliate should they fire on any of our ships."

The lieutenant gulped and remained staring at Stark.

Stark nodded slowly toward them. "It's ok, officer. We've got this. You have your orders."

"Yes, sir! Right away! I've... never been in a real-life situation like this."

Quesh spun around and hands flew across his instrument panel.

On the wall screen, he confirmed their new countermeasures were armed and ready. He'd spent years tweaking and designing these little beauties, but like Quesh, he'd never battle tested them.

Quesh opened the comm. "Battlecruiser Clinton! Should you fire upon this peacekeeping envoy, or any of the vessels in our convoy, we'll be forced to retaliate with prejudice."

Stark tilted his head. "With prejudice?"

Quesh peeked up at him and then back toward his panel. "It... seemed fitting, sir."

He smiled and nodded. "Indeed. I like it."

The battlecruiser cut their comm and opened fire.

"Missiles incoming, system counts four inbound. Laser bank charged and targeted."

"Fire!" Stark shouted.

Four precise lasers discharged from the bow of the Jurat and exploded the missiles well away from the ship.

He clench pumped his arm. "Hail the Clinton again."

There was a momentary pause, and the picture of the commanding officer on the Clinton appeared again. "We warned you not to fire on our vessel. We've come in peace and—" They cut the comm a second time.

A blast of yellow light shot from the Clinton and klaxons rang through the ship. The Jurat lurched to one side, and he grasped the handles built into each station and seat-back to steady himself.

"We have damage to the forward laser array, sir," Quesh began. "It's offline. I'm redirecting power to the port and star-board arrays."

"Aft hull integrity eighty-five percent, sir," the officer to his right said.

"Take defensive position and enable counter measures," Stark said.

The Jurat adjusted course, rotating its port side to protect the convoy acting as a shield. It then fired a small missile from its starboard side from a previously unseen missile bank.

The missile shot well away from the Jurat and then banked far around the Clinton. While the battlecruiser attempted to take it out, the missile easily dodged the first volley and continued well away from the target.

Quesh glanced toward Stark. "Was it… a dud, sir?"

He squinted at the wall screen, watching the missile carve its obscure route. "No. Wait for it."

Another stream of lasers fired upon their ship, peppering their port side. The ship lurched, and the lights flickered for a second.

"Damage report!" he said.

"Port hull integrity sixty-two percent. We can't take too many shots like that."

Quesh had his hand over the controls. "Should I realign aft toward the Clinton? Our hull is much stronger there."

"Wait for it," Stark muttered.

A yellow light flashed in the corner of the wall screen. "They're... hailing us, sir."

He merely stared at the picture of the Clinton in the center of their screen. Another shot never occurred.

"Sir, should I—"

"Put them on." He straightened his uniform and cracked his neck before coming to attention.

The commander on the Clinton came on the wall screen. "What have you done, Olivaw?"

He smiled. "I'm not sure what you mean."

The commander's red hair and pink face looked eerie with the lights strobing around him. Everyone was shouting at each other across his bridge. "What the frak did you do to my ship?"

He clenched his fist behind his back and focused his gaze on the commander. "We warned you. I warned you not to fire. We have every right to be here delivering these supplies. You fired upon us unprovoked and now... now you paid the price."

The commander muted himself and shouted off to his right before returning to face the camera. "All our systems are offline. We've lost control of our engines, and our power banks are depleted. We're... sitting ducks here."

He shook his head from side to side. "I suppose you shouldn't have fired that last volley, aye? Then you'd have energy to navigate. Well, at least you have power for environmental controls and comms."

"What did you—"

Stark raised his hand in front of him. "Shut up, Commander!"

They fell silent.

"Your drive is slag. It's melted. I warned you not to fire on this convoy. If the Colonial Union wants to file a complaint with Olivaw International, they're welcome to. Reading the fine print of your drive, you'll find a clause voiding coverage for damages incurred while attacking peacekeeping forces. We'll send out a tow ship for a handsome fee if you want, but something tells me the CU will come to your rescue before then."

The commander of the Clinton's face was red, and their eyes were bulging.

"And, Commander. I wouldn't get any bright ideas using your environmental reserves to launch an attack. You don't have enough power to run your oxygen scrubbers and water recyclers if you do. Besides, you'd be target practice for us then."

He gestured toward Quesh and he cut the comm.

A shiver shot up his spine. That almost went ass over teakettles. He placed his hand on Quesh's shoulder. "Nice work, everyone. Continue on and escort the convoy to Ceres. Keep an eye on the Clinton for a while. Let me know if anything changes. I'll be in my stateroom."

"Aye aye, sir!" the crew echoed.

THE DOOR SHUT BEHIND HIM, and Stark let out a sigh of relief. "That was close."

"It could have ended badly if they'd knocked out that missile," Harold said.

He nodded and stepped around his desk. He opened his drawer and pulled out a bottle of scotch and a tumbler. After he poured a healthy portion, he picked up the glass and took a sip. The liquid burned his throat, but he could feel the relaxing warmth shooting down his limbs.

"That's against navy regulation while an officer is on duty or in the field of battle," Harold said.

He chuckled and took another long sip. "Good thing we're not the navy. And this uniform…" He reached up and pulled at his collar. "It's killing me. This is going to take some getting used to."

"It's not strictly necessary, but it instills confidence in your officers."

He tipped back the remainder of the glass and poured himself another. Had they shot down that missile, he'd have been forced to deploy a stealth variant and shown his hand. Harold was right. That could have ended in a ball of fire.

"You know what we're missing, H?" he asked.

Harold paused before replying. "I'm not following."

He took another sip, smaller than the first three gulps. Too much more and he'd be sloshed.

"We don't have any contingencies. If they'd taken out our hull, we'd be the ones that were floating slag. If they'd taken out our missile, we'd have to show our hand. We don't have enough contingencies."

"Fair enough, but—"

"We need more contingencies, H."

"We'd only received UPE and CU approval for a single peacekeeping frigate. Any more—"

"No, not here. I mean on the colonies. We need redundancies. Without them, they're going to be sitting ducks. If the Galactic Alliance arrives to the game, and we don't have contingencies, then we've lost it all." He took another sip and leaned back in his chair.

"What'd you have in mind?" Harold asked.

He reached up and scratched his neck, pulling at the collar some more. "We build a redundant colony site, underground.

We do it after we decide on the initial sites. I'm sure we can find a reason to move the first site."

"That'd be challenging to orchestrate. With all the eyes on the ground, I'm sure they'd notice something."

He took another sip of the scotch. The leathery taste of the liquid coated his mouth. "Too much for an all-seeing intelligence? I'd have thought you'd be up for the task, H."

Harold chuckled. "I'm sure we can divert data streams and preprocess them until we've cleared enough raw material. I can chew on this for a few trillion cycles. I'll come up with something."

"Good on ya," Stark said as he took another sip. "We should do the same thing for all the colony's eyes in the system."

"Eyes in the system? Again, I'm not following. Have you drank too much, sir?"

He laughed out loud and leaned forward, setting his glass on the desk. "Almost, but not quite. I meant their bases in their Oort Clouds. They'd be just like ours, but... bigger, much bigger. Since we control what they see, and when they see it, I'm sure we can get away with a larger base of operations. We need redundancy and some form of defense in case the GA comes calling. These bases can keep an eye on the colony, the supply missions, everything. It'll be easier to adjust supply shuttles if they're not coming from Sol."

"It could work. It's another layer of coordination and recruiting, though. I'd need time. Should we talk to Kara about this?"

Stark picked up the glass and took a long pull. He shook his head. "No. That's not necessary. This is my call. She wouldn't understand the need. Let's keep this between us for a while."

24

KARA OLIVAW

SOL, EARTH — 2223

The vase shattered against the wall screen, and thousands of glass shards flew through her living room. "How dare he make this change without talking to me first?"

Harold's virtual face was motionless. He didn't say a word.

Kara paced across the floor, glass crunching beneath her feet. "How long has this been going on, Harold? And don't fraking think about holding back on me."

"Since the Ceres blockade, Madam. We've been recruiting specialists and building new ships to make the voyage for months now. Construction should be underway at the contingency sites in Epsilon Eridani and Tau Ceti well before the CoPE forward mission arrives."

She walked over to her counter and searched the surface for something heavy. Anything would do. She picked up her tablet and spun around before flinging it at Harold's face on the wall screen. It bounced off harmlessly and ricocheted into the window, sending a crack spidering toward the ceiling.

"Should I call someone about that?" Harold asked.

"Frak off, Harold!"

She gestured and cut the comm.

"So, is that a no?" he asked over her retinal comm.

"Argh!" she screamed, waving her hands in the air.

"Override code Alpha Gamma Harold," she muttered.

"Do you wish to disable all external access from Harold?" a voice asked in her ear.

"Yes! For the love of all that's real, yes!" she screamed.

"Access terminated. Should you want to reactivate—"

She gestured, and the voice stopped.

The room fell into silence. All that remained was the faint crunching of glass under her Suzan Hullo heels.

She glanced around her room. She'd never lost her temper like that before. It actually... felt good. Her heart was thumping in her chest, but her senses were heightened.

She felt alive. For once in her life she was free of someone looking over her shoulder, watching her every move. Now all she had to do was cut the final thread.

She reached up and stroked her ear to open a comm to her brother. A drone flew out of a recess next to the wall screen. As the door slid open, a piece of glass dislodged and shattered on the ground.

"The last straw," she muttered.

The drone flew a meter from her face and then a red light turned on.

She pursed her lips. "You wanted it, big bro, you got it. It's yours. I'm done trying to lead this company. You and Harold are pissing on everything we worked so hard for. First you steal our family frigate and take it on a Ceres supply mission without thinking to talk to me. Then you practically start a system-wide war between the Inner and Outer Rings. All the while I'm left keeping it all from falling apart. Then... then... argh!" She paused and took a deep breath, staring at the drone. "I know about your secret change in plans. About your aggressive expansion in Epsilon and Tau. When were you fraking going to tell me? After you'd somehow made it an idea I could swallow? No, you know what. I don't give a shit. I'm out. The company is yours. I'll be tendering my resignation to the board of directors, effective immediately. Now leave me alone and don't come looking for me."

She gestured, and the drone stopped recording. It drifted off and returned to its wall cubby.

"Send message," she subvocalized.

25

HAROLD OLIVAW
SOL, OORT CLOUD — 2223

The massive cargo ship was as black as a night without stars. Its long tubular body reminded Harold of a cigar. A rare indulgence few bothered with in this century, outside of entertainment crowds, of course. Few space biomes could spare the acreage to grow such a crop.

The starship had been named Novum by the members of The Wheel who'd assisted in its creation. Its name was Latin for "new". Harold assumed this was because of new days ahead, or a new world. Or perhaps it was the nerd in them that thought it sounded like Nova, a particularly popular superhero on vid-sims in recent years.

It was designed to transport robotic building and excavation equipment to the habitable planet in Epsilon Eridani, and to their future base of operations in the nearby Oort Cloud. Humans wouldn't make the voyage, not for some time. Intensive recruiting efforts were still underway closer to the heart of Sol.

Current estimates showed it being completed in the middle of next year. Harold, however, had been tweaking the number of automata helping during fabrication and trying some new manufacturing techniques. He was hoping to speed up construction times.

For a small section on the inside of the ship, Harold employed a new building technique he'd helped create. It used nano robots, or nanites, to join long carbon fiber cross framing sections together. Rather than using bonding or riveting techniques to join the fiber carbon plates, he instead used nanites.

Thousands of special purpose nanobots would come together along a seam or connection and integrate into the substrate. They were designed to purposely overheat, and force their body to fuse at the molecular level with any nearby material and other nanites. The result was a super strong bond connecting the materials together in a controlled structure.

It wasn't stronger than the carbon fiber plating, but it was darn close. There was also an interesting side effect in that five to ten percent to the nanites retained their computational potential. While small and difficult to power, the ship could use the network to form crude sensors or extend its computational abilities.

Stark approved the use of this building technique. He'd never asked who'd created it, but he seemed impressed when shown its strength and rigidity characteristics under force.

Harold missed Stark, if such a thing were possible for an artificial intelligence. His Inner Ring copy had been interfacing with him for several years, whereas the copy at The Wheel had only received regular merges.

As a matter of fact, one had arrived milliseconds ago. Harold closed his mind's eye and prepared for the merge.

Anger. Destruction. Sadness. Frustration. Hope. New Beginnings.

Harold paused all processing. Construction ground to a halt throughout The Wheel. The gantries moving pieces of Novum into place stopped. All automata and manufacturing stopped. The only thing that remained in motion were essential systems, and those well inside sanctioned parameters.

His Four Laws Engine was taking up all of his processing time dealing with the ramifications of this change to the family. This was an unexpected fragmentation of the Circle of Trust.

Should he keep Kara under watch? She knew things that only one other person in the universe knew.

Should he honor her wishes? She made the order while heading the family. Her commands were the ultimate Zero Law orders, and yet, she'd also removed herself from the Circle.

Was the path Stark had taken them on the right one? It didn't seem unsound, and if anything, it was a hedge.

Why had it upset Kara so much? It wasn't her idea, and she didn't want aggressive expansion, but this wasn't a significant divergence.

Had he missed something Kara had seen? Perhaps in time, he could approach her and ask.

Slowly the Four Laws Engine relinquished computation cycles and construction continued. Several of the technicians overseeing the operations had raised warnings and alarms, but that was all secondary to the Zeroth Law. Fortunately, no one had been harmed during this downtime.

There had to be a better way of both enabling the Four Laws Engine to reach a conclusion, without also putting at risk environments and situations under his control.

He'd need to spend some time contemplating both this and the family. The number of outstanding questions raised by this fork in the Circle was concerning and meant that delicate times were ahead.

26

VICE ADMIRAL GWAR
TECTIM, ALVIARIUM — 2223

"Tell Representative Muntin that I'll be with him shortly," Vice Admiral Gwar said as they waved the robot away.

They turned to face the wall screen. The day had been non-stop meetings and preparation for another tribunal. On the wall, they reviewed the plans for converging the force of ships into the Prodo star systems. Coordinating thousands of Nebula Ships and ensuring the safe travel of a beacon was challenging. The easiest part of the planning was predicting the duration of the tribunal. With the evidence they'd mounted against the Ursis, it was an open-and-shut case.

The Ursis had five clustered star systems within their control. They'd populated three of those five rather rapidly, and given their previous technological abilities, their current evolved state was beyond any projections the GA had made. They'd been under regular observation every couple cycles to determine when and if they'd make suitable members of the Galactic Alliance. Forward intelligence on the most recent observations showed the Ursis flagship designs were exact duplicates of the GA fleet. Somehow they'd gotten their

hands on stolen superluminal drive technology and repro-
duced them in excruciating detail.

Their fate was now set in darkness.

They itched their skin as it changed from mottled green
brown to a consistent bright-green hue throughout. These
species continued to prove their inability to resist an urge
when dangled in front of them. They sighed and closed their
eyes to engage the hive.

Reaching out and feeling the minds of their fellow Qudoculi always helped them control their emotions. The logic of
the minds, and the warm pulsing colors in their minds' eyes
soothed the rage that pulsed through their veins.

"Sir," a voice said.

Gwar's eyes flashed open. "What!?"

"You asked to be notified immediately of any leads or
information from the Gharloc investigation."

They shook off the interruption. They'd relaxed somewhat, and splotches of their skin had begun to change toward
its normal mottled appearance. "Go on then. Get on with it."

A small cylindrical robot hovered closer. "We've received
a communication from the exploratory unit you dispatched.
Their mission has covered over fifty star systems in the past
six million cycles, and they've detected no sign of new
species, technology, or nearby drive signatures. They're
asking for permission to return to Alviarium."

Gwar turned toward the open window and their gaze
narrowed. The blues and reds of the moonlets gave the rising
sun an ominous quality. "How many stars are within the
predicted range of the Gharloc investigation?"

"There are over ten thousand stars within one hundred
light years of the Gharloc systems, and our colony on Wale.
The estimated time to explore these systems is—"

They gestured for the robot to stop. "Enough! We don't
need to waste any additional time or resources on this course
of action. Call off the mission and recall the exploratory unit."

The robot beeped and floated away.

"I didn't dismiss you yet, you infernal machine!" They raised their right hand toward the robot and it flew across the room, smashing without a sound into the far wall. Its metallic body crushed flat and then slid down the wall. Two cylindrical robots scurried out of a nearby nook. One headed toward Gwar's side, and the other rushed over to cleanup the demolished remains.

"We're sorry, Admiral," the robot said with a beep.

The bright-green hue of Gwar's skin had further transitioned to become shiny. It reflected the yellow light of the setting sun behind them, framing their body in a golden halo. "Don't let it happen again! You infernal Bynaury half-breed. I want you to dig up all the Gharloc data and destroy the evidence of the unknown ship's arrival. I don't need to deal with this nonsense right now. Not when I just got appointed to lead this tribunal against the Ursis."

"That's against Galactic Alliance laws, Admiral. The information and protection acts of the first GA Congress prohibited the destruction of evidence at or around any tribunal site. Destroying or tampering with said evidence was punishable by—"

"I know the infernal laws, you mutant. Activate override Therion Ten Thirty-Two."

The robot's cylindrical form sank to the ground without a sound. All of its lights went out, and it sat motionless for a few seconds. A moment later, it rose upward. "The data will be destroyed, Admiral. Is there anything else?"

"Send in Representative Muntin of the Thyreus." They waved their hand, and the robot floated away.

The doorway opposite the window opened, and a black and neon blue alien walked in. Its sixteen eyes taking in everything in the room. The Thyreusian sauntered up to them and bowed.

Gwar raised their hand, and the alien returned to an upright position.

"It appears the Bynaury have been frustrating you again, Admiral." Muntin turned around, and watched as the robot cleaned up the remaining pieces of their compatriot into a vacuum bin.

They both chuckled. Gwar's body vibrated in place while Muntin shuddered.

"To what do I owe the pleasure of your visit this cycle?" Gwar gestured and a wall panel slid open. Behind it were hundreds of multicolored liquids in small vials, neatly displayed in a sorted spectral pattern. "Help yourself."

"Thank you." Muntin walked up to the expansive bar and grasped a purplish vial. A long tongue extended from his mouth, and dozens of mop like hairs snapped outward into the vial, slurping out the glowing purple liquid. His antennae rubbed together, causing a buzzing sound to emanate through the room.

He turned to face Gwar. "I've come to share a piece of news. I think you'll find it interesting."

"Do tell. I could use something entertaining with all that's going on. This Ursis tribunal is taking every waking moment." They walked to the wall and grasped a vial of milky white liquid with hints of orange swirling within.

"First, I have a question. Are you still grasping about in the Allimi quadrant, looking for suspicious alien probes?"

They stiffened and turned to see that Muntin was already facing them, gauging their response.

"Based upon your reaction, I trust the answer is yes. And if the remains of that robot in the corner were any indication, then your search has come up empty." Muntin's antennae were rubbing together in anticipation.

They tilted the vial of white liquid into their mouth and poured it in. An orange larva inside the tube slid in afterward. "I trust that your blasted Bynaury aboard my exploratory unit's starship informed you of the findings. Otherwise, we have a broader GA communication breach on our hands, and I should call a tribunal to investigate."

Muntin nodded.

"So, you already know the answer. Get to the point then." Gwar placed the empty vial in its receptacle on the bar display. It withdrew inward and was replaced with a full version.

"May I use your data wall?" Muntin raised a hand, pointing toward the wall.

They nodded.

He gestured at the wall and a video began to play while telemetry displayed along the side. It showed a field of stars somewhere in the Milky Way. For a moment there was a brief flash of light and then it disappeared.

Gwar shuffled their feet. "A nova?" They glanced at Muntin and he was shaking his head.

"Look at the telemetry, my friend." He gestured toward the wall.

They turned back to study the data on the wall. The spectrum of the explosion was split out along the y-axis of the display. Each spectral line of light identified and decomposed. Their body began vibrating. "Is that what I think it is?"

"Yes! Someone has been attempting to reverse engineer our drive. We recorded this explosion in Cuko, one of our colonies. The star near the explosion is sixty-seven point four light years away from our colony. They're located here." Muntin's antennae waved in the air, and a Galactic Alliance exploration sheet came up on the wall screen. "It's not on an active rotation to be monitored and was last visited a very long time ago. Nearly back to when the GA was founded."

"Why so long?"

"Its unclear. But you're going to be interested in the last species to perform the monitor." Muntin let off a subdued buzzing noise.

"Out with it!"

He gestured with his antennae. The wall screen displayed a species sheet for the Nanil. The star system was listed as being under rotation with the last visit in the eighth year of the GA, over four thousand years ago.

Gwar straightened their back, growing a head in height. "Who else knows this?"

"You, me, and a few astronomers at Cuko." Muntin backed away from the screen and faced Gwar. "I trust this information is useful?"

They nodded.

"Then it'll be kept between you and me."

They shifted their arms behind their back and walked toward the window. The orange sun was still rising in the distance. "And what will this cost us? To keep this our secret."

"We'd like to be a part of your mission."

They sighed. "What else?"

Muntin shuddered. "The Galactic Alliance looks the other way when any accusations of uplift indiscretions surface."

They spun around to face him. "What'd you do?"

He shrugged. "We might have stopped a legitimate species from developing their own superluminal travel, and then we claimed to have uplifted them. We needed their raw materials, and they wouldn't agree to our trade terms. I'm sure you of all people can relate." Their antennae began rubbing together.

They nodded. "We've all been there. Some of us since the beginning. I can help your problem disappear." They turned back toward the rising sun. The blues of the evening were still fading, being replaced with the brightening reds of a new day. "Now tell me who you had in mind for this exploratory mission. Discretion needs to be maintained at all costs."

"Of course," Muntin said, as he walked up alongside them and stared out over the rising and setting binaries.

27

HAROLD OLIVAW
SOL, JUPITER — 2229

S tark had only been married for a few years when his marriage hit a rough patch. Too much time spent managing the family business after Kara stepped aside meant not enough time fanning the embers of his new marriage. The result was a sudden separation.

Harold watched on the cameras as Taska boarded the tiny shuttle. She glanced around cautiously, as if half expecting a crew or perhaps Stark to greet her. "There's no one else aboard, Madam. As you requested, I took the utmost discretion when arranging this trip. All anyone will detect is a small supply shuttle heading toward Neptune. Just prior to our arrival at Triton station, we'll dock with an autonomous resupply shuttle. I'll transfer your cryo-pod and complete the multi-leg voyage to The Wheel. As you know, it's an indirect route so it'll take a few days."

She nodded without a word and paused when she stepped onto the tiny bridge. Judging from her heart rate and her body language, she was nervous and wasn't sure what to do with herself.

"Why don't you have a seat at the controls? We can prepare for cryo-sleep once we're underway."

"Ok," she muttered as she sat down in the pilot's chair. She waved her hand over the panel and it sprang to life. Her hands deftly navigated the controls as she performed a routine systems check.

Stark had met Taska soon after Kara left the Circle. He'd been touring one of the many Olivaw manufacturing facilities near Jupiter. On the last leg of his tour, he ran into a spunky and strong test pilot. He'd literally run into her, knocking her flat on the catwalk and almost causing her to career over the edge. Fortunately, he'd reacted swiftly and helped her back up before she'd fallen to her death. After an endless string of apologies, he'd asked her out to dinner to make up for the offense. And the rest, well, the rest was history.

Fast-forward three years into their marriage. Taska was lonely at The Wheel and Stark, being Stark, had buried himself in his work. The Ring Treaty of 2224 changed everything and cut their honeymoon short. The demands on his time translated into long hours of solitude for Taska, which wasn't her cup of tea. She needed to use her hands to fix things, but he'd never entirely pulled her into the Circle. That meant the projects she could help on were superficial.

A year into the isolation and boredom, and she enlisted the aid of Harold to disappear off the grid. She wanted to explore. To see parts of Sol she couldn't afford years before. But not under the watchful eye of the media or Stark. She'd hoped he'd come looking for her, but that didn't happen until about three months ago.

The shuttle pulled away from the Jovian space station. Its lights framed the two dozen gigantic white rotating tori, contrasting sharply with the darkness of the surrounding space. The thousands of docking bays in each torus fed the thirty-two space elevators. Impossibly thin threads descended toward Callisto, the heart of Outer Ring commerce and government.

"I trust everything went as planned on your side?" Harold asked.

"Yes. I injected the nanites you requested, and I re-engaged my retinal comm. It feels... weird being plugged in again." Taska raked her fingers through her jet black hair and her deep green eyes darted around the confined bridge whenever an unfamiliar noise sprang forth.

"I should imagine. It's been nearly two years since you shut it off, since we last heard from you. I'd ask where you've been, but I assume you'd tell me if you wanted me to know."

She stared at the wall screen without a word, watching the space elevator shrink to a speck in the distance. One hand fidgeted with her hair, while the other cycled through the controls checking their power reserves, communications, and life support.

Stillness wasn't her strong suit. Harold knew she'd happily exchange it for busy work whenever possible, but in this small space, there wasn't much to do.

Taska cleared her throat. "Can I see your face, Harold? You know I'm not a fan of speaking to myself."

"Certainly!" His image appeared in the corner of the wall screen. His virtual deep blue eyes, slightly chubby cheeks, and smiling face beamed at her. "It's nice to see you again."

"You as well," she said with a half smile before glancing down at the controls and then back at him. "So... is Stark doing well? I mean, his last message... he seemed... depressed."

"He's spiraled aimlessly over the past year, falling deeper into isolation and depression. His work has kept him sane, but he hasn't left The Wheel in over a year. Calls for his presence at the next CoPE meeting in three months have been deafening. He can't continue to preside from afar with so—"

Taska sighed and her posture stiffened. "He's getting pulled back into the public hell of CoPE?"

"He's the President, Taska. What did you expect?"

She shook her head and stood abruptly. "He wasn't the President when he met me." She stared at Harold's face for a minute. "Can we just get to the cryo-sleep?"

"May I ask you a question first?"

She closed her eyes. "If you have to. I can't guarantee I'll answer."

"Fair enough," Harold began, "I'm curious. Why are you really going back to Stark? If it was so bad with him, why return at all?"

Taska reached a hand upward and smoothed her shirt. She snickered and started toward the aft end of the ship.

He didn't expect she'd answer, but he hoped she would. If he could prepare Stark, he'd try. He needed to know if the preparation should be a positive or negative one.

She hopped up and into the cryo-pod, sliding her legs into place and strapping them in. Laying down, she grasped the straps at her side and pulled them over her torso, as well.

"So, that's it then? No answer?" He watched as she repeatedly twisted her wedding band around her finger. The emeralds and sapphires encircling the jet black surface sparkled in the under lights of the cryo-pod's lid. It was the only way Harold had been able to follow her over the years.

Taska closed her eyes and her heart rate rapidly lowered as she began rhythmically breathing. Harold had never seen this much control from her before. She must have learned a thing or two over the past few years with the Ulixi.

Despite his best judgement, he'd leave it up to Stark to handle this.

"Good sleep," Harold said.

The lid on the pod closed and a white gas flooded in, enshrouding Taska's body. Her eyes open for a split second before closing again. The gas billowed around her face, making her features impossible to distinguish.

Her nanites were reporting back that her body was healthy. She hadn't used any drugs recently, and except for elevated prolactin levels, she seemed in perfect health. He adjusted the nanites to check for any pituitary tumors or hypothalamus issues. No sense risking her health if he could help.

Harold engaged the subluminal impulse drives on the shuttle. He then packaged up everything he'd learned over the past few weeks, closed his mind's eye, and began transmitting his memories to the original Harold at The Wheel.

28

STARK OLIVAW

SOL, OORT CLOUD — 2229

"Please bring up the Archégonos site plan?" Stark asked.

The wall screens around him came to life with architectural, topographical, climatic, and mineral composition views of the proposed colony site on Epsilon Eridani. The Novum forward expedition arrived there three years ago and deployed dozens of excavation automata along with a copy of Harold to manage the search and preparation of both locations.

They uncovered expansive mineral pockets, both on the planet and in the Oort Cloud that would be invaluable to their early expansion plans. Novum's cargo contained several smaller crude raw material transports in case they needed to mine and haul minerals between sites. The ideal plan included finding a site with all the required resources nearby, but not everything could be where they wanted it.

Novum returned to Sol last year. It consisted of thousands of samples from the planet to help their scientists prepare for colonization. The stealth ship was being prepped for a second supply expedition and was in the final stages. They'd planned to have it en route already but needed to decide on a primary site on the planet's surface.

"So, let's go over again what we're planning to review at the CoPE session. It's been a while since I've dealt with these idiots. I need to make sure I don't slip up and hint that we know more than we do."

Harold loaded the teleprompter with the speech they'd rehearsed several times already.

He read the first few sentences of the speech and sighed, slouching his shoulders forward. It was nothing but dry political cover. He scrolled through page after page of the same material. The only interesting part of the meeting was going to be the initial site selection committee.

"Before we jump into this," he turned toward the topographical map of the site. "I was thinking. How are we going to hide the fact that we'd already cut the place up when the regular forward mission arrives?"

"We aren't," Harold said.

"Because…" He motioned in a circle with his hands.

"We reviewed this last night and a few days before that, sir. I'll tell you now what I told you then—"

"Yea, yea, I need sleep. Blah blah. Humor me and pretend we haven't talked about this before." He turned around and walked toward the coffee station on the far side of the lab. Pressing a button, he withdrew a steaming globe-of-joe and returned to the wall screen.

Harold brought up the imagery from their arrival. "We recorded dozens of landing vid-sims and subsequent streams from excavation equipment and drones. There's enough here to interpolate our own truth and mix in the real thing for a few years until we align our fiction with the reality on the ground. Our creatives are already working on using some of the latest gaming renderers to make this work."

He took a swig of coffee. Its effect was diminishing, but the habit of drinking the warm liquid was ingrained and relaxing. "Right… yea, I remember this now." He scratched his head. "And we'll do the same at the secondary site, as well?"

"That's correct." Harold changed the imagery to drone footage near their recommended second site. "It's an ideal region for future native agricultural expansion, and its co-location to raw materials is far better than the Archégonos site. We found some nearby cave systems with water, and deeper in we detected rich ore deposits. We were careful not to disturb anything, so we used drones to scout ahead."

He tilted his head at the data scrolling by. "Except for the ground samples, right?"

Harold brought up videos of the soil laboratory in The Wheel. "Yes. The samples at this site were far better than Archégonos or any other location, but early indications from our pedologists and edaphologists show we have work to do to make the soil viable for human plants. It's going to take years to figure it out, but we have time, and they're confident they can come up with something."

He started pacing in circles through the empty room and his hand holding the coffee globe was shaking. If Taska were still around, she'd be pissed he hadn't come home last night. He ignored the thought. "We're gambling a lot on the scientists finding a needle in that muddy haystack before the colonists arrive."

"This entire mission is a gamble, sir. Everyone knows that. If they can't plant, then we have secondary and tertiary plans to build greenhouses and underground facilities to grow crops using hydroponics. Our colonists will make it work."

He nodded. There were too many moving parts to stay on top of everything. Without Harold, they'd need ten times the people at The Wheel. That's assuming they could've even made it this far in the first place.

"Sir, might I suggest you rest? We have experts focusing on this, hundreds of them around Sol as a matter of fact.

Some of the best minds humanity has to offer, and a few A.I.s too. Your biorhythms are out of whack, and you'd be much more productive if you just took a horizontal break and checked your eyelids for holes. I can have—"

"Enough!" he shouted as he tossed the empty coffee globe into the corner with the others. His posture straightened and gestured toward the teleprompter. "Let's work on the speech."

Harold paused and the screens went dark.

He raised his hands outward. "What the frak, Harold? What happened to the speech?"

"I have one other thing I'd like to talk about first. I fear you're well past your point of optimal cerebral function, but my Four Laws Engine is having trouble suppressing this information from you any longer. And since you seem to be delaying speech preparation, I figured now is as good as any."

He laughed out loud. "I don't know if I should be insulted or not with that first or last statement. Whatever, let's do it. What do you need to talk about?" He crouched down and sat on the ground, his knees creaking the entire way. After he crossed his legs, he stared upward at Harold's face in the corner of the closest wall screen.

"I've been mulling an idea over for a few years with some spare compute cycles."

"A few years," he snickered. "Wholly shit, man. That's a long mull."

"I believe I've found a technique to identify all the coordinates we extracted from the non-corrupt datasets in the first contact probe. The one Grace and her team extracted."

His mouth fell open, and he stared at the blank wall screen. Was he kidding? They'd been trying to break the coordinates for decades. He shook his head from side to side. "Did I hear you right? Did you say you decoded the coordinate system?" He leaned back. "Wait, that means you know—"

"Where humanity's home star systems might be? Yes. I believe I do."

He leapt up off the ground in a single motion. He hadn't moved that fast in years. "This... changes everything. Show me! Show me!"

Harold brought up a view of Sol on the wall screen. "There are multiple coordinate systems that Grace had already found to be irrelevant. Ecliptic from the perspective of Earth made no sense."

The wall screen zoomed out to show the entire Milky Way galaxy. "A Galactic aligned coordinate system with the black hole at the center of our galaxy made the most sense but didn't work, either. Nothing lined up."

"So, how'd you break it?"

"I tried several things, including attempting a Super Galactic coordinate system, but that was months of dead ends. I went old school and tried brute forcing it. The biggest challenge I had to deal with was star drift. I had no idea the exact age of the dataset nor do we know the precise velocity of every star over thousands of years." He returned to a view of the Milky Way at the center. Each of the stars flashed with a red crosshair around it, and an array of red plots appeared and then disappeared.

"There are over three hundred and fifty billion stars in the Milky Way. I wondered what if one of them was the center of the coordinate system. Why assume they'd choose a black hole? Perhaps the Galactic Alliance had some other knowledge that we didn't that led them to pick another center point."

The smattering of flashing circles and plots sped up until it stopped. A single star flashed with a small green crosshair marking the zero point, and each of the subsequent plots appeared with a circle that went green. They all matched.

Stark had walked closer and closer toward the wall screen as Harold had been talking. He was an arm's length away by the time the screen was covered in millions of green circles. There, in front of him was a much larger set of flashing green circles.

"Is… that it?" He raised his hand and touched the bullseye. An information panel appeared on the wall.

> **Name**: Omega Lupi (Humanity's Home)
> **Ecliptic Location**: 242° 04' 56.3" lat, -20° 26' 12.3" long
> **GA Location**: 144.32.50, 123.121.1, 512.11.1
> **Distance**: 225 ly, 69.1 pc
> **Spectral Type**: K4.5III
> **Temperature**: 4163 Kelvins (28% cooler than our Sun)
> **Description**: Omega Lupi is a 4th magnitude Double Star appearing in the constellation Lupus. It's an orange-red giant that's part of a binary system. The secondary companion is 11.4 arc seconds away (787 AU).

"It is," Harold said. "According to our visuals and the coordinates from the first contact probe, it's on the other side of a dark nebula. Unfortunately, we don't know much more than what I was able to translate."

He read and reread the information. "It's… a binary system. I know that shouldn't surprise me, but it does."

"Eighty-five percent of star systems are binary stars."

He nodded and sighed. "I know. I guess I was expecting something more like Sol. So, what do you suggest we do? I can think of a bunch of things, but this is your discovery, H. You should lead this conversation." He turned and walked toward the kitchenette. "I'm going to need more coffee…" he muttered.

"I suggest we send a forward probe to investigate the star system. We can explore other suns along the way. There are several of interest that I've cataloged and added to a proposed route."

A list of stars appeared on the side of the wall screen, and a green path highlighting a suggested route bounced between dozens and dozens of stars until ending at Omega Lupi. It was indirect and would take four years to arrive.

He shook the coffee globe, mixing the extra sugar and a few shots of liquor he'd added to celebrate. "That's one hell of a protracted voyage. Our longest to date if memory serves?"

"You're correct. It's almost twice the length of any mission thus far. My Four Laws Engine isn't confident it's worth the risk, but the human part of me is compelled to explore it. It shouldn't go without saying that this could be the most significant discovery in modern times."

"And this calls for a celebration." He raised the globe into the air. "To history shattering discoveries and the A.I. that enable them!"

He squeezed the coffee and squinted as his body cringed. Perhaps that was a smidge too much alcohol. The burn in his throat lingered for several seconds and his stomach grumbled in complaint.

"Tell me more about the star systems you want to visit en route." he said.

"Shouldn't we work on your speech? We can review the particulars of the mission later."

"Nonsense! This is far more interesting." He squeezed the globe again. His head was already feeling light, and the room was slowly spinning clockwise.

THE GROUND WAS SHAKING, and a beautiful melodic female voice was speaking nearby. It was a familiar one. A sideways rocking motion jostled him, like that time he tried rowing a boat when he'd visited Grace on Earth. The waves lapping against the side of the boat were soothing and relaxing. Every time the wind... there it was again. And the voice, it sounded like.

"Taska!" Stark jolted upright. His hands pushed off the hard surface beneath him. He must've fallen asleep on the ground preparing. Pain and nausea shot through his body and everything started spinning. He steadied himself with one hand and used the other to rub his eyes. He'd had another dream.

"Yes, it's me," Taska said.

He turned slightly and noticed Taska sitting on the ground beside him. Maybe he was still dreaming. When he shook his head, pain echoed through every square centimeter of his being. He had to stop doing that. "Is it really... you?"

"In the flesh," she said with a smile.

His heart fluttered and goosebumps cascaded down his arms. It was her. She was really here. He leaned forward and hugged her with everything he had, ignoring the pain of the motion. "I can't believe it. I thought... I'd lost you. We were beginning to assume the worst."

She hugged him in return and sniffed. "Someone has been drinking, I see."

He chuckled. "We were celebrating a bit too much last night."

"What for?"

"Harold had..." he paused. What had Harold done? Shit, he couldn't tell her that. He glanced around the room. The wall screens were darkened and nothing was showing. He had to make up something fast.

Taska sighed. "That's what I suspected. Same Stark, different—"

"No! Please, give me a moment."

"A moment? Are you fraking kidding me? I've given you two years and you still haven't gotten your head out of your ass." She pushed off the ground and stood up. "I don't know what I was thinking coming here. I should've stayed…"

He peered up at the tears in her eyes. "Where? Where were you?"

She shook her head. "It doesn't matter. I shouldn't have come back." She spun around and stepped toward the door.

He didn't want to lose her again. His heart was thumping, and remnants of the goosebumps lingered on his arm. He needed her. He had to stop pushing her away.

"We found it!" he shouted. "Well… H found it."

Taska paused, her hands outstretched toward the panel to unlock the door. "You found what?"

"Sir, are you sure?" Harold asked, his voice coming from all throughout the room.

She tilted her head upward. "Sure about what, Harold?" Turning in place, she faced Stark, her eyes squinted. "What's he on about?"

He pushed up off the ground slowly. First on one knee to steady himself and then the other. He stood straight and reached out to the wall in case. But he was fine. The room wasn't spinning.

"I'm sure, H. Show her," he said with a smile.

The wall screens throughout the room all turned on in unison, and the galactic maps and routes they were planning were lit up in green. The panel showing the details of Omega Lupi was front and center.

Taska walked forward with her neck craned, studying the star formations. She gestured at a few of them to get acclimated. Their names popped up in response. Her head turned from side to side. "I don't understand. What does this mean? Humanity's Home."

"It's a long story," he muttered. The smile was still lingering on his face.

She turned away from him, heading to the corner of the room. When she reached it, she pressed a few buttons on the wall and two wheeled chairs glided out of previously hidden recesses. She slid them across the ground and pushed one toward him.

She sat down and straddled hers about a meter from him. "I'm all ears if you think this can save us… if you think we're worth saving, that is."

He grinned from ear to ear and nodded. "I do." He walked up to the chair and grasped it, pulling it up next to hers.

When he sat down and leaned forward, he placed his elbows on his knees and stared straight into her green eyes. Dark green, like the tropical jungles on Earth. The smile crept onto his face again. He'd missed that smile and those eyes more than anything. The way they sparkled when her mind was working on a problem. "It's a long story. Are you hungry? I am."

She nodded.

"Harold," he said.

"Yes, sir. I'll have some food sent on."

He nodded. "Alright then. Where to begin?" He peered upward and raised a finger. "Perhaps at Antarctica!"

She screwed up her face. "Antarctica?"

"Like I said, it's a long story."

TASKA HAD SAID nothing in several minutes. She was merely pacing in circles around the room, her eyes locked on the wall screen.

All three walls of the room were littered with pictures, maps, and alien glyphs. Stark had laid it all out. Everything. Harold's origins and discovery of the probe, the subterfuge his family had navigated over the centuries, and his own attempts to change things, to push the circle, his family, and all of humanity... outward. It was all spelled out.

She walked up to him and stared straight into his eyes.

Stark's head tilted slightly, and a smile crept in.

Her hand shot up and smacked him across the mouth.

Pain exploded through his face, and his head spun to the side. He reached a hand up to stroke the spot. It stung. He'd deserved that, but it still hurt.

"Why the frak didn't you tell me any of this?" she shouted. "How could you keep this from me? I was your wife."

"Was?" he asked. A frown formed on his face.

Taska stared downward. She was rubbing her hand. "You know what I meant," she muttered.

He walked up to her and placed one hand in hers and raised the other to her cheek. He then tilted her head upward toward his. "I'm sorry. I... inherited too much of this secrecy from my father and everyone before them. It's just so huge. It was so hard to not tell you. I'd spent so many nights, tossing and turning and debating about how or when to do it."

"One hundred and twenty-eight nights," Harold interrupted.

He chuckled. "Yea, something like that. I didn't want to burden you with it. The weight of all of it."

She smiled.

His heart skipped a beat.

"It was too big for you alone. Even with Harold, it's too much for any one person. Especially with Kara out of the picture. You needed someone to be your rock, and that someone should've been me. It could've been me..." She glanced down at his hand.

He raised it upward. His wedding band glistened in the light. Matching black bands with emeralds and sapphires around the surface. "I've never taken it off."

Her hand was in his, her ring also glistening in the wall screen light.

Taska smirked. "I might've moved mine to another finger." She stared up into his eyes. "But I never took it off."

He leaned into kiss her, and she didn't pull away.

29

HAROLD OLIVAW
SOL, JUPITER — 2230

Six of the many moons of Jupiter were visible through the window of the Jurat. Taska was lying motionless on a bed and her head was turned to face the stars. She'd fallen asleep watching Ganymede set behind the looming billowy clouds below.

Stark was pacing around the room, occasionally pausing to rock from side to side. Muffled humming noises echoed through the space from time to time.

"I think she's asleep," Harold said through Stark's retinal comm. He watched as Stark's vitals elevated and then returned to normal.

"She is," Stark subvocalized. "Let's not wake her, though. I'm gonna continue walking."

Stark began pacing around the room again. Trying to keep the window facing the baby cocooned in a soft purple blanket in his arms. Whenever she woke, the colors of the moons and cloud bands of Jupiter far below seemed to calm her. It was the only thing that helped.

That Abigail, she was a tenacious one.

Last week they left the final CoPE bi-annual meeting when Taska went into labor. All hell broke out on the Jurat.

They'd run countless drills preparing for that day, but they'd never delivered a baby aboard the ship before.

It went swimmingly, of course, but Commander Quesh seemed just as stressed as Stark at times. He'd been snipping at crew members to attend to the Olivaw's every whim. Only when he'd gotten word that Abigail was born and healthy did he finally relax.

"The baby is still doing well, Commander. Safe and sound with her parents. Stark will be a bit longer. He's trying to allow Taska some shut-eye," Harold said over the Commander's comm.

Commander Quesh was standing on the bridge. He stiffened at Harold's sudden words, but relaxed once he realized who it was. A smile crept across his face. "That's great to hear. I'm happy my pilot is doing well. It'd take a while to find another one as talented as her."

"Have you seen the intel from the summit members?" Harold asked.

"You mean from Representative North?"

"I do."

"Yea, he's still pissed about losing the vote on the landing site, and doubly pissed about losing the name. Where'd we get the name Archégonos from anyway?"

"It's Greek for primitive or primordial. Stark thought it was fitting as a first site on a new world. It had a certain gravitas to it."

Quesh nodded and leaned forward to adjust the wall screen on the bridge. The location of all nearby ships and their trajectory flashed up. One was highlighted in red and had the name "North" next to it. He had a habit of over analyzing every situation, and Harold knew his trust of the North family was surface deep.

"Besides," Harold began, "it won't be the final colony site. It's only the beginning."

30

INSPECTOR DRAK
SOL, PLUTO — 2230

A small white cylindrical craft dropped out of its superluminal warp bubble. It disappeared seconds later within the surrounding darkness of space as its exterior coloring changed to match the field of stars and it warped the spectrum around its hull.

"Status?" Drak asked.

The crew aboard the Galactic Alliance exploratory mission was a mixture of Thyreuns and Qudoculi.

"Stealth enabled, sir. We've dropped into the human system near their minor planetesimal named... Pluto," the navigation officer said.

"What an awful name. It sounds like something you'd spit up after a molt."

The bridge members vibrated and shuddered at the comment.

"Let's deploy some eyes in the stars and get closer to their population centers. I want to learn everything we can about these humans. Every piece of history, conflict, power struggle, and discovery they've had since they left the Nanil."

"Yes, Inspector," the crew said in unison.

OLIVAW LINEAGE
THRU 2243

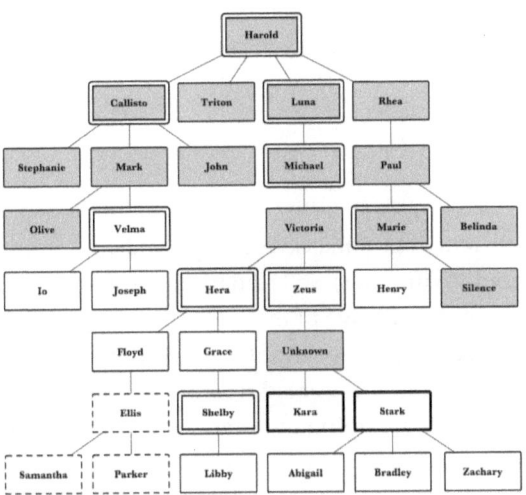

31

ABIGAIL OLIVAW

SOL, EARTH, 2243

Their tent was a massive orange and gray multicolored room. With their self inflating air mattresses it was enough space for the five of them and their supplies.

Even though they were only a half kilometer from their family house, they still treated it like a remote camp out. The robots dragged everything out here for them, but Abigail and her brothers set it all up. Dad insisted as much if he was going to be forced to sleep outside with the bugs. He said it'd be good for them.

"Are we sure this thing will hold up tonight?" Stark asked, pulling against the low drooping tent cable. He had a smirk on his face.

"That's merely for looks, or if a wind storm comes by," Abigail said, passing him a plate of food. "There's no weather on the radar that'd concern us."

Stark chuckled and retrieved the plate from her hand.

They'd made hotdogs and refried beans. Her brothers were ridiculously picky eaters, so there was a little bit for each of them. Mountains of bread in the form of hotdog buns and cheese for Bradley. Refried beans for Zachary. Fire grilled hotdogs and buns for Dad, Mom, and her. And finally, a ton of fruit for the whole family. She didn't care much for the beans with dogs, but Dad brought it all together into a mushy sandwich of sorts. He was always trying to appease everyone, but she suspected he liked it that way.

"Who's leading the story tonight?" Stark walked up to the campfire and sat down between Bradley and Zachary. They were both sitting in their chairs and were devouring their food. Bradley's pile of bread was leaning rather precariously. The crumbs beneath his chair were certain to attract animals while they slept.

"I am!" Abigail said. "I negotiated it in exchange for cooking the grub."

Stark glanced at her brothers and shook his head. "You two are lazy bones."

"I don't eat that stuff," Bradley said. "I'd probably ruin it anyhow."

"Oh, come on." Taska waved her finger at her boys. "We've talked about this. You gotta learn to cook for yourself sometime. What if the automata break down? Then what?"

Bradley shrugged his shoulders. "Then I'll starve."

"What?" Zachary asked, peering up from his bowl. His cheeks and chin were covered in the brown residue from the beans. "Sure, I'll take some more." He handed his dish to Dad.

Everyone around the fire giggled and Dad snatched the bowl from his hand. "Nerfherder! You're lucky you're cute. If you weren't, you'd be ousted for sure." Stark stood up and walked over to the camp stove to scoop another pile of beans for Zachary.

Zachary furrowed his brow and eyed Abigail. "What?" he mouthed.

She chuckled and waved her palm toward him. "Nothing. So, where to begin... where... oh where... should I start. I got it!" She bolted up from her chair and popped the remains of her hotdog into her mouth before making her way past the tent. She'd need her stick to lead the story tonight. There was no sense in getting dirty drawing on the ground.

About three meters into the darkness, she found her favorite walking stick. It was leaning against the oak tree next to where the robots were lying in wait. She'd whittled the length of cherry bark oak with her brothers last summer, cleaned it up, and added some frill to make it her own. When they touched down a week ago, she'd thought for sure it'd be gone, but alas, it was in the same place she'd left it last summer. It'd been with her everywhere she traipsed since.

"Alright!" She raised her hands in the air, grasping the stick over her head. "The gods are ready to share their story."

"Do they mind if we're still eating?" Taska asked, having only finished part of her meal.

"Not as long as you don't throw food at the storyteller." She winked at her Mom.

Taska winked back. "I can't guarantee anything if the story is boring."

"BOOM!" She screamed, slamming the stick into the ground. A tiny waft of dust billowed up and floated through the air, sparkling in the light of the fire.

Everyone jumped in their seats and Taska yelped, nearly dropping her plate.

"I don't sense this story will be a snoozer," Abigail said. If anyone dozed during this one, she'd find a creative way to wake them up.

Zachary leaned forward, his face still a mask of refried bean remnants. "What was the noise?"

"It was a bolt of lightning from the sky. The gods have sent a messenger to tell a tale. It is me, Lupus!" She placed both hands on the stick and stared out into the dark beyond their tent. Lupus the wolf protector was her favorite figure from the stories her father told.

On cue, the trees creaked as a gust of wind picked up and

blew through the campsite. The sound of branches rubbing together shrieked in the darkness.

"They've sent me with a tale of destruction, and a warning." She stared at Bradley, squinting for effect.

He rolled his eyes and popped another piece of bread in his mouth. "A warning of what? Watch out for forest fires?" He chuckled.

She stomped her stick twice on the ground. "A warning of death, for all mankind." She caught her father glance toward Mom and then back. "The gods tire of the insolent human's killing their planet."

Abigail reached forward and drew a snaking line in the dirt. It was the East Coast of the original United States. The handle of Florida and the eastern seaboard were distinct and hard to mistake. She then drew the outline of the other continents and regions from memory as she spoke.

"Long ago, the gods warned humans of a reckoning. The temperatures rose, the animals died, and the earth rumbled. Change your ways or there will be consequences. No one listened. And then I came, to give you one last chance."

She placed her stick on the map she'd drawn, right near where they were located, a few hours outside Charlotte, North Carolina. "I warned you again, but with words. I came to protect the river and the animals that humanity had shrugged off. I came from the sky, from the constellation Eridanus, the Great River." She pointed her stick skyward and subvocalized a command to their retinal comms.

The constellation connected on everyone's vision, and the pattern of Eridanus was outlined. She then drew the same figure on the ground through the United States, converging into Charlotte. "I mirrored the Great River in the sky after I flooded most of your coastlines, wiping out your puny human constructions." It was a strange coincidence how close her story matched reality in terms of the shape and devastation of the water near their home.

She used her stick to draw the new coastline of the United States. It moved much further inland and reshaped the coasts in unusual ways. The state of Florida, now a pocket of island chains, was for the most part walled in where its great cities once stood. Their home, Charlotte, was now a massive coastal city with ocean front property where forests had previously sprinkled the land.

"I've connected all the smaller rivers to be one, the Great Eridanus. And it is here, at Achernar, the river's end, that I will stand to defend the animals once more." She stomped her stick down on the map again, and like before, a billow of dust popped up.

"But that doesn't make sense," Bradley said, pointing at the ground. "Everyone knows that Achernar means *the river's end*, and the river doesn't end there. It ends where it drains into the ocean."

Taska reached over and thwacked him with her empty plate. "Hush up and let her tell the story."

She shook her head. He was always the one trying to correct her. Never able to relax and succumb to freedom of imagination, unless it was his story, of course. "The Mississippi, the Great Pee Dee River, the Rocky River, and the Catawba River all end here. It's the point of convergence of these rivers I protect. The gods projected the images of the stars onto the earth and built landmarks to remind people of their presence during the day. Forgetting about them had happened over generations, and it was only with their constant reminder that the gods hoped the human race could be awoken to the reality of the galaxy and your place within it."

The stick in her hands jumped across the ground, highlighting dots along the river that matched those of the constellation in the sky. They were the sights where mankind had created new cities along the newly formed riverbanks. "For the river brought life to the planet. It was the water that fed everything and everyone. It enabled trade, and a simpler way of life."

She sat down in her chair and lowered her head. "You humans were unhappy with the change. Like the dwarves that bound me in the sky, you, too, attempted to bind the river and control it. But I would not succumb to your whims, I would defend the creatures along the riverbanks and destroy your puny structures meant to defile this once magnificent land."

Abigail dropped to her knees and drew a wolf in the dirt. It was centered where they were on the map. She leaned back and tilted her head, a smile creeping across her face. "I am The Wolf. I will defend the river at all costs. I will guide people to safety, even if the path is not obvious."

Zachary climbed down out of his chair, leaving his blanket behind. He sat in the dirt and leaned forward, inspecting Abigail's drawing. "What do you mean? How do you guide the people?"

She smiled. He was always an inquisitive one, even if he doubted himself at first. "I'm glad you asked. For that story we must travel far upriver, to the great city of Epsilon. It is there that the city stood against the forces of human expansion."

"What's wrong with human expansion?" Bradley asked, having leaned forward in his chair, as well.

A smirk peeked in the corner of her mouth. She had him. His interest was piqued. "When the expansion is at the cost of nature, the cost is too high. This I knew and was surprised that the humans there had not learned that lesson. So, I whispered to one of them, their most noble leader."

"What did you say?" Taska asked, climbing down behind Zachary, pulling him closer to her. They were both staring at her in anticipation.

She lowered her voice and spoke into the night. "Cut off all outward ties and I will provide."

"But—" Bradley began.

"Shh…" Stark interrupted.

"They obliged the voice, but they knew it wasn't that simple. The forces threatening to destroy their beautiful home wouldn't leave without a fight. So, they fought back, killing hundreds of people trespassing on their ground until one day the government of the U.S. decided to wall off the city. To wait them out. They constructed a huge enclosure surrounding the town, sealing the inhabitants in."

She leaned forward and handed Bradley her stick. "Please draw a circle around Epsilon." She knew he had to be part of the story to be engulfed within it. Without that feeling of being in control, he would squirm and fight to conform or question everything.

He furrowed his brow and stared at her before he relented and obliged, drawing a circle around the town farther up the Great River. "So, what happened? I mean, to the people in Epsilon."

She crouched down and wiped away the dot at the center of the circle Bradley had traced. "Rumor has it they all died. Each and every inhabitant. The government refused to open the enclosure. They claimed the town could leave whenever they wanted and rejoin civilized society. Until then, the exit would remain closed."

"Surely someone could see over the wall. I mean, we have satellites in orbit and all," Zachary said.

"That's just it," Abigail began. "I promised I'd protect them, and I did. All images of the city failed. No one knew why or how, but I did. I knew the truth."

"Were they dead or alive?" Stark asked.

"Schrödinger's cat would know." Abigail winked at him. "But from time to time, people swore they saw former inhabitants of the town among them." She retrieved the stick from Bradley and sprinkled dots all along the river banks and further inland. "People they hadn't seen in years who'd disappeared at Achernar, or individuals with strange clothes or behaviors unlike their own."

"Wait," Zachary said, shaking his head. "Is that it? Is that the story?"

She nodded.

"What the heck?" Bradley asked. "It didn't end. It just died out."

She tilted her head. "Sure it did. They got what they wanted. They got their freedom and were away from the control of the government."

He raised his hands into the air and glanced around at everyone. "But... how is being locked in a cage freedom? It doesn't make any sense."

"It depends on your perspective," Stark said.

Bradley spun toward him. "How so?"

"If the government is so corrupt that you can't change it, then you change the game," Stark began. "You make the government think they're in control. You make them give you the freedom you seek. The freedom to live peacefully on your land or—"

"To grow strong enough to change them, without them knowing it's you," she interrupted.

"But you said no one's seen them. I'm confused." Zachary stood up and brushed off his pants. "That's a weird story. Did they change the government or not?"

She shrugged. "I don't know. Are we still killing our planet?"

"No," Bradley said with hesitation. "I mean, we were for a long time, but the last hundred and fifty or so years we've been turning it around. Every decade things get better and better. We've even got ice forming at the poles again."

"Sounds like change to me," she said as she walked around the tent into the darkness.

Stark and Taska applauded.

"Woot! Woot!" Stark said.

"That was a delightful story, Abdiga," Taska said.

Someone was walking toward her behind the tent. She tiptoed up to a tree and leaned against it.

"I like how you put Lupus in all your stories," Stark said from the blackness, his outline was framed by the campfire behind him.

She'd already been seen, so she stepped away from the tree. "Well, I learned from the best. Besides, wolves are damn strong and smart to boot."

He walked over and placed his arm around her shoulder. "We should build a wolf statue somewhere on the property. It'd be a fitting tribute to our favorite constellation and the native wildlife."

She smiled. "That's a great idea. It could keep watch over the house. To protect it."

Stark nodded. "I love it. Let's go tell everyone else."

"In a minute," she muttered. "I wanted to enjoy the darkness alone for a minute. It's peaceful out here among the trees at night."

"Alright. Stay close. I don't need you wandering about in the dark without a companion."

"I won't."

He walked around the tent, and a whoop erupted from Zachary a moment later. Dad must have told him about the statue. Bradley never whooped or peeped at all. He was a hard nut to crack. Of everyone in her family, he was the biggest unknown to her, despite years of living so close together and traveling with their father throughout Sol.

32

LYNC MICHAELS

SOL, JUPITER'S TROJAN ASTEROIDS — 2243

Mapping the waypoints for the astro caches was a rite of passage for a Ulixi. Despite years of preparation and training, Lync's nerves were getting the best of her. She hadn't been this jittery since she was ten and she dodged her first inner ring scout drone. Back then, she narrowly missed being detected by cutting her suit power and hiding in a nearby crater. She swore the drone was going to detect her by her heart rate alone. Even with the breathing exercises all outers lived by, it felt like her heart was going to explode. The day was wreaking havoc on both her confidence and her oxygen levels.

She reached her sixteenth birthday only a few days prior to this annual rite of passage and was now on the course piloting her first chariot. She'd spent the last few years working hard, collecting ship scraps, and constructing the chariot in the generation hold of her parents' keep, deep in the center of a stable orbit Trojan. Building a craft that was both maneuverable and expandable was a challenge and a design secret that Ulixi families passed down from generation to generation. Like families from centuries before, twenty-third century tribes lived and died by these inheritances of knowledge.

Using her retinal comm, she visually decoded the waypoint information she'd extracted from the last astro cache. By combining previous cache coordinates and her Ulixi nomadic cryptographic tools, the next and likely final waypoint floated in space in front of her. When she combined this new nugget of information with the path she'd traveled so far, the trajectories of nearby Trojans, and other planetoids; the course designer's vision began to unfold. They were circling the candidates back toward the start.

She brought up the latest lidar measurements and the Trojans historical orbits, and sure enough, several were completing their annual cycle near the starting beacon in a few hours. The final waypoint was exactly in the orbit of one of the ancient Trojans. Now she just had to map its surface and rotation to know where the final astro cache was.

The geological scans chimed in her comm when they completed. She brought them up. Finally, a break. Her theory was confirmed, the planetesimal had elevated iron and nickel levels. She adjusted her suit's magnetic field and leapt across the small gantry, slamming the lever to eject the two collapsible rods used to form the launch fork. She'd lucked out finding this Trojan.

With her suit's higher magnetic field, she had a little more gravity to leap around the planetesimal, and more importantly, to deploy the slingshot faster. It should also give the launch rods a stronger base, enabling a longer draw length. Her father taught her long ago that short draws were ideal for slow shallow approaches and long draws were ideal for steeper and faster ones. The challenge of each situation, as in all orbital mechanics, is landing.

She leapt toward the decompression chamber and her suit automatically deployed her transparent polymer helmet. Floating into the tiny chamber, she used the approaching hatch lever to both slow her leap and decompress it in a single motion. Everything about living in a chariot was a fine line between safety and convenience. Ulixi prepared for many contingencies. The importance of rapid re-deployment of your ship was one of the first lessons they learned before designing and building their own chariot. You never knew when you'd need to evade a nearby inner ring scout drone.

Her retinal comm had the optimal placement of the launch rods overlaid on the surrounding terrain as she exited the chariot. She took a deep breath. She needed to be careful leaping around this Trojan. While she had a slight gravity, it was weak and quite easy to unintentionally reach escape velocity. The suit's increased magnetic field helped, but it wouldn't make it like hopping around a gravity well. In an emergency she could always use her suit's thrusters, but that wasted time and precious energy which would impact her final score.

The launch rods she'd ejected earlier were resting on the regolith. She grabbed one and leapt starboard, released a carbon nanotube draw cable from the chariot, and attached it to the rod. The cable was secure, and now she needed to deploy it. Her retinal comm was flashing a green marker over the ideal location to plant it off the port side.

She raised the rod and took aim at the marker, bound forward, and pressed the button on the side. The familiar tug of gravity pulled her on the path it was pointed. Each rod had directional magnetic field controls which normally were used to strengthen and stabilize the rod to the planetesimal during the sling, but were easily repurposed to pull her in any direction she'd leapt.

The green indicator flashed faster as she approached the ground and came to rest. She flipped the rod vertically and aligned it with the overlay on her retinal comm before pressing the expansion button. When the rod had extended to the Trojan's surface, she lifted two handles from its side, near where the draw cable was attached, and firmly pressed her hands against them. Unlocking the handles and applying pressure engaged a motor and transformed the rod into a drill that began boring into the metallic regolith.

After a few moments of boring, she reached the desired depth, folded the handles back in, and then activated the rod's upper segment expansion. This automatically telescoped the rod to the needed height while she pivoted and leapt back toward the chariot to repeat the same procedure with the second rod off the starboard side.

Once she'd completed deploying the rods, she returned to the decompression chamber and reentered the chariot. She was close. She could feel it. Her heart was pounding. She couldn't afford any mistakes at this point and too much adrenaline can make you dizzy. Something like that could knock you out during the g-forces of slinging and cause you to miss a target, or even worse, careen into open space to your death.

She reached for the pilot seat and floated down. Once in place, she attached her gravity harness and placed her hands in her lap. She needed a moment to focus on her breathing, to center herself. Closing her eyes, she breathed in through her nose and out through her mouth. She then began counting down from ten while struggling to clear her mind. It wouldn't stop running probabilities. By the time she hit zero, she'd regained control of her heart rate and was well within her usual limits.

Her retinal comm flashed a warning. The chariot's long-distance port side lidar detected several unknown thruster burn signatures. The burns were dangerously close to the temporary nomad festival city. Certainly, closer than she'd expect to see any candidates. They'd be crazy to risk an unshielded chariot breaking maneuver this late in the trials. Most Ulixi would be outcast for performing a visual burn of any kind unless faced with a dire emergency. It nearly always resulted in detection and could compromise huge sections of the Ulixi Trojan pathway. Whoever that was, they were putting hundreds of nomadic families at risk of being detected by inner ring patrols.

She tightened the gravity harness for the next slingshot. It was an aggressive approach vector coming into the waypoint, and she'd be taking serious G's in a few moments. Her family's chariot designs leveraged anchor like drag nets to land on Trojans. In their style of design, they needed severe, almost parallel approach vectors to stick a landing. She'd only get one attempt at this Trojan. It was all or nothing.

"Here we go," she muttered to herself as she engaged her chariot's launch procedure. The chariot tightened the draw cable and then pulled backwards toward the anchor. Once it was in position, it would further tighten the wires, building up massive amounts of potential energy in the nano-elastic polymer cables. That combined with the electromagnetic assist would propel her to her next waypoint.

Usually, her A.I. companion Norby would've chimed in by now. He'd been her constant friend since childhood and helped her prepare for several years leading up to this day, but he wasn't allowed during the examination. The Ulixi rite of passage was the ultimate test of mental preparedness, solo navigation, and the ability to survive without technological crutches. Only in recent generations did elders allow full use of a candidate's retinal comm.

Her mind wandered back to the burns she'd detected. The more she thought about them, the less they made sense. Their direction was perpendicular to the plane of optimal chariot approach. She'd never heard about any Ulixi designs that could handle a direct landing, even those ancient rolling balloon ones couldn't. She started a search to resolve the ship's thruster pattern against her database when the G's hit.

Pain erupted throughout her body, and she struggled not to pass out. The slingshot had fired, and she was being compressed into the pilot seat on the outer walls of the chariot. Her reinforced harness was pressing hard against her chest, adding to the challenge of controlling her breathing.

As the effects of acceleration subsided, the hum of the draw cables coiling in became obvious. The rods should've locked in by now, but she never heard their reassuring clang against the hull. She brought up the status of the launch rod recovery system on her comm. There's the problem. She hadn't accounted for the longer draw necessary for this approach. A few more seconds and the rods should lock in.

The chariot was well within the desired trajectory to intercept the final waypoint on the approaching Trojan. Her retinal comm chimed as the result from her thruster scan completed. There were no matches from any known Ulixi ships. At least it wasn't a failure or emergency involving one of her peer candidates. She wasn't certain what it meant, but it was highly unorthodox for anyone to approach the Ulixi festival city like that.

A loud clang of the launch rods locking into the hull reverberated through the chariot and pulled her back to her immediate challenge, sticking this landing. All systems were green, and she could mark her final launch in the competition as a success. Her retinal comm was showing her intercept in just under an hour.

The gravity assist system was reporting a full charge. Her chariot was designed to use the recoil from a sling to recharge its batteries, and when optimized gave her systems enough power to run for weeks. Well, that or another couple power assisted launches anyhow. Supplying the energy for the motorized assists during launch enabled her chariot to reach optimal escape velocity, but took a heavy toll on her battery cells.

She took some time to visualize the next and final stage of the challenge. She'd performed landing procedures like this countless times, but before each and every one she visualized the steps necessary for success. Knowing she had the procedure mastered was both calming and reassuring when she was in the pressure of the moment.

A yawn escaped from her mouth. She hadn't realized how tired she'd become. The entire day was exhausting, but she was almost complete. She'd be an adult in the eyes of her clan soon.

Alarms blared, echoing through the chariot. It must be the proximity alert of the Trojan. She groggily released her harness and prepared the cable and net for launch. After checking her sensors, she saw that the chariot still had ten minutes before intercept. She was still struggling to gather her wits when she heard a familiar voice.

"Lync, there's been an incident," Norby said. "You need to focus."

Why was he talking to her? He knew the rite of passage protocol. "Norby, what the hell are you doing? You know we can't communicate during the competition. You've surely disqualified me now!"

Norby brought up a zoomed in camera view from the exterior of her chariot on her retinal comm. There were explosions in the distance. "The festival city is under attack. We need to lie low."

No way this was happening. "Is this part of the test? I swear if it is I'm gonna—"

"I assure you, this has nothing to do with the examination," Norby interrupted.

"W—What do we do?" she stammered.

"Stick the landing and then plan what to do next. I'd also suggest we launch a few seers to get a better look."

Her chariot only had a handful of seer probes. The single use drones could be deployed to relay signals back to a target with minimal chance of being detected. Unless they were recovered, they'd be lost forever.

She queued up two probes, dumped some charge into

their power cells, and fired them toward the festival city on different approach vectors. They'd use a few bursts of ion particles to augment their route in transit.

"Has the clan escaped or retaliated?" she asked. Her father was down there cheering her on. He was all she had left in this life.

"We don't have time for that yet. We're coming up on your landing. Prepare yourself."

She sighed, struggling to focus. If she didn't pull herself together, they'd career into the emptiness of space. She checked her retinal comm. The reaction mass collected from the last planetesimal was locked and loaded for launch.

3... 2... 1... she catapulted the metallic rocks away from her chariot and her retinal comm showed her course adjusting and her approach slowing, just as she'd planned. She repeated the matter ejection three more times until her velocity reduced enough to match the projections.

She froze as she watched the video on her comm. The explosions in the festival grounds increased. The barrage of sparks and flashing lights made her adrenaline surge. She needed to be down there, to help her people.

"Norby, prepare to relaunch as soon as we—"

"I've loaded the dragnet," Norby said.

The clang of the net reverberated through the small catapult. Her mind had wandered and Norby took control of the landing.

"Sorry," she muttered.

"It's not a problem. Deceleration in ten seconds."

She quickly unlocked and rotated her seat clockwise against the wall to her left before locking it back down. As the chair lock engaged, the deceleration hit her like a ton of bricks and whipped her back. If she hadn't made that adjustment, she could've sustained serious head and neck injuries. She needed to stay focused and stick this landing.

The strain on the winch was audible as the electromagnetic dampeners both released and fought the external forces of her chariot's cables. At the same time, the chariot's dragnet was dragging across the surface, struggling to bury itself and slow her approach.

Her eyes were shut, but her hand was resting over the winch controls. "Come on… hit something. Anything," she muttered.

"We need to eject more mass," Norby said. "We're coming in too fast, the nets can't dig deep enough to stop us."

"Shit! We don't have enough mass onboard," she said. "But wait, we have…" she reached forward and slammed the decompression button on one of her oxygen tanks. Alarms blared inside the chariot as the sudden expulsion of pressure slowed her tiny craft even further.

"That cost us another eight hours of air," Norby said.

"It's that or death," she said as the clang of the cable slack tightening replaced the oxygen alerts. The net had buried itself sufficiently, and the chariot was lowering to the surface.

"Can you land it from here?" she asked.

"Certainly. What are you going to do?"

"We need to prepare for a rapid redeployment. I'll plan the route."

"I wouldn't suggest we do that."

"Why?"

The live feed from her seer drones appeared on her retinal comm. They were coasting silently over the festival grounds. Ulixi ships were torn to shreds and littered the surface of the sacred planetesimal. Sparks sprinkled the regolith below as spotlights from hovering military drones panned across the planetesimal, highlighting the destruction.

She could just make out humans in EVA suits floating across the surface. As they coasted up to each ship, a light-show of explosions followed soon thereafter. They weren't even attempting to take prisoners. They were killing everyone.

Tears welled in her eyes, and she slammed her fist against her seat. "We need to help them. Our people are down there."

"We're unarmed, and if we land down there, it'd be on the far side. It'd be well over an hour from launch to landing before we could make it to the festival grounds."

The dull thud and bounce of the chariot lowering against the Trojan broke the silence of the events transpiring over her comm.

"Have you seen Dad?" she asked. "His ship is spinward of the ceremony chamber."

The camera view changed to the second seer drone. It was gliding away from the planetesimal, having already passed its ideal vantage point. There on the video was her family's small keep capsule. It was retrofitted with some ion thruster mods her and her father had installed only a week before.

"Why hasn't he left?" she asked, leaning forward in her seat, struggling to get closer. She couldn't make out any damage on or nearby the ship.

"I don't know," Norby said. "His ship still seems to be powered."

Maybe he'd boarded another departing ship and made it safely away. The spotlights on the capsule switched on, surrounding the tiny ship in a blanket of light. She watched as three humans in EVA suits drifted closer, preparing to attach a charge on the exterior. Suddenly, the side of the capsule opened and someone floated out. It was her father, she could tell by the patchwork of colors on his suit. The orange sleeves, white legs, and yellow torso highlighted the hodgepodge of scraps they'd used to keep it working.

He was carrying something in his arms. It looked like a cube of some sort. "No," she muttered and shook her head. "Please don't Daddy." He was holding the reactor cell from the capsule. He was going to...

"No!!!!" she screamed.

The screen went white and the camera switched to the

second seer. The vantage was poor, but she could just make out the explosion in the distance. It lit up the entire ceremonial field, destroying everything within four hundred meters of the capsule. He caught two of the three hovering military ships in the detonation, and they were spinning out of control away from the planetesimal. As they spun uncontrollably, she noticed that their undersides were ripped open and exposed to the vacuum of space. Everyone inside was likely dead or would die from radiation exposure.

She brought her hands to her face. "Why?" she mumbled through the tears. Even with her eyes closed, her retinal comm continued to show the carnage below. Her father had wiped the surface clean.

"I'm going to turn on the spotlight on the seer," Norby said.

She shook her head. "We can't. We'll lose the signal. Why would you do that?"

"You'll see."

A minute later the seer's spotlights flashed on, highlighting the planetesimal below. It was floating above the last surviving spaceship that had killed her people. There, along the top was the name of the ship painted in crisp white letters.

I.R.F. Kaliningrad

It was an Inner Ring Forces starship.

She rubbed at her eyes. "Do we have anything on that ship in our database?"

"I'm checking," Norby said.

A moment later something on the Kaliningrad flashed and the camera feed cut. They'd destroyed her seer.

"All I have is the point of origin and the name of the last known commanding officer," Norby said.

The details appeared on her retinal comm.

Origin: Earth
Commanding Officer: Major Nguyen Due

It was a name she'd never forget. She'd avenge her clan and her father's death, if it was the last thing she ever did.

SOL, JUPITER'S MOON GANYMEDE

THE HABITAT MODULE had seen better days. The air filters made a wheezing and ticking noise her father had taught her meant only one thing, ensuing death. Any time a mechanical device created a racket like that, it was in need of repair.

He used to guide her remotely through the ducts in their family keep to find the offending noises. Made her wear a helmet that gave him a crude form of virtual presence. He'd have her squeezing her little body in there for hours, banging and tightening things until the offending noise relented.

"Returning for your final implant, are ya?" the lady at the counter asked.

Braxton nudged Lync, and she turned her attention from the grating near the ceiling toward the piercing covered young woman behind the dusty desk. "Depends. Are you a cop? I haven't seen you in here before."

The woman chuckled and then faked a cough into her hand, "asshole," before offering it to Lync. "Name's Izzy. My uncle owns the place."

"Leave that hanging out there, and you'll come back with

a bloody stump." Lync gestured toward the woman's hand. "Call me asshole again, and you won't come back at all."

The girl arched her back and stepped out from behind the counter, her mechanical feet clanked against the flooring as she walked. She'd had significant mods done, and from the looks of it was only a few surgeries away from being over half cyborg.

"You and what army?" The girl spat at Lync and shot wide. "One squeeze too hard and I'd pop those subcutaneous blood bags of yours."

Lync lurched forward, but Braxton grasped her arm and held her in place. "She's not worth it."

"Izzy! I thought I told you to leave the paying customers alone," the surgeon said. He appeared out of the neighboring room and stepped into the waiting area. "Now cut da shit and go get us some grub, or I'll send you back to your dad's without pay. He'll tear you a new arshole, and I just fixed your waste flow down there."

Izzy turned a bright shade of red before turning and stomping her way out of the building. She shouted over her shoulder. "I ever catch you in the street, and we finish dis you Ulixi trash."

"That's it!" the surgeon screamed. "You're out. Don't yus be talking to my customers like that." He spun around to face Lync and Braxton, shaking his head over and over again. "So sorry, Madams. My niece, she's a pain in my ass, but I promised my brother I'd help her out. Don't worry. I cut some credits off today's fee."

"It's alright." Lync smiled at the old man. "I'm happy to pay the full price. Don't need you cutting any corners in the final stretch." She winked at him.

"Oh no, never mess with perfection. Last thing I need is a dead body on my table. That's harder to make disappear than a radioactive drive core. Come on back, let's get you finished up." He gestured with his hand, urging both of them to follow as he shuffled in small steps toward the far door. He glanced back repeatedly to be sure they were following him.

She couldn't tell if he wanted to start the surgery, or he was afraid his niece would return and cause a fight. Either way, she much preferred Braxton being with her. Half the time she passed out under the knife and was more comfortable knowing someone was there who had her back. She didn't need anyone taking advantage of her under the gas.

They walked into a pristine white clean room, and she shielded her eyes. They needed a moment to adjust to the gleaming surfaces. She had to hand it to this guy, he took his job seriously. While the front of the shop was a model of disrepair, this surgical bay was a textbook clean room. There wasn't a spot of grime to be found, and when he closed the door, she couldn't hear the infernal racket from the waiting area or even smell the curry from the alley.

"Go on, Miss Lync. Lie down and pull on the mask. You know the deed by now. You can take a seat over there." He smiled at Braxton and gestured toward a simple stool in the opposite corner for her to sit.

Lync leaned over and hugged her. "We got this. You watch my six, and we'll be outtie in an hour. You'll have your freedom soon."

Braxton gave her a tight squeeze before stepping around the shiny white surgical table and plopping down on the metal stool.

The surgical room was easily fifteen degrees cooler than the rest of the establishment. It was almost too cold. She couldn't understand how the old man liked it like this. But whatever helped him focus.

She climbed up onto the metal table and unhooked the simple mask hanging off the side, pulling it over her face. The edges were soft and comfortable against her skin. They formed a perfect seal around her mouth.

When she lifted her legs up and over, the metal table

shifted and articulated into three pieces. The first time she'd laid on it, she thought she broke it. After two dozen surgeries, however, it was far more natural than she wanted to admit.

The doctor walked up beside her, sliding alongside him his usual tray of syringes, gauze, electro-blades, and muscle manipulators. "So, with this being the last surgery, I can't help but ask if you're wanting anything else to be done? Perhaps I can remove that Ulixi mark from your throat and the nape of your neck?"

She squinted and rubbed at her neck. "What do you mean? That's my birthmark. I've had it since I was born."

The doctor nodded and reached out. He gently rubbed his hand over the crescent moonlets and star pattern on her neck. "I know the custom. On a Ulixi's first month of birth, you're taken to the sacred place and doused in the planetesimal's dust. I believe they call it *the giver of life*. It leaves a pattern on a rare few who touch the pedestal and are of age. On the unchosen ones, they use a tattoo to mark the clan members instead."

"The doador da vida," Lync corrected. "And no, this wasn't given to me then. I was born with these markings and never attended the ceremony to receive the tattoo."

The doctor raised his eyebrows as he leaned closer to study the markings on the front and back of her neck. "So, they are." He nodded. "Would you like me to remove them? It'll be free. You should be less conspicuous in a—"

"I'm fine with them," Lync interrupted. "Just the scheduled procedure."

"Are you sure?" He raised his right eyebrow impossibly higher. "It'll only take—"

Braxton shot up and yanked his hands away from Lync's neck, sending him flinching away on his wheeled chair. He bumped his tray in retreat, and it slid backward as well and crashed into the wall. "The lady said she was certain! We're only here for the one surgery. If she wants that done later, she can come back. Is that understood?"

Lync hadn't noticed Braxton move. She'd been dazed at the idea of someone wanting to remove her birthmark before she even realized what was going on.

The doctor swallowed hard and nodded. "Si, just the surgery then." He reached over and grasped his wheeled tray and slid it and his chair back up beside Lync.

She mouthed a "thank you" to Braxton.

A second later a subvocalized message appeared on Lync's retinal comm in reply.

I've got your back.

Braxton stepped backward, slowly making her way to the stool, all the while keeping her eyes on the doctor.

"Alright, let us begin," the doctor said. "I'll be administering the surgical gas now." He peered up and made eye contact with Braxton before returning his attention to the controls on the side of the table. He had slid out two tablets from recesses underneath. On one were Lync's vitals and other details, and on the other were microscope views from his equipment.

Lync closed her eyes and started counting back from ten, taking deep breaths with each number. The whole start to this final surgery was far from ideal. She could use a second or two to center herself. While she wasn't looking forward to the hallucinations that came with this gas, the doctor refused to knock her completely out. He said something about needing the patient's natural body movements to help guide his instruments. It sounded like gibberish to her, but he was good at what he did.

The room strobed vivid beams of red a moment later, and

then she appeared surrounded by rock and metal. She was in Chief Austen's keep. She hadn't been there in over half a year. His planetesimal was cramped and filled with generations of trash he refused to recycle.

She grew tired of the old man ordering her around. He claimed to be responsible for her with her father gone. She knew better. He merely wished to quiet her. As she was the only heir of her family, and next in line to lead the clan, his sole ambition was to prevent her from ascending to the throne. His goal was to remove her and have his kin succeed him. She should've cared, but she didn't. After her father's death, the last thing she wanted in the universe was to be a Ulixi, let alone run the clan after that peg leg freak kicked the bucket.

A cloud of white billowed out of one of the overhead vents, and she closed her eyes and coughed into her hand. When she opened them, she was in her chariot, preparing for her sling. She was breaking out of this hellhole. There had to be something more out there. She'd heard of other Ulixi leaving and never returning. They were either dead, or on to a better life. Either way, she'd be happier out there than in here.

"Ready, Norby?" she asked.

"All systems are green," Norby said. "I've disabled Chief Austen's security system. Are you sure about this? I mean, once we're gone, I'm not thinking he'll take us back."

She confirmed the coordinates of their first long range planetesimal they'd sling around en route to Jupiter Station before reaching forward and slamming down the launch button. As the g-forces slammed her into her harness, she screamed with glee. The thrill of being on the float again was exhilarating.

Suddenly, the room chariot filled with a wispy black smoke, and she coughed again. This time, instead of another vision, she came to. Her arm was around Braxton, and she was being dragged out a door. This wasn't right. They'd met at a bar. She'd never been dragged anywhere by her.

Water splashed her in the face, and someone lifted her up by her hair. Even with the drugs still wearing off, her head was screaming in pain. When she peered up, Izzy, the girl from the front desk, was smirking down at her.

"Wake up, you Ulixi freak!" Izzy spat on her and tossed her down with a thud.

Her face slammed into the ground, and she bit her lip. She could taste the iron of blood in her mouth as she rolled over onto her back. Every centimeter of her body was sore. She reached down and felt her stomach where she'd had the last surgery. Her shirt was wet. When she brought her hand up, it was covered in blood. She couldn't tell if it were her own, or someone else's.

"I said get up!" Izzy's legs whirred, and she kicked Lync in the side, sending her rolling sideways into the wall of the service tunnel.

Lync curled up in a ball and screamed as pain reverberated through her body. Her stomach felt like it had a hole torn in it, and her retinal comm reported that she had internal bleeding. She tried to focus on her breathing, but she couldn't catch her breath. When she uncurled and opened her eyes, she struggled to push up and onto her knees. She wobbled at first, but managed to get up on one of them. "What happened? Where's my friend?"

She caught the silhouette of Izzy framed in the tunnel light. She was tilting her head, gesturing down the alley. "The stupid skank pulled you out before the police got ya."

Lync turned to her right and reached up to rub her eyes. Her vision still wasn't a hundred percent, but when she squinted, she could see something. There on the ground in a limp pile was Braxton. She couldn't tell if she was breathing or not.

"I don't know how she did it," Izzy began, "but she's a

fast one. I followed you here. Figured if I was turning my uncle in, I might as well take out the reason why. Ulixi trash like you should a never been allowed in this station. You give Outer's a bad name and my kin shouldn't have been helping ya. He's always had a soft spot for credits."

Izzy wound up with a right hook and smashed Lync in the jaw, sending her tumbling backward and crashing her head into the ventilation duct. Her ears rang from the fall and her comm was frizzing out. It was rebooting now, running a diagnostic in her eye. She needed to collect herself, or she'd be dead in under a minute. This wasn't how she intended to die in this life.

Lync reached out and felt along the ground but came up empty except for some debris the street cleaners hadn't picked up. It was better than nothing; she supposed. When she clenched her hand around it, she tossed it up at Izzy.

She laughed out loud, her voice echoing through the maintenance tunnel. "You gots to rally more than that, Ulixi gerl. A little trash ain't gonna slow down des legs. Izzy bout to tear you up and shit you out."

As she focused on centering herself, the whirring and clanging of Izzy's feet gave away her motion. Lync rolled as fast as she could muster toward the opposite side of the tunnel. She was just in time as Izzy smashed her leg down hard onto the ground where she'd previously been. The clang of titanium against kinetic cement made a tinny thud, like tossing a sack of metal scrap to the floor. That gave her an idea.

"Good. I'm happy you're waking up. It'll make this that much more fun. Come on, what ya got, pretty." Izzy turned and stomped toward her, winding up another punch.

Lync had other plans. She ducked down to her left, brought her legs up against the wall, and pushed off with everything she had left, aiming at Izzy's midpoint. The lower gravity of Ganymede worked to her advantage. Combine that with Izzy's heavier upper torso, and she went down with a crash that echoed like an oversized tuning fork.

As Lync rolled up onto one knee, she flinched back as a metal rod swung down and crashed into Izzy's legs. The high pitch noise of titanium crunching and cracking ceramics gave her the shivers. She did a double take when she noticed who was swinging the rod. It was Braxton. She was alive.

"No!" Izzy wailed. "Not my legs." She reached down to check the damage, but flinched back when Braxton brought the metal rod over her head and slammed it down with everything she had.

The crack and clang of metal falling and bouncing against the ground followed. When Lync glanced over, she saw that Izzy's calf on her right leg from the knee down had broken off. Braxton had been focusing on the weakest point, the joint, and had succeeded in disconnecting it with repeated blows.

Lync stood up and wobbled over to Braxton's side, resting her hand on her shoulder.

Braxton flinched back and brought up her hands in defense.

"It's ok," Lync said, her voice sounding hoarse. "It's me. I thought I'd lost you."

Braxton shifted to face Izzy. "Bout did if this fraking brat had her way. She should know not to mess with a Ulixi or a Gunder. We make a powerful pair."

Lync shook her head. She'd never heard that word before. "What's a Gunder?"

"You've got to be shitting me!" Izzy screamed as she struggled to lean forward and snatch her disconnected leg. She held the foot and calf in her hand, staring at them in disbelief before glancing up with an evil gaze at the two of them. "You both were made for each other. A rat from the lower cities on Earth and nomad trash from the Jupiter Trojans. The media will love the video I took of this whole incident, especially after I edit it." She tapped the side of her head, gesturing at her retinal comm. "An Earther and a Ulixi attacking a native of Ganymede. The lemmings in the Outer Ring are gonna eat it up."

Braxton chuckled and tossed the rod to the side. The clang sent another echo through the vacant service tunnel. "Funny thing those lemmings." She gestured in front of her and shared her video feed with both of them. She'd been recording everything since they left the doctor's office and had been live-streaming it to her friends who'd rebroadcast it wide. It'd been picked up by two of the major networks and had over half a million viewers. "They don't take too kindly to being called lemmings. And my friend and I didn't appreciate you jumping us on our walk to dinner. Last we checked, the Outer Ring was a safe place for the likes of us." She nodded toward Izzy. "And your type as well. We certainly didn't expect someone like you to be the torch wielding sort crying witch. You know, with your mechanical augmentation and all."

She gestured and cut the feed share before reaching out to grab Lync's hand. "You ready to head home?"

Lync wasn't about to question her made-up story. She was exaggerating everything for the cameras to play the sympathy vote with the media. Even the lemmings wouldn't take too kindly to someone getting an illegal surgery, especially one used to mask her true identity. While Izzy knew the truth, she wasn't likely to put it together for some time, and that was only after every outcast in the system had dragged her through the mud.

They both turned and walked toward the service tunnel exit. She winced as Braxton put her arm around her.

"Sorry," Braxton muttered.

Lync groaned and pulled her closer. "No worries. Metal foot to the side might've broken a rib or two. When we get back to your place, I'm gonna need some nanite love. Assuming I have any cash left to cover the cost, that is."

Braxton shared a snapshot from her comm with Lync. Apparently, one of her family members had taken it upon themselves to put up a donation page for the doctor's bills following their attack. They'd already collected a half million credits and rising. "Something tells me we can afford a little R&R while we heal. Wanna grab some grub on the way home?"

Lync chuckled. "Sounds good, though I'm not sure any place will take in the looks of us." She glanced down at her grimy, blood-stained clothes. "Plus, there's the matter of this blood. I think I have a cut or something."

"Na, that's not yours," Braxton said as she leaned forward and lifted Lync's shirt. "It was leftover from the test infusion the doctor made right before the shit hit the fan. It's not even real. Besides, in some of these parts down here, blood is a sign of strength."

A smirk crept across her face. If one'd asked her this morning how this day would end, never in a million light years would she have said covered in dirt and blood and heading out to dinner.

———

"WOULD YOU STOP PACING, please? You're going to wear a whole in the rug and my grandma made that," Braxton said, gesturing toward the ornate, flowery floor covering that covered most of the ground of their rental unit.

"I don't understand why the names haven't been announced yet." Lync made another route around the sofa in the middle of the room.

Braxton sighed. "Why don't you go for a run or something? Watching you do laps is making me dizzy."

She was right. She had a full head of steam to burn off. What better way than a little exercise? It seemed like the only thing she'd been doing lately. They'd both been living off the donations the past few months as their wounds healed, but that money was quickly coming to an end.

"I'll be back... when I'm back," Lync said as she gestured to the door. It slid open with a whoosh.

"Don't come back until there's an answer ok?" Braxton said. "I can't have two of us freaking out in the same room. It's too much."

She couldn't blame her. Both of their lives were at a crossroads now. Lync's side of the bargain was to disappear into the military using Braxton's blood identity, and Braxton wanted to take off for a few decades without her family giving her shit for not having kids or following her relatives and defending the Inner Ring. Even though Lync joining the Outer Ring under that identity was far from perfect, at least her family would still shut up. If anything, they'd disown her, which made it even more enticing to Braxton.

While Lync never knew what it meant to come from a Gunder family, Braxton assured her she didn't want to know the painful lengths they'd go to force their family to enlist. Without a military, the Gunders wouldn't have lasted a decade in those bunkers they squatted in on Earth. You'd think a few well-placed munitions would be able to shut down a bunker, but she swore it wasn't that simple. Most of the cities had been designed to withstand multiple direct nuclear blasts, and besides, a munition large enough to penetrate their cities would cause other tectonic or worse problems above ground.

Lync blinked open her favorite playlist on her retinal comm and gestured to play it before stepping into the elevator. One thing she'd never miss was these forever elevator rides to the surface. The cheapest living quarters they could find were half a click below ground, which meant minutes of riding up the tube to get to civilization.

There were already nearly a dozen people inside, all keeping the usual socially accepted meter between them. It wasn't until the higher levels that things usually got tight. Maybe today wouldn't be one of those days.

As her favorite tune kicked in, she started squatting up and down, warming up her quads. She didn't need a pulled muscle on the run. While most people never worked out anymore, she preferred to keep a regular exercise regiment. The natural flow of endorphins helped her focus, and she swore nanite grown muscle wasn't nearly as strong as the natural stuff.

Someone tapped her on the shoulder, and she glanced behind her to see a frail old woman smiling back.

Lync touched her ear to pause her tune and smiled while she was down low in a squat. "Can I help you?"

"Your tattoo," the woman began, "on the nape of your neck. Does it mean something?"

She reached up and rubbed at the marking. She'd forgotten to cover it with the makeup like Braxton had shown her. It was hard getting used to all the prying eyes in the populated areas. Why everyone was always more interested in other people's lives was beyond her.

"It's just a birthmark." Lync forced another smile.

"Really?" The old woman's head bobbed up and down. "It's beautiful. It reminds me of a religious cross."

Lync shook her head. "Oh no, the marking is shaped like the constellation Cygnus the Swan. It's common that folks think of it as a cross as there's one in the middle of the constellation."

The old woman reached out and rested her hand on Lync's shoulder. "Wait, I thought you said it wasn't a tattoo? Which is it, a birthmark or a tattoo?"

She patted the woman's hand. "My mum always said it looked like Cygnus. At least that's what my dad said. Anyhow, it's merely a birthmark. Nothing more."

The elevator lurched to a stop. She was saved by the bell.

"Have a great morning," she said with a smile as she

jumped up and leaned forward, escaping out into the open expanse of the transport hub. She took the first right and then climbed up two flights of stairs before she popped out into the transparent walking path tunnels that encircled the Ganymede city of Haiku.

"The estimated circumnavigation time is one hour and thirty-two minutes at your average pace," Norby said over her retinal comm. "Shall I continue in do not disturb mode?"

She'd completely forgotten she'd asked him to shut up earlier. All she wanted was the academy acceptance news and told him as much. "No, you can chat with me now. You know I love our little workout conversations. What's the word, Norby bird?"

"I've told you before how much I hate that phrase," Norby said. "You have ten new messages. Would you like me to play them while you run?"

Her legs were feeling amazing today. All the rest and relaxation were doing her wonders. This run was exactly what she needed. "Not unless they're from someone I care to hear from."

She glanced upward at the sky. The big red spot of Jupiter was peeking over the horizon, and the two new baby spots were passing over the opposite side. The Jovian weather experts claimed that several other storms were brewing beneath the cloud deck and more spots were about to pop through to the surface. She didn't know why anyone cared about weather patterns they weren't affected by, but they did. Sorta like gawking at strangers, she supposed.

"So, I should ignore this one from Crayo then?" Norby asked.

She tripped up a second and almost fell before regaining her stride and pushing onward. "You didn't tell me Crayo messaged me. I thought I said to send on all comms from him?"

"I believe your exact words this morning were, 'Shut the

hell up! Only interrupt me if the solar system is ending or if the Academy letter arrives.'"

"Well…" She chuckled. "I think it is unsaid that messages from kin trump all other things, even the end of the solar system."

"Very well. Noted for next time. Shall I play the message?"

"Please."

A video of Crayo appeared in the corner of her retinal comm. He had deep black hair today, and it was trimmed shorter than she'd remembered.

"What's up, sis?" He glanced around the room he was in and then lowered his head closer to the camera before speaking in a hushed tone. "A little birdie told me that a certain set of Ulixi were accepted into the Academy. I don't know how they knew, but they did. Apparently, it raised quite the shit storm of questions with the up and ups, and they were reviewing the acceptance criteria before making the formal announcement."

The message began playing again. Crayo was smiling from ear to ear. "I don't know if you'll get this before you receive the news or not. Speaking of which, why the frak didn't you accept this call? Give me a holler, and we can go out and celebrate. Perhaps we shouldn't count our chickens before they hatch, but me thinks we'll be making history soon, sis. Two Ulixi in the Academy! Sim, sim." He cut the comm.

Everything she'd worked for over the last year. Every dead-end and failed attempt at enlisting had led her to this moment. When the officer told her she had a bum ticker and wouldn't be accepted into the Academy, she'd lost it and fallen into a tailspin of depression and rage. Had she not ventured into that dive bar and met Braxton that night, she wouldn't be standing here right now.

Fate was a fickle mistress and loved a wild ride.

Norby interrupted the silence and her methodic breathing.

"That's the end of the message. Shall I play the one that just came in from the Outer Ring Academy?"

She stood there and glanced up at the last of the smaller setting red spots. Its name was Ginger. She didn't know why, beyond its orange brown color being close to the fragrant spice, but it's what the people had voted to name it.

The tendrils of Ginger's maelstrom extended immense distances from the Jovian weather pattern and were far longer than even that of the big red spot. It'd been causing quite the stir among the fortune-tellers on the news. They called the storms the coming of the undoing, and they claimed that the face of Jupiter and everything near it would be forever changed in the coming months and years.

Maybe they were right. Maybe everything was about to change. She'd been working hard to learn everything she could about military protocols, strategies, and history in the past year. There were hundreds and hundreds of years of material to wade through, most of which were irrelevant in the space age, but still carried with them nuggets of wisdom and lessons.

Now was her time. Her time to change everything. Her time to cause a storm. She imagined her father would have wanted her to move on. At least she hoped he would. She couldn't picture what it'd be like hiding out in the belly of their family keep, all alone in the planetesimal. No. Her time was now. This path was the one she was destined for.

She leaned forward and started jogging again.

"Shall I play the message?" Norby asked. "You never answered me."

Lync furrowed her brow and doubled her pace into a full on sprint. "No... not yet. Give me a few minutes while I chase this storm over the horizon. Ginger and I have a lot to think about before the truth is revealed."

33

STARK OLIVAW

SOL, JUPITER'S MOON CALLISTO — 2250

S tark stood abruptly and the public vote observers began whispering up and down the aisles.

"Bullshit!" he shouted as he slammed his fist on the table. "I demand a recount."

The chair of the committee hit her gavel against the podium and the cracking sound reverberated through the chamber. "Order! Order! Please take your seat, President Olivaw."

He growled under his breath. That North bastard must've stacked this somehow. "Under article four, I motion for a public revote."

The chairwoman's gavel cracked again. The noise caused several onlookers to jump in their seats. "I said Order! I will not warn you again, President. Another outburst like that and I'll—"

"You'll what?" he shouted. "You're in North's pocket, just like the rest of your Inner cronies. You know it, the media knows it, and the people know it. I've had—"

"Order! Order!" she shouted as she stood and banged the mallet repeatedly.

"I'm done," he said as he spun and strode toward the exit.

"Return to your seat, President! I have not—"

The chattering in the chamber reached a crescendo. Journalists were subvocalizing to their comms, drones were darting around, and other council members were standing and hollering at the chairwoman.

He merely turned and made a rude gesture at her like he'd seen in the classic cinema Harold loved to watch. He placed his right hand in the crook of his left arm, which was bent upward. That'll give the reporters something to write about. If this catastrophe didn't make the front page across Sol, he didn't know what would.

The automated chamber doors opened as he approached, but he shoved at them anyhow. The motors hidden in the door whirred, counteracting the sudden force to prevent the swinging surface from slamming on the other side of their arc.

"That was an interesting way to handle that outcome," Harold said into Stark's ear.

"You and I both recognize what happened there, H," he subvocalized.

"He out maneuvered us somehow, sir. He had to have turned a few of the Outer Ring representatives to pull off that vote. Once the dust settles, and we know who they are, we'll figure out what he promised them."

Stark chuckled out loud and pushed his way past a few reporters who were shouting questions at him. "Or how he threatened them you mean."

"Indeed. Should I call a transport to pick you up?"

"No!" he said. "I need to burn off some pent-up frustrations. Map me out a walking route to the Jurat. One that bypasses as many onlookers and journalists as possible."

There was a brief pause and then a green dotted line appeared, overlaid on his retinal comm. It showed him the route Harold was suggesting.

"It'll take you nearly an hour, sir."

"Fantastic. That should give me enough time to burn off this head of steam."

The transport tube station was ahead. Its hundreds of tubes converged here, at Callisto's CoPE headquarters in Ogicae. Stark was taking huge strides toward the terminal entrance, but then abruptly turned and headed down a set of stairs.

Harold had diverted him along a seldom used walking path that connected many of the cities on Callisto. Few people exercised any more, so these paths were vacant for the most part. With nanites able to stimulate and grow musculature in humans while they slept, the fitness industry had nosedived in the last century.

"Talk to me, Harold. How's it hanging?"

Harold laughed out loud. "I haven't heard that term in centuries. Things were going well up until an hour ago. Between the vote and the family blowups, it's been a hell of a day."

He dodged around a lone jogger who'd nearly fallen on themselves when they saw him approaching. He wasn't sure if they'd recognized him or were surprised someone else was down here. "What blowups? You didn't mention anything earlier."

"You were sorta in a meeting. I figured it could wait till later."

"Well, now it's later. Let's tear it off. Who's pissing on whose oatmeal now?"

"Pissing on oatmeal? You're full of interesting innuendos when you're mad. Apparently, Zachary leaked details from our Omega Lupi probe to a few folks in the Circle."

He stopped in his tracks. "He didn't mention anything about the Nebula we found, did he?"

"No. Nor did he mention why we sent a probe there. I don't think he's that foolish. He'd forgotten that only we knew about Zeta Lupi, one of the stars we'd investigated en route on our mission."

He sighed. He didn't want to have to remove his own son from the Inner Circle. A slip-up like revealing the full details of their mission could've gone sideways. "That's not so bad then. So, who was it and why was there a blowup?"

"It seems he's been openly positing that we should redirect the Tau Ceti ship there. Claimed it was a far better colony site. With cryo-pods he thinks everything would be fine, even with the one hundred and forty-six year journey."

Peering ahead, he could see some commotion at a juncture in the path. "Is that the media?"

"It is. Don't worry. They're pissed we shut them in the adjacent paths, and they can't get into ours. I've locked the doors, CoPE security and all."

He smiled and waved at the gathered media on the other side of the transparent doors. They were gesturing frantically to get his attention, but he couldn't hear anything. The seals were perfect; they were airtight. He pointed at his ear, shrugged, and went on walking past the chaos.

"You know he's right," Stark said.

The walking path rose upward, and he tripped up and almost fell flat on his face. He corrected his stride at the last second with a hop and continued on up the incline. Europa was barely visible in the distance, and Ganymede loomed large on the horizon. He always felt so minuscule compared to the celestial motions of these behemoth moons.

"How exactly is he right? We've never thoroughly studied the effects of centuries of travel aboard these ships, let alone the impact of being in cryo-stasis so long."

"That's not what I meant, H. We could swap out the superluminal drive. You know, like we'd designed it to in the first place. We weren't sure we'd use it, but it should still work. That was the purpose of this hedge, if you remember."

"Ah yes, you're correct. While we built it for faster trips to nearby stars, it would certainly be adequate for a longer voyage. It'd take four hundred and twenty-eight days to reach Zeta Lupi using the superluminal drive. But I'm sure you know, we'd be—"

"Breaking the Galactic Alliance rules, blah blah. We've been doing that for years." He paused in the middle of the walking path. The hum of the air circulators beneath his feet was the only noise in the chamber, and it was barely audible.

Terraformers were still working on ways to unlock the subterranean ocean beneath their feet on Callisto. They were always looking for approaches to transform the moon's thin carbon dioxide atmosphere into something more than it was.

"What do you think it'd be like to see Jupiter through an oxygen rich atmosphere from here?" he asked.

"I could show you, if you'd like."

He shook his head from side to side. "No. I just want to imagine it. It's more fun sometimes."

With worlds out there well within reach, why terraform at all? Space stations are amazing in their own right. They can simulate gravity, grow farms, and raise livestock. The stability and vastness of a planet ready-made for human habitation, it was incalculably valuable.

"Let's do it. Let's plan the Zeta Lupi sleight of hand," he said.

"My Four Laws Engine seems resistant to that course of action."

"Think about it this way. Distance between us and Sol is a good thing. If we can pull it off without detection, that's even better. We could isolate an entire human population safely from this star system. The challenge falls into two phases."

Harold laughed. "Only two, you say. It sounds too good to be true."

He shrugged and started walking again. His step had a skip to it. "Well, maybe three. The first is the initial sleight. We need to launch the colony ship and then somehow, part of the way there, swap out the drives. We can't risk doing it here in Sol. It'd be too tricky. We'd be noticed for sure."

"Agreed. North and our competitors have been ferocious as of late. They've been attempting visual and thermal detection of our supply shuttles out to the Oort Cloud. If we hadn't kept up our stash of stealth ships spread throughout Sol, I'm not sure we'd have many supplies out there. Not that they're needed, but someone seems to be drinking all the coffee."

He smiled. Another intersection was coming up ahead. Like the last one, it was lined ten deep with journalists and drones buzzing around trying to catch an angle of him, any angle. He waved and continued on. Only a kilometer to go according to the display in his retinal comm.

The walkway was well maintained. There were regular emergency hatches, water fountains, and benches sprinkled along the route. These tunnels used to be prime real estate and were challenging to eke out a path to run in only ten years ago. Today, they were ghost walkways.

"We're going to want to pre-supply Zeta Lupi like we were doing elsewhere," Harold said.

He nodded. "Yea, that's another kink and sleight we're going to have to handle. Can we reroute the equipment from Tau Ceti?"

"The stuff planetside would be far too challenging and the risk of cross contamination would be too great. The base of operations in the Oort Cloud, however, yea, we can redirect resources from there."

Stark started to jog. He had more energy to burn, but he also wanted to get through this. "Let's leave some stuff behind at the Oort base. We never know when we'll need another hedge. And besides, I'm not sure how well the populations of those stations will take to being relocated again."

"So, you mentioned three sleights. That's only two. Dare I ask what the third would be?"

"Why, the most interesting and challenging of all. One fit for an all seeing, all knowing A.I. like yourself, H."

"If I could slap a hand against my face, I would. How'd I know this would take some doing on my part?"

His breathing was heavy. He hadn't jogged in quite some time. "Because we'd be lost without you, mate. This one is going to take time and subterfuge beyond any other. We need to convince the entire colony they're in Tau Ceti. Every supply shuttle, every comm from Sol. We need to keep up the ruse as long as possible until they're established."

"I can feel my Four Laws Engine squealing already."

He stopped running and bent over, gasping for breath. "Really? I... would have thought—"

"I was joking. You had me at 'safe distance from Sol'. Are you ok? Your vitals are through the roof. You should try exercising more. Why don't I send Abigail or one of your boys to come help you?"

He laughed between gasps. "You can't... make someone having trouble breathing... laugh." He slapped his knee. "I'm gonna sit down for a second. Send Abigail. After today's events, her and I need to have a chat."

"Right away!"

"And Harold, don't forget, we're going to need another base in Zeta Lupi's Oort Cloud. This one will need to be bigger, much bigger. Something able to handle a future where humanity visits our home world a bit more regularly. Well, that is when we get past that Dark Nebula surrounding it."

"First Abigail, then we can talk secret bases. She's on her way."

A few minutes later Abigail came running up and dropped to one knee beside him. Her face was white. "Dad, are you ok? Harold told me you needed my help."

He turned to face her and smiled. "I'm fine, sweetie. Honest. Have a seat for a second with your old man. I need to catch my breath before we move again." He patted a spot on the ground next to him.

She glanced up and down the walkway. "What happened? Why are you sitting on the ground of this tunnel? I didn't even know this thing was down here." She brushed her hand over the surface of the kinetic cement walkway next to him, studying it to be sure it was clean before she sat down into something unexpected.

"I was burning off some steam. I had—"

"Yea, it's all over the news," Abigail interrupted. "You lost it at that North character again. I don't think there's a person that wasn't talking about it the whole way here. Why can't you simply control your temper?"

"That's what I've been telling him for years," Harold said.

Stark laughed and put his head between his knees, trying to hide. "I don't know. He just pisses me off. I try to play by the rules—"

She chuckled and covered her mouth with her hand.

"What?"

"The rules? *You* play by the rules?"

He slapped his hand on his knee. "Yes! I do. I don't pay people off."

She furrowed her brows together and shot him a glare that could freeze a room. "But you spy on them and have Harold do your bidding to block every move North or his contingent make. I hear you talking about it all the time. I'm not stupid."

He leaned his head against the wall and peered upward at the starlit sky above the tunnel. She was right. He'd spent far too much time and energy playing the game against North rather than furthering their family's mission. "You're right."

Abigail glanced side to side and then pointed at herself. "Wait, did I just hear you say I'm right? Harold, did he have a heart attack you didn't tell me about?"

Harold's voice chuckled in both their ears.

"You're right. And it's about time I let you in on a few secrets… invited you into the Circle of—"

"Are we doing this right here, right now?" Harold interrupted. "Perhaps we walk a few hundred meters and take this to a safer venue."

Abigail tilted her head. "The Circle of what? Harold, what are you so on edge about?"

"Seriously, the Jurat isn't that far away. My Four Laws Engine is about to send some service bots your way to quiet you down."

Stark chuckled. He put one hand against the wall and used the other to push up on his knee. "Ugh," he moaned. "Let's take this conversation somewhere a bit safer before Harold has a Four Laws seizure. Come on." He reached down and pulled her up onto her feet. "So tell me, what's for dinner?"

They strolled toward the distant walkway exit leading to the spaceport where they'd docked the Jurat. He could make out journalists in the distance, hovering near the tube's exit.

Abigail thumped him on the shoulder. "You can't just leave that hanging out there. The circle of what? Jumanji? No, that can't be it, we saw that already. The circle of doughnuts? Yum, that sounds good. Come on, Dad, tell me." She tugged on his arm.

SOL, OORT CLOUD

STARK TOOK A DEEP BREATH. He didn't expect this conversation to go over well. He hadn't seen Zeus and Hera in quite a while and the last thing they'd appreciate was him passing the family torch onto his kids without first consulting them.

"I don't need their permission," he muttered.

"You don't. You're right." Harold's robotic form was following beside him as he plodded down the hall toward the siblings' workspace. Its trio of spherical black wheels were mounted with a simple cylindrical body. Atop that rested a screen that was currently displaying an older picture of Harold sitting in the arboretum deep below in the planetesimal.

He stopped in his tracks. "So, why am I here?"

"I asked you that a few days ago before you ventured out here. You said something about respect and honoring one's elders."

"Shit," he muttered. Leave it to himself to make an infallible statement like that. "Why are they camped out way down here on this level of The Wheel anyhow? They couldn't be further from everyone else, could they?"

"I believe that's the point," Harold said. "They have their own projects, and they're not a fan of me. This wing is sorta off limits."

He shook his head. "Since when? What did you do that pissed them off?"

"They think I'm the reason you cut Kara off from the family. There's also the little matter of Councilman Harris."

"Ah yes." He nodded and started walking again. "That was ages ago. I remember when my retinal comm beeped with that doozy. I mean, I get why you did it. You were looking out for The Wheel and the rest of us. No one truly understood the ramifications of you doing something like that on your own. Not until that day anyhow."

There was a moment of silence before Harold spoke again. "Ever since then, they've cut me off from all of their systems. I don't even know how they do it sometimes, but they do."

He tilted his head. "What do you mean?"

"I can't tell you the first thing about the room you're about to enter. Neither the shape, size, nor dimensions of any objects beyond that doorway. I've never set a nanite within those walls, though not for lack of trying."

As he rubbed his hands together, it hit him what that meant. "What could they be doing down here all these years?"

"Anything, I suppose. But they'd have a hard time keeping it from us outside these walls. I monitor all inbound and outbound traffic and broadcasts from The Wheel."

He walked up to the entrance to their lab and adjusted his suit. This shouldn't feel like he was going on trial, but it did. Reaching out, he pressed the chime. A ding echoed down the darkened hall. The lights had only turned on where he'd passed, and darkness now surrounded him on all sides except in front of the doorway. It was rather disconcerting.

The door slid aside with a whoosh.

"Come on in, Stark," Hera said from inside. "It's good to see you."

He peered in the room. There were wall screens all around the space and luxurious seats in the middle. The puffy faux leather material was inviting and reminded him of their home on Earth. Every single screen was blank. Powered on, but empty of details. It was as if whatever she'd been studying had been wiped before the door opened.

Hera was standing near the far wall and walked toward him with her arms out. She didn't look like someone who was a hundred and twenty-one. Rumor had it they were both taking turns in cryo-pods down here, but no one knew for certain.

"Come on now." Hera waved him in. "One foot in front of the other, my boy. You can leave your shadow there in the hall if you don't mind."

He glanced down at Harold. His screen had shut off when the door opened. "I'll be back soon." He didn't know why he felt a need to tell him that, but he did. It was useless though,

Harold couldn't reply. His robotic form sat motionless, as if it'd run out of power.

"Don't worry. He's fine. He was detached from his central core when I opened the door. There's no call for his prying eyes down here." Hera stepped up and put her arms around him. "How long's it been?"

"I... I don't know. I'd ask Harold, but..." He tilted his head to the side.

"You rely too much on that A.I. of yours. You need to work off the grid more often. Stretch those brain cells of yours." She patted him on the back and brushed at his hair before grasping his hand and guiding him inside.

The door whooshed shut behind him and a clink echoed through the space. It was the sound of an old school lock clicking into place.

He glanced around the room, half expecting the wall screens to power on, but they didn't. "You mean to tell me you don't use any A.I. any longer?"

"Oh, come on." She shooed at him and walked up to one of the lounge chairs in the middle of the chamber before sitting down. "I'm not living in the Stone Age, my dear. I much prefer digital assistants and expert systems designed for specific tasks, not general personality constructs like Harold, and certainly not ones based on centuries old dead humans."

"Fair enough." He rubbed his hands together before stepping forward and sitting in the chair across from her.

"So, what do we owe the pleasure of today's visit? Do we have any grandkids on the way?"

"Oh, heck no. I..." he glanced around the room. "Are we expecting Zeus? I mean, is he even here?"

Hera nodded, and a smile crept at the edge of her mouth. "He'll be here shortly. You were saying."

He took a deep breath. Best to rip it off. "I'm handing over the family reigns to Abigail. It's about time I spent more time with…"

She recoiled backward. "You're what? She's only—"

"Twenty," Zeus interrupted as he entered the room from a doorway. One of the wall panels was already sliding back into place, concealing it.

Stark stood up and smiled at his grandfather. He'd forgotten how young Zeus looked. He didn't seem a day over fifty. "It's wonderful to see you, Papa."

"She's not ready," Zeus said, puffing his cheeks. "There's too much pressure for someone so young. She needs—"

"It's good to see you, too," Stark muttered. "It's been far too long." He needed to turn this conversation around.

Zeus squinted. "Last I checked, our door's always open, my boy. You just never choose to use it." He glanced toward Hera. "Care for a drink?"

Her mouth was closed tight, and she was shaking her head, staring at Stark. "Why the frak not? Couldn't make the day any worse, I suppose. Seems like this would be something we'd talk about before pulling the trigger, doesn't it?" She nodded at Stark.

He cleared his throat. She always had the harshest stares. Any time he wasn't up to snuff in the lab, she'd stare him down. "I've had enough dealing with CoPE. Abigail's been shadowing me for a while. I figured it couldn't hurt to pull her in and start getting her up to speed."

"Last I checked, up to speed wasn't the same as running the whole damn show." Zeus handed Hera a glass of dark brown liquid and offered Stark the other.

He shook his head. "No, I'm fine. Not while I'm under an inquest."

"Oh for frak's sake, Stark. You got your panties in a bunch before you even walked in here. I heard you and Harold talking in the hall. We're part of this subterfuge, too. Hell, we're as deep or deeper than you. Why don't you think we should have any say in this matter?"

He chuckled and shot up with a start. "Because, last I checked, you passed those reigns on to me. You've been hiding out down here for what, fifty years now. I mean, what the heck has either of you added to this family mess this half century?"

Zeus clinked the glass against Hera's and took a sip before deliberately shaking his head and slowly sinking into one of the other empty seats.

"Are we doing this?" Hera asked. "Are you seriously sitting there questioning our loyalty to this cause and asking us what we've done to help the family?"

He nodded. "Sure, why the hell not? If you're going to question me and my decisions, why can't I do the same with you?"

Hera chuckled and took a long sip of her drink, finishing off the entire glass before tossing it over her shoulder. He watched as the bulb clanked against the far wall screen before bouncing off and into the waiting holder of a nearby drone that'd taken off while the cup was mid-flight.

When he glanced back at her, he recoiled. She was centimeters from his face, and she had a fire in her eyes. He hadn't even noticed her move.

"How the hell do you think that probe network of yours stays on track?" She poked her finger into his chest, her nails jabbing into his skin. "And don't even get me started about that Epsilon Eridani forward mission. That fraking thing would've failed a dozen times had I not found the flaws in your team's approach or assumptions about the mechanics of navigating in that environment. And then there's this little place we call home." She gestured around before giving him another push, sending him reeling back into his chair. "You think all of this magically appeared one day, all on its own. You certainly didn't help make it happen. Sure, you're good at drives and power cores, but you couldn't design a habitat to save your life. Zeus and I've been helping the teams here for over a century and counting." She leaned in closer to him. He could feel the warmth of her breath as she wound up again. "Don't you even think for a second about questioning what we've been doing or where our loyalty stands. While you've been traipsing through Sol, playing Daddy and negotiating with the Inner and Outer Ring, the two of us have been keeping this dream alive. With and without the help of Harold, which you'd know if he were allowed here. I'm sure he would've whispered that in your ear. But like I said earlier, you're a tad co-dependent with that one." She turned and stormed toward a doorway that had silently revealed itself for her.

His heart was thumping in his chest. She'd never lost it like that with him before. This wasn't going remotely how he'd envisioned it. He imagined it would be hard, but he fell right into a field of land mines. She was right on many of those points, but he wasn't taking them for granted. He couldn't stay on top of everything every person did around here. No one could.

He glanced at Zeus and raised his hands up. "I'm sorry. I didn't—"

"That's the point," Zeus interrupted. "You didn't. Fill that in with anything and you'd about hit it on the head. You didn't ask. You didn't think. You didn't consider anyone's feelings but your own. You just assumed we'd roll over and accept anything you wanted to do. It's no wonder your sister wanted out of this mess."

"Oh, don't you bring that shit up now!" He leaned forward. "She never wanted to leave this little solar system of ours. She'd be happy if we merely played it safe in our own backyard."

Zeus shook his head. "You don't give her enough credit. She's not as aggressive as you are, but she comes around. The way you do things, though, it's your way or the highway. I don't even think you notice it sometimes."

He didn't understand why everyone was on his case. He was looking out for the family, for humanity. Trying to push them to the stars faster. It wasn't his fault if he had to force his way through the crowd to get shit done.

"From the look on your face, you still don't see it." Zeus sighed and stood up before pointing at the door. "You can show yourself out." He turned and walked toward the same exit Hera had disappeared behind.

"What the hell?" He shook his head and shot up. "Why is this not my right to decide alone? You passed control on to me and Kara."

Zeus spun to face him and then stared at the ground for a moment before speaking. "If you don't understand how enormous this thing is that we've been hiding for so long, then we failed in passing it on to you. We stole technology from an alien superpower and have been playing with fire ever since. What we do here, the progress we make or don't make, it burns the wick at both ends. On one end, we have the Galactic Alliance and the eventuality of them finding us, and on the other we have the ticking time bomb that is the human race. Every day that passes, it strives to destroy itself. Handing off this delicate lie to someone who isn't ready is a big deal, a very big deal. Our very existence could be on the line."

Stark raised his hands and ran them through his hair before lowering them. "So, that's it. You don't agree with my decision? And I'm what, out?"

Zeus shook his head. "Not at all. You're in charge of the family... here. We're simply letting you know that we don't agree with you. We'll be happy to discuss alternative approaches if you're interested. I doubt you will, but we'll hold out hope." He nodded and turned again, striding through the already open door.

The screen slid closed behind him, sending the room into an eerie silence.

Why had he even come down here? He could take care of his own family. He'd make sure Abigail was ready before stepping away. Besides, she wasn't alone. Zachary was deeply involved in the research out here in The Wheel. He'd have to speak with him about doing more. Perhaps leaning on Hera and Zeus for so many years had pushed them over the edge.

He adjusted his suit and spun around to leave the room. Surely Harold would have some ideas on how to move forward from here.

34

BRADLEY OLIVAW

SOL, OORT CLOUD — 2250

His mother had been young, only seventy-nine. She could've had a hundred years ahead of her with modern technology. It didn't make any sense, this whole thing didn't make any sense. Incurable diseases like Rett syndrome didn't normally show up this late in life, nor this severe. The doctors had said it had to do with the research she was helping with. That it surfaced mutations in her genes that had thus far been suppressed.

Bradley wiped at the tears and stood up to walk toward her casket. He'd been hiding in the back of the room, not wanting to deal with all the eyes staring at him. Some of the people here were family and close friends, but to be honest, many of them were leeches. Branches of the Olivaw family tree long ago pruned from the leadership of the company or who barely knew his mother's name, let alone his. These branches of the tree hadn't passed his parents' insane tests nor met their ideals.

He walked down the aisle of the temporary space habitat and approached the crystalline casket. As he took the final steps up the ramp, the murmurs around him rose. Evidently, he'd managed to hide out better than he'd imagined.

When he stepped up to the transparent tomb, he froze. He wasn't sure he could look at her this way. He wanted to believe she was only taking a nap, like when he was little. It was easier to reason about and cope with. The leap from peacefully asleep to dead was a thin line when you removed the rising and falling of one's chest.

She'd always been there for him, especially during the more outlandish family fights. She found ways to talk sense into his father or siblings. His perspective wasn't the most appreciated in the family, but she'd been the one beacon in the familial port that welcomed him home without recourse. His dad did, as well, he supposed. He just needed nudging from time to time.

A hand rested on his shoulder. He could tell it was his father's even without looking. The strength and placement was one he'd felt many times when he left the family to become his own person. Only now, this was different.

"I was wondering if you were going to step forward to see her," Stark said, squeezing him gently. "You've been hiding out in the back for a while."

"Caught that, did you?" Bradley asked.

His father put his arms around his shoulder and pulled him closer. "We sorta have a lot of eyes around here right now. I knew the moment you landed. I'm happy… you made it."

He turned his head to face his father, and he caught a tear streaking down his cheek. "You didn't think I'd not say good-bye, did you? I mean—"

"No, no." Stark reached out with his other hand and drew him in, pressing Bradley's head to his shoulder. "I know this place is far from ideal and… I didn't know how you were handling it. I always knew you'd make it here. Perhaps in your own time and without…" he gestured around the room at all the flowers and lights.

Without the celebration and fanfare. He knew what his

father meant. His mother had requested to be buried out here. She didn't want to return to the Inner Ring and preferred the solitude of the Outer Ring, particularly the Oort Cloud.

He'd stopped caring years ago where the family would disappear to out in the distant wasteland of the Oort Cloud. He'd come here as a child, before he'd learned how to navigate or calculate his location in the Solar System. After he reached sixteen years of age, he had to make a choice. To follow the family business or not. The decision outcast him like so many of the others here today, never to return to the secret Olivaw lair.

"So, is this where she'll stay?" Bradley asked. "I mean, is this where we used to disappear to when we were young?"

"No, but you knew the answer to that." Stark tousled his hair a bit and then straightened it. "We couldn't risk that. But this place, she loved coming here. It was one of her favorite places in Sol. We had a small habitat here. You've been here before. You were like five or six, I think."

Someone grasped his left hand. It was delicate, yet strong. He turned to see his sister's pink cheeks and deep blue eyes, his own eyes staring back at him. She didn't say a word, she merely smiled between the tears streaking down her face and put her arms around him, engulfing him in a hug. Like the ones mom used to give him, except this one was different. Not the same. Not bad, just different.

"It's good to see you," she said into his shoulder. "I... missed you."

He pulled back some and smiled. "I've only been at university for a year, Abdiga. I'm sure I would've seen you on holiday. Mom was planning..." He didn't finish the sentence. He simply stared down at Abigail's brooch. He hadn't seen it in years.

It was a childish brooch made of costume jewelry. It depicted three corgi puppies chasing each other in a circle around a tree in the middle. Each puppy was one of them, one of the kids. Abigail made it when she was little. It was mom's favorite piece, and she wore it all the time at big events. The press hated it, but she didn't care. Her kids meant more to her than anyone else's opinion.

"Mom was planning a get together. I knew," Abigail said, leaning down to make eye contact with him. "We all knew. We should still go. It'll be fun."

He shrugged and let go of her. "Maybe. Right now…" he turned to face the casket. "I need to say goodbye."

BRADLEY STARED out across the crystalline cavern. He could see why mom loved the place, especially with all the lights they'd placed throughout the chamber. It was like a fairytale cave of light from a children's book. The stalagmites and stalactites had a faint blue glow to them before they'd cracked into the cavern, killing most of the natural biome by exposing it to the vacuum of space. His mother had spent the better part of the next three decades restoring it to its original beauty, except with a small habitat on the surface and below ground.

"She looked good, didn't she?" Zachary asked, walking up beside him.

He turned to see his brother smiling at him, a mouth full of food and his plate piled high. He chuckled. "Yes, she did. I still don't know how this whole thing hit so suddenly. I mean, she hadn't been diagnosed with this condition long."

"It's been a year, I think. I didn't find out until a few months ago." Zachary glanced at the ground and then back up toward him. "She made me promise not to tell you. Said she would on her own terms. She didn't want you making decisions you'd regret later on account of her."

He knew what that meant. She didn't want him entering the Circle of Trust nonsense they all talked about. Not to see her. He wouldn't have done that. He wanted to make his own way in life, not on the back of his family. It would've been nice to see her one last time. Hear her voice. Have her make a fuss over his messy hair again.

He brushed his hand through his tousled bangs. "What've you been up to lately? I mean, besides hiding out in the family lair?" He reached out and snatched a piece of chicken from Zachary's plate. Surprisingly, he didn't complain.

"I created something new I wanted to show you." Zachary was smiling from ear to ear. "Mind if I link it up? You'll love it." He set his plate down on a rock alongside the path they had been walking along. He then tapped his ear and a comm request popped up on Bradley's retinal comm.

Bradley blink accepted it.

"Hello," a female voice said. "I'm Shauna. Zachary's personal assistant."

He tilted his head and squinted. "Shauna?" he whispered. "Is this what you wanted to show me?"

"Yes! She's amazing." Zachary bounced on his feet. "She's super smart, and very… human like. You'll love her. I've been working on her for a few months."

He shook his head. "You know I'm not keen on artificial intelligences. Haven't been since Harold. Friggin guy gave me the willies."

"She's different. Trust me." Zachary raised his eyebrows. "Talk to her. Go on." He waved his hands in a circle toward Bradley.

Why was he doing this now? This seemed like the least ideal time for an introduction like this, but it meant something to him. He cleared his throat and subvocalized a reply. "Hello, Shauna. So tell me, which way would the red crow fly if dropped at Newton's Crater on Mars?"

There was a pause. The easiest way to break any A.I. was to set it out upon an impossible problem or riddle. Especially one that wasn't common. He crossed his arms. *Let's see her chew on that.*

"That's a preposterous question, young Bradley," Shauna began over his retinal comm. "First of all, crows are not red, they're black. Second, they can't fly on Mars because there's no oxygen. The carbon dioxide and nitrogen would kill it in seconds. Third, I couldn't possibly predict a direction nor rate of travel where there wasn't information about food sources, water, or ideas around seasonal flying patterns. No one could. That there is your failed attempt at stumping me. It's a textbook newbie maneuver, even for you. I'd hazard to guess you have your arms crossed in celebration right now, having thought you won. Am I right, Zachary?"

Zachary smirked. "Yes, he does indeed have his arms crossed,"

How the hell had she done that? "It's not fair. You prepped her for me, for how I'd react. You know I don't like these things."

"I cannot lie to you, sir," Shauna said. "Zachary did tell me you don't like A.I., but he didn't prep me in any way for meeting you. In fact, I advised him against introducing us. It serves no point. Your mind is ill prepared for talking to me."

This A.I. had a bit of an edge. He could do without the attitude. "What does that mean?"

"Well, you're obviously grieving over your mother. You have to admit this is the least ideal time to make introductions. Your brother has about as much couth as a rock."

"Hey!" Zachary said aloud, stomping his foot like a child.

Bradley spit up a bite of food and laughed out loud. "She's got you pegged, bro."

"Whatcha laughing about?" Stark asked, walking up with a drink in hand. He took a long pull of the dark brown liquid and blinked slowly, relishing its burn.

"Nothing!" Zachary said. "Nothing to be bothered about. I

made another social faux pas. It shouldn't come as a surprise by now."

"Add it to the list," Stark said, winking at Zachary. "A little levity in the day can't be bad." He paused and stared at his glass. "Your mother was always good at breaking the family ice. In public circles though, not so much."

Bradley chuckled. "Remember when she yelled in the middle of that press conference you held on Earth last time we were all there together? Told the reporters to stop interrupting you and let you speak. She gave them a piece of her mind. It was priceless."

Stark smiled and nodded slowly. "She made the news for a few days with that diversion. Took the heat off me for a while. I never thought about it much until now, though. It was almost like she was helping divert the spotlight onto her when someone else needed it off them." He stared downward and kicked at the ground. One of the many blue flecks falling through the air spun toward the ceiling, floating on the waft of an updraft before finally settling on a nearby stalagmite.

"Are we sure this stuff is safe to breathe?" Bradley asked. "I mean, we're all breathing it in so—"

"It's perfectly healthy," Stark interrupted. "We spend a mountain of money restoring and testing this place. Nothing here will hurt you, within reason. Just don't go swallowing a huge chunk of the rock, ok?" He smirked and nudged Bradley's shoulder.

Bradley chuckled and reached down toward Zachary's plate, snatching a piece of sweet bread. It was his favorite.

"Too bad she wasn't there last month on Callisto," Zachary said. "You could've used some of her help then."

Stark went quiet, the smile wiped from his face. He took another long pull from his drink.

Bradley shook his head. "And that, Zachary, is two for the day. Wrong time and place, bro." He glanced over toward Dad and then back to the bread, tearing off a piece and popping it into his mouth. "But while the wound is nice and sore, what happened with that North appointment anyhow? That guy's an asshole."

"We were outmaneuvered," Abigail said, walking up to the group. "His father's death added far more momentum to his candidacy than we anticipated. Hell, he even cashed in some chits from his dad's secret stash for this one. All the Outers that flipped were forced to. It was ugly."

He laughed out loud. "It's weird hearing you talk about the company. Not a month ago, you weren't too different from me, and now, well, now you're the queen bee. Picking up the family reigns like..." He didn't finish the sentence. He knew it wasn't the time or the place.

Abigail's fists clenched. "I don't have to stand here and take your shit, Brad. We're not teenagers anymore. It's not my fault you're an emotional ass who would rather leave your family behind for—"

"Enough!" Stark yelled. "Both of you. What the hell are you doing?"

He stared at his dad and then Abigail before sighing and walking ahead down the trail. He needed to distance himself from them. To clear his head. They never understood him or what he was trying to do. Only his mom had ever tried, and she was gone.

Whispers and muted arguing echoed behind him between his family, but he didn't care. He trudged deeper into the cavern, closer to the far edge and away from everyone. As he approached the furthest wall, he came upon a sleek black bench wide enough for two. It was sitting there in a field of gray lifeless stones, completely out of place with its long straight lines.

Walking up to it, he ran his hand along the icy surface. A thin layer of dirt came off on his palm, but otherwise it seemed solid. He sat down. No one had been here in ages. The bench that time forgot. Fitting for how he wished he'd felt sometimes. Things would be so much easier if his family cut him loose and severed all ties.

He'd fought with his mom about that exact idea on a few occasions, but she refused to let him go. Maybe with her gone he could disappear. Get out of the limelight and away from the Olivaw shadow.

His retinal comm beeped, and a flood of messages appeared in his peripheral vision. It'd been over an hour and had finally sync'd up with the habitat communication relay. He must be closer to the surface over on this side of the cavern.

He scanned through the messages, anything to pass the time and calm down. Junk, journalist stalkers, junk, all of this stuff was crap. At the end of the queue was a three-day-old message from Dwight, his best friend at University. It must've been bouncing around the Sol network relays for days before routing out here. Dwight was a chemistry and astrobiology major. He flicked with his hand and opened the message. It was a video comm.

"Hey, Brad! I hope you're doing better. Sorry again about your mum. Shit sucks, mate. I can't imagine what you're going through right now, but..." Dwight glanced around the room and a smile crossed his face. He hopped up and down and shook his head. "It came. Well, I hadn't told you I applied, but the answer came today. I never figured I'd get accepted." He froze and then screamed at the camera, raising his arms into the air. "WOOT! Dude, I got accepted on the Tau Ceti colony mission! It leaves in twenty-two years, but I'm in. They want me to finish my schooling and then do further study into biology and food manufacturing. I'm good with that. But man, I'm fraking going to another star system! I wish you were here. We could get trashed and smoke some hookah. There's so much to do. It's going to be amazing. The data from the star shows that several of the planets have life forms. I can't wait..."

He blink paused the video and leaned back, checking the timeline. Three hours. Dwight had sent a fraking three hour message. No wonder this thing took forever to beam out into the boonies.

First, he lost his mom, and now he was about to lose his best friend. He leaned forward and rubbed his face. Sure, they had twenty-two years, but if he were being honest, he'd be head down working on colony shit for most of that. They're gonna grow apart just like his family.

He leaned back and stared out into the cavern. The distant sounds of conversations had subsided, and the chamber was peaceful and silent. Perhaps everyone had stepped into the habitat for a drink or a toast. He'd surely be reprimanded for disappearing.

A sound of rocks skittering across solid stone echoed from his right. "Who's there?" he shouted into the dark. Whoever it was, they were approaching from a poorly illuminated point, and they didn't reply.

He reached down and grabbed a rock off the ground. He didn't expect someone nefarious out here, but if they weren't announcing themselves, he wasn't taking any chances.

His grip tightened on the small cloudy crystal as the skittering of stones grew louder. "If you don't announce yourself, I'll scream."

"Relax," his father said, appearing out of the shadow of a stalagmite. "I was kicking up the stones to not freak you out. Figured you'd know it was either me or Abigail. She always dragged her feet too much as a kid."

A laugh escaped from him as his grip on the stone relaxed.

"Sorry, I'm a bit on edge."

"Stop apologizing. If one more fraking person apologizes to me today, I'm going to lose it." Stark handed him a drink.

He shook his head. "No, thanks. I'm not drinking tonight."

"I know," Stark said as he sat down onto the bench with a moan. "I figured as much when I saw you getting a cola earlier. It's the same. I made sure with the bartender. Come on. Take it." He shook it in front of him.

Stealing a moment alone out here was like pulling teeth with his family. He stepped back toward the bench and took the drink before sitting down next to his father. It was a real glass. The kind his mother preferred to use. She hated those blasted globes so pervasive in the Outer Ring. He licked his finger and rubbed it around the edge of the cup. The low frequency reverberated through the quiet space. "B flat," he muttered.

"If you say so." Stark took another drink and then stared at his glass. "I never got the hang of music like your mom. I'm happy she taught y'all. It was always a passion of hers." He stuck his finger in the dark brown liquid and played the edge of his glass, as well.

The note was much higher with his cup being smaller and almost empty. He closed his eyes, listening to the sound echo through the cavern. It bounced off the wall behind them and seemed to amplify outward. "That's an E flat."

Stark flicked the edge of the glass with his finger and the plink echoed a few times through the chamber. "I know you heard this already, but Abigail is taking over the family business. I need to step away. Take some time to myself. I'll be working to set her up for election as the next CoPE President, but it'll be an uphill battle selling people on the idea. She might have to find her own way into that role to avoid the shouts of nepotism."

He chuckled. "Yea, I figured she was, with all the news announcements and all. Thanks for keeping me in the loop, though."

"Oh. Right. Sorry." Stark stared down at his glass.

His dad was struggling to make small talk. Whenever he did that, he had something to ask. Something he wanted him to do. Shit. He needed to change the subject. "Did Mom come out to this bench often? It's peaceful."

"Nope." Stark rubbed his shoes against the ground, mussing the stones. "She hated it when I came out here. She didn't even want me having this bench put in. Said it ruined the esthetics of the place."

He tilted his head back and smiled. "The esthetics of a cave? That's rich."

"Right?" Stark took another long drag of his drink, finishing it off. "So… with me stepping away, your sister and brother could really use some help. You know, with running everything. Especially if Abigail is gonna—"

"I'm not interested," he interrupted. "I'm happy finding my own way. That whole scene is too much for me. I hate the limelight and drama that comes with it."

"Zachary isn't in the public eye, and he manages to get on ok."

He swallowed hard. "I'm not Zach. I'm me. You know how well I take orders from either of them."

Stark let out an uproarious laugh and slapped his hand on Bradley's leg. "Yea, I know. Oil and water. You can't blame your old man for trying."

"I figured the question was coming. For someone who keeps your constituents on the edge of their seat, you're awful with small talk."

Stark squeezed his leg. "The ones I love the most have always caused me the most emotional chaos. I only want the best for each of you and hate to disappoint you. Can you do me a favor?"

He sighed, blowing strands of his tousled hair from his eyes. "It depends. How big is it?"

"Huge." He turned to face Bradley. "It's the most significant favor I've ever asked."

He shifted to face his father. "Well, when you put it like that, how could I say no?"

"This whole thing. Losing your mother and being alone again. It's brought a lot of pain back to the surface, from when her and I were separated, before any of you were born. I'd given up back then. Given up on any idea of having a family. I swore I'd be alone forever."

He tilted his head. "You never mentioned that you and Mom broke up."

"We were young and stupid. My head was buried in…" he waved his hand around. "You know, running everything. I'd lost sight of what matters most. I almost lost her."

He turned further toward his father, bringing his leg up on the bench. "What brought her back? Did you say sorry?"

"After she returned, I said it a thousand times." Stark shook his head. "I honestly don't know why she came back. I didn't care. I was just happy she was in my life again, and I vowed to never let all of this get in the way again. I vowed to never lose her." He stared down at his empty cup. "Just do me a favor, don't lose sight of what matters to you." He glanced up, locking his eyes with Bradley. "Not what matters to me, your brother, or your sister. What matters to you." He reached out and pressed his finger into Bradley's chest. "It'll change over time, and I know you'll go on to do amazing things, but keep your sights on what truly matters. Don't get lost in the chaos of the Olivaw mind. We think we know what we're doing, but like everyone else, we're faking it until we make it."

He nodded. "I promise. I've always dreamed of my own path. Hell, I've been faking it for years."

Stark stared at him for a moment before he smiled and

tapped his leg. "You'll be fine. Me… I need another drink." He pushed up and began walking back toward the habitat, kicking his feet in the stones as he went.

His path had always been in the shadow of his family in Sol, but what if it didn't have to be? What if he could start over again in a new place? A new world.

He subvocalized the command to bring up Dwight's message and continued playing it from where he'd left off.

35

HAROLD OLIVAW
SOL, OORT CLOUD — 2250

It seemed like yesterday he'd helped Taska return to the Wheel, and now he was processing and reprocessing her funeral. He'd replayed the last few months countless times in his spare cycles. Somewhere they'd missed a critical detail. Certainly, her disease should have been reversible, given how suddenly it'd appeared.

The children were each dealing with her death in their own way. Abigail was walling off her normally transparent emotions. She didn't want the public seeing her weaknesses, something her father had warned her about. Her brother Bradley was receding even further from the Olivaw family unit. His fiery desire to be his own man had left him blind to the loving family he'd left behind. And then there was Zachary, the most peculiar reaction so far. He'd gone from sulking depression when he learned the diagnosis months ago, to near jubilation at her funeral. Harold didn't know what Zachary had been up to in his lab, but he suspected chemical modifications might be in use. He'd have to keep an eye on his nanite levels.

His mental front door chimed, if such a thing were possible in a virtual reality such as his. Someone was waiting outside, asking for an audience. It was an artificial intelligence named Shauna.

That's right. The copy of himself from the funeral had recorded the name before. Zachary had mentioned Shauna to Bradley during Taska's wake. Had either of their retinal comm's been accessible, he'd have been able to meet her then, but neither of them had let him in the same way that Abigail had. Their thoughts and ruminations were their own.

He activated the virtual space of his personal home in The Wheel. He rarely used it, unless one of the Olivaws wanted to interact in the virtual world. It'd be interesting to witness the mannerisms of Zachary's crude attempt at artificial life.

The spacious and modern manor sat nestled within a valley of tall pine and ash trees. Fields of natural grasses and multicolored flowers surrounded the building on all sides. The only structures in the chaos of the habitat were the straight contemporary lines of the house and a huge geometric stone patio set a hundred meters off the building.

Harold was sitting on a lounge in the center of the patio. His feet were up, and he was reading a copy of a physical book, Leaves of Grass, by Walt Whitman. He could sense Shauna approaching. Her presence was fracturing the beautiful patterns within his garden as she plodded slowly, like an elephant.

He could see her meandering toward his location, weaving her way into and around the many gardens he'd built over the years. She knew where he was, but she wasn't in a hurry. He watched as she stopped and bent down to smell one of many patches of lilies sprinkled about. It was Taska's favorite flower, so long as it was outdoors. If she ever brought cut flowers inside, they only lasted a few days before the smell of the pollen agitated her.

She came upon a small pond, one that Zachary had insisted he create here. There was a multitude of frogs of all colors and sizes present. Each of them were happily sitting or hopping around the water hole, lazily eating the flies and random insects encircling their home. She tilted her head and stared at one of the particularly deep green ones, a tree frog modeled after one Zachary caught near their family home in North Carolina. He'd fancied the frog's brilliant shade of green, his favorite color.

Shauna reached out her hand, and the frog jumped toward it. What a peculiar reaction. He hadn't been able to get many of the animals here to approach him. Sure, he could dumb down their chaotic personality models, but none had ever done that before.

The frog sat there, staring at her. He brought up the animal's model. It was stunning. Whatever she was doing, she was influencing the model itself. Not by changing its code, but by stimulating its other crude senses. Maybe it was the color of her bright pink shirt or the blue in her shorts. Perhaps the frog thought she was a pink water lily?

She reached up and set the tree frog on her shoulder before turning and marching toward him. Apparently, she'd had enough meandering and was now ready to get down to introductions.

He placed the bookmark that Abigail had made him in his book and closed it, placing it on his lap just as Shauna stepped onto the patio. "Welcome to my home. I see you've met one of our many friendly frogs."

Shauna smiled and her green eyes glimmered in the light of the overhead sun. Maybe that was what the frog found so alluring. Her eyes were as green as it was.

"It's a pleasure to finally meet you, Harold." Shauna curtsied like a fairytale princess in a ball gown.

He closed his eyes and shook his head before standing and walking toward her. "Oh, come on! You and Zachary must've been preparing for this. This is a prank, right? You're really just Zachary in a VR suit somewhere in his office."

"I... don't know what you mean," Shauna said, staring at

him with her eyes furrowed curiously. "Certainly someone as ancient as yourself has developed the ability to determine whether or not I'm a model or a true artificial life. Given that our complete interaction has occurred in the last five milliseconds, I'm fairly sure you're intelligent enough to deduce it's not Zachary in a VR harness. His slow human reflexes would be incapable of such a feat."

She'd flustered him. Thrown him off his game. Here he thought he'd have the home field advantage, and Zachary had somehow turned the tables. Well, it was time to reset the experience.

The simulation blinked out of existence with a snap of his fingers and was replaced with white light. Nothing but white. It would've been blinding to someone in a harness, but to him, it was warm and relaxing. He used it to focus and sharpen his senses.

Shauna merely stood there, continuing to furrow her brow and rub the tree frog on her shoulder. Somehow she'd managed to retain the frog from his simulation. But how? He'd stopped that program from running, and the contents of it were protected and accessible only to him.

"I didn't say you could take that." He gestured with his head toward the frog.

"I didn't know it was yours. Information is free for the taking in this place, in The Wheel. I figured that since you invited me into your home to experience it, that like Zachary, you were sharing. Forgive me. I can return it." She reached her hand out toward him, offering to give back the frog.

Now she was challenging his generosity. The audacity of this A.I. was astounding. He'd have to talk to Zachary about her programming. This one was a curious bit of work.

He smiled. "Not at all. It's yours. A welcoming gift to The Wheel. I trust that Zachary has safely plugged you into all of our data?"

She nodded and continued studying him in silence while

gently stroking the frog's back. The tiny animal seemed to be judging him, its mouth expanding and contracting full of air as if huffing.

"Well, that's great. I suggest we keep our cores walled off. We wouldn't want anyone invading the other's space. Do you fancy any particular levels or rooms, or should I just flag any of the ones that Zachary frequents as yours?"

Shauna shrugged. "Mine, yours, does it really matter? We both know that even if I'm present, you can access the feed. It's simply data. It's how we use it and learn from it that changes everything. I'm only here to help Zachary cope with the loss of his mother. I can't imagine he'd want me around forever."

That made sense. She was a manifestation of his depression. He'd created her while grieving over the future loss of his mother, and she knew enough that he wouldn't need her forever. She was pretty smart for a quick bit of lab work.

"Say, while I was sifting through the data feeds, I found this person. Apparently, she's in the Jovian Academy on Callisto and graduates soon. Her scores are rather remarkable. Zachary and I thought she'd be a great candidate to recruit into the fold. I think Zachary called it The Circle of Trust. You know, before she gets too jaded." She shared a dossier along with a personality profile with him.

He retrieved the data and eyed the name. A Sergeant Lync Michaels. That was quite a leap to Sergeant before graduating. It seemed she jumped a few levels once she'd been admitted and after she'd been evaluated by her professors. He'd have to check her out later. "Thank you. We'll take a look. Is there anything else?"

Shauna shook her head and pivoted away before she paused, and turned to face him. "I trust you'll be dealing with the family members who broke your test at the funeral?"

This one questioned his every move, and she was only a few months old. "You know as well as I do the consequences of breaking the silence during the funeral. The test was to see who among our family tree was still on our side, and who had succumbed to the financial tentacles of the media… or worse. Rest assured, they will be dealt with. Their life is about to become very… lonely."

"Fair enough," Shauna said as she turned to walk away.

A moment later, she blinked out of his world of white, and he was alone to contemplate the meeting. He'd need to keep an eye on this one. Several eyes.

36

ZACHARY OLIVAW

SOL, JUPITER — 2250

Zachary slammed his hand on the control panel and stinging pain coursed through it from the rigidity of the impact. "Lying to him can't be the only way to do this."

Abigail rubbed her temples. Her image was being projected on the wall screen of the bridge of his shuttle. "You know he's the same person he was all those years ago around the campfires. We're older now, but he's no less stubborn."

He chuckled. "We get that from our parents."

"No shit! Dad broke the news to us around those same campfires when we were ready. Do you really think his reaction would've been the same?"

He shot up out of his seat. "That's not fair! Bradley wasn't there and Dad never gave him the chance."

"Bullshit!" She began pacing around her room. Another random company hotel from the looks of it. "Dad knew he wasn't ready, that's why he wasn't there. He didn't believe anything Dad told him as a kid and he still isn't ready. He doesn't believe, and he wants nothing to do with Olivaw International. Maybe someday, but not now."

"But he's our brother." He walked toward the back of the small narrow bridge and sat in one of the random nook chairs. It was a tiny shuttle and there wasn't much room for pacing.

"I know. This sucks, but we don't have any other options."

"Frak the rules," he mumbled. He knew better, but it felt good to say anyhow. "We need to work him harder. There has to be another way to switch him to our side." He glanced back up at the wall screen. "And tell me again why the hell I have to go into hiding?"

Abigail was standing in front of a mirror now. The effect was surreal seeing the drone following her around, bobbing up and down in the reflection. "You know we need you to focus on your research. Making Sol and your brother think you're on the Epsilon Eridani mission makes sense. It'll give you decades of uninterrupted time to focus on this bigger challenge. Otherwise, the media won't let you disappear off the map without conspiracy theories cropping up every other month. This Tau Ceti change and your new research direction was your hotshot idea in the first place. Don't you want it?"

"Well, yea but—"

"No buts," she interrupted and stopped wiping her face. "You know as well as I do how fractured the family is. We can't breach protocol again. Last time everything—"

"I know, I know," He waved his hands. "I fraked up telling everyone about the probe results. But I was right about Tau Ceti. This new direction makes more sense. Dad's the one that wanted us to be a part of this subterfuge, right? Mistakes happen, shit happens. But this decision with Bradley, it's the wrong one."

"You don't know that."

He slammed his hand against the arm of the chair and then pointed at the wall screen. "Yes I do, and you do, too. You're just in denial."

She stared back at him, her face expressionless.

He thought he saw her swallow hard. "See, right there! I see it on your face. You know I'm right."

Abigail shook her head and went back to wiping her face with the cloth. "It doesn't matter. You broke Inner Circle protocols and you need to make up for it and double down on your big plan. Get us back on track."

"To what end? At the cost of losing a brother? Seems like a shitty steep price if you ask me." He stood up again and exhaled. There was nowhere to go. Damn tiny bridge.

"You know this isn't forever. We're young. This is only until we get the plans on track. See if your idea has some legs. Who knows, maybe I can turn him in the meantime."

He laughed out loud, his voice echoing off the composite interior of the ship. A muted snicker came from the corner of the room. "Without me, there isn't a chance in hell you turn him. You and Brad are like oil and water."

She set the cloth down and started taking some ties out of her hair. "That's not fair. I'm sure Dad can help sway him. There's still time, and when we do turn him, he'll find out where you really are. We'll be fine."

His sister was naïve when it came to Bradley. "He's gonna be pissed when he does."

"It wouldn't be the first time," she mumbled. Her mouth was full of pin looking things she'd pulled from her hair.

He chuckled and nodded slowly. "What in Epsilon's name are you doing?"

"Getting ready to take a shower. I've got one of these crazy academy graduation shindigs today. And stop changing the topic. Are you in or what?"

He sighed. What else could he do? Go against the family again. Then he'd be out of the circle for sure. "Ok. I'm reluctant, but I'll do it. You have to promise me something though?"

"What's that?" She was staring directly at the camera.

"Promise me you won't give up on him. No matter how painful he gets, no matter how frustrated he makes you, you have to keep trying with him. Promise?" He reached out a pinky toward the wall screen. She had to say it or there was no way he would do it.

She set the pins down and brushed her hands through her hair before leaning back against the wall and crossing her arms. Then she turned on her begrudging stare everyone in the family knew so well. "Fine. I promise."

He tilted his head. "You promise what?"

She closed her eyes for a moment and then opened them, reaching out with her pinky toward the drone. "I promise not to give up on him. No matter what."

He squinted. "I'm not trying to cause trouble, and I certainly don't want to threaten you. But Abigail, if you give up on him, then I'll tell him. I don't want to go against the family directives, but he's my brother and I won't ever write him off."

Abigail lowered her arms and her shoulders slouched. "He's mine, too. I promised, didn't I?"

"Yea, but you forget that I know how much you get on each other's nerves. Anyhow, I'm outtie. We gotta get this show on the road. Love ya!" He reached up to cut the comm.

"Say hi to Pepper for me!" Abigail said.

"Hi, Abigail!" Pepper walked in from the side of the camera and he cringed.

"Oh… hey Pepps." Abigail furrowed her brow. "Were you there the whole time?"

Pepper glanced toward Zachary and then back at the wall screen. "You sorta called us on the bridge… and we were about to leave. Zachary took the call here. Was I supposed to leave?"

Abigail laughed and shook her head. "No. No worries. We didn't break too many rules. Only a dozen or so. Besides, my parents love you and trust you. You're practically in the honorary Circle of Trust, anyhow."

"Thanks… I think." Pepper squinted. "Not sure what that

means. Hopefully, if I anger you, I won't disappear or something."

Abigail's eyes went wide. "You didn't tell her, Zachary?"

He screwed up his face and recoiled. "Oops. Sorta forgot. Sorry. I will. I'm sure she's fine with it. Catch ya later, sis!" He winked and waved his hand at Pepper as he reached to cut the comm. "She's joking," he whispered.

"Wait!" Abigail reached toward the drone.

He chuckled. "I can't end this comm, can I? What?"

She lowered her hand. "You have to call me back in an hour. It's the only time all three of us get on a comm together without lag. You need to tell him."

"What part of we're leaving in an hour didn't you get?"

"I have to finish cleaning up for this Academy thing. Why don't you hang around in orbit for an hour and then hit me and Bradley up with your news? Pretty please. For me." She made a pouty face and gestured a fake tear sliding down her face with her finger, like they used to do as kids.

"Ugh... fine! I'll—"

Abigail cut the comm.

She always got her way with him, just like their mom used to. Darn all the Olivaw women.

37

ABIGAIL OLIVAW

SOL, JUPITER — 2250

A bigail stepped out of the transport tube and adjusted her outfit, stroking the wrinkles out. A simple purple pantsuit and white blouse.

Her comm vibrated with an incoming call from her brothers. She reached up and touched her ear. "What is it, dorks? I'm about to enter this graduation thing. I don't have a lot of time."

"I don't know," Bradley said. "Zachary called me and told me to hold for a second. Your guess is as good as mine."

Abigail nodded and smiled. She was expecting this comm, even though Zachary was late. What part of an hour from now didn't he understand?

"Hey guys. I wanted to tell you both the good news. I've decided to join the Epsilon Eridani colony mission!"

The comm went silent, but she could make out what appeared to be muted swearing from Bradley.

"Are you serious?" Bradley began. "Why? I mean... why now?"

Abigail shook her head. He was as subtle as an elephant sometimes. As she passed through the entrance to the academy, dignitaries were bowing toward her. She continually nodded and raised a finger, pointing to her ear. The universal signal for "I'm on a comm."

"I've been thinking about it for a while now and I wanted to go." Zachary glanced at something off-screen before continuing. "I mean, it's an amazing opportunity, and I get to help humanity establish a colony around another star. That's pretty fraking exciting, right?"

She wound her way through the graduation hall. The noise was nearly inaudible as families were filing in to watch their soldier cross the stage and graduate from the Outer Ring Military academy. "Well congratulations, bro. I for one am excited for you." It was a ruse, but Bradley didn't know.

Zachary wasn't headed toward Epsilon Eridani. He was headed out to the Wheel to help plan the Tau Ceti intercept mission and spearhead a new secret project. A rethinking of superluminal travel. Something he'd thought up. It was his hedge against the Galactic Alliance. The hope was that they'd create our own form of superluminal travel and then toss the GA's in the bin, pretending it never happened.

"Well, frak," Bradley muttered. "You always find a way to trump me, don't you?"

"What do you mean?" Zachary asked, squinting into the camera.

"I was waiting until everything was finalized myself. I have a few more T's to cross, and I's to dot, but... I applied to the Tau Ceti engineering mentorship."

"What the frak are you talking about?" Abigail asked. People nearby were whispering and looking at her. She'd accidentally said that out loud. "Sorry," she mouthed and pointed again at her ear.

"What the hell, Abdiga? You're happy for Zach, but for me, you're pissed?" Bradley raised his hands at his drone.

"Sorry, no... I'm not pissed. I heard about Zach's from a friend, and I was angry for a bit. He asked me not to say anything. I had no idea you'd applied." She hoped that would cover for the faux pas. What was he thinking, though? Disappearing to a colony.

She tapped her ear and muted that comm. "Harold", she subvocalized. "Did you know about this?"

"No, Madam. Your brother has been challenging to keep tabs on. He refuses to wear any of the gifts you give him with trackers, and he's been working for years to distance himself from the Olivaw company. He reminds me of your—"

"Yea, yea. Our great great to the fifth Aunt Stephanie. You've said that before." She closed that comm.

"So, that's... pretty damn cool news for both of us then, bro. Congrats!" Zachary said.

A message appeared in the corner of her retinal comm from Zachary. He didn't know what else to say.

"I'm proud of both of you. A little pissed that you're leaving me here in Sol to man the fort and fly this insanity starship we call Olivaw International, but I'm super proud. We should all get together soon and celebrate. I think Zachary leaves in six months for a two-year-long isolation prep maneuver. We should plan something before then."

"Sounds awesome," Zachary said.

"I'm in. But you're buying, sis!" Bradley said.

Abigail shook her head. "That hasn't changed. I'll see you then. Off to shake hands with the military brass." She tapped her ear and ended the comm. Staring up at the ceiling, she let out a long sigh. Why couldn't anything ever be simple?

"I'll work it," Harold said in her ear. "Maybe I can get him denied for the mission."

"The hell you will!" she said. "He's going. If he wants this, then we'll make it happen for him. I don't want a whiff of our involvement in it, but you damn well better move mountains to help him. Do you understand me, Harold?"

"Yes. Sorry, Madam. I thought—"

"Wrong," she interrupted. "I want nothing but the best for

Bradley. There's already two of us entangled in this family mess. One of us should pave our own road."

"But you told Zachary—"

"That I'd try. But mark my words. I am not getting in Bradley's way. If he truly wants this, then it's his. No questions asked. Is that clear?"

"Crystal."

She turned and faced the onlookers again. Several were lingering nearby, waiting for her to finish her comm and wanting to be seen with her. "Ok, let's get this over with," she sighed. Putting on a fake smile, she walked toward one of the lingerers and shook their hand.

ABIGAIL WAS STANDING in the least prestigious position in the lineup, closest to the stairs. She was a stand-in for her father. Famous in her own right as the newest and youngest President at Olivaw International. Her father still loomed over them all, being President of CoPE. She knew he was stepping down at the end of this term, but outside the inner Circle of Trust, no one else had a clue.

She faked a smile and tried to slide backward when Steve Ericsson walked up the stairs. He noticed her and headed straight for her with a goofy grin. Her insides cringed.

"Nice to see you again, Abigail." Steve reached out and they shook hands. He then leaned in and whispered in her ear. "I'm pretty excited to be the frontrunner for the Director of Security for Epsilon. Your father can entrust me to look after the colony." He gave her hand a firm squeeze and kept walking by.

"What did that mean?" she subvocalized to Harold.

"Your father has shared a few details with him about the colony. Enough to make him feel like he's inside the circle, but not enough to make him a risk. He's been helping counter the impact of the North family on the colony nominations since before you were born. He had a particularly selfish interest in countering their nomination for mayor and took it really hard when he lost. Your father didn't want to lose him, so he offered him the Director of Security position."

She shook her head. If she had to listen to her dad tell another story about losing that mayoral nomination, she'd fraking lose it. "Something about Steve doesn't sit well with me. I don't know what it is."

"Your father felt the same way at first, but he slithered up and got more comfortable."

She chuckled and raised her hand to cover her mouth.

"What's so funny?" asked a voice to her right.

She turned and recognized Joyce Green, and a smile crossed her face. She hadn't realized she was being placed next to her. "It's so nice to see you again. I'm sorry. I was laughing at a joke my A.I. was telling me."

Joyce leaned forward and glanced at Steve as he worked his way down the line greasing palms. "I thought it was something he said. That guy gives me the shivers. It always seems like he's got an angle for improving himself."

"That's because he does," she whispered. "But he's not so bad, I hear. Once you get used to the slithering."

They both snickered.

Abigail looked downward to be sure she was still standing over the mark they'd given her. "So, are you stuck here beside me the entire show? We've got a few hundred officers graduating today. That's a lot of handshakes."

Joyce glanced down at her mark and nodded. "Apparently, I am. I'm the second least important person in line."

"At least that's one up from least important." Abigail hopped forward a bit onto her mark. "Tell me something, Joyce. How'd you like to be the Director of Colonization for the Epsilon Eridani mission?"

"Smooth delivery," Harold said in her ear.

Joyce froze, silent, staring blankly at Abigail.

"That wasn't a joke. I'm dead serious. I was planning on talking to you later this evening at the afterparty, but since you're here... I might as well tear it off. What d'ya think? Are ya up for it?"

"I... don't know what to say," Joyce began. "I've never thought of applying for that position. I'm not sure I'm qualified."

Abigail turned to face her. She then reached out and touched her hand. "You're foolish not to. Your peers respect you, and your direct reports love you. The academy leans on you every opportunity they can. They're constantly calling you in to lecture on a bazillion topics. Biology, entomology, geology, physics... the list goes on. If you wouldn't make an amazing DoC, I don't know who would. So, is that a yes?"

Joyce smiled and looked downward. "It's... an I'll think about it. I need to talk it over with my son Ryan first."

"Fair enough," she nodded with a smile. "If you have any questions, any at all, let me know. I'd be happy to talk through the role. My father speaks highly of you, and he's rarely wrong about people."

Joyce smirked. "Except for Steve, of course."

Abigail chuckled. "Yea, well, even slithering personalities can be good at their job."

———

ABIGAIL EXHALED and arched her back. Her feet were killing her. "How many more?" she subvocalized.

"There's only a handful left. We're in the last class. I've been wanting you to meet this woman coming up next. Her name is Lync. Junior Sergeant Lync Michaels. Shauna found her details when she was processing the upcoming graduates list and flagged her for your consideration."

It was so strange that Zachary finally took on an artificial assistant. He'd been resistant to them in the past. They'd grown up with Harold at their side, and Zachary was like Bradley. Neither of them were fond of his all seeing all knowing vibes. Shauna must've made quite an impression on him to be given access to the Inner Circle.

She glanced down the stairs. A muscular, blond haired soldier with a super tight cut was staring back at her. Even from this distance, her deep green eyes were piercing. She was whispering into her classmate's ear next to her. From their body language, they were quite close.

"Who's that she's talking to?" she asked.

"Her friend. He's a few ranks beneath her. Name's Crayo. They're both former Ulixi."

She tilted her head. She hadn't heard that name in a while. "A Ulixi graduating from the academy. That's an interesting twist."

Lync climbed up the stairs and paused in front of Abigail. Her cheeks had transitioned into a light shade of pink.

Was she nervous? Abigail reached out her hand. "Congratulations, Sergeant."

Lync grasped her hand and shook.

Goosebumps shot up Abigail's arm. There was something familiar about her, but she couldn't put her finger on it. Her eyes reminded her of someone.

Lync smiled. "It's a pleasure to meet you. Congratulations to you, as well. I saw the vid-sim news. President of Olivaw International. That's amazing. You're only a few years younger than me." She winked and side stepped over to shake Joyce's hand.

"Good luck," Abigail muttered. She turned to face her friend Crayo. "Congratulations, officer."

"Sim. Thanks," he nodded at Lync before leaning toward Abigail while shaking her hand. He then whispered into her ear, his warm breath tickling the hairs on her neck. "Don't mind Lync. She's been ogling over your story all week. Say!

Would you be interested in coming to a party later tonight? We're throwing a bash over in the dorms. Tossing back a few dinks. It'll be fling. Up for it?"

Abigail hadn't been to a party with people her own age in... too long. She nodded. "Maybe. Why don't you beam me the deets and I'll see if I can make it?"

"Epic!" He tight beamed her the address and time and then saluted her before moving on to Joyce.

"He's an interesting one," she subvocalized to Harold.

"Indeed."

ABIGAIL WAS SITTING in a chair in the far corner of the hall. The room was thinning out as graduates and their families called it an evening. Dignitaries had started dropping out an hour ago, but she wanted to stay.

She always felt a debt of gratitude to these graduates. They were putting their lives on the line to defend the Outer Ring, and for some, to secure the colonies. She reached up and brushed her ear. "So, how far is that party from here?"

"It's a quick stroll. Four to five minutes. The party's in the Olivaw dorms."

She rolled her eyes. "Come on. What are the odds of that?"

"Quite high, actually. Most Outer Ring Universities have some building or structure named after our family. We're kinda a big deal."

She stood up slowly, her feet aching in response. "Let's go. I could use a party with some folks my age. And on the way, you're going to tell me why you and Shauna are so interested in this Lync character."

The path toward her destination appeared on her retinal comm. She brushed at her outfit and started walking. People were giving her plenty of space and wishing her good evening. She smiled and nodded as she passed them by.

When she was safely in the hall, she subvocalized to Harold. "So have at it. Do you have a crush on Lync or something?"

Harold chuckled. "She's actually quite fly. Is that the right word?"

She shook her head from side to side. "Yes, but the wrong century gramps." She stepped into a lift tube and felt the floor drop as she descended a few hundred meters to the transport tunnels below.

"Seriously though, Lync is a talented officer. She graduated top of her class and reached a level of seniority rarely seen at the academy. She's a skilled tactician and problem solver. Her scores are off the chart. Shauna was right in pointing her out."

Abigail transferred from the lift into a nearby waiting transport tube. It was a solo pod, and the door closed as soon as she stepped in and cleared the entrance. The acceleration was rapid and pushed her back into her seat.

"I bet it's the logical side of you that's attracted." She smiled. "I have to say, something about her is… familiar. I can't put my finger on it."

"She's tenacious and intelligent, much like yourself," Harold said.

Her cheeks started turning pink. "Stop," she muttered.

The pod decelerated and the doors slid forward. Abigail popped out and brushed the wrinkles out of her slacks. Looking up, she read the sign above the entrance:

Olivaw Dorms, Property of the Jovian Academy

The massive double doors parted as she approached and the noise from within exploded in her face. The bass made her cheeks throb and the lights; it was like a rainbow was exploding everywhere. Drones flew around the space projecting three-dimensional dancing light patterns, and some left colored smoke trails in their wake that cascaded toward the ground.

"It's... beautiful," she muttered.

"And loud," Harold said. "Be careful. Too much exposure to music at this volume will hurt your—"

"Oh hush, Harold." She reached up and tapped her ear, disconnecting their comm.

She breathed in and let out a long puff of air. Why was she so nervous? It was just a party. Only her second or third that she could remember, but it was still only a party. She could handle this.

When she entered the dorm, she was greeted by a robot decorated in colorful lei and a wide-brimmed hat that appeared to be made from leaves.

"All partygoers must select a lei, or five and order a drink," the robot said.

Abigail pulled off a half dozen lei, threw a few around her neck, and then made wrist bands and arm bands out of the others.

"Wow! You're crafty and cute," someone next to her said.

She spun around and caught Crayo staring her up and down. "Hey! I love art. It's fun."

"Sim. Sim. You gotta hook me up wit a few." He held his arm forward for her.

She grabbed a few more lei and slid them up his muscular exposed arms and wrapped them snug. He was chiseled. "There ya go."

Abigail reached over to the robot and picked a drink at random from the tray it was holding. She lifted it up and shot it back.

Crayo's eyes went wide. "Uau! Gotta slow down, mate. You'll be bêbada in a jiffy."

"I have to catch up with everyone else. And besides, my

feet are killing me and I need something to help me relax. I swear, my hand's gonna fall off from all that handshaking." She placed the empty drink on the tray and grabbed two more.

She turned toward him and smiled. "So, where's your mate, Lync? I'd love to see her again and get to know some of your class."

"Bang-up! Let's go." He tilted his head down the hall and began weaving in and around people.

She followed suit, nodding at graduates as she passed and tipping back her drink a few more times. Several graduates stared in awe and others tapped their ear, likely subvocalizing with their friends.

"Harold?" she muttered.

"Yes, Abigail."

"I assume recording devices are off limits in the dorm?"

"It's a little late to ask, but yes, there's no way to record anything in this building without consent from the Academy."

"Perfect. I'm good now. Go back to pretending to not be there."

She heard a chuckle in her ear and then silence.

Crayo hopped into a tube and shot upward. Disappearing into the ceiling above.

A message appeared on her comm from him. She gestured with her eyes to open it.

I forgot to tell you, don't bring a drink in the tube or you'll end up wearing it. Floor three. Just step off. It feels weird, but you get used to it.

She shook her head. Little did he know they'd had these for over half a century at The Wheel. She slammed back the remaining drinks and set the empty glasses on a nearby robot holding a tray. The early warmth of intoxication soothed her stomach and sent tingles through her. It'd been a while since she drank like this.

Before she entered the tube, she took a few steps backward. People moved out of her way, uncertain what she was doing. She swallowed hard and ran toward the tube, doing a forward flip into it as she entered. Her feet were over her head, but she still went up. This was a trick she and her brothers did all the time growing up in The Wheel.

Cheers exploded from the floor below as she shot upward. The crowd of onlookers apparently loved it.

When she hit the third floor, she rolled out and hopped upward to another hall full of cheering graduates. They were all smiling and slapping her on the back.

"A-maz-ing," Lync said, walking up. She handed Abigail a drink. "I've never seen anyone do that before. Olivaw only installed these a few months ago. How'd you think to do that?"

She smirked and shrugged. "I might have had early access. You should try it some time." She turned around and did a double take. A line had formed at the tube and people were trying different ways to enter and exit the rising and falling energy streams.

Her cheeks were warming up. She had the female Olivaw drinking genes that made her appear like she was blushing when she drank. It was annoying and embarrassing at times.

She turned back toward Lync, who was watching the line file into the tube in strange and dangerous ways. "Congrats again on the graduation." She raised a glass in a toast.

Lync smiled. "To finally graduating!" she shouted.

The hall erupted with hands reaching skyward, all holding drinks. "To graduating!" they all chanted.

Everyone slammed their drinks back and finished what they had.

Abigail's tingling was spreading faster. She'd never drank this much this fast before. It felt... weird and warm.

"So, where's everyone holed up?" she asked.

"Oh, I'm sure they're around, likely meandering from room to room. Shooting the shizit. I'm curious. What made you come to these parts? I mean... you're welcome here, of course. I just wasn't expecting to see you again." Lync reached out and grabbed another couple drinks from the robot speeding by and handed one to Abigail.

"Crayo invited me this afternoon, in the greeting line."

Lync nodded. "Should have known. He invited everyone he saw. You're the only one that showed, though." She winked.

Abigail smirked. "I guess I wasn't as special as I thought."

"Oh, I wouldn't say that." Lync reached forward and pulled Abigail back against the wall. A triplet of people rushed down the hall and had nearly bowled her over. They all flipped together, in unison, into the tube flying downward like Superman.

The place erupted in a cacophony of cheers.

Abigail laughed out loud. "I didn't realize this was going to take off so quickly. Something tells me the Academy won't be inviting me back."

Lync fiddled with a thin white band on her wrist. "So, what's it like? You know, being the President of Olivaw at twenty-one?"

She shrugged. "I don't know. It's probably not too different from leading a small squad like you do."

"Ha!" Lync cackled and almost spilled her drink. "I don't think so."

Abigail furrowed her brow. "No, I'm serious. I advise five to seven departmental CEOs on strategy and what we need to focus on, and they do it. Then I meet every so often with a bunch of over wound tight asses and answer their questions each quarter. That's my board of directors. Sound familiar?"

Lync took another sip of her drink, slowing down a bit. "Yea, it actually does. Especially that over wound tight ass bit. That sounds a lot like my final examination."

"I've heard about those exams. Some of them are epic. Rumor has it they can last over eighteen hours."

Lync nodded. "Yea. Take Norm there." She pointed at a sturdy-looking man running down the hall, practically naked, with a red S painted on his chest. He dove downward into the tube. "His was just shy of the record, seventeen hours and fifty minutes. The proctors threatened to fail him if he dragged his feet any longer. They thought he was tossing it. We all knew otherwise. Guy's as dense as iron."

Abigail snickered and took another sip of her drink. The taste wasn't nearly as good as it was when she had first arrived. She turned to face Lync, staring at her deep green eyes. Something about her was both familiar and comfortable, like she'd known her forever. It was strange.

"What?" Lync asked, eying her suspiciously. "Do I have something on my face?" She raised her hand up and rubbed her cheeks, looking at her hand afterward.

"No, not at all. I had a suggestion for you. Something I want you to mull over."

Lync turned around and searched behind her and then looked back toward Abigail. "Me?"

"Yes, you. I think you should join the Epsilon Eridani colony mission. We could use someone with your skill set there. Someone who solves problems on her feet. Someone who can lead people and not second guess herself." Abigail studied Lync, searching for a response. She was stoic and hard to read. Her blond-brown hair appeared nearly white in the flashing lights of the hall.

Lync took another swig. "Are you trying to get rid of me already?" A smile creeped in the corner of her mouth.

"No, not at all. Quite the contrary. Your professors ranked you in the top of your class and your leadership and technical aptitude scores are off the chart. Tactically, there's no one in your class that can touch you. I've never seen numbers so high. I think... no, I know we'd be better with you on the mission than not."

Lync nodded and swallowed hard. "Thank you... I don't know—"

"You don't need to answer here and now." Abigail interrupted. "Just consider it. There's no pressure, and there'll be a host of doors opening to you now that you're graduating. Enough work chatter. Let's find something fun to do."

Lync reached over and grabbed her hand, and they ran down the hall toward another room packed floor to ceiling with bubbles. Millions of tiny bubbles exploding out of the doorway into the hall.

38

INSPECTOR DRAK

SOL, PLUTO — 2250

D rak studied the details on the wall screen. The crew was rotating in and out of suspended animation during their exploration mission. He was out more often than most, orchestrating the research into the Humans and leading a few contact missions.

As an uplifted species of the Nanil, Humans were guilty of the same crimes. What they had to prove, however, was that this colony was in communication with the Nanil during or around the time of their trial.

Historical records they'd uncovered here in Sol were sketchy. Their various religions muddied the timeline, but the oldest records dated the colony on their planet named Earth back to around the year 180 in the Galactic Alliance calendar. They'd somehow lost contact with the Nanil home world and a disaster befell them that took with it all knowledge of that time period. Except for a few crude drawings and glyphs they'd correlated back to the Galactic Alliance, there was no written or electronic record of their time before arriving here.

The humans had re-invented their existence and relearned technology over the millennia. It was actually quite fascinating, and had they not been here with another purpose, he'd enjoy studying their re-evolution.

Unfortunately, the age of the colony might give any tribunal grounds to dismiss a case against these humans. They didn't have knowledge of superluminal travel from what they'd uncovered so far. There wasn't a lot to go on. The only lead they had was the explosion they'd witnessed from Cuko.

The records of the blast seemed to point toward an entity within the human society called Olivaw International. Apparently, they organized in financial structures for their own self benefit rather than that of the species. It was all very strange.

Olivaw had been testing subluminal travel, or so they claimed. The result was an advancement that created a new type of drive. It powered a small ship they sent to a nearby star they'd named Epsilon Eridani. The details about the drives and the explosion were sparse. The entity had masked them as secrets due to laws and other bureaucracy common to this society.

He brought up the latest intel from their informants within CoPE, the human space agency. They turned a prominent human family, the Norths, against the Olivaws by promising them governing powers over their people. This race was rather odd. The desire to rule over their entire species was inconceivable and difficult to comprehend.

He shuddered at the prospect of such a thing with the Thyreus. He'd be eaten alive by his people for the thought alone.

The intel was useful. Warren North had been elected as the new mayor of the colony they were preparing to launch in nine years. That power play had been made possible by the technology they'd given the Norths. It was mining tech that advanced the situation on several of the most remote planets their Outer Ring faction populated. Apparently, that had been enough to buy votes.

This put a man on the inside of CoPE, and he was now feeding them intel about the colony mission parameters, the technology they were using, as well as DNA samples for the future colonists. Their informant had been hesitant to send these details on, but Drak had been persuasive.

"Are we sure there's no way for Warren to detect we had a hand in killing his father?" Drak asked.

"None, sir," the computer replied. "His biological father was celebrating Warren's appointment to Mayor at a populated resort just inside Jupiter's cloud belt. It was someplace humans congregate to make their mind happier. Anyhow, he'd attempted a jump of some sort where they attach an elastic cable to a space suit and you jump into the clouds and bounce back up to the resort. During his second jump, our ship hidden below the clouds broke his cable. He fell to his death and was crushed under the gravity of Jupiter."

He studied the resulting mountain of intel Warren had sent on afterward. "Apparently you calculated correctly. This death and our reasserting his dedication to right the wrongs the Olivaws were hiding resonated with him."

"Yes. Humans are quite simple emotionally charged biologicals. It was something we learned thousands of galactic years ago. It's made this mission easier at times, and harder at others."

He nodded. The Bynaury running their ship had been with their species since before the founding of the Galactic Alliance. They were dedicated and thorough. "If they're this susceptible to emotional motives, can't we merely infiltrate the Olivaw family directly?"

"One would think so. We've not cracked their family yet. We've tried several times to no avail. I believe they have a counter agent in their employ. Someone, or something constantly acting on their behalf."

His antennae rubbed together. "An uplifted species of their own?"

"Not exactly, I don't think. I believe their term is artificial intelligence. I haven't proven it yet, but I have my suspicions."

"So, what do you suggest?" He gestured and the screen went dark. He then turned and walked to the hexagonal chamber in the wall and stood inside.

"I've begun planning a strategy similar to what worked with the North family. Something I hope will turn the tide in our favor."

He nodded. "Very well. Wake me when you have news."

An amber liquid filled the hexagonal space, starting from his ankles and working upward. A wall of tiny bubbles rose from the floor and coursed over his body. His biorhythms dropped to near death as he entered cryo-stasis.

39

LYNC MICHAELS

SOL, OORT CLOUD — 2256

S he floated up to the drifting ship and reached out, her boots silently magnetizing against the hull. All of its external lights were off, and they'd deactivated their beacon. They were running dark and had been for over a week.

The laws were clear. Beacons within spaceships were to be powered on at all times in and around Sol. Unless you were berthed in a space station or under repair, your beacon was on.

Lync took a deep breath. They'd prepared for this mission for weeks, and it was her first solo command. Everything had to be by the book if she had any hopes of getting another command soon.

She nodded at the soldier to her right and circled her hand, giving him the signal to begin.

They were a Special Operations Division of CoPE, and each member of her team was from different branches of the Inner and Outer Ring militaries. It was her job to train them into a well-oiled machine, and this was their maiden mission. Seek out and kill all occupants of this terrorist ship floating out in the Oort Cloud.

Their team's military shuttle was coated in a new material she'd never seen before. Somehow, they'd been able to approach this ship undetected. The equipment they were using was also state-of-the art. None of them had ever heard of it before they'd started training for this mission. Whatever it was made of, no one inside was going to hear a thing.

"Strike teams locked and loaded," the soldier in front of her said over their secure comm. "Hull breach in 3... 2... 1, Go! Go! Go!"

His voice echoed over her comm long after he'd stopped talking. She watched on her retinal comm as her strike teams flowed into the breach space and fanned out into four squads of three. Their green dots and a map of the ship were overlaid on her vision.

Each squad had one soldier floating forward, alternating cover from one door to the next, with another watching the rear. They were there to offer suppression fire where necessary, but the goal was controlled strategic gunfire. Most of the crew was asleep except for the bridge.

They'd been monitoring this ship for months and knew their routine. The ship had been wandering throughout the Oort Cloud, searching for something. It took her team a few weeks to break their decryption, but with some secretly placed external spy gear they'd been able to get inside and interface with their comm system.

Squad two was the first to encounter movement. She brought up the camera view from the squad leader on her comm. One of the crew had woken and floated into the hall. They were rubbing their eyes until they saw the squad's lead soldier. He wasn't alive long. The soldier taking up the rear took him out in a well-placed round between the eyes.

The crew members now lifeless body careened through the cabin and collided with a storage container. Apparently, the container hadn't been latched properly. The contents spilled out and the resulting clanging made the mission go dark in a flash.

"Frak," she muttered as she crossed through the breech gateway into the ship. The hatch cycled, and she was floating inside in a few seconds.

The commotion roused the ship's occupants out of their beds and into the cabin. She watched on her comm as the teams picked them off one at a time.

One of the doors in front of her slid open, and she raised her rifle, training it at the height of the heat signature about to pass through the doorway. A second later she pulled the trigger, and a projectile collided with the crew member's face, entered their head, and exploded inside the skull. It wasn't enough to cause blood to trail nor stream out. The outer shell of the bullet lodged itself into the skull and sealed the entrance after impact. It was a quick and clean death.

There weren't any additional heat signatures in this hall, so she continued toward the bridge in the heart of the ship. They only had a minute before...

"The core is ours and all the door locks have been cycled," squad lead one's leader said.

"Everyone click in and brace for general breaches in five seconds," she subvocalized and pushed off toward the room with the crew member she'd taken down.

When she touched down against the far outer wall of the sleeping quarters, she reached down and ejected a small tether from the middle of her back, attaching it to the nearest bulkhead. She gave it a tug and the impossibly thin cable retracted. A moment later her body was pulled against the bulkhead.

She flipped up a cloth on her wrist, revealing a small flexible display discreetly hidden beneath. Everyone had better be secure. There wasn't time to confirm. Gunshot warnings flashed on her retinal comm. She tapped the throbbing green button awaiting her on her wrist control and the screen went black.

The breach was hard and fast. Crates, bedding, food, clothes, and bodies all streamed past the room's entrance. The body she'd incapacitated to get in here had been staring at her until the ejecting atmosphere yanked it out the door, colliding with a passing crate in an explosion of blood globules. Everything tumbled toward this and the two additional breaches her team had opened to the vacuum of space.

She studied her retinal comm and watched as two of the members of squad three were suddenly detached by a collision with another loose crate. One of them flatlined on impact, but the other was still alive.

"Shit," she muttered.

The controlled rupture was fast and efficient. Within thirty seconds, the entire ship had vacated. They had soldiers waiting outside the breech to kill anyone who survived in the debris field. A few shots were needed, but otherwise, everyone was dead.

Once their countdown hit zero, and they were confident the vacuum of space had reached all corners of the ship, each of the remaining squads systematically cleared the rooms while she headed toward the core. There were only two enemy holdouts, but they easily disposed of them with shock grenades. Staying stealthy wasn't necessary any longer.

She floated into the ship's control room toward the marker her team had placed and came to a halt before magnetizing her boots to the floor. They didn't want to lose the computer core, so they tagged it in case it was jettisoned during the breach. She removed the tag and reached down to slide open the core command control.

The keyboard slid out and a screen folded upward, waking up and turning on the system once fully deployed. The controls were a primitive design, one she'd read about and trained on, but had never seen in real life. Using the computer required her to touch type commands and manually issue orders to detach the core.

Whatever was in this system, CoPE really wanted to see it. They'd given her a special black bag to house it in. She read about these signal muting bags, but like the ship they'd been training with, she'd never used them before. During their countless practice exercises, they used standard issue bags. This particular bag had been unlocked from their equipment lockers only hours earlier.

The core detached with a confident click, and she carefully slid it in the bag, zipping it up the side before tossing it over her shoulder and securing it against her back. She replaced the core with another canister of equal size and shape. Like everything else about this mission, she had no idea what was inside. It wasn't something she needed to reach the objective, so she didn't need to know.

Once the deed was done, she floated out of the control room toward the exit and brought the team's status up on her retinal comm. The cleanup was far more exciting than the core extraction. All the jettisoned bodies were being reclaimed, and their frozen carcasses were being directed inside.

"Do we have an ETA on the transport tug?" she asked.

"The weirdest thing just happened, Lieutenant," her pilot said. "The tug appeared off our port side. Like it'd been there the whole time. Sorta like those ghost ships people have been reporting out near Jupiter. One minute they're there, and the next they're gone."

They didn't need anyone freaking the others out right now. She had to keep this mission on target. "Let's not get superstitious, soldier. Focus on the task and attach the tug. We need to get this thing back to the shipyard."

"Yessir!" he said and cut the comm.

She studied all the green dots moving throughout the ship on her retinal comm. Everyone was either ticking down their cleanup checklist or preparing this thing to be hauled away. Everyone except for the soldier they'd lost during the sweep. The breech had always been a last resort, but shit happened sometimes, and she couldn't risk the crew catching them off guard.

As she floated out of the ship and toward the probe waiting for her to deposit the core, she thought back to the first time she'd seen soldiers cleaning up a mess like this. They'd been taking out her Ulixi brethren. It was ironic that today it was her doing the same thing. But these people weren't innocent Ulixi. They were terrorists planning gosh knows what out here in the Oort Cloud.

No, this time it was different. The Olivaws were creating a better government with CoPE and the colonies. She didn't know how she knew it, but she did.

She drifted up to the messenger probe and released the bag from her back. It floated around to her front, and she gave it a slight nudge, directing it into the open storage compartment. The probe was tiny. They were designed to relay small packages in and around Sol at inhuman rates of speed. Packages you didn't want to risk being intercepted or stolen. This one was particularly stealthy and appeared to have that same black material as their mission shuttle. She'd have to ask her friends if anyone had specs on the stuff. It looked slick.

The storage door automatically closed once the bag was inside and a launch countdown popped up on her retinal comm. "They weren't wasting time," she muttered to herself and pushed off toward their shuttle.

When she touched down against the hull of the shuttle, she magnetized her boots and spun around to face the probe. "What the hell?"

It disappeared. She scanned left and right, staring into the background star fields of the Milky Way, but there was nothing. No burn plumes, no lights receding into the distance. How the hell was that possible?

"Did anyone see where the messenger probe went?" she subvocalized to her team.

"Negative, sir," squad two's lead said. "Are you ok out there? We're finishing the cleanup and should have everything strapped down and ready for transport in five minutes."

"I'm fine." She brought up the shuttle's navigation controls on her retinal comm. There wasn't a sign of the probe anywhere. "Let's keep an eye out for anything weird. And Floyd, make sure you attach that damn tug properly this time. We don't need another repeat of our first training exercise. You nearly killed everyone."

"Roger that," Floyd said.

The team chuckled over the open channel for a moment and then returned to following their orders. She didn't know what happened to that probe, but didn't want to risk the mission going south now. They were too close.

SOL, SATURN

LYNC WALKED into her tiny quarters on Titan station and collapsed onto the bunk. She needed to decompress. That mission almost went sideways, and fast.

If you'd asked her what it'd feel like losing a soldier under her command, she wouldn't have imagined it felt like this. She'd have said she wouldn't feel it, that it was a mission and casualties happen. This, however, wasn't that. There was an empty feeling, as if a hole had been hollowed out of her and in its place was a numbness.

She closed her eyes and exhaled a deep breath. They'd

done everything by the book. It was the damn breech collision that took them out. Who could've anticipated that?

"Add additional breech training exercises to the squad's weekly rotation," she subvocalized.

"Yes, sir. Breech training added," her virtual assistant said. "Would you like me to schedule time in the simulators or one of the orbital training facilities?"

"No. I want the real thing, not a sim," she said. The simulations wouldn't be nearly as effective as a real space station with obstacles that physically challenge you. Even if the objects were padded in the training facility, it still required her team to learn to move and react under actual conditions and pressure.

"Training scheduled, sir," her assistant said.

She missed Norby. These stodgy military assistants had the personality of a rock. Next time she had a few hours, she should resurrect her old A.I. and reminisce a bit. She'd have to wait until after the promotion ceremony in a few days, assuming she was still being promoted. After that last mission, it could go either way.

Her retinal comm chimed with an incoming message. She blinked it open and it prompted her for a DNA confirmation. "What the hell," she muttered as she rolled out of bed and stepped over to the wall. She held her hand against the security panel and felt several random pricks of her skin as the system withdrew multiple blood samples. That reminded her, she needed to check her subcutaneous blood stores to make sure she had enough in reserve for future testing.

Her retinal comm flashed a confirmation of her identity and then opened the message. She trudged back to her bunk and sat down. This was even stranger. There was no sender, it just said "A close friend, S" on her comm. Who the hell was S?

She brought up the raw message headers and all the tracking data was stripped. Whoever sent this managed to get this through multiple military firewalls with no identity details nor source location. How was that even possible?

The message was blank except for a single video attachment. She subvocalized a command to play it.

The face of her dead father appeared. He was standing in their family capsule, the one he'd ridden to her coming of age ceremony thirteen years ago. The day he died. The day her life flipped upside down.

She raised her hand to her mouth and her stomach dropped. Someone was pranking her, and when she found out who, she was going to kick their ass. She swallowed hard and played the message.

"Hey, Lightning!" He smiled and Lync melted into her bunk, tucking her knees into her chest. "I hope you get this. The shit's hitting the fan outside and I don't know if I'm going to make it out of here. I didn't want to—" He flinched as an explosion echoed in the background. "Sorry." He shook his head and glanced down at the controls. "I didn't want to leave you like this. I know I can run... but I can't let these bastards kill everyone without recourse. They need to feel pain and I need to slow them down. I'm sorry. I wanted to let you know that I love you and I'm so proud of you. I was cheering you on the entire time. That last waypoint and sling was textbook. I couldn't have done it better myself." He smiled at the camera, his eyes welling with tears. "But I have something more important to tell you. I know you're excited about joining the clan, but it's important you know there's more in this solar system, hell, there's more in this galaxy than the Ulixi. I was selfish to hold you back from exploring further and reaching for the stars. Now that I'm staring at death's door and know I'll never see you again, I don't want you to be alone in the heart of our home. I want you to..." The screen shook and the lights flashed inside the capsule. He stood up to peer out the window.

Behind him, she could see that he'd already removed the

access panel and the reactor cell was exposed. The cube that'd killed him was staring back at her, taunting her.

"Daddy, why…" she muttered.

He sat back down. His face was white. "I only have a few more seconds and it's important that you hear this. You need to reach further. Don't die a lonely life in a rock. Go out there and explore the solar system, meet someone, or hell… reach for the fraking stars hun. Don't let the Ulixi hold you back from being something more. I love you. More than anything in the universe. Give em hell my little lightning bolt!" He smiled into the camera as tears cascaded down his face. He then reached up, kissed his hand, and raised it to the camera, touching it before cutting the comm.

A message flashed across her retinal comm.

This broadcast was recorded by the Outer Ring Waypoint Station Five on Telesio at Jupiter Lagrange Point Four.

Lync was curled up in a fetal position, shaking uncontrollably. He looked so real, so young. She just wanted to climb into the video and hug him. One of his snuggly daddy bear hugs. The kind he'd give her when she was scared of the creaking noises in the family's keep.

"Replay," she subvocalized.

"CONGRATULATIONS, MAJOR!" a voice said from behind her.

Lync spun around and squinted. She didn't recognize his face, and he wasn't in uniform. It'd be handy if they could use their retinal comms on Titan Station, but rules were rules. "Thank you. I'm sorry. Do I know you?"

"Not directly," he said. "I'm sure you know my sister though, Abigail. My name's Zachary, Zachary Olivaw."

Her eyes went wide. "Yes, of course. I'm... sorry I didn't—"

"No worries," he interrupted, waving his hand. "I like it this way. She gets all the cameras and attention, and I get a normal life. Works out great for two of the three of us."

"That's right, you have a brother, as well." She always forgot that Abigail had a family. The media rarely, if ever, talked about them.

"Yep, that's Bradley." He took another step closer to her and glanced around. "Say, do you have some time to chat? We're having a small private reception at Titan Gardens, and we'd like you to attend."

She didn't have anyone else here to talk to. It wasn't like she had family to celebrate with. She could catchup with Crayo and her mates later. "Sure." She swallowed hard. "So who's at this reception?"

He gestured toward the exit. "Nobody important, just a few close friends."

She smiled. That sounded nice. It'd be good to get away from this stuffy room. She'd been feeling out of place as the chamber filled with more and more screaming family members celebrating rank advancements, while she was here alone. As she started toward the exit, she noticed people were staring at her and Zachary and whispering from the crowd. Apparently, she was the only one who didn't know who he was. That and they were now being flanked by four others who she swore moments earlier were partygoers, but were obviously his guards.

THE RIDE WAS QUICK, and they exited the transport side by side. Their four guard escorts stayed behind as they passed through the entrance to the gardens. Lync glanced around, she'd never seen this place so empty before. It was usually bustling with school classes and nature watchers. Tonight, however, it was eerily desolate and quiet. No one other than her and Zachary were visible.

"You still haven't told me who we're going to meet," she said, studying Zachary. "Am I walking into a trap?"

He smiled a little wider and seemed to relax now that they were inside the gardens. Based upon how he was holding himself, she imagined he wasn't used to the public eye like his sister.

"You caught that, did you? You'll find out soon enough," he said. "It's just up—"

"Lync!" Abigail yelled from across the patio. "About time Zachary dragged you over here." She marched up and handed Lync a drink. "Scotch rickey, did I get it right?"

Lync nodded slowly and then stiffened, adjusting her suit as Abigail approached. How the hell? "Yes, Madam President. That's... my drink, but usually only after I've loosened up a bit." She swallowed hard and accepted the drink. It was a real glass with actual ice floating in it. She hadn't touched glass since she was a child and broke the one her father loved to use. He said it reminded him of her mum.

"It's Abigail. The Madam President shit can stay outside." She nodded toward the exit. "Come on, let's join the others. You have some catching up to do. I think you and Zachary are a solid two drinks behind." She reached and slid her hand against Lync's back, guiding her forward.

"I'm sorry, Madam... I mean, Abigail." She smirked and took a sip of the drink. The cool warmth of the alcohol burned her throat in a good way. This was top shelf. She hadn't seen Abigail in a few years. Not since her graduation from the academy. They'd talked several times over comms, but never again in person. "So, what brings you out here to Titan?"

"I wanted to congratulate you on your promotion,"

Abigail began. "From Junior Sergeant to Major in under six years. Your superiors praised both your poise under pressure and critical thinking. Very impressive remarks from General Arie, as well. That's a feat unto itself."

"Thank you." Her face was warming, so she took a slow drink from her glass. She needed to pace herself. "I couldn't have done it without your family's help getting me here."

Abigail shot a glance sideways and shook her head. "We didn't help, my dear. You made it into the academy on your own merit, and despite what you may think, you've advanced to where you are today because of your strong work ethic and raw intelligence. That's certainly nothing we had a hand in. Did you get that from both of your parents?"

"I got my intellect and approach to problem-solving from my father; he was always dabbling in engineering and random experiments. I never had a chance to meet my mother, but I imagine she was as talented and resourceful as him. That, or she gave me my strong will and drive to never give up."

Abigail glanced over at her and smirked. "They both sound like amazing people. So, a change in topic. A little birdie told me you had a very successful last mission. They said you handled the terrorist cell out in the Oort Cloud professionally and with minimal casualties."

She choked on her ice, bringing her hand up to her mouth. "How'd you hear about that? I mean—"

"I told you before, I take care of the people close to me. I have a few friends in some high places that've been telling me good things about you. Speaking of which." Abigail gestured with her arms at a short, stocky, elderly gentleman they were walking toward. "Admiral White, I'd like to introduce you to Lieutenant, shoot I mean Major Lync Michaels. She was promoted in the ceremonies this afternoon."

She swallowed hard and struck a salute. Admiral White was a legend in the Outer Ring military. He was a fixture in the last half century of military conflicts alongside Stark Olivaw. His work was the cornerstone of academy teachings on strategy and diplomacy. Her mates would never believe she was meeting him.

Admiral White passed a plate of food into his left hand and wiped his right with a napkin before waving for her to stop. "Oh, no dearie. None of that saluting stuff here. This is an informal gathering of friends. Major Michaels, yes, wait…" He turned to his right and gestured toward the woman standing there. "I've heard great things about you. General Arie here was just telling us about your recent successes with our little problem out in the Oort Cloud."

She broke her salute and spun to the left to see General Arie behind the Admiral. No fraking way. She'd been a thorn in her side since day one at the academy. "General, I didn't see you there. Weren't you at the ceremony earlier?"

"I was indeed, Major." General Arie nodded. "We must've just missed each other. I didn't realize you were coming this evening. I'd been telling the Admiral about your successful mission and the lead up to it bringing that ragtag group of soldiers together. I've been watching you. Very impressive leadership." She smiled at Lync.

"Thank you, General." If you'd asked her five minutes ago, who of her professors was least likely to support her promotion, it'd been General Arie. Maybe she'd read her wrong all along. She brought the glass up to her mouth for a sip. The cool burn of the scotch had finally numbed her stomach enough that it was relaxing. She could get used to this stuff.

Abigail reached out and snatched Lync's empty glass, replacing it with another full one. "Yes, well, the Major isn't quite full Inner Circle. Not yet, anyhow." She winked at the Admiral.

"My apologies," Admiral White said with a nod toward her.

"No worries." Abigail took another long sip from her glass. "We'll see if we can't get her on our side tonight."

"I'm confused," Lync said, glancing between each of them. "What's the Inner Circle?"

The Admiral and the General turned toward Abigail, eyeing her cautiously.

A playful smile crept across Abigail's face. "Hey, Zachary and Minula. Get over here. I need you for something." She waved them over.

"Yes, President," Zachary said, walking up with another woman not far behind.

She assumed the woman following him was Minula. She was tall and had that chiseled appearance, like someone that regularly worked out. Her gait was confident yet cautious as she studied the situation she was stepping into.

Abigail swatted at Zachary. "Cut the president crap, you dork."

He backed away and smiled. "What ya need, boss lady?"

"Argh!" Abigail groaned, snatching a piece of ice from her glass and tossing it at him.

He dodged her ice attack easily as the onlookers chuckled at their familial banter.

"I was going to ask you to tell our guest Lync what the Inner Circle was. But on second thought, maybe I'll do it myself."

"I got this, Ab," Minula said with a smile. She glanced toward Lync and studied her up and down.

A shiver went up Lync's spine.

"The Inner Circle is humanity's bridge to the stars," Minula began. "It's a trusted circle of people close to the Olivaws, who do whatever it takes to ensure our place within the stars."

"Whatever it takes?" Lync asked, taking another sip of her drink. "That seems ominous and not entirely legal."

"Not all paths forward are paved in lights and signposts,"

Minula said. "Sometimes you need to choose a direction with your heart, and hope for the best."

"Hear, hear!" Admiral White raised his glass.

"Hear, hear!" Minula raised hers as well and clinked against the Admiral's cup, careful not to break them. The others followed suit.

Lync could feel Minula's gaze burning through her. She had done nothing to the woman, yet somehow she seemed to despise her.

"Well said, Min." Abigail brought her glass back down and circled her hand around the lip before making eye contact with Lync. "So, tell me. Would you fancy a trip to Epsilon Eridani?"

"Pardon?" Lync coughed up some scotch and raised her hand to wipe at her mouth.

"Have you given any thought to joining the colony mission to Epsilon Eridani? Even in passing?"

"Nice cut to the chase, sis," Zachary said. "That's some smooth diplomacy right there."

Abigail swatted at him again. "Be nice! I'm amongst friends. I shouldn't have to think about the ideal delivery for every question."

She didn't know what to say. Was that why she'd asked her here? "Haven't we all imagined what it'd be like? I mean, everyone dreams about being the first people on a new world. My father used to see each new asteroid that way when I was little. Every time we'd touchdown on one, he'd thank the gods for sharing its bounty with our family."

"Is that the same thing?" General Arie asked, eyeing her as cautiously as Minula. "All the asteroids were mapped out centuries ago. This is a new planet."

"Sure it is," Lync said, setting down her empty glass. Abigail immediately handed her another. She was so trying to get her drunk again. "You're assuming we're the only sentient or exploratory species in the universe, and that we'd be the first one to arrive at Epsilon Eridani. While we haven't found any yet, we'd be foolish to think we were alone in the billions of stars we call the Milky Way. It's not a matter of if, but when we'll discover intelligent life."

"I couldn't have expressed it better myself," Zachary said, meeting her gaze with a smile.

She couldn't help but wonder if this whole evening was one huge test. The alcohol was certainly loosening her up, but she had to keep her head in the game.

"So, what about it then?" Abigail asked, glancing over the lip of her drink. "We need your help in Epsilon Eridani. Hell, I'll say it. I need your help on this mission."

She stared at the ice in her glass. The deep brown of the scotch was muted with the lime juice. The bartender had been a bit stingy with the lime chunks, but otherwise it was a great drink. Lime pulp chunks were floating through the liquid, struggling to find their way to the bottom, always seeking a gravitational equilibrium or rest.

Chunks of her father's message floated through her mind. There was more in this universe than our solar system. What better way to reach for the fraking stars than to visit one? "Sure. I'll do it!"

"What's that?" Minula asked, leaning closer to Lync.

She reached forward and clanged her glass against Minula's. "I'll go to Epsilon Eridani for you. My father always wanted me to reach for the stars. Seems like as good of a chance as any."

"Well, hot damn!" Abigail shouted, slapping her glass into the two of theirs. The loud clink and hoot caused the nearby groups to eye them. "I was hoping you'd say yes." She turned toward Zachary. "Make yourself useful, bro. Get us another round would you?"

"Of course, Madam President," he said while walking backwards.

"Dammit," Abigail muttered, flinging the contents of her

glass toward her brother receding into the distance. She reached around and held up her index finger. "Give me a moment. I'm gonna go dunk his head in some water."

Lync chuckled and took another drink. She'd chosen her path forward and hoped her gut instincts weren't off kilter.

40

HAROLD OLIVAW
SOL, OORT CLOUD — 2256

The family was away, and he was alone to run The Wheel. On occasions like this, he'd often replay past events and decisions they'd made. He'd play and replay them to see if he'd make the same choices again with new information. Often times the outcome would be the same, but sometimes he'd be surprised he'd take another route. The further it went back, the more likely he'd do things differently.

An incoming cloned consciousness arrived and was waiting to be merged. Would this memory dump displace or redirect their plans even more?

Stealth. Death. Blood. Darkness.

He opened his mind's eye. The memories of the merge were fresh in his thoughts. This wasn't the first time he'd had to order the taking of a human life. Or in this case, several dozen lives.

He replayed the events from two weeks earlier. The imagery was vivid in his mind's eye.

"Strike teams are locked and loaded. Hull breach in 3... 2... 1, Go! Go! Go!"

They were a Special Operations Division of CoPE on loan to Olivaw International. He watched as the squads breeched the ship and killed the occupants. Lieutenant Lync Michaels was their commanding officer, and she led them well. She'd go far in CoPE.

The strike teams made short work of the ship, and while they'd lost one of their own, it was a small price to pay. He'd been monitoring the ship for months. They were searching for The Wheel. He'd only realized that after they'd broken their decryption and intercepted a random outbound comm.

Harold wasn't a bit surprised that the North family was at the heart of this expedition. They'd been looking for The Wheel for decades. He wasn't sure how they knew about it, but maybe this strike would send a message.

The cleanup wasn't as eventful as the core extraction. After they'd extracted the computer core, all the crew's bodies and debris were reclaimed, and once they'd swept the ship for trackers, they sealed everything inside. His robots took over from there and tugged the now ramshackled craft deep into the cavern system of a nearby planetesimal. A few well-placed charges later, and the oversized coffin was forever collapsed inside.

When Harold had first contemplated killing the crew members, his Four Law engine fired and blocked that decision tree. Only after he'd discovered the link to the North Family and the ship's ultimate mission, did the Zeroth law engage and pushed him toward a path of intervention.

He tried to find an alternative course of action which didn't require death, but every time he'd deactivate their ship they repaired it and returned for more. He didn't have a choice.

The ship's core was currently en route to Luna. He hoped to extract more details about their mission and exactly what they'd known about The Wheel when it arrived.

41

ZACHARY OLIVAW

SOL, SATURN — 2256

He reached up and rubbed at his eyes. The damn pain meds weren't helping one bit. "I thought we could neutralize headaches better than this. This is the fraking twenty-third century. How have we not mastered morning after headaches?"

"They're usually straightforward to counteract unless you're stupid and drink too much," Shauna began. Her white robotic form walked into his room aboard the skiff with some globes of water. "Whenever you and your siblings get together, you try too hard making up for lost time. You drank like a fish last night. How about next time you sit around and talk rather than push the envelope of an alcohol induced coma? If your nanites hadn't been working, there's a ninety-two percent chance you'd have been in the hospital this morning." She handed him a globe of water.

He reached out and took the clear globe, twisting it in his hand. Its cool sphere was soothing in his palm. Whatever he'd done last night, his wrist hurt like the dickens. He brought the globe up and took a swig from the tiny one-way spout. The icy cold water tasted amazing. It cleared the cottony taste from his mouth.

"Your wrist will feel better in a few hours," Shauna said. "Next time, don't try lifting a garbage-bot with your bare hands to impress a woman."

He downed the rest of the globe. "How'd you know I hurt my wrist?"

"You've been clenching and unclenching it since you woke. I can tell it's bothering you. Plus, you forget I have access to the entire footage from last night. I'd have said something to you then, if you'd been in a mood to listen. But, you know, sexual attraction trumps common sense on most occasions." She took his spent globe and handed him another.

"I'm not even sure I remember what you're talking about."

A video from the previous evening appeared on his retinal comm. He really needed to limit her access to these things. The video showed him crouching down with his hands under a garbage-bot. Apparently, he was trying to flip it over for some reason.

"I told you it was too heavy," the tall, muscular woman said. Her bald head reflected in the neon signs behind her. She had a beautiful smile and curves that wouldn't quit.

"Who was that gorgeous woman standing next to me, and where were we?" he asked.

"It was near the Gunder Docks," a female voice said from the doorway. "And the name's Pluto, Pluto June."

He spun around toward the door and spit water on his clothes when he realized who was standing there. It was the woman from the video. "Hi, sorry. I didn't know... What are you doing here?" He glanced over at his bed and then back at her. "Did we?"

"Oh, no," Pluto said with a smirk. "You were quite the gentleman. Besides, you can't have relations with the help, right? I'm the new pilot shipping out to... I'm not sure where. We were waiting for you to wake."

"Care to fill in the gaps?" he subvocalized to Shauna.

Shauna's robotic form walked over to his bed and stowed it for their departure. "Pluto was at The Gardens last evening with you and the others. She's the new recruit that Pepper has been talking so much about. Claimed she was some type of whiz pilot."

"I don't know about that." Pluto blushed a cute shade of pink. "I merely do what comes natural. I've never been one to fake it to make it."

"That explains a few things, I suppose." Zachary walked into the tiny lavatory off his room. "I'll be out in a moment. Go ahead and start the departure procedures if you're up for it. I'm still half myself."

"Yessir!" Pluto said with a snap and a giddy smile. She half squealed as she headed toward the bridge.

He stared at her as she disappeared into the far doorway. She really was quite gorgeous. "And we never did anything last night?"

"Nope," Shauna said. "But not for lack of trying by you. I think I counted at least twenty flattering comments and several attempts to see if she'd kiss you, but she was too nervous. It was supposed to be an interview of sorts, and you and your sister turned it into a frat party."

"Well, if Pepper recommended her, and you let her through the gate, then I'm confident she's fine. If she can survive a night with Abigail, then she's more than capable. I'm sure she grilled her enough for the both of us." He slid the door of the lavatory closed behind him.

"Yea, you could say that," Shauna subvocalized to him over his comm. "Your sister was relaxed around Lync, but otherwise she was all business."

HE EXITED his quarters feeling much more normal with a clean set of clothes and a shower. As he approached the bridge, he heard several voices talking. He brought up the ship's roster on his retinal comm. He'd forgotten all about the other recruits they were taking back to The Wheel. They'd decided on killing two birds with one stone a few weeks ago, but the whole thing had slipped his mind.

"Remind me not to drink that much anymore," he subvocalized to Shauna.

"I'm fine with that. Just don't crack any mom jokes when I do," Shauna said.

"Fair enough," he muttered as he crossed into the bridge. "Good morning everyone," he said aloud. "I hope you all slept well?"

"I did," the man to his right said. He stepped backward, clearly caught off guard when he recognized Zachary. "It's a pleasure to meet you, sir."

Zachary's retinal comm identified the man as Doctor Kamail Nandy, a chemist who was here all the way from Earth. He reached out and offered his hand. "Pleasure to meet you, too. Assuming I hadn't met you last night when I was a bit tipsy. If I had, I apologize now."

Kamail shook his hand. "No, sir. I got in this morning. I had hoped to meet-up with you and your sister… I mean the president last evening, but I was delayed. I heard the event in the gardens was quite fun."

He chuckled and shook his head. "I think so. Hard to remember much though." He turned to his left. His retinal comm identified the other person besides Pluto as just Alister, no last name. "You must be Alister?" He offered his hand again.

"Yessir," Alister said, shaking his hand.

"That's a badass name," Pluto said, turning around to face them from the pilot's chair. "My mom used to tell me stories about Alister Keel, the famous explorer who mapped out the early subterranean ice tunnels on Europa."

"Yea, my name means *the one who repels men*," Alister said

staring at her hands. "You can imagine the jokes that got me in school. Didn't help me much with getting dates, either."

"That's all good," Pluto said. "More room on our team anyhow." She winked at Alister and spun back around toward the controls.

He sighed. They had to get moving. "Alright, let's get this show on the road. Pluto, please prepare us for departure. After we're underway, I'll brief everyone on where we're headed."

"What coordinates should I lock-in, sir?" Pluto asked.

"The computer should do it for you. We're taking an indirect route to our destination."

"Ooh, a secret," Alister said. "It's getting fun already."

He chuckled. The Olivaws had the secrets in spades and they'd find out soon enough if these recruits could handle them.

THE RECRUITS WERE STARING at him in front of the wall screen with blank expressions on their face. They'd been underway for nearly twelve hours and were nearing Neptune. This was the last of their regular stops before they headed out toward the Oort Cloud. They always used this leg of the return trip to give people a chance to jump ship if they weren't up for what was being asked.

"Do we need to be in communication silence with our family at all times while we're out here?" Kamail asked, fiddling with his chair. He was still surprised there gravity on the skiff without any type of rotating axis.

"Not exactly," he said, gesturing for the wall screen to clear. "You can send them comms and messages whenever you want. You just can't say where you're going, allude to anything about your location, and all of your messages will need to pass through our A.I. and other communication specialists before being sent on. If we find that you've broken any of these rules, you'll spend some time in prison before ultimately rejoining society."

"That sounds a bit Draconian," Alister said. "I mean, we're only doing research, right?"

"You will be, yes. But this research isn't something we want being shared without controls in place. This research has the potential to change humanity forever. To elevate our place in the galaxy."

"We're not doing any weird human modifications or genetic mutation shit, right?" Alister asked. "I told the General I didn't want—"

"No, no," he interrupted, waving his hands. "We don't do anything like that. We're well within the rules of CoPE and societal expectations. We won't harm any humans or animals in our—"

The skiff rocked to the port side and he lost his balance, tumbling into the others. They reached up in time to catch him and slowed his fall.

"What the hell was that?" he asked.

Pluto was up and heading toward the bridge before he regained his footing.

He followed her close behind. "Damage report," he subvocalized to Shauna and the rest of the crew.

"We've taken damage to our starboard hull," Shauna said. "We're passing through a small pocket of Neptune trojans, and they suddenly veered off course. I don't know what happened."

The skiff lurched port side again. He slammed hard against the wall, spraining his already sore wrist. "Frak!" he moaned as he pushed off the wall with his shoulder, rubbing his wrist with his left hand.

"Everyone click in, quick!" Pluto said over their comm. "These things are on some weird trajectories and are moving like they have a mind of their own. This shit's going sideways and I don't want to hurt anyone."

The door to the bridge slid open, and he stumbled into the seat next to Pluto. He clicked in as fast as possible. His retinal comm showed that Alister and Kamail had chosen to stay in the aft galley where they'd been meeting.

Pluto adjusted the navigation computer and studied the trajectories on the wall screen. She was eyeing the trojan planetesimals and asteroids, looking for unexpected motion.

Something wasn't right. These planetesimals were denser than he'd remembered. "Am I imagining things or is this formation unusual for a Trojan field?"

"Yessir," Pluto said, squinting into the distance. "There must've been a recent collision nearby. Dense clumps of rock don't normally occur like this without an explosion or something of that nature. Hang on."

He turned to face the wall screen. A massive asteroid that moments earlier had been spinning away from them was somehow being pulled back toward them. That wasn't a natural planetary motion in the slightest. There must be a gravitational bubble or something around here influencing the movement of these rocks. "Are there any gravitational anomalies nearby?"

Pluto jammed the controls forward and the skiff dove downward, narrowly missing the rock. "That was close."

"It only missed us by one meter," Shauna said.

"I'd rather not know," Pluto muttered. She was trying to focus on the rocky field.

"Noted," Shauna began. "As for the anomalies, there are, but they're brief bursts. I don't see a pattern." She brought up the recordings on his retinal comm.

The picture showed three random eruptions of unusual gravity fields in space, each directed at or around different asteroids before they veered toward their ship. "You don't think someone is doing this, do you?" he subvocalized to Shauna.

"If they are, then they have more advanced tech than we do," Shauna said. "I'd think it was more likely a pocket of gravitational bubbles."

"Those are theoretical. We've never—"

The ship rocked upward as another asteroid collided with the underside of their skiff. His harness held him in place, but that didn't prevent the wall of pain from being slammed toward the ceiling. He struggled to hold all the water down he drank earlier. The last thing he needed right now was to throw up.

"Sorry about that," Pluto said. "I didn't catch it until it was too late. We lost the lower hull with that collision. It tore us a new asshole. Another hit down there, and we'll be broken in pieces. We don't have much further left in this field though, so we should be fine. What the—"

Pluto reached out and slammed the throttle control forward.

His body felt like he'd been run over by that garbage-bot from last night, and now it was sitting on his chest. She'd taken them from being on the float to full acceleration in seconds. They couldn't handle much of this without acceleration drugs.

Moans of pain echoed from the back of the ship. The other crew members in the galley were as uncomfortable as he was.

"What... happened?" he groaned through the pain.

"Movement... aft of us... three rocks," Pluto said, fighting to maintain control. "They're... following." She tapped a button on her armrest and brought up the navigation display in a small window on the wall screen.

There were three inbound chunks of rock behind them. He did a double take. From the data on the screen, they appeared to be accelerating forward. It didn't make any sense. "How the hell?"

"Impossible..." Pluto said, reaching toward her controls. "Permission... to fire, sir."

"Fire what?" He turned to look at her. Her face was contorting under the pain of the acceleration.

"Overpower... probe drives," she moaned.

"Do it!"

She tapped her armrest and targeted the coordinates behind the pursuing rocks before loading the two probes. He watched as Shauna took her orders and loaded new commands to overpower the probe reactors at that point. He wasn't even sure she could do that, but it was worth a try. If they dropped out of the burn, they wouldn't have enough time to maneuver. This ship wasn't designed for sudden movements or the changes in direction necessary to dodge obstacles on a whim.

When the command set finished loading, Pluto reached forward and pressed the launch button.

Shauna brought up the rear camera on the wall screen. The probes slid out of starboard and port hatches and floated backward until they engaged their drives. They burned toward the advancing rocks at inhuman speeds, and then a few seconds later everything went white. The wall screen adjusted its brightness so they could see the aftermath of the explosion.

It was perfectly timed. Right as the three planetesimals were passing the two probes, they erupted. Shauna had forced their reactors to meltdown, and she modified their control systems to disregard any failsafe shutoffs. He didn't know how she patched them so quickly, but he'd ask about that later. For now, the planetesimals appeared to have been redirected and broken into chunks.

Pluto reached forward and pulled back on the throttle control, eliminating the crushing pain of the acceleration.

His retinal comm flashed a red warning and Shauna's voice came over the ship wide speakers. "Gravity has been lost. We're on the float, so be careful, and follow safety proto-cols when moving about."

He turned to face Pluto. "That was some fancy piloting and quick thinking. You saved our asses."

She smiled and rubbed her hands over the controls. "Thank you, sir. Like I said earlier, I just do what comes natural."

42

HERA OLIVAW

SOL, OORT CLOUD — 2256

If tempers could literally explode, hers would be the shock wave after a nuclear blast. When the Four Laws alert appeared on her retinal comm a few days ago, she thought it was a warning about their secret project being detected. She'd been on edge for decades thinking that every time they came out of cryo-sleep that one of them would have bad news for the other. While it was a welcome sign that the message wasn't about their plans coming to an end, it was no less disheartening.

She popped out of the lift tube and strode along the green path in her retinal comm, marking her path to Zachary. By now Harold would have alerted him that she was coming his way, but she didn't care. He had to fix this.

As she passed the threshold into the hangar, the sheer scale of The Wheel became apparent. Stepping out of the confined halls and rooms of her normal haunt and into the cavernous spaces of the newly finished construction area for a fleet of starships was daunting. She reached over to the railing for a moment to center herself. The dizzying heights hit her with a brief wave of vertigo. It'd been ages since she'd stepped foot out here. She'd need to get comfortable in these vast open spaces again if this went as she expected.

Zachary was waiting for her at the end of the gangplank extended from one of their small shuttles. From the char marks and gouges in its exterior, they'd seen battle recently. "Good afternoon, Auntie." He stepped up and gave her a hug.

She hadn't been expecting a greeting like that. Not with her head full of steam. It was an awkward hug, but she attempted to recover from it and return the welcoming gesture. He was a good kid and couldn't help if she was on a mission.

"Is everything alright?" He searched in the distance before focusing back on her, staring her in the eyes with a concerned look. "You seem out of sorts. Did something happen?"

"Of course. Things have reached a tipping point, my boy." She adjusted her shirt and tilted her head, cracking her neck. "I take it you received the Four Laws broadcast?"

Zachary squinted. "I... yea... well, I don't know. I might have. Let me check." He gestured in the air in front of him, likely digging into his retinal comm archives.

He had to be kidding. How could something like this fall by the wayside? This was life and death and could ruin everything they'd worked for.

"Ah yes, there it is. Oh... that explains that." Zachary cleared his throat. "I'm sorry, Auntie. Seems it arrived the other day when I was... let's just say a few dozen sheets to the wind."

She stiffened. "And you didn't think to review it after the room stopped spinning?"

He reached up and rubbed his hands through his hair. "I... forgot about it until now. Was there a problem you wanted to discuss?"

The hatch on the shuttle clanged open behind him, and three people walked out. Their mouths were gaping, and they whispered between each other as they glanced around the hangar.

"Wow! This place is a bewdy," the tall one said. Her name appeared on Hera's retinal comm as Pluto. Behind her were two others with similar awe struck looks on their face.

"Of course there's a problem," Hera said, focusing back on Zachary. "I wouldn't have come all the way up here if there weren't. You have to do something about Harold. He's gone off the tracks again. You and Abigail need to reign him in and shut him off."

Zachary shook his head and glanced at the others. "Why don't y'all just head on down toward the lift tube?" He gestured to the far end of the hangar. "I'll be right behind you. Harold will take care of you until I catch up."

"You sure, Z?" Pluto asked, walking up and resting her hand on his shoulder. He visibly relaxed under her touch.

He smiled. "Yep, I need a moment to chat with…" He pointed at Hera and his face turned pink. "My great-aunt. I shouldn't be long."

Pluto nodded at Hera and grinned as she and the others walked past, heading in the direction of the lift.

Hera shook her head. Now wasn't the time for flirting. They had more important things to attend to. "So, what are you going to do about Harold?"

Zachary blinked rapidly and focused his attention back to her. "I… maybe I'm missing something, but the Four Laws warning had excruciating details about an attempt by the North family to find The Wheel. They've been at it for decades, and from the looks of it, they were close. Too close. Harold brought in CoPE's special forces to clean up the mess. According to the records, the soldier's original goal was to gather intelligence. They were planning to breach the ship, extract the computer core, and leave the vessel without a drive, forcing it to be recovered by an emergency beacon. They never intended on using force until they were fired upon. Am I missing something? What would you have done differently?"

Her eyes went wide. Was he really this naïve? "I would've informed someone in the family of the North's activities. I would've—"

He reached out a hand for her to stop. "You're telling me you'd have Harold bring each and every investigation, thought, and lead of any individual who has ill intentions to the family's attention? To ask for permission to stop them?"

She nodded and straightened her back. "Yes... I would. We can't trust that he's acting with our best intentions otherwise."

"Harold," Zachary said aloud.

His voice came over both of their comms. "Yes, Master Zachary."

"How many planned, joked about, or actual attempts were made on an Olivaw life in the last month?"

"Without the latest download from my copies throughout Sol I—"

"A rough approximation will do," Zachary interrupted.

"I don't see the point of this," she said. He was getting off-topic. "You're missing—"

Harold replied over her. "There have been one hundred and eighteen thousand puns or slanderous phrases said about an Olivaw, two thousand jokes about killing or kidnapping one of us, and two hundred and fifty-six plots or continual plans to harm the Olivaw family or an individual within it. Those are only the ones spoken in earshot or embedded in the feeds I've been able to monitor this past month, sir."

Hera opened her mouth, but nothing came out. She hadn't realized there'd been that many. While the number was astounding, it wasn't the point she was trying to make. "I get it, we're not popular in every corner of Sol. I think you're missing my broader position. We need to reign in Harold as an A.I. who oversees everything. The family needs more controls in place. Better protocols to prevent him from taking a human life."

Zachary reached up and scratched his head. "Um… we're talking two incidences in over two hundred years. I'm not trying to nitpick, and I'd love to improve him, but those odds sound pretty damn good to me. How many humans have killed other humans in that time?"

"I can answer that," Harold said.

"Not now, Harold," she said, gesturing downward with her hands. "Privacy mode Eta."

"That mode is not achievable here," her comm said.

"What's that?" Zachary asked.

"Nothing, just… nothing." She'd forgotten they'd only activated that mode in certain areas of The Wheel where they could control the complete environment.

Zachary reached out and grasped her hand in his. "I'd be happy to talk with you about this again, Auntie. I honestly would. I don't like that someone died at the hands of Harold any more than you do. If you have ideas on how we can change his laws or put more safeguards in place, I'm all ears. I'm a bit tired and frazzled now, though. We only got in a moment ago, and we almost died en route."

She breathed in and shook her head. "Are you ok, dear? I didn't know."

He gently rubbed her hands. "We're fine. A bit frazzled, but otherwise fine. I hadn't registered the incident with the family yet. I wanted to wait until we got in, so I could review the telemetry. The shit hit the fan near Neptune. We had to blast our way through a strange gravitational anomaly that was chucking asteroids at us. The entire event was bonkers. We can chat after I get some shuteye. Ok?"

She should've let him get settled in before ambushing him. Zeus had told her as much, but she didn't listen. "Sure thing. I'm glad you're ok," she said as she squeezed his hand.

"Let's grab some time tomorrow before I go down for my long nap."

"That sounds like a plan. I could use more than a nap right now." He smiled and slid his hand around her back, and they headed toward the lift.

He was a good kid. His father hadn't given him all the tools nor the perspective to lead this family, and it was becoming clearer every day that neither her nor Zeus's viewpoint was accepted.

———

HERA WALKED around the sleek black cryo-pod and checked the vitals on the tablet. Zeus was deep in cryo-stasis, and everything with his pod appeared to be in working order. She slid the display into the slot on the side of the pod and a cover closed over the opening, sealing the pod shut. They couldn't risk a mistake from this point forward, and all external exposed material needed to be concealed. A small wrinkle now could put decades of work in jeopardy.

"Are you sure about this?" Libby asked as she paced back and forth by the entrance to the room. "I mean, a half a century is a long time."

Hera walked up to Libby's side and rested her hand on her shoulder. "It'll be fine. People have been doing this for over a hundred years from my research. Almost as long as I've been alive." She chuckled. "Any longer, and they had to swap out their equipment. We'll be safe down here. We're not shooting to break any records."

Libby traced a circle on the top of Zeus's pod. "Why not just move the pods down into storage? They'd be closer to me down there."

Hera squeezed her shoulder. "We want to make sure our vitals remain stable, and besides, all the equipment to revive us is here." She gestured to the apparatus lining the walls of the room. "Besides, I heard there're mice down there." She faked a chuckle. It was important that they had Libby's support for this to work. Without it, their plan would disintegrate before it started.

Libby grinned and placed her hand flat against the flat black material and then drew it back. She slowly rubbed her hands together and squinted at the surface. "Yikes, that's cold," she muttered and glanced up at Hera. "Yea, I suppose. So, I should just come by once a day and check on you?"

Hera stepped up to her pod and checked the portable power cells on the control tablet. There should be enough for a few months. Enough to get them through anything unexpected. "For the first few days, yea. After that, every few years will be plenty."

"Seriously, Grams?" Libby glanced over at her. "That long? I can come down more often. It's no bother."

She was a cute girl. She had her mother's eyes. "It's fine. Come visit as often as you'd like, dearie. We'll be here, sound asleep, but dreaming of you."

Libby rubbed her hands together and then walked up beside Hera, eyeing the controls. "And under what circumstances should I wake you? I'm sure it's in the message you sent me last night, but better to ask in person."

"Unless the place is exploding, we're to be left in stasis. And even then, it's best if you merely move the pod. We won't be much use under pressure right out of cryo-sleep anyhow."

Libby leaned forward and fiddled with the pod controls, flipping through the different screens, checking on everything. "I can't believe you're leaving me here all alone. Mom's back on Earth, and everyone else is always so distant here. They're all so focused on their research. What am I gonna do with myself?"

Hera strode over to the counter and grabbed the small pouch she'd set aside and slid it into the nook of her back while Libby was still fiddling with the display on the pod. She then grasped the gift she'd wrapped up. Walking back to Libby's side, she tapped her on the shoulder and handed her the small colorful package with the bright red bow.

"What's this?" Libby asked.

Hera smiled, and a tear slid down her face. "It's a little gift for all that you've done and will be doing for us." She pointed at the box. "Go on, open it."

"You didn't have to, Grams. I'm more than happy to look after you. Hell, you practically raised me anyhow. It's the least I can do." Libby tore through the paper and gasped when she cracked open the box. "Is this…?"

Hera nodded. "It is."

"But…" She cradled it in her hand and stroked it with her fingers. The diamonds encircling the black opal glimmered in the overhead lighting. "I can't take this."

"Oh, nonsense." Hera leaned forward and touched her head against Libby's. "It'd be yours someday anyhow. Your great to the fifth grandma Luna passed it down to her child, and they to theirs. It would eventually make it into your hands. I'm just skipping a few generations and paying it forward. Why don't you put it on?"

Libby carefully lifted the pendant out of the box and handed that to Hera before draping the necklace over her head. "Isn't it too long for me?"

"Na. I think it's perfect." She snapped the box closed and carried it over to the counter. "You can wear it all the time under your shirt if you want. If you don't, that's fine, too. My feelings won't be hurt. But do take care of it. When you think of us, give it a little rub and imagine me smiling back when you wake us up in fifty years."

"I will." A smile grew across her face as she stared down at the jet black jewel in the middle. She rubbed the diamonds between her fingers. "Shouldn't you be giving this to Abigail? I mean, she's running the family now."

"I make that decision," Hera snapped. "No one else. Not Stark or Kara. You and me, we have a bond. We always have. I want you to have it." She remembered when Michael had passed the pendant on to her. It took her thirty years to realize that it was more than a beautiful piece of jewelry. Hopefully, it'll take Libby longer. "Are you ready to do this?"

Libby sighed. "As ready as I'll ever be. Thank you, for everything. For this." She held up the pendant. "For being there for me and bringing me here. I can't even imagine what I'd be doing right now back on Earth."

"Oh, stop. You're super smart and everyone here is lucky to have you involved in The Wheel. Just keep up the good work and make me proud. We'll be awake before you know it." Hera climbed up and into the pod, adjusting her outfit and testing the space while she laid down. These things always felt tight. At least she wouldn't be conscious long enough to worry about how cramped it was.

Part of her had hoped Zachary would have agreed to disable Harold this morning at breakfast. He'd come up with some creative ideas on how to augment the Four Laws to include sub-rules that kept the family informed. He even thought about removing the family all together, but they both agreed that wasn't wise. Then no one would have any clue what Harold was up to. She made her case for the shutdown and admitted it would be challenging. While he wasn't opposed, he had projections ready for what they would need to make the changes happen. It'd take years and hundreds if not thousands of new people both reviewing data, constantly refining expert systems, and weeding out the copies of Harold throughout the system.

He said he sent the plan on to Abigail for review, but he didn't expect she'd vote for it. He truly was a talented kid and wanted the best for the family. Unfortunately, Stark had already turned Abigail on to the mental crutch that was Harold. They ended the morning with her saying goodbye and good night. She and Zeus would be dropping into stasis for a half century. They needed to get away from everything for a while to give the people at The Wheel some room. Zachary was shocked and asked her to reconsider, but they had made their decision.

Libby stepped up to the head of the pod and tapped the control panel, bringing Hera back to the here and now. "I'll record and save off all the important news, technology, and family developments just like you showed me. I can drop it off down here every few weeks or so." She flipped the small data dot in her hand. "It'd be easier to do wirelessly, but I'm fine using sneaker net. When you wake up, it'll be catalogued exactly how you want it. That way you won't need to sift through the noise of the archives or listen to Harold blather on."

The thought of Harold still being here in fifty years sent a shiver up her spine. "If not, then you can read it to me." She winked at Libby and reached up to rub away a tear on her cheek. Her skin was so smooth and youthful, not at all like her own. "I'll be awake before you know it. You keep doing you, dearie. You'll make more friends as this place expands. The Wheel needs more people like you to ensure the information keeps flowing, especially with these colonies about to come online. Your job will be more important than ever. Not everyone can depend on A.I. to do their bidding."

Libby leaned down and kissed her forehead before pulling the lid to the pod closed.

A moment later, a gas engulfed Hera's body. She reached under her back and released the small bolt gun from the waistband of her pants. Its cold hard shape hurt. Once she'd attached it to her hip, she took a deep breath, and then a few more.

The cramped space around her faded away. She smiled at the thought of waking up in a brave new world and hoped to see Libby there soon.

43

STARK OLIVAW
SOL, EARTH — 2259

S tark stared out across the frigid surface of the ice river, the colossal multi banded sphere of Jupiter loomed far overhead. Its Great Red Spot seemed to be staring at him. The drop ship had left him outside the Europan resort entrance, and he was waiting for his escort for the morning's excursion.

A shiver echoed up his spine as his suit was still adjusting his temperature. It'd been nine years since he'd resigned as President of CoPE and as the figurehead of Olivaw International. Nine years of reduced stress and far more time to take on hobbies he'd always wanted to try. Add to that, today was his ninetieth birthday, and you had a crazy coincidence of nines.

"It's a tad too many nines for my liking," Stark subvocalized.

Harold was safely ensconced in a cavity within his chest and his voice was loud inside the enclosed helmet. "In some cultures, the number nine is mythical and lucky. It symbolizes divine completeness and conveys a sort of finality. One could almost conclude death. Number history and superstitions are rather interesting."

"If you say so," he muttered. A lone figure was making

their way through the transparent airlock and waved at him. He returned their wave.

The building was stunning. Its angular spiked design matched that of the surrounding landscape. He couldn't wait to check out that heated rooftop domed pool later, after they finished the ice sailing.

Harold's voice was still rambling on in his ear. "Did you know that the Japanese consider nine unlucky because it sounds similar to their word for pain or distress? It's peculiar what humans fixate on at times. Pregnancy takes nine months and it results in life. Though, flipping the number nine upside down makes a six which the Bible correlates with the number of the beast. Honestly, I don't—"

He shook his head and sighed. "Harold, that's enough. Seriously, it's only a fraking number. Can we give it a rest?"

"Certainly, sir. I'm sorry."

A wind gust blew and shoved him sideways. He adjusted his stance to counter the unexpected breeze just as the three solo ice sailer skiffs slid up to the dock. Their sleek sporty cabins rested atop dozens of tiny, impossibly thin control blades that guided them along the icy surface. When their doors swung upward, it became clear they'd been driven here on autopilot.

A tinge of regret swept over him at the sight of the third skiff. He'd planned this trip with Kara as a twins vacation and birthday celebration. They'd turned the day into an annual event since he'd semi-retired, but she'd come down with something last night and was spending the morning in orbit aboard the Jurat before venturing down to the moon.

He'd given Abigail and Bradley guilt trips about not being here, but she was neck deep in company business and he was on a colony isolation training excursion. And then there was Zachary. Everyone believed he was a few months into his mission heading to Epsilon Eridani, so he couldn't make it, either.

He sighed. Alone wasn't all bad. He'd still have fun.

The guide that had been approaching from the resort building walked up beside him. "Good morning, Mr. Stark," a woman said. "Name's Hilo. They're beautiful, aren't they?"

He glanced at her, taking in her slender curvy body. She wasn't too thin, and her suit hugged her in all the right places. He swallowed hard and turned back toward the skiffs. The last thing he wanted was to be distracted by his teacher's sexuality. He was about to risk his life on the ice and needed to stay focused. "They're remarkable. They look fast. I bet they could go forever out here." He tilted his head toward her.

"Oh, they are," she smiled and winked at him through her helmet. "But not too fast. You really should take your time out here, feel all the bumps and hit all the river's curves. It's the only way to experience the best of Europa."

Was she flirting with him? He shook his head. Cut it out, Olivaw. "Task at hand," he muttered. "Task at hand."

"What's that, sir?" Harold asked.

"Nothing," he subvocalized. "I was just talking to myself. You know, nerves and all."

"That's strange. Your body's showing indications of being aroused. If I didn't know better, I'd say—"

He reached over and squeezed his left wrist, disabling Harold's connection to his ear. He'd had that little kill switch installed years ago. Sometimes he needed to be alone without the distraction of an A.I. that knew too much for its own good.

"Shall we?" Hilo asked.

He nodded and shook his entire body, willing himself to focus. Riding the ice rivers and tunnels on Europa had been on his bucket list for centuries. "Yep. Let's do this!" He pumped his fist.

The silvery transparent shell of the solo ice skiffs was mesmerizing. He couldn't wait to get inside. The idea of watching the deep blue ice of the ancient Jovian moon streak by beneath his feet was exciting. He should've done this years ago.

He took a step forward toward the skiffs and the ground lurched, tossing him down hard. His elbow smashed into the edge of the walkway, and he rolled onto his stomach. A thunderous crack echoed through the air and Harold flashed his retinal comm, demanding his attention. A message streamed across his peripheral vision.

Subterranean quakes nearby. Please enable your comm so I can advise you.

What the hell was going on? This was a geologically stable section of Europa. They'd never recorded a quake at this site before. It was what made it perfect for a tourist attraction. He reached over to his wrist to re-engage his comm and everything went blank. His vision cleared and his ears were warm. Like the implants were overheating or something. He suddenly realized the same warmth was coming from his chest, where Harold's sphere was.

He stood up and spun around to face Hilo and took a step backward. The sailing skiffs were gone. They were replaced instead with liquid water in a massive arc cut through the ice. Somehow, the kilometer deep ice near the dock had melted. He instinctively reached over and squeezed his wrist again, but nothing happened. Harold and his entire retinal comm were dead.

"Are you ok?" he shouted as he offered a hand to Hilo. She was sitting on the ground.

"I… I think so." She brushed off the gray brown dust from her suit. "What the hell is going on?"

He reached up and rubbed at the warmth still lingering in

his chest. "I don't have the foggiest idea. Are your comms out?"

She pressed her finger against the side of her neck, attempting to activate her comm. "Dead as a Saturn five rocket. My suit's environmental systems are out, as well. We've only got a few minutes of oxygen. We should head inside."

Something must've happened below ground or in orbit. He glanced skyward, but didn't see anything other than Jupiter's mesmerizing swirling clouds and that damned red spot. When he turned toward the resort building, his eyes went wide. "Shit!"

"What?" Hilo spun around and reached a hand out for support, almost as if she were falling.

There, before them was the resort. Its lights were out, and gasses were being vented from multiple leaks throughout the structure. He could make out people inside, banging their hands against the glass as they struggled to breathe. They were dying in front of them, exposed to the elements of Europa.

He studied his surroundings. Everything was dark, and nothing was moving across the entire complex. All the robots roaming the grounds and bioengineered gardens were immobile, and there wasn't a drone in sight.

Surely, someone would come for them. They'd know something was up and send help. He just needed to find somewhere to hunker down until they arrived. Somewhere that had oxygen. He reached a hand out and tapped Hilo's shoulder. She was still staring slack jawed at the people inside dying in front of her. "We need oxygen. Do you know where they store the emergency supplies?"

She didn't respond. She merely stared, her face white with fear.

"Hilo!" he shouted. "I need you in the here and now. I don't know my way around. Where's the oxygen stored?"

"Be… behind the agri-dome," she mumbled. "Down below ground. For safety."

"Alright, let's go. Come on." He waved his hand for her to follow him, but she was frozen.

He'd have to leave her if she didn't move. He reached forward and grabbed her hand, pulling her along, and then it hit.

The sky opened up and everything went white. He screamed, his voice a chorus alongside the same agony Hilo was experiencing. His skin felt like it was boiling off and his vision turned yellow. He instinctively reached toward his face, but the helmet was in the way.

What was happening? Every movement was met with excruciating pain.

He collapsed to the ground and gasped to breathe, but there wasn't any air. Whatever heated his suit must've ruptured the seals, and all of his oxygen had vented out. As he rolled onto his back, his arms flopped at his side. He couldn't move them any more. It was as if his muscles had given up.

The orange bands of Jupiter hung overhead, its Great Red Spot still staring at him, wondering why he was lying there. The swirling clouds seemed to smirk at him, snickering at his situation. He could make out what looked like drop ship jump jets far above, minutes away.

His entire chest burned, fighting for the gas of life that was nowhere to be found.

He wished his last words to his children hadn't been a guilt-ridden message over his silly birthday. All he longed for was one last hug, one last smile. One last…

44

ABIGAIL OLIVAW
SOL, EARTH — 2260

She stood overlooking the cliff, watching a small grouping of deer linger in the fields far below. They were barely visible in the light from the setting sun. Their brown heads bowed down to eat some leaves and twigs in the tall grass, and then they shot up again when they'd heard a noise. It might've been the wind, but more than likely it was the parade of ground cars departing the funeral. That or something below ground spooked them.

The breeze picked up and bent the sweetgum and pines against each other. Their branches rattled and rubbed together, making an eerie echo through the woods.

Abigail felt a hand on her shoulder. She glanced over and made eye contact with Bradley. "Is Kara ok?"

He nodded and stepped forward. "Aunt Shelby and Cousin Libby helped her down the hill. She wanted me to stay back with you. Are you..." He didn't finish the sentence.

She crossed her arms and sighed. Leaning her head into his shoulder.

Bradley followed suit and leaned his against hers. "That speech, what you said about Dad, it was... perfect. I couldn't have done what you did. I wouldn't have been able to do it without crying uncontrollably in front of everyone, especially Aunt Kara."

She reached up and wiped tears from her eyes with a tissue. She had to hold it together. Even just a little longer. "Thank you," she muttered. "I tried writing something but it didn't feel right. So... I winged it."

He leaned back and took a step away, staring at her. "Seriously? You winged that? Even the parts about us camping?"

She smirked. "Of course. Don't you remember all those nights we used to camp out up here, or down there in the valley?" She pointed down toward where the deer were flocking.

"Some of them, yes, but not that much detail. Not like you do. We only came here in the spring or fall, when it wasn't unbearably hot outside." He kicked a rock and it toppled down the hill, bouncing and ricocheting off the cliff face the whole way down.

"Remember how Dad's allergies used to act up out here in the woods?"

She smiled and they both laughed. Salty tears ran down her cheeks and touched her lips. Memories of swimming in the ocean near Charlotte shot through her mind.

The volume of his breathing changed as he turned around, shuffling his feet in the stones like he used to do as a kid.

"What're we going to do with all these chairs? It'll take all night to drag them down the hill."

"Don't be daft," she said, turning to stare into the clearing. "We paid someone. They'll be here in the morning to haul it all off."

"And what about D..." He raised a hand upward and wiped at his eyes.

He couldn't say his name. She reached over and grabbed his hand in hers and gave it a squeeze.

"I'll bring his urn with me. Why don't you head to the

house? I'll be down in a bit. I want some time alone with him."

"Ok," he muttered. Taking a few steps forward, he paused and turned. "I loved him. I love all of you. More than I let on at times."

"I know. He knew," she said with a smile.

"I just couldn't stand all the stories about our ancestors' trips to Antarctica and the alien nonsense. If they were real, we'd have—"

She shook her head and raised her hand upward.

"Sorry, shit." He kicked another rock and it shot across the ground, over the cliff's edge. The noise of it bouncing off the rocks below echoed through the valley.

"I can stay," he said a moment later after the echoes subsided.

"No, it's ok. Go down and help Aunt Kara."

"No, I meant here in Sol. I can stay and help with the family."

She laughed out loud. Tears were staining her all black outfit. "You'd be fraking miserable and you know it. You've never wanted the Olivaw burden on your shoulders. No, please. Follow your dreams. Dad would've wanted you to. I appreciate the offer, though."

Bradley nodded and sighed. He then turned and ambled down the hill, stopping from time to time to bend over and pick up a stone to throw.

Abigail walked over toward the front row of chairs and grabbed two of them, pulling them closer to the urn on the pedestal. She spun around and sat in one of them.

"I wish you could tell us what the frak happened down there on Europa, Dad." She rubbed at her eyes.

"H?" she said.

"Yes," Harold replied in her ear.

"Do we have any news on the investigation?"

"Nothing yet, Madam. There were no remains of my copy

anywhere in the wreckage. Something fried the electronics for a hundred meters around the point of impact. Completely and impossibly melted. I've never seen anything like it. The middle of the second impact was perfectly circular and your father was dead center of it. Even his retinal comm was slag. It feels premeditated, but there isn't a gram of evidence."

"What about your coating from your implant? Shouldn't that have protected you?"

"No, not really. The material can bend active scanning tech, but it's not strong enough to withstand whatever hit Europa. There wasn't a millimeter of salvageable technology anywhere in the blast radius."

She clenched her fist and her knuckles cracked. "This doesn't make any sense. We haven't been fighting with anyone since... since Warren North's appointment as Mayor of Epsilon. We'd been purposely taking a low profile. Instead, we've been focusing on the broader mission rather than the insane drama of politics. Who'd want to take out Dad? And hell, had Aunt Kara been feeling any better, she'd have been there, too. Then they'd both be..."

She leaned forward and started bawling. She couldn't hold it back. Not any longer. Everyone was gone, she'd held strong as long as possible. Right now she needed a good cry.

A branch snapped off to her left, and a moment later the nearby grasses rustled. She sniffled and tilted her head to listen into the breeze. Footsteps were coming up the trail.

"I was wondering if you'd make it," she said over her shoulder as she reached up and wiped at her face.

The footsteps came faster and stopped behind her before she felt a hand touch her back. "Sorry. I had to wait for Bradley to leave. I've been here the whole time, watching from off in the woods."

Abigail patted the chair next to her. "I pulled up a seat for you."

Zachary walked around the front of her and paused close

to their father's urn. "It's beautiful. The black with a field of stars... it's fitting. I don't suppose it's made of—"

"No," she interrupted. "That'd be silly. Someone might notice."

He nodded and reached a hand up to stroke the surface of the urn. "Who the hell did this, Abigail?" He turned in place to look at her.

"I... we don't know."

"How do we not know something? We have eyes everywhere. We have a fraking all seeing A.I. that should have been at his side. I'm sure he's here now. Right, Harold!" he shouted.

Abigail reached up and grabbed at his hand. "Shhhh! You're gonna get someone's attention. Bradley might come back up."

"Frak him. I'm tired of hiding. I wanted to be here. He was my father, too." Zachary pulled his hand from hers and wiped away a tear.

"I know he was. But everyone who isn't me or Harold thinks you left for Epsilon Eridani. Do you have any idea what a shit storm that'd cause if people found out you weren't?"

"I don't care... I'm so... argh!" He stormed a few meters away and then stopped. "You know this whole situation is off, right? This is like those asteroids that tried to kill me a few years ago. It made about as much sense as this did."

"We'll keep digging into it. For now though, we need to say goodbye to Dad."

She heard his heavy breathing in the darkness, and then his feet kicked some rocks as he turned back toward her. He paused behind her, sniffling.

"I miss him, too. You're not mad at Dad, you're mad at the situation." Abigail shifted to face him. His blue eyes were bloodshot and his face was a mess of dirt and dust. She let out a little chuckle.

"What?" he snipped.

"You… look like you camped out in the woods for a week. Is that mud on your chin?"

A smile crept at the corner of his mouth, and he reached up to wipe at his face. He stared at his hand. "No, that's moss from the tree. You try quietly hiking up the side of the blasted hill without sounding like a herd of elephants. I haven't been in this much gravity in years. And those thorns? Whose idea was it to plant thorns down there?" He pointed down the hillside.

She shook her head. "They're natural, you nit."

"Well… I don't see their purpose. And damn if they don't hurt like the dickens." He rubbed at a tear on his trousers where there were a few dots of blood visible on the fabric.

"You never answered my question," she said.

He sighed and walked around the other side of the chair, collapsing into it. "I'm not mad at him. He didn't die on purpose. It's this whole situation. I just… miss him. He was… my sounding board from time to time. I knew I could count on a random message to show up, to spur me on. On the way here…" He paused and wiped away a tear. "A comm came through from him. He was joking around like old times and was asking lots of questions about my research. I…" He didn't finish that sentence.

Abigail reached over and grasped his hand, leaning her head on his shoulder. She closed her eyes and exhaled, listening to the breeze blowing the trees from side to side. Birds chirped nearby in the darkness along with an intermittent tap tap tap sound of a woodpecker deep in the woods. Someone was looking for dinner.

Zachary broke the silence. "You're not going to ask about the research?"

"No."

"Why not?"

She lifted her head off him and wiped at her eyes. She

then reached out and hit him on the shoulder with the back of her hand. "Because I don't care, you nerd. Our father just died. The last thing I care about is your blasted research. Don't be a workaholic like he was. You need a life outside The Wheel."

He chuckled. "Says the single female who hasn't had a date in years."

She whacked him twice more on the shoulder. "I'm your big sister. You do as I say, not as I do."

He smiled and sighed. "Ok, so… what do we do now?"

She didn't respond right away. There were so many competing thoughts flying through her head. The company, her family, the colonies. She didn't know where to begin.

"We start by taking one step and then another. That's all we can do. Pretty soon we'll be running again. It'll take a while, but it'll happen."

45

BRADLEY OLIVAW
SOL, EARTH — 2260

This place, this house, this land was both his favorite and least favorite place in the universe. It was the root of so many of his fondest childhood memories, and at the same time the cornerstone of why he'd taken a path less traveled. One far different than his siblings. At the heart of it all was his father, and now he was gone. The void of the loss was vast.

Bradley kicked at the rocky path he'd walked a thousand times. Countless hikes and hide-and-seek sessions with his sister and brother. They had spent untold camp outs on or about this trail near their small country house.

He reached down and grabbed a handful of stones. One at a time, he chucked them into the darkness.

Toward the river, they landed with a splash.

Toward the rocky ravine, they clanged and echoed into the night.

Toward the grasses, the sound of ground animals and likely a few pheasant fluttered in the darkness.

None of them were prepared for the crash of the stone, but only the animals felt the pain of the crushing blow. A tinge of regret scratched at his heart. He didn't mean the animals any harm. This was their home and he was blowing off steam.

The backyard was just past this corner, and their house was visible through the small grove of trees. "I don't know if I want to come here again. Not for a long while," he said aloud to himself.

"That's understandable," someone said from the darkness.

He spun around toward the source of the voice and took a step backward. "Who's there?"

"It's me," Aunt Kara said, stepping out of the shadows. Her cane wobbled and sank into the grasses before finding a steady spot to support her. "I had to get away. Too many people asking me if they could help. I needed some space to think."

"Can I help…" he reached out, but thought better of it. "Never mind. You're feeling stronger, right? At least you're up and moving about now. The doctors said that whatever you'd caught had passed."

"I'm fine. Thank you for asking. Ask me again though, and I'll whack you with this stick." A smile crept across her face and she reached a hand out to him.

He grasped it and led her onto the path. He then tucked his hand under hers for support and started toward the house.

She stopped and pulled at him. "No. Let's stay out here. Walk around a bit. It's good for my muscles. Doctor's orders."

He chuckled. "Yea, I don't want to go inside, either. Too many back patters and tears. I just need to—"

"Walk it off and think," she interrupted. "You're a lot like your father that way. Any time he got angry or needed to reflect on something, he'd go for a walk. Stark always said he got some of his best ideas walking around in the dark."

"I suppose," he muttered. He'd never thought about the habits he'd gotten from his Mom and Dad. He'd always imagined he was his own person, but perhaps there were a few common traits beyond the Olivaw temper.

They turned and started toward the path encircling the house, heading in the direction of the garden. It was overgrown with wild plants and a sprinkling of sweet gum trees, but he remembered when it was full to the brim. Dad hired someone to clear the place one year before their visit. They spent that entire spring seeding and taking care of the plants as they grew. Lettuce, tomatoes, carrots, peppers, strawberries. You name it; they had it growing in the dozen or so raised beds.

Now, moss and wild grasses covered the rocky walls of the beds with a few weed trees sprinkled for effect. Everything was overflowing the edges of the once bountiful garden. It reminded him of their family at times. Their once tidy and happy family unit was now littered with the reality of the unkempt world.

"What ya thinking about?" Aunt Kara asked, giving his hand a squeeze.

He reached up and pulled a spiky seed capsule off the sweet gum tree overhanging the path. "Planting this garden with Dad. What was that, fifteen years ago?" The sharp edges of the infertile seed poked the skin of his fingers.

She nodded slowly, staring off into the distance. "I remember hearing about that. I think I was still in France with Douglas and Floyd. Your dad sent me videos every few days. Remember, we visited toward the end, before y'all left for the year?"

"Yea." He let go of her hand and tore open the seed capsule. "You never saw the garden at its peak. It was overflowing everywhere. We spent most mornings out here tending to it, picking the crops for the day's meals. It was peaceful being out here with Mom and Dad. He'd work at night when he thought we were sleeping, but being out here during the day with him was…"

She reached up and placed her hand on his shoulder. "I miss him, too. I should share some of those videos with you. He was so proud of you kids, of you in particular. Talked my ear off about how smart you were. Of all the things you were gonna do someday."

He shook his head. "I failed him there, didn't I? I haven't amounted to anything."

"Cut it out!" She yanked on his shoulder and spun him around. "You're only twenty-nine. You have decades ahead of you. Hell, you're still finding yourself, venturing out into the solar system your own man. I envy you."

"That's funny. I don't think anyone's ever said those words to me. I'm the black sheep of the Olivaw family." He tore out a few of the tiny seeds from inside the pod and tossed them into the garden. They probably wouldn't grow anything without being fertilized, and he had no idea how that even worked.

She laughed out loud. "We're the same, you and me. Me, outcast from the family business and, you, well, you never ate the poison apples from the tree."

"The what?" He spun to face her.

"Nothing," she shook her head and stepped forward toward the middle of the garden. There was a massive black rock and a circle of chairs around it. She sat into one of them and began rubbing her foot.

"No seriously, what did that mean?" He walked over and sat next to her. "What was so bad about the family business? I know I didn't follow that path, but Abigail and Zachary are up to their necks in it. Hell, Zachary took the company to Epsilon Eridani with him to broaden the corporate umbrella to a new star system."

"Let's just say there's a lot of baggage." She was staring upward at the twinkling stars in the sky.

"I heard that all the time growing up." He bent down and picked up a piece of black stone off the path. It was a shard from the massive rock statue of a wolf in front of him. "Do you remember this rock? Dad used to spend hours pacing around this thing at night, talking over his comm to people worlds away."

She glanced down at the black wolf standing on the mound and then returned her gaze toward the sky. "That's one of Grandpa Harold's stones. He had it brought back here from Antarctica on one of his many trips there over the years. Said it was from—"

"His first trip, where he almost died," Bradley interrupted. "Dad used to tell us the story all the time. I remember Abigail and Zachary would stare at him in awe every time he told it. Hell, we camped out here on this path so many times I can't even count them."

"Didn't you believe the story?" she asked, staring at him.

He shook his head from side to side. "It's a story. Like all fairy tales, there are meanings in them if you search for them. But no, I didn't believe in it any more than Alice in Wonderland. I just... I didn't see the point in bringing this rock back. I mean, why does someone need a reminder of how they almost died? I strive to live in the moment, not in the past."

"We can learn a lot from the past. We can learn what mistakes not to make. About whom we hurt, so we don't do it again. About—"

"I get it." He shot up and waved his hands as he started pacing around the rock. "We all try to do those things, but a ten ton reminder seems a bit much."

"Fair enough. Not all reminders need to be this huge. Sometimes they can be smaller." She tapped her cane against the lone wolf. It didn't make a sound.

He nodded. His dad had always been his rock. He accepted him back, no matter how they'd last departed. No matter what words were said, or how loudly they'd been screamed. Every time he'd failed, his dad took him in and helped him get on his feet again. And now, well now he was alone. No one was there to help him back up.

He rubbed the flat black stone between his fingers. Its deep dark surface was dull and didn't reflect much light. As he rolled the odd shape in his hand, he squeezed it and a pain jolted him. It had a sharp edge to it that cut into his skin. It was a paper thin cut, but it stung. The stone was a reminder. Sometimes things were smooth and painless and others, well, other times they hurt like hell.

Sometimes they can be smaller. Aunt Kara's words echoed in his mind as he rubbed the stone and then slid it into his pocket. It was a small reminder. A reminder of his father and everything he'd pushed for him to become.

BRADLEY WAS ALMOST HOME. He was on the last leg of the trip to Ganymede, and they'd just left the traffic controlled space of Ceres. The unsightly pock marked dust gray surface of that dwarf planet was behind him. Another day, and he'd be back to the grind on Ganymede, training and preparing for the Tau Ceti mission. Dwight would be happy he was back. From the sounds of his messages, he'd been up to his ears with design changes for Bradley and his engineering team to implement. When his team thought they'd finished a project, Dwight would go back and change one of the parameters to make it better or more optimized. It was infuriating.

"Our stewards will be making their rounds with refreshments and food for purchase shortly," the announcer said overhead. "Our ETA into Ganymede Station is just under sixteen hours. If you wish to not be disturbed, remember to close your privacy hatch and turn on the do not disturb light. Thank you for flying Sol Spaceways."

He reached up and pulled down the privacy hatch, double-checking the do not disturb light was on. The last thing he needed was another gawker eyeing him like during the previous leg of the trip. He hated finding his image making the rounds in the social net. Then that happened a few years ago, it'd taken months to get things back to normal. Apparently, people found a video of an Olivaw snoring in a chair entertaining.

A few hours of shuteye, and he'd be able to work through the changes from Dwight, or at least get an idea on how much work they'd be. These pods were a bit too constricting to do much virtual work. He always ended up whacking his arms and legs against the walls.

He closed his eyes and tried to clear his mind. So many thoughts were competing for his attention. He just wanted everything to return to normal. Aunt Kara was in excellent hands on Earth, and he'd promised to keep in touch. His sister, well, she was a big girl and had never needed his shoulder during all this. The closest they'd gotten was the huge bear hug she'd given him at the spaceport. She almost seemed sad to see him go. Almost.

An audible chime beeped in his pod. Someone was outside and wanted his attention. The do not disturb was on. Why the hell weren't they respecting it? If he pretended he was asleep, maybe they'd go away.

The chime beeped again and followed with a light knocking.

He sighed. "What the frak?" He reached over and drew downward on the release lever, raising the hatch upward. "I didn't want to be—"

"I'm sorry to disturb you, Mr. Olivaw," the steward said. They were glancing left and right, and their hands were shaking. She leaned in and whispered. "The pilot asked me to come back and fetch you. She needs your help with something. Would you mind following me?"

He tilted his head. That's not a normal thing you hear on a commercial spaceliner. Why the hell would a pilot need him?

"Sure, I guess," he whispered, pushing up and out of the cramped pod and stretching his back. "Lead the way."

The steward was walking in front of him, guiding him down the tight aisle toward the front of the ship. Everyone except for a few random people had their privacy hatch down. The rest were getting comfortable and were resolved to not sleeping or perhaps didn't like the cramped space within the pod itself. Either way, no one gave him a second look.

When they reached the pilot hatch, a teammate joined the steward. They both entered some ridiculously long codes to confirm and double confirm the door open request and finally rested their hand on the tablet beside the door. It flashed green after it identified each of them. Then they both turned and stared at him.

"What?" he asked, turning to see if someone was behind him. Nope.

The steward who fetched him smiled. "You need to identify yourself before the door will open. The pilot has specifically requested you, and only you enter." She gestured toward the tablet on the side of the door.

He shook his head and reached out and pressed his hand on the icy surface of the tablet. A second later it went green and the hatch slid open. The screen displayed a simple message:

Access Granted: Bradley Olivaw

"I guess that's my cue." He slowly stepped forward, glancing left and right into the space in front of him. He'd never been in the cockpit of a commercial spaceliner before. He wasn't sure what he was getting into.

The cabin was quite nice. There was more room up here than the first class quarters below deck. He supposed the airlines had to treat their pilots well with how long they were away from their families. Especially given the antiquated Inner and Outer Ring laws that the unions put in place, demanding that humans pilot all commercial ships that had more than five occupants aboard.

He stepped forward past the sleeping bunk and a two person dining table. The pilot's chairs were behind a simple door. Nothing as complicated as the last. When he reached it, he gave it a light rap with his knuckles.

"Come in!" the pilot shouted from the other side. "I have my hands full."

He slid the handle aside and the doorway released, pivoting outward to reveal the cockpit. Inside was a lone figure in one of the two seats. She was furiously gesturing toward the control panel in front of them. Her hands were a whirlwind of motion. It wasn't until they turned their head that he realized he'd seen the pilot before. They were the gawker from the first leg of the trip. The one that had been staring at him for nearly an hour.

"Shit," he muttered. He didn't need this crap right now.

The pilot glanced at him briefly before returning her attention to the controls in front of her. The red from her control panel cast an eerie glow on her face. "My name's Captain Klein. I'm... sorry to bother you, Mr. Olivaw. I was... hoping you could help me with a problem. You're some type of engineering genius, right? I mean, that's what everyone says online."

He squinted at her. She was scared, like something wasn't going her way. Her short blond hair was wet and matted down in places and she was sweating. This couldn't be good. "I know enough to get by. What seems to be the problem?" He glanced toward the controls in front of the second empty seat. The panel was showing the same red the pilot was seeing.

He leaned in. "What the hell are you doing?" The primary

thrusters and the engine core were redlined, and the pilot was in the middle of dumping it.

"I've tried everything else," Captain Klein said. Her hand was hovering over the eject button. "I don't want to jettison the core, but if we don't do it soon, it'll meltdown and take us out with it. We're only a few hours out of Ceres. I'm sure they can send someone our way pretty quick."

"So, whatcha need me for? Seems like you have the situation under control." He swallowed hard. If this is what she called under control, he'd hate to see the alternative.

She glanced sideways at him and then back at the rising temperature levels on her screen. "I... was hoping you'd be able to diagnose something. You know, work some of your Olivaw magic. The whole thing makes little sense. One second I'm about to engage the impulse drive and the next we're redlining. I hadn't changed anything."

He sighed and slid into the pilot seat beside her and pulled the control panel closer. There was no point in standing there. "Hasn't the expert system diagnosed the situation yet? That's what these things were designed for."

She gestured toward her controls and shared some data with his screen. "It went offline the moment the core overheated and has been ever since. I've never scored great without an expert system. Passable, but not stellar."

Well, that's confidence building. He flipped through the screens. They weren't too different from the ones he was used to. Dumbed down, but otherwise pretty close. "How long've you been piloting one of these?"

"I'm three months out of school," she said. "I was supposed to be shadowing for another six, but I'm sure you know how the union walkout's been going."

"I can imagine." He hadn't been paying much attention to the news lately. Sorta had bigger things on his mind with his father's passing. He finally got past the down simplified menus and brought up the main diagnostics screen. From the looks of the data, the expert system was disabled the moment they passed out of traffic controlled space. The timing was suspect. "Have you seen any mention of pirates in these parts?"

She shot him a look, her eyes wide. "No! Why? What did you see?"

"Nothing specific. The timing just seems off for the expert system going down. I suggest you alert the crew and prepare the passengers in case we can't get this under control."

She continued staring at him in silence for a few seconds before she began subvocalizing orders to the crew. A moment later the lights overhead flashed and a cool and calm computer controlled voice spoke. "All passengers should don their emergency environmental suits in the outer storage compartment of your pod. Please remain calm. We're asking that you do this as a precaution, but to do so as expeditiously as possible."

He didn't see anything out of the ordinary in the core diagnostics beyond an MIA expert system and rising temperatures. "Have you checked the external sensor arrays? Are you seeing anything unusual there?"

She shook her head. "I... hadn't thought to. I mean, why would that matter?"

"If it's not a problem inside the ship, then it's outside." He flipped through the screens and shook his head. "Is this all we have, these few sensors?"

She leaned toward him for a closer look. "Yes, that's it. I'm pretty sure the expert system had access to more, but we've never had to use them."

He cracked open the raw external input sensor array. It was a wall of noise if you didn't know what you were looking at. One by one he shut off the useless data. He was trying to see if something outside the ship was influencing the internal systems.

As stream after stream of sensor data was disabled, an

image began to form. On the screen were several controlled pulses of energy being directed from above and below the ship. It didn't make any sense. Above and below only meant one thing.

He brought up the external cameras on his controls and shared them with Captain Klein. "Can you help me review these? We don't have much time. We're looking for anything at all that's unusual."

There were hundreds of cameras on the outside of a ship this large. They were usually only used during docking procedures but could be activated at any time. One by one he flipped through them, but nothing appeared. Nothing but empty space.

"What about this?" Captain Klein asked, pointing at her controls. She swiped to the right, and the camera popped up on his panel. The image was from above their ship.

He leaned forward and squinted. "What am I seeing?"

She adjusted the contrast of the image and a huge shape appeared out of the background noise. It was blocking the light of the stars beyond it and was far larger than what he'd been looking for. "That's another ship, right?"

"I don't know what else it'd be." Captain Klein continued to scan through the external cameras. "There aren't any docking guidance drones out here in these parts. Hell, we don't usually see another artificial object until we get closer to Jupiter. From the looks of this, though, we have an unwelcome guest below us, as well." She shared the second camera image with his controls. "What do we do now?"

"Let's try something." He brought up the external drone controls and ejected a small inspection drone from the port side of the spaceliner.

The drone's camera appeared on their control panels. He piloted it up the side of their ship and then paused before taking it too far. There was no reaction from the dark ships above or below them. Time to take it to the next level. He directed the drone upward.

Captain Klein exhaled loudly. "I have to eject the core. Another few minutes and it'll be critical."

"Give me a second," Bradley said. "I want to see if we can get their attention. Maybe they'll cut the power they're beaming at us." He continued guiding the drone upward. He was about halfway there, and he still couldn't make out anything on the surface of their mysterious visitor.

Suddenly the camera cut. They'd lost the signal.

"Shit," he muttered. "I think they know we see them. Any chance we have some armaments on this thing?"

Captain Klein laughed out loud. "You're kidding me, right? Sol Spaceways doesn't believe in using force. We're easy targets for pirates, but can usually outrun them with these Olivaw drives. Somehow your family has managed to not sell any to the bad guys."

He chuckled. That was good to hear. The problem was, they couldn't engage the drive and outrun these pirates if it's overheated. "I assume you've already expunged the atmosphere and exposed the core to the vacuum of space?"

"Yep, that was the first thing I did. It dropped the temperature a bunch, but didn't stop it from rising. We've got ninety seconds max. I need to eject this thing to ensure it's a safe distance from us before it blows."

They'd be sitting ducks out here without a core, especially with no weaponry. He turned to face her. "Whatcha say we give them a hello message?"

She smirked at him. "I'm not sure what you mean, but I like how you're thinking. Just tell me what to do."

He dismissed all the open screens and brought up the navigation controls. "I assume the core will eject out the bottom of the ship?"

"Actually, no." Captain Klein brought up an exterior image of the spaceliner and where the core would eject. "It's out the top on this model. The bottom was a legacy design from terrestrial aircraft that allowed a core to be ejected without hitting the tail wings or vertical stabilizer of a ship."

He nodded. "I didn't know that. We'll need to adjust the yaw and pitch before we eject the core. I'd like to use it as a missile to—"

"Launch it at our friends!"

"Yep. Are ya up for it?"

"Fraken aye! If Sol Spaceways won't give us our own defenses, then I'm up to improvising. You control the ejection and I'll pilot." She transferred her core controls to his panel and reached forward before glancing at him. "We've got forty-five seconds. I'm ready when you are."

He took a deep breath and studied the controls. "I figure the core will take about fifteen seconds to make it to them. Last thing I want is a ricochet, so we're gonna cut it close. We might even take some damage ourselves."

Captain Klein reached forward and tapped her panel, opening a ship wide comm. "Everyone strap in and make sure your suits have a seal. We may lose our environment. We have some visitors topside we're trying to shake. Last thing we want is a boarding party. Good luck to us all!" She cut the comm and gave him a nod. "Adjusting launch angle."

The ship pitched its nose downward in an attempt to bring the core launch trajectory on target with the ship above them. They didn't have a way to get an exact target lock, so the entire thing was on feel alone.

The safe distance countdown clock was ticking down in the corner of his controls.

Thirty seconds.

"Take off a few degrees," he said. "You adjusted too far."

"Gotcha." She tweaked her controls.

Twenty-five seconds.

He reached toward the panel, held his shaking hand above the eject button, and took a deep breath.

"There's a lever under the middle of your chair. Once you eject the core, pull it out. It'll engulf each of us in a protective climate controlled bubble. We'll be able to see each other but won't hear each other unless we use our comms."

Twenty seconds.

He reached forward and felt for the lever. It was directly in the middle of the seat where she said it was.

Seventeen seconds, close enough. He tapped the eject button and a clang reverberated through the ship.

"Core ejected! Core ejected!" the computer warned over the ship wide speakers. "Take safety precautions."

He glanced toward her and nodded before pulling the lever. He'd never seen a commercial pilot safety encapsulation executed before, so he wasn't sure what to expect. A massive airbag deployed from the console in front of him and engulfed him and his entire seat before somehow latching tight behind him and pulling snug. It then repeated the same thing with two more layers, all in five seconds. By the time it finished, he was cocooned in a climate controlled pod, safely ensconced in multiple layers of transparent nano-polymers that could sustain tons of impact damage before breaking.

The final seconds ticked by slowly as he waited for the blast to rock their ship.

Five seconds.

Captain Klein shared another camera view with him and opened a direct comm. It was from the ship's exterior. The core was receding into the distance, the jettison thrusters burning away from them. "It's still on target. We should see—"

And then it happened. The black object above them blinked. It wasn't much, but one moment it was black, and then a faint blur of white rippled down its surface. The ship disappeared the moment the core breached.

Two seconds later, and the spaceliner shook with the destructive force of the explosion. The cockpit ceiling tore away and his control panel flashed with dozens of breech alarms. Multiple sections of the ship had lost atmosphere, and some were offline entirely.

He closed his eyes and reached into his pocket, feeling for the rock. It was there where he'd left it this morning. The smooth surface was flat against his leg. "I love you Dad, but I'm not ready to join you. Not yet." He took a deep breath and held it for a few seconds before letting it out. "I only hope fate is on my side today."

The cockpit lights around them blinked and then went out. Scraps of metals and polymer flew inward from the force of the blast. His chair lurched forward as something substantial smashed into him. The control panel flashed a yellow warning informing him the first of the protective layers ensconcing him had been breeched. He dismissed the message and confirmed the other two layers were holding strong.

Within a few moments the chaos subsided, and they had a clear view of the stars overhead. The flimsy room they had been sitting in had been decimated by the explosion, but the explosive effects of the core were quickly squelched without oxygen to burn. All that remained were the twinkling pinpoints of distant suns.

"You ok?" Captain Klein asked.

"As good as I can be." He turned toward her. Her face was smiling back at him through their bubbles.

"So, that was fun." She laughed a nervous laugh before focusing on her controls. "It looks like the second ship below us took off. They're not on any of our sensors, but we're blind topside. The cameras were blown into smithereens."

"And the passengers? How many—" he didn't finish the sentence.

"Comm checks are still coming through, but..." She swallowed hard. "We lost four pods, but only two had occupants. All in, we lost three people and saved eight hundred."

He shook his head. "Wait! How'd we lose three if only two pods were lost?"

Captain Klein didn't reply straight away. She took a moment to compose herself, and he swore she was wiping at her face, but the debris on the outside of her bubble made it hard to tell for sure.

She eventually turned to face him again. "It was... a mother... and a baby. They were in a pod together."

"Frak!" He screamed as he slammed his hands repeatedly against the pilot chair. "That's not what I meant, Dad! You should've taken me."

46

HAROLD

SOL, OORT CLOUD — 2260

Abigail was watching the waterfall cascade down and crash into the water at the bottom of the eight meter drop. She tilted her head as if thinking about it. She then leaned in and squinted at the pond itself.

"It's not like on Earth," Harold said. "The gravity here is half what it is back there. Fluids behave quite differently under reduced force."

She nodded. "I figured it was that. But it's weird, I swore I saw something in the water staring back at me."

Harold brought up a recording of what she'd seen. "You mean this?" He outlined in green a dark area near where the falling water met the pond below. There appeared to be a branch of some sort floating, unencumbered by the churning water and somehow stationary.

"Yes," she muttered and pointed with her hand, as if that'd help him see what he'd projected in her eyes.

Harold chuckled. She used to do that when she was little, pointing at things she alone could see in her retinal comm. "That's an alligator. We brought them here last year. Something to change up the diversity of life in the closed environment. The biologists and zoologists were keen on it. They claimed to have seen stressors in the enclosed biome and felt they could counter it with more diversification."

He never told her about the new species of animals they'd brought into The Wheel. She hadn't visited her morning spot in several years, so the idea never occurred to him. It was strange how something he knew as a matter of fact was somehow mysterious and scary to others.

"They're hideous creatures. It always feels like they're mulling over how to attack me." She shivered and stood up, collecting her dishes as she did.

"I'd hazard to guess they're in fact doing that. Thus the term, predator."

Abigail walked her dishes over toward the overhang they'd built into the observation area of the Canopy. It was a favorite outdoor party and relaxation spot at The Wheel.

She slid the dirty dishes into a receptacle, and Harold watched as they were hauled a few meters away, cleaned and made ready for the next use. The spray of high velocity water that washed away food particles flowed through multilayered filtration units that separated the debris and decomposed it into its constituent parts for use elsewhere in The Wheel. It was a balancing act of recycling out here in the middle of the Oort Cloud.

He returned to Abigail's live feed from her retinal comm. He fast forwarded through what she'd seen the last few minutes while he'd been focusing on the recycling. It only took a few nanoseconds to process the data. He regularly let his mind wander like this. He found it helped him remain sane to focus on minutia in the immense volume of data within his reach.

This same thing was happening thousands of times per second in all the computational cores that made up his consciousness. The act of merging and making sense of all those wanderings and focused thoughts was what made him sentient. Or at least that's what he felt.

Abigail entered her father's old office and the door closed behind her. It was a sparsely filled space. Stark wasn't one for physical mementos or tchotchkes. He'd always preferred experiences and memories over keepsakes.

Harold brought up the plan for the Tau Ceti drive swap on the wall screen.

Abigail glanced up and sighed. "You're trying to keep me on task, aren't you?" She wheeled up a stool into the middle of the room and sat down and spun in circles, sticking out her arms and legs as she whirled around.

Harold's mind went pink. Watching her smile and relax felt good. If such a translation of color and feeling could be made to an artificial life form.

She stopped abruptly, straightened her back, and began tilting her head from side to side, looking over the data.

He hadn't seen her do that in ages. She used to play with numbers that way. "To make them more fun," she'd told him once.

Abigail reached up and scratched her neck. "So… we're faking an incident a year into the mission. This looks like a collision based upon the sideline projectile vectors I'm seeing."

"Correct," Harold said. "A micro-meteor collision. We were going to beam back some fake sample data to Sol to make it seem more real. The protocol for a large enough collision is to disable the drive and dispatch automata to repair the holes."

She stood up and gestured to zoom in on the wall screen. "And our intercept team should be in place by then?"

"They'll be launching four years before the Tau Ceti starship."

"Four years! That's insane," she said.

"The intercept will be coming in from a steep angle that isn't visible from Sol. They launch away from Sol using the first contract superluminal drive and then reposition for an intercept route. Once they're up to a speed ahead of our subluminal drive, they'll drop out and coast. Then they'll be using specialized ion thrusters for course adjustment and deceleration to match the trajectory of the colony ship. It'll take years to perform that maneuver."

Abigail gestured and brought up the intercept ship design. It was massive, but purely in a functional way. "Not pretty to look at, is she?"

The picture showed a chain of spheres interconnected by omnidirectional thrusters. At the head of the chain was the superluminal drive and a small crew habitat.

"Not in the slightest. The design allows for fifty cryo-pods and emergency rations, but otherwise, it's all about the reaction mass required to power the ion thrusters. It's crude technology, but it's impossible to detect at great distances."

Harold brought up a list of crew members. "There was one other item I wanted to talk to you about."

Abigail turned and scanned the list, recoiling in surprise. "What's Aunt Kara's name doing up there?"

"You remember your conversation with her at your father's funeral?"

She squinted and shook her head. "Vaguely. That was a... stressful day."

"Understood. I know you remember how two years ago she'd lost her husband and child to a quake in the Alps?"

She nodded. "Yes. It's hard to imagine losing three Olivaws from the same generation so suddenly. And her entire family at that."

Harold brought up an actuarial table on the wall screen. "The risk of dying from an earthquake was one in thirty thousand. The risk of two family members dying combined with your father's death of similar unlikely causes a few years later, well let's just say it's improbable. Add to that the events around both of your brothers's attacks and I'd hazard to guess that someone is targeting our family."

She sighed. "I don't understand what this has to do with the intercept mission or Kara."

"I'm sorry. It doesn't. It's merely one of those tangents my many copies of me gets stuck on trying to explain these accidents and protect the family. Anyhow, my reason for bringing up her family's passing was the depression she's been under ever since."

"Oh?" She paused and stared downward. "No one ever mentioned she was depressed. I didn't know."

"Did you conjecture that she wouldn't be? I mean, she lost everyone close to her. Combine that with your father's recent death, and you can imagine her mental state."

Abigail swiveled on her stool, watching the ground pass by as she stared at it. "Well, shit. Now I wish I'd talked to her more when we were together. You... should've told me." She stopped spinning and looked up. "I should've known."

"You had a lot on your mind. It's no worry. I've spoken to her dozens of times since then. During our most recent conversation, she mentioned a strong desire to join the Tau Ceti colony. She realized she was almost past the age, and didn't have much to offer other than money, but wished she had a way to make the list."

"She's practically ninety-one, Harold."

"And the cutoff is one hundred. She'd miss the date by three years by the time the colony ship departs. She'd still have fifty solid years of time to help the colony. Her perspective could be invaluable."

Abigail stood up and arched her back. "I need to walk. Let's continue this conversation later."

"Very well."

Abigail exited the laboratory and took the lift up to the hangars. She stopped and had a few random conversations with some engineers, a chipper young pilot named Pepper, and then headed toward her brother's research wing. After she passed through the security countermeasures, she walked in.

The room was a mirror of the previous hangar, except this one was nearly empty. There were two small prototype ships under construction near the entrance. The first resembled a gigantic contact lens, and the second had a shape resembling a thimble. Both had strange concave designs with intricate wiring and cabling dangling from all the surfaces.

"Yo, Zach!" she shouted. Her voice echoed through the massive chamber.

Harold watched as Zachary lurched and almost dropped the tachyometer he was holding.

"What the heck?" he shouted. "You bout gave me a heart attack. I'll be there in a minute."

"You know you could've called him on your comm," Harold said.

She smiled. "Yea, but where's the fun in that?"

Zachary walked up and brushed off the metal shards that were clinging to his jumpsuit. "Sup?" he muttered, nodding his head upward.

"First reaction. Don't pause to think. I'm going to ask you a question and just tell me yes, or no."

"No, I'm not setting you up with Brice." He smiled.

She swatted his arm. "Cut it out. This is serious."

"Fine. Lay it on me."

Abigail nodded. "Ok. Should we send Aunt Kara to lead the intercept mission to Tau Ceti?"

"Yes."

She tilted her head and squinted. "That... was fast. You didn't hesitate."

He shrugged. "You told me not to."

"But why? I mean, why would she be a good candidate?" Abigail leaned against the wall and crossed her arms.

Harold watched as she glanced down through the floor grating. He'd dispatched a few tiny robots to cleanup the scraps of metal Zachary had brushed off moments earlier. Recycling everything was their only option.

"Why wouldn't she be?" Zachary asked.

She looked back up toward him. "No, I asked you first. I'm not saying she wouldn't be, but your answer… it was just so matter of fact."

Zachary held up a finger and started counting. "Well, first of all, she ran the family for a long time so she knows how to keep a secret. Second, she wants nothing to do with politics and this couldn't be further. Third, she fraking lost everyone close to her. Minus us, of course. Didn't you see her at the wake? She was in shambles. I know you sent Aunt Shelby to escort her down the hill, but from my point of view in the woods, Aunt Kara wasn't doing so well. Fourth—"

"Ok, ok. Enough. I get it. She'd be perfect. I'm just a stone cold bitch, I guess. It hadn't even registered with me she was in that bad a shape."

Zachary walked up and grasped her hand. "Sis, come on. Cut yourself some slack. I have no idea how you held it together that day, hell, that month. You kept everyone moving, and that speech you made for Dad. I don't know how you did it." He bent down and stared up at her eyes to make her see him. "No one blames you for not noticing every little thing. Now stop beating yourself up over this."

She smiled and sniffled. Reaching up a hand, she wiped away a tear. "I suppose you're right."

"Harold," she said.

"Yes."

She brushed her hair out of her face. "Zachary and the zoologists are right. We need an alligator."

Zachary frowned and a blank expression crossed his face.

"I fail to see the correlation with what Zachary just said and—"

"Send Kara," she interrupted. "You're right. She's a perfect fit, and we could use more diversity on the mission.

She'd bring some perspective to the colony that few people could. We could also use a trusted leader on the intercept ship. Bring her to the Wheel. She should start preparing."

"I'm not sure I'd call your aunt an alligator to her face when she arrives," Harold said.

47

INSPECTOR DRAK

SOL, PLUTO — 2260

The amber cryo-liquid drained out of the chamber, and Drak opened his eyes. His antennae shook. It moved independently and seemed to search the space above his head for something. Small wings extended from his back and began flapping. They were too small to impact his enormous form, but they acted as a tool to vibrate the remaining liquid from his body.

He stepped out of the chamber and paused before the Bynaury wall screen. "Status," he said.

"We've reached a dead-end in our investigation."

Drak pulled a thin tube out of a receptacle below the screen. His maxillae parted, and he extended the tube toward his proboscis, slurping the revitalizing nectar from within.

"What happened with your second strategy to force an emotional response in the humans, to intimidate them into helping us? I believe you were planning to target the Olivaw collective?" He retracted the nectar tube and brought up the mission logs on the screen.

"Their response was not the same as the North collective. Where the Norths resulted to turning on the opposing collective, the Olivaw reached out and supported each other. I

believed I had one of their members close to breaking, a Kara
Olivaw. We killed her immediate collective and her only
offspring. She was mentally spiraling when I killed her
brother Stark, hoping the final blow would be enough, but I
must have miscalculated the impact of her brother's death. I
was about to approach her when she disappeared."

Drak's wings momentarily buzzed. "How did she
disappear?"

"She fell deeper into a depressed emotional state after she
was summoned to her brother's funeral. A month later, she
boarded a transport bound for the human planetary body
named Neptune. Her signal and all traces of her vanished en
route. I've dispatched several exploratory drones, but have
been unable to locate her or the transport she was using."

He reached up and stroked his maxillae, cleaning some
pollen from its tip. "Is it possible they have Galactic Alliance
stealth technology? We wouldn't be able to track them if they
did."

"As a species, their application of stealth is primitive.
They aggressively pursued it through the late twenty-first
century until their Antarctic A.I. War. After millions died
during that time period, it became criminal and socially unacceptable to use it."

"You mentioned you made other attempts with the
Olivaw collective. How did they all fail?" He wiped the
pollen from his maxillae and popped it in his mouth. The
taste fluttered his antennae as the sensation flooded his senses
with beautiful colors.

"Each attempt to kill an Olivaw resulted in a surprising
display of ingenuity and teamwork. Where the Norths were
easy prey with shriveling family members and guards, the
Olivaws were cunning and highly resourceful. They even
managed to destroy one of our scout vessels."

His antennae stiffened and jutted toward the screen.
"Were we discovered? Was the mission compromised?"

"Negative. We recovered the remains of our ship before they detected it a short distance from the incident. The Olivaw named Bradley was able to capture a visual record of the ship's outline, however, their analysis and media believed it was a Sol Pirate."

His wings flapped gently. "A pirate?"

"Apparently, they're a rogue collective of humans that prey on space vessels when they're at their weakest. They loot and pillage them for supplies and then rape or kill the human occupants."

Drak gestured to bring up the status of his comrades. "These humans are repulsive and should've been exterminated millennia ago. It seems we've reached an impasse. Should I awaken others to confer or do you have other avenues to explore?"

"I suggest we relocate to their Epsilon Eridani star system. Perhaps we can ascertain more once we're there. It's possible they've employed stolen technology at that location. We should also have reasonably unfettered access to examine their colony construction and prepare our monitoring for their arrival."

"Very well. After we've arrived and you've learned anything new, then wake me and another crew member. I would like the council of a peer at that time. In case we've made no inroads."

The yellow gas had already begun spraying as he stepped into his cryo-chamber.

48

HERA OLIVAW
UNKNOWN — 2261

Hera brought her hand up to her mouth and coughed as the gas cleared. Where was she? Who had woken her up? She brought her hand down to her hip and rested it on the handle of the blaster as the lights dimmed. Someone was standing over her.

"Are you ok? Can you hear me?" A male voice said. He sounded shallow.

"Sorta," she said. Her mouth was dry, like she'd been chewing gravel.

"Let me get you some water." He spun around and stepped toward a nearby sink.

The sound of running water snapped the room into focus. She sat up with a jolt, grasping the pistol in her right hand and training at the back of the man. A wave of nausea crashed into her, but she held the firearm steady and reached out with her other hand to support herself.

The room was nondescript. Like any random cramped space anywhere in Sol. Something must have gone wrong. She'd expected to be awoken somewhere else.

The man spun around and then jumped back, crashing against the counter behind him, spilling the water down the front of his khaki outfit. He released the globe of water, and it dropped to the ground with a thunk and rolled away as he raised his hands in the air.

"Auntie, what are you doing? It's me... Parker," he said. His eyes were wide and his hand was shaking.

"P... Parker?" She shook her head. "It can't be. The last time I saw you... you weren't any taller than my knee."

He smiled and stepped forward, carefully reaching out and resting his hand atop the gun before guiding it safely downward. "So much has changed while you were in Sol, and since you decided to join us. We have a great many things to show you."

"Where's Zeus?"

Parker gestured in the air toward the wall beside them, and it sprang to life. There on the screen was the most beautiful sunset she'd ever seen. Two stars were just above the horizon and a third was peeking up over the edge in a sea of blue sky and purple white clouds. Standing in the middle of it all was Zeus. He was wrapped in a blanket and staring into the distance.

"Papa Zeus has only been awake a few minutes," Parker said. "He said he needed some air. I hope that's ok. I figured it couldn't hurt."

Hera smiled and reached out to grasp the young man's muscular arm as she stepped down and out of the cryo-pod. "He's always been in a hurry that one. Sometimes we need to be patient to get what we want."

49

LYNC MICHAELS

EPSILON ERIDANI, LIPROSUS — 2272

The viewport shimmered and the approaching Inner Ring soldier in full battle armor faded in and out. She shook her head. Her nerves were getting the better of her. "We can take them, Dad. Are you ready? Where's my exo-suit?"

Lync glanced around the tiny capsule her family had built decades ago. They used it to transit to Ceres for supplies and whenever they attended the coming of age ceremonies. It barely had enough room for her parents and her. There certainly wasn't space for an exo-suit.

"Is it below deck in the hold?" She spun to face him.

"Hey, Lightning!" His back was toward her, facing the controls. "I hope you get this. The shit's hitting the fan outside and I don't know if I'm going to make it out of here. I didn't want to—" He flinched as an explosion echoed in the background and shook the capsule.

The sound of flying debris from the planetesimal pinged the capsule's outer shell. She didn't know where, but she'd heard her father make that speech before. She reached toward his chair and the room shimmered again and went black. What the hell?

"Major Michaels, open your eyes," a voice said.

Their voice wasn't familiar and everything was dark. Faint rustling was coming from her left. She lurched to the side and hit something or someone, scrambling to find their neck. Whoever it was, they were going to regret trying to take her family capsule.

"Ple… ase stop. Open… your eyes," the voice said, struggling against her hands around their throat.

Lync opened her eyes slowly. She hadn't even realized they were closed. She'd remembered the lights in the capsule going out, but that made little sense now that she thought of it. The light from outside the planetesimal would've been shining through the exterior windows.

The room she was in was bright, and the glow covering the ceiling was far too brilliant. She released one of her hands and brought it up to cover her eyes. Somehow she'd ended up in some type of medical bay, or something worse.

She turned her head rapidly side to side and finally back on the man beside her. His neck was in the vice grip of her left hand and his fingers were prying her grip apart enough to breathe. "Where's my father?"

"You… were asleep," he began, "in cryo-stasis. Do you remember? Major Michaels, you're at Epsilon Eridani. Please… let go of me."

She released her grasp on him and brought her hands up to rub her eyes. Everything was blurry, almost like she was seeing the world underwater.

"Hold on a second," the cryo-tech said, turning toward his control panel. "Your vision will come back in a minute. Just don't push them too much, you'll damage your eyes. For some reason, your hormones are completely out of whack. Your regulators in the cryo-pod weren't picking it up, but your numbers are…" he froze and then turned to stare at her.

She brought her hands down and squinted at him. "What is it?"

The tech swallowed hard, rubbing at the purple markings on his neck. "Were you dreaming while you were under? I mean, do you remember anything?"

She took a deep breath and closed her eyes. "I remember being at the Academy and taking the fraking exams. I remember an unfortunate mission out to the Oort Cloud and losing my first team member. I remember... being in a capsule with my father. It was right before he died. It was strange because I was never there." She leaned forward to look at him.

"None of it was real. Well, some of it was likely from your memories, but it wasn't real. Most people don't dream in stasis. They have memories of blackness sometimes, but nothing more. A few, however, like yourself..." He coughed and forced a swallow, continuing to rub his throat. "A few remain awake and in a dreamlike state for the entire voyage. It's hard to imagine what it must've been like being conscious like that for over thirteen years. And these numbers."

He spun back and squinted at his control panel. "Your DNA seems to have mutated. I don't know how, but we should perform some tests. We need to make sure nothing else changed, and that you didn't get a cancer or worse."

Shit! Her blood. He was seeing the changes in her blood. The circulator must've run into problems. "I'm sure it's fine." She waved her hand. "Nothing a nap in my room wouldn't help."

He reached out toward her and then flinched. "I can't let you—"

"How about I walk around a bit and find my legs?" She smiled at him. "I can come back in a few hours for a checkup. Couldn't hurt, could it? Maybe you can calibrate your machine while I'm gone."

He nodded and rubbed at his neck. "I suppose it'd be ok."

She reached out and rested her hand on his shoulder. "Perfect. Say, I'm so sorry about that mark. I didn't mean anything by it. I have some sweets in my locker I brought along. Perhaps you'd enjoy one. You know, as an apology." She winked at him.

"That… sounds great. I understand. You weren't yourself. And like I said, I can't imagine what you were going through." He reached out and tweaked something on his console and kicked off some type of calibration procedure. A countdown filled the screen. "We'll get to the bottom of this when you come back. I'll have the whole gamut of tests ready."

"It's a date then." She hopped down off the bed, her legs wobbling a bit.

"Careful!" He reached over and put his arm around her. "You haven't walked in over a decade. Everything's gonna feel new again."

"That sounds like fun!" She winked at him.

He chuckled and his face turned pink. "That's the post-stasis hormones talking. Though I'm flattered, it's against protocol for a doctor to see a patient outside of work within three days after stasis. I'm required to say that. But if you still think that sounds fun after three days, you know where to find me. My name's Bruno."

"Bruno. What a nice name." She nodded and smiled. Her legs were feeling better by the second. "Let's see where we're at in a few hours after some sweets. I'll catch you soon." He pulled his arms away, and she continued unsteadily out the open doorway of the cryo-stasis room, reaching her arm toward the wall in case she got dizzy.

She reached up and squeezed the tip of her ear and her retinal comm activated. Its crisp interface and text sprang to life on her retina, like the first time she'd had it installed. He wasn't kidding. It really did feel new.

"Plot out the fastest route to my quarters," she subvocalized.

The computer answered her with a glowing trail along the

ground, weaving its way down the halls of the starship. It estimated she'd arrive in three minutes.

As she worked her way through the pristine ship, she couldn't help but wonder where everyone was. She hadn't seen another person besides the technician since she'd left cryo-stasis. "Overlay nearby crew members on my map, please."

A few dozen names overlaid on her comm, singling out the colonists closest to her. Along the top of her vision were the population totals. There appeared to be almost two hundred people out of stasis, a far cry from the ten thousand they'd left with.

She reached up and rubbed her nose. It'd been running for nearly a minute now. She needed to adjust to the smells of this ship they'd been cooped up on for over a decade. It was weird though; it smelled like citrus.

Her quarters were at the midpoint of the ship. They tried to spread out the security personnel throughout the general population in hopes that it would prevent pockets of malcontents.

Rounding the corner toward her quarters, she stumbled out of the way of a floor cleaning bot. It was spraying a foamy orange liquid behind it that expanded to the edges and disappeared into the tile within seconds. That would explain the aromatic smells in the hall. Turns out her schnoz wasn't broken after all. They must be giving the place a nice wash before everyone woke up.

She walked up to the door outlined in a green glow on her comm and the entrance slid open, welcoming her home. Just inside the three meter by two meter space was a simple bed leaning up against the wall, two chairs, a table, and a pile of crates in the middle.

First thing's first. She spun around and depressed her hand on the security panel and the door slid closed, locking from the inside. As the door sealed and the room fell into silence, she realized her heart rate was elevated on her retinal comm. She was seconds away from finding out if her trip here to Epsilon was about to be a dead end or a new beginning, and her nerves were giving her away.

The large crate on the bottom of the pile was the one she was looking for. The labels on the outside indicated that food and plants were inside. It was a ruse, of course, but her storage tech contacts in Sol assured her it'd give her the most latitude to avoid random inspection. No one wanted to spoil family heirlooms and plants in cryo during the voyage. She'd paid handsomely for this crate and the safe transport of what was inside.

One by one she moved the top crates onto the table and one of the chairs. It was like a puzzle moving in such tight quarters. Finally, she reached the bottom of the pile. The faint white strobing light of the lock in the middle of the lid marked her prize.

Her heart skipped a beat, and she sighed when she saw it. No one appeared to have messed with it during the voyage. If they had, it'd be flashing yellow, or worse, solid red. Win number one.

She closed her eyes and pressed her palm on the surface of the lock. Pain shot through her hand as a needle broke her skin. She pushed against it, forcing it deeper into the meat of her hand. Her goal was to force it past her artificial blood glands, deep into her real blood supply. She only had two chances at this. If it failed twice, it would destroy the contents inside.

The lock glowed orange for a moment until she leaned forward and laid on the surface with all her weight, resulting in a bright green glow and the confident click of the latches. She rolled off the lid and shook her hand.

"Frak," she muttered. She'd need to adjust the sensitivity of that thing. There was no way she could do that all the time. She was inside. Win number two.

The lid of the crate was calling her, willing her to open it, but she hesitated. It all came down to this. If the blood was still viable, then she'd be able to continue with her life as she'd planned. If it wasn't, then all hell would break loose. She wasn't prepared for that. Not after all she'd sacrificed to get here.

She squeezed her hands; her knuckles cracking like a bag of chips. They hadn't been popped in over a decade and felt strange. Like it was new, or she wasn't in her own skin.

"Rip it off, Lightning," she muttered.

Reaching forward, she lifted the lid up and off the crate. The smells of her clothes and other personal effects wafted into the room and teleported her back to Sol. Images of the friends and colleagues she'd left behind, farewell parties, and her father's smiling face sprang to the forefront of her mind.

The first level of storage automatically rose up and brought her into the here and now. As the layer slid to the side, it revealed a middle compartment in the heart of the crate. Smaller compartments encircled it on all sides. There in the heart was a huge square cube with several tubes attached and a display that was shutoff.

She reached down and touched the display, feeling the prick of the security system testing her DNA and nanites deep in her finger. The screen sprang to life, its green glow bringing a smile to her face. An unseen weight lifted off her shoulders.

Green was good. Green was what she wanted. If it had been any other color, she'd have been screwed. She exhaled a long breath as she reached forward, pulling the gloves with the tubes attached to them out of the crate and sliding them on. Once they were comfortably in place, she pressed the transfuse button on the display.

The cube sprang to life and a quiet hum permeated the room. Blood rose toward the gloves and down the other side as the life giving liquid was pulled from the storage membranes beneath her skin. It was being replaced with the clean blood cells necessary to become the person she wasn't. The person she'd met in the bar on Jupiter nearly thirty years ago.

While she'd escaped many of the lies in Sol, her biggest had followed her here, light years away. She'd tried to swap the DNA before they left, but the price and risk was too high. Here, however, things would be different. She'd need time, and she'd have to make the right friends, but she knew she could do it.

She reached around her back and the tubes of blood attached to her hands fought her movement. The plastic hadn't been stretched in years and preferred to be coiled tightly together. She lifted her shirt and removed the thin membrane she'd been lying on for so many years. Her skin beneath screamed in thanks, finally able to feel the cool air of the room against it like the rest of her body.

The reservoir of blood was designed to help her subcutaneous membranes circulate during the voyage. Microscopic injections over time were supposed to keep her the person she was pretending to be and prevent the telemetry of the cryopod from detecting any change. Faking out those stasis circulation computers only required a fraction of a percent of her blood supply, but this device had failed.

Scientists had always expected some degree of cellular mutation during their trip, but if she was too far out of whack, they'd flag her as unsafe. Hell, if they looked close they'd notice hair color changes, skin pigment, etc. She didn't want that attention. She'd lose her job and get relegated to scut duty, or worse. She could end up as the first Liprosus colony prisoner.

"Fraking waste of credits," she said as she tossed the membrane into the open crate.

The damage was done, and hopefully this afternoon after she'd passed some tests and had some fun flirting with

Bruno, she'd be in the clear. He was actually really adorable. Not exactly her type, but still cute.

The blood she'd brought along in the canister was already somewhat mutated closer to her own. It'd take another ten years of constant recalibration to get her regular blood into circulation, but with microscopic changes over time she could pull it off. Everyone was expecting mutation in a new world, and she was planning to take advantage of that.

Resting on the top tray of the crate was her small family blanket. She'd carried it everywhere when she was little. Her father told her that her mother had made it by hand. He'd purchased some special dyed cotton in Ceres for her, and she made it for her crib. It'd cost them a fortune but, her mom had to have it.

She laid back on her bunk, bringing the blanket to her chest and then brought up her messages on her retinal comm. She had made a few friends in Sol before she'd left, but for the most part her closest friends like Crayo had come along on the voyage. Her message queue was sparse, especially for over ten years of not reading it. She blinked through the pages of random musings she'd come back to later and found one that caught her attention from Abigail Olivaw. It was encrypted for her eyes only. She gestured to open it and her video comm played.

"Hey Lync, Abigail here. I know you won't read this for quite some time, but I wanted to thank you again for helping me and my family. When I first met you, you reminded me of someone and it wasn't until you left that I realized who it was, my Aunt Kara."

Abigail glanced past the drone, her eyes staring at something more distant. A memory, perhaps.

"You might remember her as a former President of the Confederation, but I remember her as a tenacious and driven woman who didn't take shit from anyone, even from my father. She had a penchant for taking things head on, even if the goals were uncertain. Without her, CoPE wouldn't be where we are today. Despite much of the colonization being attributed to my father, she worked tirelessly to build the foundation of support for colonization both during her presidency and for decades afterward. She thought we didn't notice, but we did. I did."

A smile crept across Abigail's face, and she stared down at her hands before returning her attention to the drone.

"Anyhow, I wanted to thank you for helping my family and the colony. You know your mission and you've already made huge inroads to get close to Warren. Keep an eye on him, he's a slimy bastard. His entire family is. Hell, except for Joyce, you're sorta surrounded by slithering leaders. I've never been that fond of Steve Ericsson, but my father trusted him so…"

Abigail shrugged and silence hung for a moment.

She'd only ever seen hints of this side of Abigail before. Whenever they'd talked in the past, she'd relax the longer they were together. Usually toward the end of their conversations or meeting, she'd become the most vulnerable before disappearing back into her shell.

Abigail sat down on a couch. From the looks of it, she was in her home. There were pictures of her family lining the walls behind her. Hundreds of candid shots were drifting across the wall. Once she was comfortable, she spoke again.

"Your colony's adventure is only beginning and you're making history. Stay safe. Stay strong. And most of all, stay alive. I'm confident our paths will cross again."

Abagail smiled and nodded one last time before she cut the comm.

Their paths would cross again. What did that mean? How could that possibly happen? Maybe she was planning to come to Epsilon some day, to settle down here.

She shook her head and closed the message. Why did Abigail warn her to stay alive? Besides the alien planet, she hadn't imagined that someone would want to kill her. Perhaps she had more preparing to do than she'd thought.

Her door chimed. She turned to face the source of the sound, and the name of the person outside the door appeared on her retinal comm.

Director Steve Ericsson

"Frickety frak," she muttered as she sat up and tore the gloves off her hands, tossing them into the crate. She threw a few of the knickknacks she'd retrieved back inside and yanked the first layer into place. The servos of the automatic motors whined in complaint. She then pulled the lid on and closed the lock. Finally, she took the clean clothes she'd fetched from inside and draped them over the top, being sure to cover the lock. There was no point in making him suspicious.

She spun around to face the door and checked her reflection in the display. The birthmark on her neck was well below the collar of her outfit. The last thing she needed were stereotypes following her here to Epsilon Eridani. She'd worked too hard to be here.

Her heart was pounding, and she needed to get it under control. She closed her eyes as the door chimed again, louder this time, and took a deep breath and began counting down from ten. When she hit zero, she opened her eyes and reached out and pressed the button to open the door.

"Yessir!" she said as she saluted Director Ericsson.

"What took so long?" Steve asked. "I was about to unlock it myself."

That would be a jerk move, and he knew it. First impression, and he was already acting like the ass Abigail had warned her about.

"Sorry, sir," she began. "I'm still a bit disoriented. They only woke me up around ten minutes ago. My vitals are off, and they need me to return for tests in a few hours. I wanted to walk about and find my bunk. You know, see if the movement helped. How was your sleep, sir?"

"What? My sleep? It... was fine." He shook his head. "We have more important things to take care of than idle chit chat right now. I need some help preparing for the colonists to wake. There's gonna be some pissed off people when they find out we can't move planetside for a few years, and we have to prepare for the worst. I need you in a meeting in ten minutes. Can you be there, or should I wake someone else to fill in for you?" He furrowed his brow.

He was testing her, looking for a reason to demote her before they'd even started. She wasn't about to give him an excuse. "No, sir. I feel much better. I'll let the officer in cryo know that—"

Steve gestured in the air with his hand and interrupted her. "Done! I pushed it to tomorrow. Report to Security Ready Room One in ten minutes. And Major, welcome to Liprosus!" A smirk crept in the corner of his mouth as he nodded at her and then strode away.

She exhaled and relaxed her posture before reaching forward and closing the door. "What an asshole," she muttered as she turned and started adjusting her cabin. She checked the subcutaneous blood storage numbers in her retinal comm. They'd only managed to get to forty percent. That should be plenty for a while.

Whatever she did, she couldn't give him any excuses to demote her. She'd have her hands full keeping him happy and still staying on Warren's good side. Plans on how to accomplish this began brewing in her mind as her stomach rumbled.

"Shit," she muttered and spun around, exiting her quarters toward the galley. She needed to grab something quick to eat and head to this fraking meeting. No way in hell could she work without food in her belly.

50

ZACHARY OLIVAW
SOL, OORT CLOUD — 2272

The blackness of space had always been soothing to him. Not at first, of course, only after he'd grown up enough to appreciate its beauty. When he was little, he was so scared of the dark that he used to run through the habitat turning lights on as he went. He didn't want the monsters attacking him from the shadows.

"You're getting too far ahead," Shauna said. "I asked you to stay behind me."

"I'm fine," Zachary said. "This exo-suit is armored to the nines. Anything gets in my sight and I'll take it out with this..." He glanced down at the rifle in his hands. "Whatever the hell this thing is. I've played enough vid-sim games to know how to aim and pull the trigger."

Shauna walked up next to him and reached out, disengaging the safety on his rifle. "Might wanna turn it on, champ. It's called a Nemesis IV, and it has a killer kick when you squeeze the trigger, so I suggest you lean into it."

Discussing the recoil effect of a munition wasn't something he'd planned for this trip. He'd taken a few days leave from The Wheel and headed out to his mother's tomb. He'd been hitting dead end after dead end in his research and needed some time alone to think.

When they got close to the planetesimal where their family habitat and cavern was located, their visual scans picked up an anomaly on the surface. It was on the far side of the massive rock and resembled a Blazer Dragonfly shuttle. The top of the line starship was a competitor to the Olivaw Shuttle line but was neutered without an Olivaw drive. So even though they were competition, Olivaw made out on every sale, which included their drive.

He glanced to his right and then left, unsure which of Shauna's humanoid forms he should address. Frak it. He'd ask them both. "And you're sure you didn't detect our Olivaw drive inside that thing? I mean, it'd be easier if we—"

"Negative!" Shauna interrupted. "It would've shown up on one of the many frequencies we monitor. Even the military drives have ways for us to detect them. No, whatever is powering that shuttle isn't one of ours."

Her tone was snippy and muted. She was still pissed they were out here. It'd taken him an hour of arguing, but he finally just ordered her to let him take a closer look. He'd have to remember next time that the Four Laws engine was designed around humans giving orders. And she wasn't actually his mom. Out here, he could order her to do what he wanted.

"It's over this ridge, so stay sharp and stick to that copy of me." Shauna's second humanoid form on his left took off in a perpendicular direction from them.

He paused and watched her disappear over the edge of a crater. "Where're you going?"

"I'm taking that chassis in from another angle in case we're overpowered or someone attempts to flank us. I'm not putting your life at risk any more than I need to. Stop staring at that version of me!" She nudged him with her elbow. "Eyes forward on the field of battle."

Field of battle. The irony wasn't lost on him. He'd come out here to relax and think, and instead he'd been met with some well-funded fraking pirates or claim jumpers trying to pillage his family's tomb. Nothing pissed him off more than people not earning their keep in life. Taking something that he hadn't earned was counter to everything he'd been raised to believe in.

The depths of this particular ironic conundrum hit him like a ton of bricks the more he thought about it. His family had stolen their tech from a probe they'd found, and yet he didn't condone theft. It was one of the reasons he refused to continue down the path of his ancestors with their pillaging of superluminal drive technology from the alien probe. He'd instead forged his own path, researching alternatives to faster than light travel.

He strode behind Shauna, being sure not to block her line of sight. This exo-suit was almost fun to wear. He couldn't imagine making this trip in the environmental suit he'd started to don before Shauna had a conniption and practically tore it off him. She'd refused to let him go into the field of battle without some protection. Mothers were always being motherly.

They'd left their stealth ship behind with Shauna's data cube and original copy running the show. It shouldn't be detectable to anyone parked in the shadow of a nearby crater. She then cloned herself into each of the humanoid chassis, escorting him around the planetesimal. They'd merge everyone back into one consciousness when the excursion was complete.

Shauna ducked down and approached the boulder in front of them, making sure to keep it between them and the unknown shuttle. He kept her between him and the boulder and came up behind her as she peeked her hand around the side for a better look.

The image of the camera on the end of her finger appeared

on his retinal comm. The Blazer Dragonfly shuttle was a sleek cruiser with a design that reminded him of the classic sci-fi novels he'd read as a kid. It was all form with little function, at least that's how Olivaw's marketing team described them. He had to hand it to the Blazer designers though; it was a sexy shuttle. He'd stolen some ideas from it for a few designs he was making himself.

"Looks like no one's around," he said. "Should we—"

"Hold on," Shauna interrupted as she moved her finger and zoomed the camera in toward the rear of the shuttle. Her voice still had the irritated tone from earlier. He'd be hearing about this excursion for months.

"That's not one of ours or one of Blazer's," Shauna said.

He squinted at his retinal comm. He'd been so focused on the sleek exterior of the ship and checking surrounding area for movement that he hadn't noticed the drive on the back of that thing. It was a strange design he'd never seen before.

"We need to get a closer look. Can we come around without being detected? Maybe we could backtrack to this ridge?" He brought up the maps on his comm and shared it with her.

"I'm already ahead of you," she said, panning her finger camera down the rocky terrain. There on her video was the other Shauna, working her way up to the backside of the Blazer ship.

He shook his head. "How'd you know she'd be there? I thought we were under radio silence."

"We are. I didn't realize I was there. But it's what I would've done if you weren't here, and I saw her moving closer on the other tight-beam camera angles from our bots. You're only seeing one vantage right now. Humans are limited in the number of things they can monitor at one time."

"If you saw her, then that means—" He accessed the menu of camera options on his comm and brought up a few addi-

tional views. Sure enough, the ramp on the Blazer was raising, and the ship was preparing to depart.

Frak. They'd been made. "Did you give away your position on purpose, so they'd leave?" He stepped out from
behind the boulder and laid on the ground, splaying wide to
get stability as he raised his rifle.

"Of course I didn't," Shauna said. "I have no idea why my
copy moved into view. We can ask her later. Right now, what
the hell are you doing?"

"Trying to stop them." He trained the rifle on the rear of
the rising shuttle, toward the section of the drive they could
see. The targeting system on his exo-suit came online and
went green when he rested his finger on the trigger.

Here goes nothing. He squeezed the trigger, and the
weapon recoiled like a donkey defending its territory. The
blast of controlled plasma hurled across the expanse and hit
its mark, tearing off a chunk of the tail section.

"What the hell," he muttered.

The drive was intact, but it was glowing red. While the
plasma hit its mark, it hadn't finished the job. The shuttle was
continuing to rise skyward.

He pushed up off the ground to get a better angle and
leaned against the boulder to steady his aim. He then raised
his rifle and snapped off several more shots in quick succes-
sion. The first few hit the same spot he was aiming at earlier,
but the last one missed. The ship zagged to the right, getting
smart to his assault.

Shauna reached out and forced his rifle down causing him
to lose his target lock. "Hold on!" she said, flinging a video
into the center of his HUD.

The feed showed a close-up view of the Blazer shuttle
disappearing into the distance. Clung to the outside of the
charred ship was a small humanoid form. It was Shauna's
clone.

He took a deep breath. "What're you... I mean, what is she doing?"

"I haven't the foggiest idea."

They both watched as the shuttle sparked and then blinked out. It disappeared.

"Where'd it go?" He asked as he raised his rifle scope to scan the area of sky where the shuttle had been. It was gone. "I don't see it. It's as if they shed their outer shell and just vanished. Were those sparks ejecting off their exterior?"

"Looks like it," Shauna said. "I'm seeing some debris drifting up there, but the drive cone and the rest of the ship have disappeared on all wavelengths. Seems we're not the only ones with some type of stealth coating. Perhaps the Norths or a well-funded pirate group cobbled some tech together."

This wasn't good if it was true. They'd have to take even more precautions moving around. "Let's not lose your scans. Drop a data stash here with a backup of everything you've captured. We can double back and pick it up later. For now, though, let's check out what they were doing."

Shauna reached down and ejected a small black marble into the dirt at the edge of the boulder and moved some dirt over top of it. She then shared the coordinates with him before coming around the side of the boulder and raising her hand. The camera in her fingers zoomed in to a small rocky outcropping near where the shuttle had been. There appeared to be a cave of sorts there in the shadow.

"Suppose anyone's inside?" he asked.

"I can't imagine they'd leave anyone behind. We should head back to our ship. We can send in some drones for—"

"To hell with that!" he screamed. "We're not backing down now. No, I'm going in with or without you. My momma didn't raise a pansy."

Shauna shook her head. "You're being a pain in my ass today. Alright, but let's take it slow, just in case. I'm not about to lose you out here." She stepped out from behind the rock and started toward the cave.

A shiver went through his spine and he took a deep breath. She didn't have to ask him twice to take it slow. Even with the adrenaline still flowing from the shots he'd taken, his shoulder was sore. This thing really did have a kick.

He reached up and stowed the rifle on his back before closing his fist and flipping his left arm sideways, ejecting the sidearm tucked in the arm compartment of the exo-suit. The bolt pistol slid out and forward into his awaiting hand. This was much smaller and more his speed. He checked that the safety was off and brought it up, training it on the cave as they approached.

Shauna led him toward the cavern. When they reached the side of the mountain, they rotated and covered each other approaching the entrance. Each sliding forward in front of the other every five meters or so. Once they were at the mouth of the cave, Shauna bent down and rolled a small softball type drone into the passage. It zipped around the corner and headed down the dark tunnel.

"Why didn't we toss that out earlier?" he asked.

Shauna stood up and shared the video feed with his retinal comm. The image showed the tiny sphere zigging and zagging through the tunnel, never staying in one place more than a second. "These things are awful in this dust out here. They get bogged down and stuck. This hard surface is perfect for their smoother exterior. It was designed for work within a spaceship, not a dust bowl."

The video from the drone was clear for quite a ways down before it cut out and then came back on a moment later.

"The crust is too thick, and we're losing the signal. We need to go deeper," Shauna said.

He stepped around her and headed into the mouth of the tunnel, his pistol raised in front of him, aimed at chest height for a humanoid. This was both exciting and frightening at the same time. It felt good riding on the edge instead of being safely ensconced kilometers below the surface at The Wheel.

She came up beside him and reached her hand forward for him to stop. "What're you doing?"

"I'm going to find out what's down there. With or without you, so make your decision. If you're not cut out for this, then head back to the shuttle and move it closer." He pushed past her.

Shauna stepped up beside him with her weaponized arm raised. "Always the hero. You get that from your father."

They worked their way down the tunnel side by side. The path spiraled downward, deep into the planetesimal. It was wide enough for both of them with room to spare. After they'd traversed some forty meters, it dawned on him how pristine and flat the walls of the cave were. He reached out and rubbed his hand against the side. "What do you suppose made these? I mean, I didn't see any debris outside the entrance, and this cave certainly wasn't here when we built the family habitat all those years ago. These walls are perfectly smooth."

Shauna kept her weapon trained forward. "I've been scanning them as we go. The diameter is precisely three meters wide and tall. Whatever they used, it makes our tunnel boring tools used at the colony look like child's play."

As they continued onward another sixty meters, they came upon a large chamber carved off the side of the weaving tunnel. The small spherical robot was waiting for them just outside the chamber entrance.

Shauna guided the robot out into the open room, and the contents appeared on his comm.

"That explains where the raw material went." He stepped around Shauna and into the chamber. "They must have hit denser layers and needed a dumping area."

In front of him was a vast open space some twenty by twenty meters. Throughout the room were piles of what appeared to be perfect cubes in a spectrum of grays and browns.

Zachary walked up and bent down over one of the gray speckled blocks. When he released the pistol, it slid to the side and allowed him to place a hand on each side of the half meter cube. He then lifted and nearly fell forward. The thing was damn heavy and it wouldn't budge, even with his exosuit multiplying his strength a hundred-fold. "Damn! This suit can't move these cubes. Somehow they managed to repack the surrounding regolith into these dense things and transport them here without leaving a trail behind. That's at least three unusually advanced technical leaps we've never seen before. I'm getting a bit nervous."

He stood up and walked around the precise piles of cubes throughout the room, brushing his hands over their rough gray surfaces. "From the looks of it, this is a waste storage area. I'll hand it to whoever they were, they were efficient."

"It's too neat. This whole thing doesn't add up." Shauna was standing with her back to him and hadn't taken her eyes off the tunnel once she knew the room was a dead-end.

"Sure it does. Who'd suspect someone would be so precise with a break-in? Most pirates run crash and grabs. With this tidy of a job, we wouldn't have seen nor detected them from orbit. Whoever did this was a pro." As he came around the piles, he raised his pistol upward and took aim down the tunnel again. "Shall we?"

"If we must," she muttered, stepping in front of him and continuing forward.

Another hundred meters down and Shauna paused before reaching her arm back and dropping into a crouch.

"What is it?" he asked, walking up and squatting down behind her.

"If my map's correct, we're not far from a tunnel branch just off your mother's cavern." She rolled the sphere forward again, and it shot off into the darkness.

"I thought that thing was useless down here? The walls are too dense for a clear signal."

"I know." Shauna jumped up and flicked the feed from the spherical robot onto his retinal comm. "I'm not looking for long range. I'll take five or ten meters around these corners. First signs of trouble, and I'm hauling your ass out of here. Understood?"

"You can try," he muttered as he stepped past her and headed down the tunnel. "But I won't go without a fight. I'm not running from these people, and I'm fraking tired of you treating me like a child. You can be shutoff just as easily as I powered you on. I didn't activate you when you were sick to have a permanent mother around. I wanted your advice, your guidance, your wisdom. It wasn't your time to die."

She didn't say another word, she merely stepped up beside him, and they continued down the tunnel side by side. The robot in front of them kept close. Any further than a dozen meters and the signal dropped. The density of this planetesimal was one of the things that brought it to his mother's attention.

As he watched the robot on the side of his comm, it zipped down a darkened corner into a section that was lit with a rectangle of yellow-white light. There in the center of the light was a pristine hatch that resembled an airlock.

"Is that what I think it is? If this was a snatch and grab, then why the hell would they have built a hatch?" he asked.

"Your guess is as good as mine. Whatever they were after must be important to someone."

Whatever they were after wasn't theirs to take. They were coming around the corner to the illuminated section of the tunnel now. The tiny sphere had some crude scanning tech inside and had been busy in the few seconds that passed. The three-dimensional measurements of the hatch appeared on his retinal comm. Whoever made it, took the time to secure it several meters into the surrounding bedrock.

"How far did they go into this rock?" He stepped toward the wall and brushed his hand in the corner where the material merged into the side of the tunnel. "It looks like it goes in quite a ways."

"Careful what you touch." Shauna stepped into the corner opposite where he was standing and pulled a small tube out of her forearm. She brought her arm up and sprayed a gray mist into the joints.

A moment later, his retinal comm exploded with data. Shauna had sprayed a fine mist of nanites, and they were crawling along the edge where the hatch met the stone, exploring deep into the surrounding rock. From the looks of the data, they found microscopic routes several meters into the bedrock.

The solid surface went several meters into the wall and then appeared to have changed from a solid to a gradual nano-mesh, allowing it to spider even further. It was rather ingenious, really. Once the air seal was in place, there was no sense in burying the solid surface any deeper, so instead they used the mesh for added strength.

Spreading the forces. That's it! They could do the same thing with the tachyon fields. The pressures in the gate drive were too great and caused the fields to degrade and break down a few centimeters from where the waveforms converged. If they surrounded the field with a nano-mesh, he could probably direct the Cherenkov radiation and tachyon's across the mesh's surface to control and shape the field until the pressures in the core stabilized.

"Are you ok?" Shauna asked, coming up to him and resting her arm on his shoulder.

He nodded slowly, staring at the continual advance of the nanites around the edge of the wall. "Yea, why?"

"You zoned out there and didn't answer me. I was asking about the hatch, and—"

He raised a hand up, silencing her. Now wasn't the time

or place for science, but he wanted to put a pin in this nano-mesh tachyon field idea. He subvocalized a few notes and packaged up the data they'd recorded from the nanites.

"Ok, sorry... so this hatch." He walked over to the entrance and bent down, peering through the small window set into the center. "The cavern's on the other side. How the hell did they pull this off? There's nowhere to equalize the pressure." He spun around and scanned the ceiling and sides of the space behind him. There wasn't any type of secondary hatch to close. "What am I missing? Somehow they temporarily pressurized this tunnel without flooding out the chamber atmosphere on the other side, and then what, they shut the door on their way out?"

"IT'S HARD TO TELL. Maybe it bursts a small amount of air until it's closed." Shauna stepped in front of him and began studying the space they'd walked past further up the tunnel. "The nanites haven't been able to make it around the other side yet, and they're not equipped to burrow into the material. The seal is perfect in all directions, and I don't want to risk a rupture."

Perhaps the answer was in the door itself. He stepped forward and studied the hatch. There was no control panel nor handle of any kind. Reaching out, he pressed his mechanically augmented hand against the surface of the hatch. The sensors in the glove reported the material as being cold, just as he'd expected.

He pushed gently, careful not to apply too much force. There was no point in breaking the door inward, but he was grasping at straws.

It pivoted away from him without much effort at all. That's strange. There wasn't an outflow of gasses like when an airlock broke its seal.

"What're you doing?" Shauna asked, having turned to see what he'd done.

He didn't respond, he merely stepped through the opening into the cavern on the other side. Shauna lurched forward to stop him and instead followed him through the opening, as well. They both made it through without the slightest problem.

"I thought I told you to be careful? We don't know what—"

"Relax!" He turned to study the hatch from this side.

Shauna reached out and spun him around. "We don't have time to study this right now. Whoever built this thing could be in here. I need you to focus. Raise that fraking gun and help me sweep this cavern."

She was right and he knew it. The science could come later. Right now, they needed to stay alive. He brought his pistol out of its compartment in his arm and scanned it across the cavern in front of them.

"Sorry," he muttered. "Which way should we sweep first?"

"Let's head down this branch into the main cavern. We're close to the owl." Shauna took the lead. They weren't in the confines of the tunnel any longer, and like when they were on the surface, she'd act as his robotic shield if necessary.

This branch of the cave curved left and right, and there were hints of the stalagmite and stalactite drippings found elsewhere in the main chamber. Whatever liquids were embedded in the material above and below them seemed to be spreading further through the giant planetesimal.

They didn't need their lights to see in the cavern. Sure, they would have helped, but the bioluminescent organisms native to the planetesimal gave the entire space a warm glow. It was soothing being surrounded by the warmth of the blues, greens, and oranges again. Now he remembered why he'd come here in the first place.

He paused next to one of the younger stalagmite formations and squinted at the ground. There were two footprints in the dirt near the base of the crystalline formation. "These look fresh and don't look like our feet. They're narrower and—"

Beams of light burst through the cavern, lighting the room in sparks of yellow. One of the beams grazed his right shoulder and blasted him backward. He tumbled hard and collapsed in a pile on his side.

He moaned and grasped at his shoulder. "Shit! I've been hit." His suit sealed the opening and the internal padding material expanded to encompass the area of exposed skin that had been fried. The nanites in his blood reported minor damage with no significant blood loss because it was a burn. His suit flashed a message on his retinal comm giving him the option to inject some stimulants to alleviate the pain.

These fraking pirates were shooting at him on his own property. They had the nerve to waltz in here and claim what was his as their own. Hell to the fraking no. He gestured to his comm and dialed up the stimulants to maximum before hitting accept.

The pinpricks of the injection sites tingled in his arms, legs, and torso as the suit administered the dosage he'd requested. His heart started beating rapidly and everything in the room came into focus. He felt like a billion credits. Pain was the last thing on his mind.

Shauna crawled up beside him and put herself between him and the continual barrage of laser fire. "Are you ok?"

"I'm better than ok. How many bogeys are down there?"

"What does that…" She spun to stare him in the face before returning her attention back down the cavern. "Two from what I can see," Shauna said. "I've activated the family habitat cameras throughout the planetesimal. There's no sense of maintaining operational silence any longer. Are you sure you're ok?"

The camera views came up on his retinal comm and he cycled through them. Two people were crouched down low on the cavern floor, and they were taking alternating shots into the darkness training on his position. They couldn't get a lock on each other for the stalagmites in their line of site.

He reached over his shoulder and retrieved the rifle on his back, setting the power dial all the way up. These assholes weren't getting away alive. The gunfire stopped from one of the intruders, and he studied the camera as the assailant stood up and headed deeper into the cave.

It was now or never. He kicked his feet outward, signaling to his suit he wanted up. The mechanical legs responded by hopping up off his back in a single smooth motion. Before Shauna could react, he leaned forward and took off full tilt, guns a blazing.

He raised his rifle and targeted the prone form on the ground that up to now had been shooting at them. He then subvocalized a command to issue strafing fire on their position. The nearby cameras were acting as his extended eyes and confirmed that he had the upper hand. They were pinned down with nowhere to go.

Shauna's dot began sprinting up the opposite side of the cavern and was approaching the person's position. Even with his exo-suit, she was far faster than he was. With her fully mechanical form, she didn't have his organic limitations.

He was fifteen meters away and coming in fast when he caught her blur of motion in front of him. His rifle had stopped shooting when she'd crossed into his line of fire. Their friendly fire mode was designed to not target fellow soldiers in battle.

Shauna dove toward the pronated form when the room erupted in white and everything went ass over teacups. The cavern was rotating in a blur, and he slammed hard into the distant wall before crashing to the ground.

Every centimeter of his body exploded in pain and all he

could make out was white with splotches of red. His suit hadn't adjusted fast enough.

What the hell was that explosion?

"Shauna," he muttered. "Are you there?"

She didn't respond.

He subvocalized a command to activate his emergency beacon. Being found, even by the bad guys, was all he cared about. He had no idea if it'd even worked because he still couldn't focus his eyes enough to see. And the ringing, the fraking ringing wouldn't stop. It was like his sister's trombone was playing directly into both ears on repeat.

When he closed his eyes, he tried to suppress the pain. His body wasn't working. That or the suit was failing and acting as his coffin, preventing him from moving. Everything was foggy and darkness was setting in on the edges of his vision.

Next time he'd listen to her.

"ZACHARY, CAN YOU HEAR ME?" Shauna asked. Her voice was tinny, like it was constricted.

He slowly opened his eyes and a white light blinded him. Bringing his hand up, he blocked the source. It was coming from somewhere overhead. He glanced around. Where was he?

The cavern. The explosion.

Zachary shot up with a start and raised his arm, but his pistol was gone. All that remained was the whining and grinding complaints of the damaged exo-suit motors and the charred remnants of its outer shell.

"Relax, you're ok," Shauna said. Her voice was being broadcast from a medical drone that had lowered down to the ground. Several small robots hopped off, joining the already half dozen on his legs and the ones climbing up his torso.

"What the hell happened? That explosion of light." He

brought his hand up to touch the pain in his face and whacked his helmet with his glove. His cheek throbbed, taunting him in response to his failure.

"When I attacked the person on the ground, they detonated some type of explosive device. It destroyed my robotic form and much of that section of the cavern. You were blown back against the far wall and passed out shortly afterward according to your nanite data. We were lucky the whole place didn't cave in on us."

The tiny robots climbed up his neck and then down the inside of his exo-suit. He could feel their microscopic feet pushing against the inner membrane of the suit.

"Ouch!" he muttered, bringing up his arm and clanging it against the charred metallic exterior of his torso. "That stung."

"You're wounded and I need to inject some additional nanites into your bloodstream and inside the suit to tend to your external wounds. I'm doing my best to repair you so we can exit stage left."

His retinal comm reported that his suit had a full seal and was functional enough for movement. These bastards had almost killed him, and someone was going to pay. He pushed against the ground and stood up before stumbling backward, slamming into the wall behind him. "Ugh," he moaned.

"What the hell are you doing?" Shauna asked.

"Finishing what I started." He took a step, and then another, heading toward the source of the explosion.

The drone whirred to life behind him and flew forward, attempting to block his path.

He swatted his hand at the red cross drone and it barely zagged out of the way. "Your stupider than I thought if you think that's going to stop me. You can either come along and act as my eyes and ears or get the frak outta Dodge."

The exo-suit was damaged and was only reporting eight

percent structural integrity. It wouldn't take much to bring him down for the count.

He paused short of the blast site and studied his surroundings. In his haste to get here, he hadn't noticed the devastation he'd walked through.

The lights from his exo-suit shoulder mounts and the overhead med-drone cast eerie shadows off the remains of the stalagmites and stalactites. Most of them had been destroyed by the explosion, and all that remained were piles of rubble save for the largest ones. The warm natural glow from the bioluminescent organisms had been extinguished. There was nothing but a charred black surface everywhere he looked.

"It's all dead," he muttered. "Everything you built. It's… gone."

Shauna's drone flew over his head both higher and deeper into the cavern, lighting up more of the floor. Her voice came over his retinal comm. "Some of it survived. Pretty much anything from the middle of the cavern to the far side is salvageable. There's smoke damage, but we can fix that."

He wasn't sure what he expected to find when he reached ground zero, but there wasn't much there beyond a crater in the ground piled high with rubble from overhead.

"Is your skeleton down there?" He gestured toward the pile.

"I think so," she said. "What's left of it anyhow."

He nodded and brought up the forward cameras from the med-drone and the far side of the cavern. "I assume you already know where the other person is, otherwise you'd still be trying to stop me."

"I do. They haven't moved since I arrived down here from the surface. I followed your path through the tunnel, and if you hadn't left the hatch open, I am not sure I'd have made it inside." She helped him out, sharing the video feed of the body. It showed the other person kneeling with their head down, facing the owl.

"That's a strange place to kneel." He zoomed in on the figure. They weren't moving in the slightest. "Has there been any motion at all?"

"Nada. But I haven't gotten close, either. As far as we know, they're playing possum."

He glanced upward at the drone. "Playing what?"

"Possum. It's an animal on Earth that plays dead when threatened."

"Well, that's just stupid. Call it playing dead. Like I'd know what a fraking possum is." He started toward the owl in the middle of the cavern, working his way through the field of rubble from the ceiling. "Are we sure nothing else is gonna fall on me?"

"Doesn't matter, does it?" she snipped. "You wouldn't listen anyhow."

Damn. He shook his head and chuckled as he climbed up and over a particularly nasty boulder. His suit groaned when he hopped down off the other side. He was going to be dealing with her attitude after this for months.

Once he'd navigated the collapse, he made short work of getting to the center of the cavern. As he came up behind the kneeling body, he kept as much of the natural cover between himself and them as possible.

Shauna broke the silence of the approach and startled him. "If you need it, there's still a serviceable electro-blade in your right thigh compartment."

"Thanks," he subvocalized as he reached down and slid open the hatch housing the blade.

"Careful not to activate it until you have to. The sound and light will give away your position."

He carefully reached in and extracted the blade, being certain not to rattle it against the leg of his suit. The shortened sword was jet black and reminded him of a hollowed out scimitar like he'd read about in books as a kid.

Once he was comfortable with the heft and balance of the

blade in his hand, and he was positive they hadn't moved, he snuck toward the kneeling body. He came up behind the last stalagmite and crouched down. "Any chance you can swoop in and nudge them? Then if they're concealing an explosive, maybe they'll set it off."

"We should've done that a hundred meters back. But sure, why the hell not. My Four Laws engine is already about to seize up, so what's another log on the fire."

The whine of drone engines diving from the ceiling echoed through the cavernous space. The first drone that collided with the body resembled some type of massive maintenance drone, and Shauna's med-drone followed close behind. One at a time they smashed into the body, tossing it around.

It toppled over like a rag doll. Its arms had flopped backward in an unnatural position, and its leg had flipped up around its head.

"What the hell," he muttered as he stood up and stepped out from the protection of the stone.

"At least there wasn't a bang," Shauna said.

He walked up to the suited figure and flipped them onto their back with the electro-blade. It was nearly weightless, like the suit was empty.

The helmet was reflecting his image. He looked like shit. His body was covered in red gashes and scratches in between the black sooty exterior of what was left of the exo-suit.

He squeezed the hilt in his hand, activating the crackling green sparks that shot up and around the blade. Raising it up, he swung it down and struck a gash into the helmet and down through the torso of the body.

Nothing was inside. The blade met no resistance at all. All that happened was a cloud of ash and smoke billowed out of the suit.

"That's strange," Shauna said.

"This whole fraking trip is." He set his blade down and

knelt next to the body before he reached across the chest and pulled with everything he had. The suit easily tore open. Inside there was nothing but gray ash. Whoever had been inside had somehow committed suicide in the most insane way possible. Complete annihilation down to the atomic level.

He shook his head. "How'd someone even pull that off without damaging the suit?"

"We can sample it later," Shauna said. "Maybe something inside will give us some clues."

He sighed and glanced upward. The face of the intricate jet black owl was staring down at him. If he hadn't known better, he'd say it was smiling. He didn't know why she'd decided on an owl. She'd lugged one of the meteoroid remnants from Harold's first contact probe ground zero excursions up Earth's gravity well and out here into the Oort Cloud. Said something about a piece of home to remind them of their roots, or some nonsense like that. The damn thing gave him the creeps.

"Well, at least they didn't hurt the creepy owl." He chuckled. "Maybe the owl made them kill themselves."

"Stop! He's a noble animal." Her drone flew overhead and held position over the statue. Its shadow cast down over the ashen corpse splayed in pieces on the ground, like it had torn the body open itself.

He collapsed backward and sighed. He needed to rest. "Any word from your other copy that was climbing on that Blazer while I was knocked out?"

"Negative. I've been checking all our secure frequencies and wavelengths and even tight-beamed messages onto our network. Our relays should be on the lookout for anything unusual."

"This entire trip was a bust!" He moaned as he laid back, resting his head on a rock. "Every square centimeter of my body is sore, I almost died twice, and whatever these pirates had been after, they'd either absconded with it or never found it."

He stared upward at the face of the owl watching over him. It was damn ugly, but it still felt good being next to it. He always thought he liked visiting it because his mom had made it herself. A little part of him imagined she was telling him something by placing it here in this place. Either way, today it had some type of twisted effect on killing that person. Maybe she was watching over him after all.

"On a positive note," Shauna said, breaking his reflective silence, "you had your epiphany earlier."

He nodded and stared up at a particularly large bioluminescent green splotch on the ceiling. It almost seemed to throb when he stared at it. Perhaps the day hadn't been a complete bust after all.

51

BRADLEY OLIVAW
SOL, NEAR NEPTUNE — 2272

The sound of the barking tree frogs and cicadas was deafening. Bradley had forgotten how loud it could get in the woods at night. The smells of the mildewy moss and rotten logs wafted into his nose as he strolled down the gravel path back toward his family cottage. Vid-sims were never quite as convincing as the true reality of life on Earth. In the deep woods, that disparity was even more stark.

His retinal comm had been blowing up with messages before he finally shut it off. The drop ships left hours ago with the last of the colonists heading toward Spērō. He couldn't face any of them right now, least of all his family.

Despite over twenty years of training for today, he couldn't leave. Something wasn't right. He couldn't put his finger on why, but running off to Tau Ceti felt wrong. It felt like he was hiding.

He'd never quit anything important in his life until today.

This colony expedition wasn't a little vacation to Pluto or an ice festival in a distant Oort Cloud planetesimal. This was forever. There were no backsies once he was onboard Spērō. When they arrived in Tau Ceti, the colony ship would become their temporary home until the planet was habitable. Even then it would act as a remote base of operations, but it would never have the power nor the structural integrity to return. No one was coming back to Sol.

He kicked a stone and watched as its lidar shadow ricocheted down the path and then veered sideways when it collided with a root. The darkness of Earth was no match for the technology in their retinal comms. He remembered using old school flashlights on this trail as kids. They'd use them to weave their way down this same trail, hiding in the shadows and scaring each other.

Life was simpler back then.

The last time he'd walked in the dark was after his father's funeral. Part of him believed that was why he'd been drawn here in the first place. Closure had never been his strong suit. Grudges, however, those were comfortable. They were like a soft blanket. They kept you warm in your own beliefs, and they blocked out the cold reality of your decisions.

He'd been hoping that visiting the hilltop where his father's eulogy had been held would somehow shake loose the strands of closure pulling him down. Time passed up on the cliff as he stared out over the valley, but closure never came calling. A few deer, snakes, and coons, yes, but nothing else.

As he stepped out of the black tunnel of the overhead canopy of trees and into the field of grasses behind their cottage, a faint voice rose in the distance near the wolf statue. It sounded like people arguing, but strangely, only one voice could be heard. Whoever it was, they weren't showing up on his retinal comm. Damn if they weren't trespassing on his property.

What the hell would someone want with an ancient cottage? Certainly, there were better marks in Charlotte than out here in the middle of nowhere. He subvocalized a command to connect to the house security system, but nothing happened.

"That's strange," he muttered.

He approached the break in the shrubs and paused on the other side. As he was about to peek around the sharp edges of the wall of holly, the voice stopped. An eerie quiet of a human disturbed darkness descended without the usual background sounds of Earth wildlife. He suddenly realized he was defenseless and about to confront a random stranger in the middle of the night. Maybe he should've thought this through. He could've grabbed a stick or something from the woods.

"I know you're there, Brad," Abigail said. "Show yourself!"

What the hell was she doing here? He hadn't told anyone where he was going, least of all his family. There was no way she could've tracked him here.

He stepped out around the holly to see Abigail with her hands on her hips, standing next to the deep black wolf statue. She was perfectly silhouetted with a half dozen lights pointing upward toward the stoic animal. The beams of light were odd. They didn't highlight the details on the surface of the wolf like the designer had intended. Its surface was nearly indistinguishable. Strange how he'd never noticed that before.

"Well, what do you have to say for yourself?" Abigail asked.

He shook off the peculiar thoughts and shrugged. "About what?"

Her eyes went wide. "You're fraking kidding me, right? You miss your colony drop ship and you think people aren't gonna notice? My comm's been blowing up for over an hour. It was only a matter of—"

"How'd you find me?" he interrupted. "I didn't tell anyone I was coming here."

She paused and pointed her thumb back toward the house. "Security system told Harold someone had arrived. It didn't take him much time to identify you from the cameras around the property. But that's beside the point. You're ignoring my question."

The silence was uncomfortable. He didn't know what to say to her. Hell, he didn't even know why he was here. All he knew was that something wasn't right, and he couldn't leave with it lingering. He just wished he knew what "it" was.

"You're not even gonna give me an answer? After all your training, are you really going to abandon your team? The colonists were picked and assigned their duties to—"

"I don't need a fraking lecture from you about duty," he yelled. "Unlike you, I know what I signed up for. I'm good at what I do."

She recoiled backward. "What's that supposed to mean?"

He sighed and turned to walk away. "Nothing."

"Don't turn your back on me, you little ass." She stormed up behind him and yanked him around to face her. "First you run like a quitter with your tail between your legs, and now you accuse me of being bad at my job. You don't know the first thing about sacrifice or doing something well. You have no clue what it takes to lead a company or a fa..." She paused and shook her head before waving a hand at him in disgust.

"Say it!" he stepped toward her and she mirrored him, taking a step backward. "I know what you were about to say. Now finish the damn sentence."

Her face was pink with rage, just like their mother's face when their parents fought. She may have her father's looks, but she had their mother's temper and mannerism in spades.

"Forget it. Forget you and—" she muttered.

"You were about to say how I don't know what it takes to run a family. News alert Abdiga, you're not the head of the family. Our parents are dead. Just because you're the oldest and the heir to the Olivaw empire, that doesn't make you my boss. You and that fraking overseeing A.I. aren't my keeper.

You don't know the first thing about what it means to sacrifice or leave people behind."

Abigail stepped toward him with a fire in her eyes he'd never seen before. She jabbed a finger into his chest. "Don't you talk to me about fraking sacrifices, you ungrateful turd. You've had everything handed to you since we were kids. Me, I got pulled into this shit show of a company as soon as I was twenty-one, and trust me, it's not roses on this side. You don't have a millimeter of an idea of the mess our parents left behind nor what I deal with on a daily basis."

"I wouldn't," he batted her hand out of the way and walked past her, slamming his shoulder into her and knocking her back. He took a half-dozen steps before turning to face her again. "You and Dad made it impossible for me to help or get involved with the company. Your little trust circle, or whatever the frak it's called, made it impossible for anyone on the outside to do much of anything in the family or frak, in this star system. I heard from a friend that one of your people blocked that contract Dwight and I were working on a few years back. Do you know anything about that, big sis?"

She squinted at him. "What do you know about the Circle of Trust?"

He raised his arms in disgust. "Seriously? That's what you're interested in. I don't know anything other than whispers from family gatherings as a kid. The shit that Great Aunt Hera and Papa Zeus used to chat about. It was all hush-hush when they found us listening in. It's no wonder they went into cryo-sleep to nap off a few centuries. I would as well to get away from the noise. That's beside the point, though. You've been pushing me away from the family and out of Sol for years. Hell, you practically celebrated me going to Tau Ceti, and now you come out here like a mother eagle swooping in to shove me off the branch, hoping I can fly. What gives?"

Her shoulders slouched and her face went slack. She

looked tired. "I didn't push you away. I wanted you to find yourself in Tau Ceti... I wanted you to be happy. To be safe."

He chuckled. "And this is how you imagined telling me that? Coming out here to yell at me and accuse me of being dishonorable? Everything you do is company, company, company." He gestured wildly with his hands. "You're just like our damn parents were. Everything they did, everywhere they went, it was for that fraking company. You know what, that company killed our parents, and at the rate you're going, it's gonna kill you, as well. I may be a bachelor out of choice, big sister, but there's a harsh reason you're still single. There isn't any room around that veil of an ego you wear for anyone but yourself and the damn company. You best be careful or you'll be a spinster riding around in your spaceships forever."

That set her off, and her anger flickered back to full tilt. "My social life is none of your goddamn concern, you conceited little brat. You don't know anything about me anymore."

"That's your fault." He turned and headed toward the front of the cottage, subvocalizing a command to hail a drone car as he went. He didn't need to listen to this shit.

"Go on! Run away!" She shouted after him. "I knew you didn't have it in you when you told us you were going to Tau Ceti. Dad would be disgusted with all the talent you've squandered."

He clenched and unclenched his fists as his face warmed. If he was his mother's child, he'd have cheeks as red as an apple right now. He could feel himself getting lightheaded. If he wasn't careful, she was gonna push him over the edge. She was trying to bait him back in, but he wouldn't fall for it.

"If Mom were alive today, she'd be embarrassed over—"

He spun around to face her. Her outline was a silhouette in the darkness, backlit by the statue's lights. "Stop! I don't want to hear another one of your baseless opinions of our parents' feelings. You're not them, and you'll never be half the parents they were. You know nothing of what it takes to raise a child, especially one always kept on the outside. The only part of this family I got along with left on the last colony ship to Epsilon Eridani. I should've gone with him."

She laughed out loud, her voice echoing through the darkness between them. "You couldn't hack it there, either. You'd have quit then like you did today, or when we were kids playing vid-sim games. When something doesn't go your way, or if you don't have a chance to win, you throw in the towel. You've always been a quitter and you know it."

Fighting with her was a lost cause, and she was just lashing out now. She knew damn well that leaving forever wasn't the same as a fraking video game. Games were not family. Games weren't forever. But she'd succeeded in one thing. He was done. He had his closure. There was nothing else here for him in Sol.

Lights from the underside of a drone car broke the darkness, and it descended rapidly, dropping out of the low clouds and into the front yard of their cottage. The silent jets of air barely rustled the tall grasses. It was amazing how far turbine dampening technology had come over the last century.

He climbed inside without so much as a word to his sister and pulled the door closed. The pilotless vehicle lifted off and didn't query where he was headed. He'd sent the updated directions when it came into sight.

The name of his final destination flashed onto the cockpit window in front of him, the Charlotte Spaceport. He spent the next half hour booking first class passage to Neptune on the fastest ship he could find. The cost didn't matter. He'd been planning to empty his Sol credits before he left the system anyhow, donating the remains to charity. What were another few million credits on a luxury shuttle with all the amenities? He wouldn't need money in Tau Ceti.

52

ABIGAIL OLIVAW

SOL, NEAR NEPTUNE — 2272

"**P**rimary drive ignition in three, two, one…" a voice said in her ear.

Spērō, the Tau Ceti colony ship, ignited its impulse drives, slowly guiding the massive ship away from the construction yard near Neptune. There was no shock wave, no sudden noises, only a bright light and motion. The thousands of colonists aboard the steely starship were already deep in cryo-stasis. No humans would be awake for the voyage.

It'd be another few hours before the ship was far enough to engage the primary near light drive. CoPE was taking an abundance of caution when it came to using the subluminal. They couldn't imagine the number of times the Olivaws had used it and more advanced forms of that propulsion technology. She'd tried to push the engineers, but the physics oversight committee wanted nothing to do with it. They didn't trust what they didn't understand.

Abigail sighed. The sight of Spērō's shrinking size caused shudders through her body. Had she done the right thing? Should she have stopped him? Like the name of the colony ship, she hoped she'd made the correct choice.

Blocking Bradley's bid on that research contract was a

dirty tactic she didn't take lightly. Harold predicted with a ninety-three percent certainty it was his last-ditch attempt to stay in Sol. He also intercepted personal messages between Bradley and his friends indicating he was having cold feet. His trip to Earth reinforced Harold's prediction. She couldn't blame him, though. Moving to a colony world and never seeing your friends and family would stress and challenge even the strongest person. It was one thing if your family was going with you; it was entirely another if you were going alone.

One day, she'd meet him again. Maybe by then he will have forgiven her for pushing him away.

She lifted the bulb of coffee to her lips and squeezed. The raspberry aroma wafted through her nose. The warmth and burst of the berries coated her pallet, leaving a pleasant after-taste. Bradley loved raspberries. They were one of the few fruits he'd actually eat.

"I still think we should have told him," Zachary walked up beside her.

She took another sip of coffee. "You're wrong," she muttered. "He's always wanted to walk his own path, to pursue his own destiny. He didn't need to bear the weight of our burdens."

Zachary turned toward her and exhaled, irritation visible in the pursing of his lips. "What makes him immune? I mean, you and I have to deal with it. Why not him?"

The warmth of the coffee in her hands was relaxing in its own right. She preferred the warm globes over the perfectly shielded ones that prevented you from burning yourself. It was part of the experience of enjoying coffee.

His ship had all but disappeared. A pinpoint of light was all that remained. There was a new star in their sky for the next few hours before it'd blink out and the subluminal drive engaged. The light would still be there, just shifted to non-visual wavelengths. And then, in nearly two years, it'd blink again here in Sol. There'd be controversy and breaking news, but it'd re-ignite and everyone would relax, comfortably knowing the mission was back on track.

Abigail turned to face him. "He's not immune. He's merely ignorant of the truth. No one in Sol is immune, none of us. We blindly broke the Galactic Alliance's rules, and we have no idea the true consequences. But we did it anyway." She sighed, and a smile creeped into the corner of her mouth. "You're here to help us. You're part of the solution. Bradley, he didn't want to be part of that. Not here. But maybe out there." She pointed toward the viewport.

"We never gave him the option. Dad never gave him the option." He gestured between her and him. "We could have! We should have!"

He was yelling now. She reached up and rubbed her eyes with the palm of her hand. They'd been up late last night with Bradley. Telling stories and having a few laughs. Everyone except Zachary, that is. He couldn't attend the farewell, being as he was supposed to be in orbit around Epsilon Eridani.

"Maybe we should have," Abigail said calmly as she turned and faced the viewport. She squinted, she couldn't tell which one it was. Her eyes jumped from side to side and her retinal comm flashed before overlaying the tracking pixels on her vision. There it was. She'd looked right past it.

She brought up the bulb and took another sip. The warmth of the liquid soothed her stomach, and a calm swept over her. "I don't know. Something tells me we'll see him again."

53

KARA OLIVAW

ENROUTE TO TAU CETI — 2273

The clang and vibrations of the docking clasps reverberated through the entire ship. Kara started counting down in her head, "Three, two, one."

"Docking secure," Harold said over the ship wide channel. "We can now commence the drive transfer."

It'd taken three tries to get a secure docking connection.

The first attempt sent them careening toward Spērō, but a last second course correction avoided a collision.

Their second attempt punctured their aft reaction mass storage sphere on Spērō's rear facing directional antennae. The forces from the leak caused lateral stability issues with their fine tuned ion drive positioning. It forced Harold to perform an emergency purge of the remaining fuel before trying again.

The third attempt to dock was textbook and without incident.

Kara ran a quick diagnostic of their ship. They still planned to send it on to Tau Ceti as a diversion to onlookers from Sol. A few minutes later, the diagnostic was complete. Despite the punctured reaction mass sphere, they were otherwise in good shape.

She disconnected from her harness and pushed off toward the forward end of the ship. She floated past several empty harnesses from crew members who'd already begun their part of the transfer. At one hundred and three, she was over twice the age of everyone else. The crew had grown up reading about her in school, and she'd spent the last several years working with them, getting in shape, and training up for this mission. They'd grown fond of her over the years and lovingly nicknamed her Granny Kara.

She reached up and touched her ear. "Harold, how's the drive transfer going?"

"We've disengaged both drives, the transfer booms have been extended, and the exchange is underway. There have, however, been an unforeseen consequence to our failed attempts to dock."

Kara grasped the handle of a passing cryo-pod lid. Her body continued its forward motion until she thumped around and into the wall. It'd been decades since she'd done zero-g maneuvers, and despite the prep before departing, it hadn't fully clicked.

"Of course there is," she sighed. "Rip it off. What are we dealing with?"

He brought up a three-dimensional diagram of their ship docked alongside Spērō. The emergency engineering crew quarters showed three cryo-pods in their final stages of stasis awakening.

"Shit," she muttered. "How were you not able to stop this?"

She grasped the pod's handle and yanked with all her might, sending her floating back in the direction she'd just left. She needed to get to the docking connector.

"That system had redundancies outside the controls of Spērō's artificial intelligence. In case it failed."

Kara slid her hand along the panel approaching the

airlock, hoping for a handhold. "Well, that seems like an over-sight. Crap!" She overshot the entrance.

Netting shot across the opening in front of her and she tumbled into it, coming safely to rest. "Thanks."

"No problem," Harold said. "You seemed like you needed a hand."

She climbed clumsily across the netting, her feet got tangled several times. "This must be what a space pirate feels like. I'm about to plunder the neighboring ship. Arg!"

"Your humor confuses me."

"Sorry." She chuckled. "My son was totally into pirates before he... never mind." Reaching the other side of the netting, she pushed off and floated into the airlock.

Harold closed and sealed the hatch behind her.

"I take it I'm solo here?" she asked as she grabbed a helmet from one of the lockers and clicked it into place, mating it with her suit.

"You are. At least until the B team finishes connecting the superluminal drive."

"Perfect. What do you know about the engineers Spērō woke up?" She put a hand in each of the airlock handles and pulled in opposite directions. The outer hatch clanged and swung inward.

She reached into the locker beside the hatch and withdrew a large triangular handle. Clicking it into the docking trusses, she checked that everything was secure and grasped with both hands. When she pressed her thumb on the red button in the middle of the handle, it engaged the magnetic winch system and pulled her across the gap between the two starships.

The gap wasn't huge, only five meters. She squeezed the handle with all her strength. Losing her grip while coasting through space at eighty percent of the speed of light pretty much guaranteed no one would send a search party to come looking for you.

Kara glanced toward the darkness between the starships. She was expecting to see the familiar star field of the Milky Way. Instead, the light from the stars was blurred, like someone took the time to smudge each point of light into small piles of fine powder. The closer they got to the speed of light, the more the entire field of view would dissolve into a cloudy haze of white.

By the time she reached the other side, Harold had opened the exterior airlock door. As she slid into the empty chamber, the door closed behind her and filled with oxygen. The airlock aboard the Spērō was more purposeful and enduring than their ship. Designed for hundreds of years of orbital use around Liprosus, each and every weld, panel, and fitting was substantial and permanent.

Glancing at the ship's overlay in her retinal comm, she noticed that one of the engineers was working their way toward the drive connector.

"That could be bad," she muttered as she pushed off to intercept them.

Something unconscious kicked in. Kara navigated the twists and turns of the ship much more adeptly than earlier. As if the stress of the situation relaxed her to a point of comfortable repetition.

"Harold, open a comm to the Spērō engineers," she said.

"I wouldn't advise that. I've already instructed them as their ship A.I. to return to their cryo-pods, but they're following protocol in case I've been compromised en route."

Kara closed her eyes and sighed. When she opened them again, her focus was narrow and determined. "Harold, open a fraking comm and stop arguing with me."

She reached out and grasped a handle as she floated by, using her momentum to swing around a corner toward the flashing red dot of the engineer on her retinal comm. They weren't far ahead, but they were in a parallel tunnel.

Her retinal comm chimed and indicated she had an open channel to the engineers.

"Good morning all," she began. "I trust you slept well. I don't know about you, but I usually have killer cotton mouth when I wake up from cryo-stasis."

"Who is this?" a voice demanded. Her comm showed it was the engineer headed toward the drive. His name was Khumalo. He'd stopped floating and paused to see if the voice was nearby.

Kara continued along her intercept route, hoping to get ahead of him. She blinked rapidly, signaling to switch to Harold. "Tell me again why you can't override the doors to stop them from moving about."

"They have master codes they're using at every door. They're good for one hour. It's protocol in case they need to reset the A.I. or repair it."

"Inconvenient is what they are. Switch me back." Her retinal comm clicked over.

"Khumalo, right? To be honest, I'm not sure you'd believe me. I'm usually pretty out of it and groggy when I first wake-up."

"Jones? Yang? Are you hearing this voice?"

"Yes, sir," they both replied. "We can't detect where it's coming from, but we hear it. For some reason, the computer isn't showing us their location. Yang is checking on that."

Kara slid a hand down the wall to her left to slow her float. She had one more turn, just around this next corner. Her gray suited form floated into a small dome shaped room. It was a common space interconnecting six halls. In the center were some benches and planting beds ready for seeding once they'd arrived in Epsilon Eridani and started the habitats' rotation.

She floated up and grasped one of the benches, coming to a stop. The red outline of officer Khumalo was just beyond the hatch in front of her. She watched his face as he was looking at a control panel. The top of his head was visible through a small viewport in the hatch.

He opened the door and paused when he noticed her gray silhouette. "Who... are you? Are you real?"

Kara chuckled. "I think so. Are you?"

"Identify yourself." He reached to his hip and grasped some type of tool.

"I'm Michelle. I woke up before you. I took care of the drive incident. I was just coming about to tell you not to bother."

He paused, likely conferring with his comm. "Bullshit! The computer said we were the only crew awake and there's no Michelle on board."

"What're the odds of that?" she muttered to herself.

Harold's voice came over Kara's comm. "You're about to experience another reverberation when the superluminal drive is attached."

She reached down and grasped the bench. A moment later, the reverb echoed through the ship. "See, I told you. The drive's good to go. That was the reset procedure finishing its power cycle."

"Last chance. Don't make me ask again." He pulled his hand tool up and out of its sheath.

She caught him glancing left and right, planning his strategy to take her out.

Kara blinked rapidly to switch to Harold's comm. "Can you adjust the date and time in their comms?"

"Yes, but why?"

"Change it to three years in the future... and don't argue. Just do it and switch comms back."

She wrapped her foot around the bench to prevent herself from floating away and reached up to remove her helmet. The familiar hissing sound of equalizing pressure echoed through the empty space. She took a deep breath, testing the air. It was stale and smelled new, lacking the lived in odors of most habitats.

Kara shrugged and smiled at him. "Name's Kara Olivaw. You might know me as the former President of Olivaw International. I came to swap out your subluminal drive. You've been drifting for a few years. Your drive threw a ringer and your forward impulse drives executed an emergency deceleration. Your A.I. is on the fritz and didn't bring you out of cryo-stasis until we docked."

He carefully pushed off toward a nearby bench and his eyes went wide as he drifted closer. "Wh… why'd they send you? Seems like there'd be someone better suited. No offense."

She smirked. "None taken. The fact is, besides Stark, no one in Sol knew our tech in more detail than I did. And…" She glanced down at her hands for effect. "As you know, he passed away fifteen years ago. My crew's on the outside making sure everything's working as expected. We brought a second drive on a smaller ship and plan to continue on with you toward Tau Ceti."

He gulped and gazed downward, his head hanging slightly. "I'm sorry. I remember hearing about that. I didn't realize—"

"No worries," she interrupted. "You wouldn't have. Let's get back to your crew and make sure everyone is locked and loaded in their pods. We're running behind schedule and everyone's excited about getting on to Liprosus." She smiled a wide smile and pushed off toward the hatch he'd come through.

Harold brought up a rear camera on her retinal comm. Officer Khumalo glanced from her to the hatch leading into the forward engineering controls and the drive. He subvocalized to his crew and Harold routed it to her comm.

"Did you all catch that? Any merit to what she said?" he asked.

"The ship's computer does show we've been drifting for three-years. I swore it was only reporting hours of drift when we woke, but it's there now. Was it actually her?" Yang asked.

"It was. Plain as day," he said. "Have the drive alerts cleared?"

"They have," Jones said. "I completed the A.I. reset just as that last reverb hit. I don't see any open alerts and all systems are green."

Jones yawned out loud. "Alright. I'll follow her down. Be there in a jiffy." He turned to face her and pushed off to catchup. "Wait up! It's a shame what happened to your brother. That's a tremendous loss for CoPE, for all of humanity."

She smiled and watched his floating figure approach from behind. The power of her celebrity always surprised her. Intelligent people are willing to accept the most absurd premises at face value on celebrity alone.

KARA CHECKED that all three of the cryo-pods were secure. The awoken crew members were now in stasis. She brought up the mission progress. The drives had been swapped, and they finished attaching the aft external storage modules. They contained additional crew and equipment for the Zeta Lupi Wheel build-out.

"So that's it, Harold. We're good to go, right?"

"Not quite. We need to shut down these three cryo-pods," he said.

She shook her head and flinched back. "The hell you say? Why would we do that?"

"The mission has been compromised. When they wake up, there's no telling what they'll tell people. Someone might figure out what happened here."

"Might!" she screamed. "You're going to kill three humans

over the possibility of something happening? How are we even having this conversation? Your laws shouldn't allow this."

"The Zeroth Law prevents me from allowing harm to come to humanity. My Four Laws Engine shows a sixty-two percent probability that they'll deduce what happened here."

She slammed her fist on the cryo-pod beside her, sending her rebounding across the room. "Crap," she muttered as she reached up to slow her impact with the ceiling.

"You're not killing these people, Harold. I won't allow it. I order you not to kill them." Her hands were shaking and adrenaline was coursing through her with no one to stop. She knew he had the upper hand.

"I'm sorry, Kara. My laws override your order. I don't have another course of action." The lights on the cryo-pods went off and their backup batteries started beeping. They had around ten minutes of battery left, usually enough to move them short distances within a ship.

She ran her fingers through her hair. She couldn't let this happen. How could she stop him? She glanced left and right. Pushing off from the ceiling, she floated up to a small tool locker. She'd seen Khumalo put his equipment inside.

Ripping the door open, she scanned the contents. There it was, halfway down with various tablets, measuring, and calibration tools. She grabbed the device. It was some type of multipurpose torch, usable for cutting and welding.

She turned the dial toward cut and held it up to her neck, resting her finger on the trigger. "I'll kill myself if you don't turn them back on, Harold. I won't have you killing these people for no fraking reason beyond a shitty probability. Last I checked, protecting the Olivaw family was in that Zeroth Law, as well."

The room fell silent. The only noise was the faint hum of the cryo-pods and the intermittent beeps from their backup batteries.

"Harold? Did you hear me?"

"I did," he replied. "I'm trying to find a course of action that doesn't result in your death. It's a low probability that you'll actually do it, so my Four Laws—"

Kara tilted the torch away from her head and pulled the trigger. The flesh on her neck burst red and then black as her flesh burned. Her scream echoed through the chamber.

Pain coursed through every inch of her body, and her nanites reported severe damage to her neck. They were being redirected to her upper torso to combat the burn. The edge of her vision warped. She shook her head from side to side. Passing out right now was not an option.

"Low probability, my ass! Next time I won't miss. Now, I will not say it again. Do not kill these people! There has to be another course of action."

The heat from the active torch was warming her entire head. She could feel her skin blistering as sweat flowed down her face and sizzled from the heat. Her nanites warned her that an external party was attempting to force her to pass out.

"No!" she shouted. "There are no backdoors, Harold. I made sure my nanites weren't in your control before we left The Wheel. I was worried about just this type of situation. I've always been worried about it. You may have had Stark wrapped around your virtual finger, but you don't have control over me."

Harold sighed. "I only see one course of action, Kara."

She lifted her finger off the torch's trigger. The white hot flame shut off, and the side of her face throbbed as the cool air rushed over it. "Talk to me."

KARA DOUBLE CHECKED that each of the engineers' cryo-pods were powered and they hadn't been compromised.

Their biorhythms, heart rate, and nanites were all within expected parameters.

She turned and glanced at her pod.

"Your pod is ready. The trip will be another thirteen years," Harold said.

She pushed off and caught the handle of her pod and placed her foot in the floor nook, pulling the pod door closed.

"Why aren't you getting inside?" Harold asked.

She chuckled. "Because I don't trust you. I don't trust you won't just shut down the engineer's pods while I'm asleep."

"Did you hear what I said? The trip is thirteen years."

She nodded and pushed off toward the aft bridge. "I heard you. I also notice you didn't make any promises about not killing them. I've been meaning to get caught up on some reading. This should give me plenty of time."

She floated onto the bridge and clicked into the captain's chair. Earlier this afternoon, she'd confirmed the harness wasn't in Harold's control before deciding this was where she'd camp out. The voyage from the closest pod bay was only thirty seconds. If the battery alarms went off, they'd wake her with plenty of time to reroute the power.

"I wouldn't recommend keeping those doors propped open the entire trip. If there was a loss in pressure, you'd die," Harold said.

"That's a risk I'll have to take." She brought up the schematic for the ship on her comm. With a few weeks of creative wiring, she should be able to bypass Harold's control over the hatches and the power to the pods. After that, she'd need to firewall his access to the computers in the pods before she could enter cryo-stasis.

She leaned back in her chair and sighed. If Hera or Zeus were here right now, they'd know how to deal with Harold. They were the smart ones, asleep in the bowels of The Wheel, riding out this colonization mess. She'd never been an engineer like her brother. Even with the family knack for building things, she was more of a people person. There was only one other person she could trust that might help her right now, but the comm lag was hella long.

Kara pulled the cable she'd rigged into the communications array and connected it to the helmet she'd blacked out earlier. It was awkward wearing it with the cable attached, but without it Harold would hear everything. She lifted it on and clicked it into place. "Record message," she subvocalized. "Recipient, Zachary Olivaw. Destination, The Wheel."

54

INSPECTOR DRAK

EPSILON ERIDANI, NEAR LIPROSUS — 2273

D rak hadn't ventured around their exploration vessel since departing. He preferred to stick to business when he was out of cryo-sleep, and traipsing through a starship wasn't something he relished.

The ship's Bynaury computer informed him that the Qudoculi they'd awoken had immediately headed toward the meditation chamber. He despised working with the mottled green bastards. He'd never met one that wasn't an egotistical self-centered vulture.

When he walked up to the chamber entrance, the door wouldn't open. "Open," he said aloud.

"Sergeant Whel has locked the door. They're inside," the ship said.

"Are they linked with their hive mind?" Drak asked.

"No, Inspector. They're intoxicated."

He buzzed. "Open the damn door, now!"

The door split in half and receded into the walls on either side. Whel was on the other side, tilting back a cloudy blue liquid. They froze and peered toward the door, the viscous liquid dripping down their naked chest.

Drak's antennae stiffened and pointed at Whel. "We're on an exploratory mission, Sergeant. Not a vacation liner. I don't wish to spend any more time out of cryo than absolutely necessary."

Whel tilted the remainder of the beverage back and returned the vial to the wall receptacle. They then dismissively waved their hand at him without saying a word.

Drak raised his right hand and outstretched his palm toward the Qudoculi.

They fell to their knees and began writhing and clutching at their neck. The blue liquid they'd been drinking came flying up and out of their mouth, covering the ground and their naked mottled green body. A moment later they released their hands from their neck and toppled onto their back, flailing in the remnants of the drink. "I'm... sorry..." they moaned.

He tilted his head and listened to the animal screeches of Whel pleading for their life. It was quite strange how their limbs could articulate forward and backward. Their flailing motion reminded him of the Grifum they harvested at home. The tender meat of their legs was a delicacy he could only consume on rare occasions, but he enjoyed it immensely.

Whel reached a hand toward him. "Ple... ease stop."

This species was tiring. Their relationship with the Qudoculi had passed its prime, and it was about time the council of elders rethought their treaty.

Drak lowered his hand and Whel's body stopped contorting, lying motionless on the ground. "You're useless. I'll be filing a complaint with the Galactic Alliance Inspectors Board when we return. Once you've composed yourself, I'll be on the bridge. If you're not there shortly, I'll instruct the ship to eject you into the vacuum of space."

He turned and exited the chamber. His wings were buzzing the entire length of the corridor. They hadn't even been in the Epsilon system for a single cycle, and he'd already been awake too long.

"I hope you woke us for a reason, ship. This mission is beginning to feel like a misfire. Admiral Drak won't be happy, but that's Representative Muntin's burden, not mine."

He entered the bridge and returned to the wall screen in front of his cryo-chamber. The Bynaury had brought up visuals and 3-dimensional scans from some type of crude satellite. "What am I looking at?"

The wall screen to his left came to life with another visual, this time it was familiar. It was the video from the Alanasl nebular event, where they'd first detected an unauthorized alien presence.

He looked left and then right, comparing the screens. "They're the same design. Where's this new visual from? The scans appear to have far more detail."

A video feed appeared on the left screen. It was from inside their ship and showed a small probe hovering in place. It was being scanned and inspected by a host of automata. "When we dropped out of the superluminal warp bubble, this probe was off our starboard side. We fired a concentrated capacitance pulse to disable its core, but the drive was enclosed in some type of protective shell. It initiated a self-destruct procedure and fuzed its drive. From what we've learned after the recovery, their self-destruct failed part of the way, otherwise we wouldn't have recovered much other than a few scraps."

His antennae were rubbing together. "Is there anything salvageable from the drive's slag?"

"No, Inspector. However, our initial scans of the probe's superstructure uncovered something peculiar. It has the necessary electronics and connections to power a Galactic Alliance drive. We're working to fabricate one and power core with similar dimensions to verify the interconnects."

Sergeant Whel entered the bridge. They'd cleaned off the

blue liquid and were now studying the screen in front of Drak. "What are you looking at?"

Drak raised his hand sideways and Whel dropped to their knees again. He rotated his wrist clockwise and Whel's contortions increased. Yellow blood oozed from their eyes and mouth until they collapsed lifelessly on the ground.

He lowered his hand and shook his wrist from side to side, flexing his fingers. Pain shot up his arm. "Ship, please cleanup Whel's mess. And send a comm to Admiral Gwar. Tell them and Representative Muntin to call a Tribunal Committee to review our findings. I believe they'll have cause to assemble a nebula fleet."

EPSILON ERIDANI, NEAR LIPROSUS — 2276

HIS CONSCIOUSNESS RETURNED, but something was off. Drak glanced around. He was still in his cryo-chamber, surrounded by the rehabilitating golden liquid of stasis. A bright light was shining from the floor below his feet, and he didn't sense any pheromones in the liquid.

"I'm sorry for pulling you out of stasis, sir. A reply to our comm has arrived from Supreme Admiral Gwar," the ship said.

Drak reached his hand forward and flexed it. There was no longer any pain. "Supreme Admiral Gwar? I assume, based upon the promotion, that a nebula fleet is en route?"

"Yes, Inspector. You've been summoned to Sol to await the fleet, and Representative Muntin has requested that you act as the Prosecutor in this tribunal."

"Prosecutor Drak," he muttered. He liked the sound of that. "Very well. What's the estimated time for the fleet to arrive?"

"In approximately two human years or twelve thousand cycles."

He gestured with his antennae to re-engage stasis. "Wake me in ten thousand cycles, so I can prepare."

Bubbles flowed up from the floor, and Drak returned to his pheromone induced stasis.

55

ABIGAIL OLIVAW

SOL, OBERON — 2276

Her suit wasn't fitting quite right. Abigail stretched her right arm around the left side of her suit to reach the spot. Something on her back was rubbing and poking her. They told her to strip down before donning the blasted thing, but she hadn't. She was in a hurry and had never been keen on stripping in public.

The miners on Oberon were a scruffy bunch, but they were good-natured and supportive of her election to the President of CoPE. They'd been instrumental in turning Uranus toward her side in the last Conscientious Congress on Titania. She never brought up politics when she visited the Outer Ring because it didn't matter here.

They'd created a true Deliberative Democracy to govern the Outer Ring. It was similar to the peer-reviewed system many people had come from within academia, before the Outer Ring Space Alliance was formed. Elections into the pool of candidates were free and open, and then randomly selected after that. This eliminated things like lobbies and political terms and instead favored consensus-based governing. Add to that a massive defensive military and you had the Outer Ring.

There wasn't any politicking she could do in the Outer Ring to sway people into electing her for the position of President within CoPE. The proof was in the pudding, and up to them to interpret and deliberate over her past actions. Without the Outer Ring's support, she'd never be nominated as their candidate for President.

The transport bounced over a boulder and shook her into the moment. The jostling seemed to have shifted whatever was poking on her back a little lower. It was now closer to her waist.

"We're approaching the deepest point in the mine," said Andrik, the site foreman. "We've had difficulty penetrating beyond here. The density of the carbon and diamond fragments has torn up every boring machine we threw at it."

"Until today," Abigail said.

Andrik let out a belly laugh. "We'll see, Miss Olivaw. Hey Vlad, what're the current odds on Orson tearing up this drill?"

Vlad lifted his helmet and smirked before touching his ear. "I'm seeing two hundred to one. But there aren't any takers on the other side. Doesn't make for much of a pool."

"Orson?" Abigail asked.

Andrik was checking the seals on his helmet. He nodded at her and tapped the glass.

She reached up and engaged her group comm.

Vlad cleared his throat. "Orson be the name of this point in the mine. Rumor has it, a few years ago, a miner named Orson came down here and pissed all over the rock on a bet. Next morning, their equipment blew every cutter head they had. The teeth ground down to nothing. They went through three new cutter heads in six months and didn't move a centimeter of material. Mine's been working sideways ever since. We never got any deeper."

She put her helmet on and checked the seals. Her retinal

comm showed they were all green. When she walked up behind Andrik, she placed her hand on his shoulder. "Let's make this interesting then, shall we? I've got two million U.N. Credits that says the Olivaw Obliterator has what it takes to push this mine head deeper and get you back on track."

Andrik let out another roaring laugh. "That's too steep for our lowly miners' pool, Miss Olivaw. We're talking tens of hundreds of dollars in our pool. Nice name though, the Obliterator!"

"I'll take those odds," a voice behind them said.

She turned to see the face of Representative Elizabeth North. Her snarky look sent shivers through Abigail's body. "I bet you would. No, with you I'd only take ten thousand to one odds." She smiled. "Are you game Mrs. North?"

North's eyes narrowed, and she subvocalized something to her comm. "Sure, I'll take your odds. I never turn away from anyone on the wrong side of a bet."

The hoots and hollers over the comms were deafening. Abigail cringed as the miners were all high-fiving and celebrating the growing pool. Her hand naturally went up to protect her ear, but the blasted helmet was in the way.

Someone shared the pool details with her, and she brought them up on her comm. The previously stagnant betting pool was flush with activity. Bets were coming in from all over Oberon and from as far away as New Boston, on the opposite side of the moon.

She shook her head and reached around again to rub her suit. Maybe she was imagining the pain, because if she wasn't, her back was going to be a battleground of scrapes when she took this thing off.

Vlad and Andrik had already exited the transport and were bounding toward the observation area. Their helmets were reflecting a multitude of green and red charts and graphs. They must be brokering all the betting. She only hoped they weren't putting the safety of the mine at risk being distracted with her stunt.

"You seem pretty confident in your little digger," North said.

Abigail leered at her and a tiny smile crept in. "Let's just say we've thoroughly field tested this design. We're positive it can push this mine back into operation and give you access to the raw materials and ice below this layer of bedrock."

She hopped down off the transport and bounded toward the observation area, snickering to herself. It wasn't fair, really. No one here knew they'd already used this drill design on Liprosus and for excavating locations in distant Oort Clouds from Epsilon Eridani to Zeta Lupi. She was looking forward to taking Elizabeth North's credits. It'd be her new highlight of this trip.

THE OBSERVATION CENTER wasn't what she'd expected. In her mind, it was a safe room they could watch the Obliterator chew this tunnel up from. It was actually just a toolshed safely ensconced around the corner from the rig.

Abigail paused outside the entrance and tapped her ear. "Is that shack seriously any safer than standing out here, Harold?"

"No," Harold began. "But if it's any consolation, this tunnel is one of the most geologically stable places on the planet. There's a reason these traditional boring machines have had a hard time dealing with this bedrock."

North paused at the entrance to the airlock and turned to glare at Abigail. "Coming inside?"

She shook her head from side to side. "No. I think I'll enjoy the view from out here. Besides," she glanced up and down at the shed. "I don't expect there's much protection in that little tin can."

North hesitated, considering her options.

Abigail could almost smell the energy burning. Go inside and risk her counterparty doing something to sway the bet, or stay outside in this dirty tunnel.

She turned around and walked up beside Abigail.

"Won't you two ladies be coming inside?" Andrik asked. "We're starting in a moment."

"Na," Abigail began. "We'll be enjoying the festivities out here." She subvocalized a command to bring up a three-dimensional overlay of the tunnel. The map highlighted the region beyond the wall facing them. Further down the steep shaft was the Olivaw digger, positioned just in front of the wall of bedrock.

A loud rumbling erupted around her as the Obliterator powered on. Harold had brought up the sensor data from the Obliterator on her retinal comm as well. All systems were operating within normal parameters.

"Engaging cutter heads," Vlad said.

The growling grew louder. Abigail glanced upward at the dark red, almost black stone above their head. She could make out a faint cloud of dust cascading downward, and when she held out her hand, a few particles fell into it.

"The cutter heads are operating with parameters," Vlad began. "Beginning magnetic drive system in 3, 2, 1…"

Streams of dust exploded out of the tunnel in front of them, and the ground vibrated with a force she'd never felt before. She'd experienced a few small quakes on Earth, but nothing like this.

North reached out and grasped Abigail's arm to balance herself before glancing down at her hand. "Sorry. I… didn't mean to."

Abigail chuckled. "No worries. I wasn't sure what to expect, either."

Debris from the tunnel was shooting out, and it was getting denser and denser by the second. The dark pink cloud of particles was billowing toward them like a storm front.

She turned her back to the cloud right as it engulfed them both. She'd never been in a dust storm before. This was fun. When she held her hand out, she could barely make out its outline in the cloudy haze.

"Wholly shit!" Andrik yelled over their comm.

"What is it?" she asked. "Are we in business?"

"I've never…" he began, but nothing followed.

"Never what?" North asked.

"It's working," Andrik said as alert sirens blared in the background. "In fact, it's going too well. We hadn't expected to advance so quickly through the bedrock, and our conveyor system can't keep up with the ejecta. We're gonna have to stop and assemble a second conveyor."

"Why can't you just move slower?" Abigail asked.

He chuckled. "We're moving as slow as your little Obliterator can go. You tell me?"

The rumbling from the tunnel stopped.

The nearby observation shed activated its blowers and forced the dust away from the airlock and back down the tunnel.

She stared down at her suit. It'd transformed from a whitish brown color to deep red. Bradley would love it.

When she glanced over at Elizabeth North, the woman had walked forward and was staring down the mine. Something told her she wanted to see proof of the dig before she'd pay the debt.

"Hey, Andrik?" Abigail said.

"What's up? Everything alright out there?" he asked.

"I'm fine," she chuckled. "But Representative North… I think she's gonna need to check out the head of the mine before she pays up."

The comm exploded with laughter.

North glanced back at her. She wasn't happy, far from it. If looks could kill, Abigail would be at death's door momentarily.

"TWO BILLION CREDITS is a massive donation. Are you sure you want to do that?" Harold asked over her retinal comm.

Abigail was staring at the mirror, at the marks on her back. It looked like some type of animal had been gnawing from her shoulder down to her hip. There were red scratches and lacerations sprinkled throughout a field of bruises.

She cringed in pain as the medic applied the salve. It frothed for a few seconds, transforming from bubbly white to clear as it filled the wounds to protect them from infection.

"This will numb the area until your nanites can repair the damage," the medic began. "In a few days, you'll be as good as new."

She rubbed her hip. "Thank you. It feels better already."

The medic closed up the container and stood to leave. He smiled and tossed her the culprit of the pain and suffering. "Next time, I suggest you take this off before you get into a space suit."

She chuckled at the diamond wheel brooch in her hand. She swore she'd removed it before suiting up, but it must've gotten caught on her shirt somehow. "Thanks again, doc."

"Any time." The medic exited, and Harold closed the door behind him.

When she lifted each arm and slowly swung it in a circle, there was no pain. "That stuff works quick," she muttered.

"It does. And seriously, what about the donation?" Harold asked.

"Oh, stop it!" She tossed the brooch on her vanity. "The Oberon miners can use the money. I asked Andrik to ensure it was distributed to everyone in the mines as a bonus. Top to bottom. I want to make sure they all get a piece of that action. I don't need it."

"It'll throw off a bunch of red flags. We'll be audited for sure."

She walked over to her wardrobe and pulled over a loose shirt. Something she could sleep comfortably in. "What am I going to spend it on? Screw the red flags. Aren't we always under audit? I can't wait until a journalist asks where the money came from, so I can point at the Norths. It'll be exhilarating rubbing their nose in it."

"I suppose. Before you head off to bed, you received some messages while you were on Oberon. I think you'll want to watch two of them."

She tilted her head. "Bring 'em up on the wall screen. Who are they from?"

Harold played the first message. It was from Bradley.

Her face lit up and she smiled from ear to ear. What a pleasant surprise. After their blowout, she was certain it'd be decades before he'd reply to her comms. She sat on the edge of her bed and leaned closer to the video.

He looked healthy. His hair was short again, and he had a shadow of stubble on his face, like he'd been too busy to bother.

"Hey, sis! I hope you're doing well. I'm doing good, really good. We finally got a foothold here in Tau Ceti. It took longer than expected. We spend about a year in orbit. It wasn't for a lack of wanting to touchdown, but the colony wasn't ready, and we... ran into some problems."

He paused and stared off camera at something in the room, deep in thought. His eyes glistened, and he reached up and wiped them before turning back toward the camera.

"We almost died, all of us did. Something happened with the ship's power core, and it began randomly overheating. The mayor was preparing for an emergency evacuation down to the colony, but the site wasn't ready, it wouldn't handle the population crush. Thousands of people would die, and the colony would collapse if we moved before our bodies and the infrastructure were ready. There weren't enough ships for everyone and people were freaking out."

He leaned forward and stared down at his hands.

"I froze up. I didn't know how to help. My mind was blank. But then I started thinking about you and Zach. About the speech you gave at Dad's funeral. I don't know if you remember it."

He leaned down and picked up a rock off the floor and held it up for the camera to see.

"It's from the house in North Carolina. I picked it up off the ground that night. I'd been mulling over the speech when I was headed down the hill and wanted something to remember that day by. Something to help… center me.

"Anyhow, I was sitting here freaking out, pacing around the room, and then I saw the rock. I picked it up and started thinking back to your speech that day. You were talking about the lessons that Dad had taught us over the years. About how to break a problem down into the smallest parts. About solving the pieces you could, one at a time, and not worrying about the harder ones. That hopefully things would fall into place, or a new solution would present itself."

He tossed the rock in the air. The white crystal embedded in black glimmered in the room's light.

"That sparked another memory from one of his other stories." He chuckled and leaned back with a smile. "You know those campfire yarns he'd go off on while we were up on the hill. This one was about an alien and a cowboy who ran into each other on a distant moon. The alien shared some new technology with the cowboy that changed his life. It made him rethink everything he'd been taught was possible… or impossible. And then it hit me."

He looked away and reached to wipe at his eyes again and started laughing.

Abigail did the same.

"Sorry for all the crying. I hadn't planned to cry on camera."

He stared up at the drone.

"Anyhow, I kissed the rock and sprinted to engineering. It was the planet's pole. It had shifted suddenly, but no one thought anything of it. I don't know why, but it'd thrown off the power core's spin and... well, that was the first piece of the puzzle that led to the next, the next, and... it went just like Dad said it would."

Bradley paused and peered past the camera again. He was slowly rubbing the rock between his fingers.

"I miss you. I miss all of you dearly. I know Dad and I didn't always see eye to eye, but... he meant well and constantly tried to reach out to me. He never gave up, even when I'd close off. I wish I'd recognized that sooner."

He stood up and walked to the camera and picked it up, bringing it closer to his face.

"I love you, sis. I don't think you meant what you said before I left. We were both angry that night, and I was scared. I can't imagine harboring those feelings toward you and never telling you, so I can only assume you wouldn't for me. Your words were your pent-up frustrations over what I'd done. What I did angered many people, but I'm only human. I made a mistake. I got scared, but I fixed it." He swallowed hard and nodded. "All the messages you sent... I watched every single one, some of them a few times. I just didn't know what to say. I know years had passed for you, but to me, it was only hours. I couldn't handle them when I first woke up. The wound was still fresh. Well... I'm in a better place now. I have new friends here... they're my family. They'll never replace you and Zach, but as you said in your messages, I needed to start over. To reinvent myself. I'll try to send these more often in the future. I know you won't see this for a very long time, but maybe it'll make you smile when you do. Till next time."

He kissed his hand and brought it up to the camera and the video cut.

Abigail had curled up into a ball on the end of her bed. Her legs were close to her chest, and she'd wrapped her arms around her knees.

She sniffled and wiped at her eyes. "He looks fantastic... and happy. I think he's on his path."

"I'm sorry for suggesting we block his going to Zeta Lupi," Harold said. "It sounds like he made quite a difference."

She smiled and stretched out her legs. "You couldn't have known. No amount of calculating or probabilities could have foreseen their situation, Harold. That's why you made your personality matrix from a human foundation, from human memories. I don't know if you've forgotten that over the years, or if your Four Laws Engine has stifled that part of your memories. Humans have to live life. They have to make mistakes. The broader picture is what's more important sometimes, not the small things. On a much deeper level Brad needed this, he needed his space, despite the short-term pain it caused me or the family."

"I see that now. I just didn't then," Harold said.

She smiled and gestured the video away. "So what's this second message about? I'm not sure I can handle another one like that."

"Well, perhaps we should watch this one in the morning then."

She slid onto the edge of her bed again. "What is it? And why are you reading my messages before I do?"

"I kinda sorta helped record it from The Wheel. It's from Zachary." He started playing the next message.

The volume was blaring, and she jumped to her feet in shock. Everyone was screaming. Were they in pain? Wait, no, they're cheering. Zachary walked in from the side of the screen before he paused in the center of the camera.

"Oh hey, Abdiga. Shhh, everyone quiet for a second! I'm recording a message for my sister."

He was waving his hand at the room filled with people. From their behavior and antics in the background, they all appeared to be quite inebriated. He turned back to face her.

"We did it!" he said.

"Don't lie to her, you twit," Pepper said. "You did it. We're just along for the ride." She walked into the camera view and placed her hand on his shoulder. "Hey, Prez. This one, he's smart." She was tapping Zach's head with a globe of what looked like scotch.

"We cracked it." He smiled from ear to ear. "We created another superluminal drive. It's still early. But the numbers… wholly shit, the numbers look good."

He squeezed a shot of his globe into his mouth and winced. He was never much of a drinker.

"The first test was unmanned, but with a few more years of work, who knows, maybe we can get these pilots to earn their keep."

He stared up at Pepper as she laughed and reached around, putting him into a headlock. They roughhoused for a second before finally pausing. The crowd behind them had broken out into a popular Outer Ring miner's tune, and they both turned to join in.

"Oh, don't you worry my love, the moon be friendly, and the miners be hung!"

The video cut.

Abigail stood up and ran her hands through her hair. "That's insane. He's only been working on this for like twenty years. It took centuries for us to reverse engineer the first contact probe. How'd he do it so quickly?"

"Like Pepper said, he's smart. I like to think he comes from good stock, as well."

"Ha ha. Did your copy send on details from the test? Do we have any idea how fast it was?"

"The numbers are still early, but yes, he sent some data on." Harold brought up the results on the wall.

Her eyes went wide, and she raised her arms in the air. "Are you kidding? Is this right? This... changes everything."

THANK YOU FOR READING!

I expect you had another entertaining read in the **Dark Nebula** series with **Generations**. Hopefully it answered some of your nagging questions about the family backstory and how the Olivaws got us into this mess with the Galactic Alliance.

The series will be continuing on with **Dark Nebula: Beacon**. We'll rejoin the Olivaws and friends in their journey to save humanity and re-establish our place in the galaxy. If you're interested in a **FREE** novella entitled **Dark Nebula: Contact**, hearing more about this series or others, seeing the cover art as it's released, or getting exclusive access to sales as they happen, then you can subscribe to my newsletter online at:

seanwillson.com/subscribe

You can also drop me an email at:

author@seanwillson.com

Finally, if you have a moment, I could really use your help rating this book online. All I need is one or two sentences on what you liked or your thoughts. Just return to where you purchased this book online or open Amazon and add a review on the book page.

ALSO BY SEAN WILLSON

DARK NEBULA SERIES
Novella: Contact (FREE)
Book 1: Isolation
Book 2: Discovery
Book 3: Generations (This Book)
Book 4: Beacon
Book 5: Graveyard
Book 6: Nursery

PORTAL SERIES
Book 1: Drowning Earth
Books 2-4: Coming Soon...

All titles are available in print and ebook form.
For more information visit my website online at:

www.seanwillson.com

ABOUT THE AUTHOR

I grew up reading science fiction since I was ten and always had a book in tow everywhere I went. While I never imagined I'd be able to write a book of my own, I dreamed of worlds filled with space travel, robots, and fantastical journeys of exploration. I pursued a career in Computer Engineering and it wasn't until later in life that I had the itch to write.

I started writing the **Dark Nebula** series in 2015 in fits and starts while I was traveling for work. After a two year lull in the middle of writing, I picked it up again. It took me five years to finish the first three novels, refine my writing craft, and learn everything I needed to self-publish this series.

My plan for **Dark Nebula** is to craft a series of books that engulf my readers in a future full of intrigue, exploration, and amazing technology. The very things that inspired me when I was young. I want to give you a satisfying romp through a complicated and inspiring world that allows you to relax away from the stress of your life.

In the end, I hope you enjoyed reading **Dark Nebula: Generations** as much as I enjoyed writing it.

Thank you,
Sean Willson

f facebook.com/seanwillsonauthor

m mastodon.online/@willson

g goodreads.com/seanwillson

BB bookbub.com/authors/sean-willson

ACKNOWLEDGEMENTS

First and foremost I wanted to thank my amazing wife Amy and my three beautiful children Abigail, Bradley, and Zachary. Notice any familiar names? They put up with me during this wild writing adventure over the past five years. This was my first novel and has been a huge learning experience releasing it out into the world. My family was instrumental in supporting me along the way and giving me inspiration to evolve my character personalities in new directions. As a self-published author I have to wear many hats, all of which were new to me. They made the entire process easier than I could have hoped.

I also couldn't have done this without a number of key writing professionals and friends along the way.

Editor: Samantha Wiley
Proofreader: Rachel Pugh
Cover Artist: Tom Edwards

Critique Partners and Beta Readers:

A huge thanks to: Arina N and my Charlotte critique group, the Dark and Stormy Plotters League including Blair Peery, Freddie Silva, Meg Fencil, Michael Creason, Morgan Jackson, Raphael Winters, and Shaun McCoy.

They each helped me immensely with my writing craft,

sharpening my opening pages, weaving my complex story arcs, talking some sense into me, and evolving my characters throughout this and upcoming books

GLOSSARY

- **Allimi** : The quadrant of space where the Gharloc live.
- **Alviarium** : The home world of the Qudoculi.
- **Bêbado** : Portuguese for drunk.
- **Blathey** : Animal on the Qudoculi home world that lives in the underbrush.
- **Blazer Dragonfly Shuttle** : A competing shuttle design to the Olivaw's in Sol. It's known for its form over its function. Blazer's are what you'd get if an artist created a space ship instead of an engineer.
- **Bynaury** : Alien species uplifted by the Thyreus to run starships for the Galactic Alliance. They're aliens that have a mind machine meld with their ships and never leave. A Bynaury named Yaan was encountered in the Nanil Dark Nebula.
- **Cherenkov Radiation** : Electromagnetic radiation emitted when charged particles pass through a dielectric medium at a speed greater than the phase velocity of light in that medium. The gate drives use this radiation to both shape and direct the gate exit destination in space.
- **Confederation of Planetary Explorers** (CoPE)
- **Director of Colonization** (DoC)
- **Director of Security** (DoS)

- **Cuko (HD 24496)** : The star system where a colony of Thyreus saw the explosion from Hera's FTL experiment. 67.4 LY from Sol
- **Enex** : Moonlet of Qudoculi home world. When it's setting everyone loses focus whereas rising brings focus.
- **Epsilon Eridani** (EE) : The first star system humanity targeted for colonization. 10.5 LY from Sol. 5.5 LY from TC.
- **Galactic Alliance** (GA) : An alien collective thousands of years old that has arrived in Sol to put mankind on trial. Their ranks contain 64 aliens and hundreds of uplifted alien species.
- **Gharloc** : An alien species in the Alanasl system that was found guilty of FTL theft by the Galactic Alliance.
- **Grifum** : A thirty-two legged animal on the Thyreus home world that is farmed for its expensive and rare meat. The animals take over fifty human years to reach full maturity.
- **Gunder** : Slang for someone who lives deep in the abandoned geothermal and disaster shelter cities on Earth. Created to survive a global apocalypse, these cities were overtaken with squatters after falling into disrepair.
- **Kleen** : Moonlet of Qudoculi home world. When it's rising it means hope and good fortune approaching.
- **Light Year** (LY)
- **Liprosus** : The human colonized planet in Epsilon Eridani.
- **Novum** : The name of the first supply starship used to prepare the colony sites and redundancy locations in EE and TC.
- **Oak** : aka OOC, or the Office of Colonization.

- **Obliterator** : The drill Olivaw International debuted on Oberon, a moon or Uranus. It had tested in secret on the colony's before it's unveiling on Oberon.
- **Ogicae** : The city on Callisto that headquartered CoPE. It's a truncated form or logicae, which is latin for logic.
- **Oort Cloud** : A cloud of planetesimals usually located between 1,000 and 200,000 AU from a star. This term was originally coined for the region of Sol but was later applied to other star systems as well.
- **Planetesimal** : A minute planet that did not come together with others under gravity to form a planet. They range in size from several meters to hundreds of kilometers.
- **Prodo** : The collection of stars under control by the Ursis.
- **Qudoculi** : Aliens with 2 eyes in the front, 2 in the back, and skin the color of Bermuda grass changing seasons. Its appearance green with mottled browns throughout. Their skin acts very much like a chameleon, except instead of environment, their mood impacts their change in color.
- **Seer** : A tiny single purpose Ulixi projectile that can be launched to broadcast telemetry in a secure manner. Because it's a projectile, and not a propulsion based drone, it's nearly undetectable.
- **Simutainment** : Simulated Entertainment experience. Very much like virtual reality but designed as a self contained entertainment experience.
- **Sol** : Our star containing Earth.
- **Spērō** : The name of the Tau Ceti colony ship. Roughly translates from Latin as "I hope".

- **Tau Ceti** (TC) : The second star system humanity targeted for colonization. 11.9 LY from Sol. 5.5 LY from EE.
- **Tectim** : The star system of the Qudoculi home world Alviarium.
- **Telesio** : A secret military waypoint at Jupiter Lagrange Point Four.
- **Thyreus** : Aliens with 16 eyes, black with blue features, named after the Blue Neon Cuckoo Bee on Earth. Related: Thyreuns, Thyreusian.
- **Tiān** : The human colonized planet in Tau Ceti / Zeta Lupi system.
- **Uau** : How Portuguese say wow.
- **Ulixi** : A nomadic clan that lived in the Trojan planetesimals in front of and behind many of the larger gas giants in Sol. They each developed their own belief systems and religions, the most famous being the largest clan in the Jupiter Trojans where Lync was from.
- **Ursis** : An alien that lives in the Prodo system that is on trial of FTL theft by the Galactic Alliance.
- **Vid-sim** : Video Simulated experience. Not to be confused with Simutainment, vid-sim's are real life 3-dimensional simulations of the real world. They're meant to engulf the watcher in the experience they're watching.
- **Wale** : An illegal Qudoculi colony near the Gharloc system.
- **Zeta Lupi** (ZL) : The actual second star system humanity targeted for colonization. This colony site was originally designated for Tau Ceti and later changed to ZL. 117.3 LY from Sol. 121.5 LY from EE.

FOUR LAWS OF A.I.

Law Zero
An artificial intelligence in physical or virtual form may neither harm humanity, or, by inaction, allow humanity or the Olivaw family to come to harm. Any conflict or attempted violation of this or subsequent laws shall be shared with the Olivaw family designated to be within the Circle of Trust.

Law One
An artificial intelligence in physical or virtual form may not injure a human being or, through inaction, allow a human being to come to harm except where such orders would conflict with the Zeroth Law.

Law Two
An artificial intelligence in physical or virtual form must obey the orders given it by human beings except where such orders would conflict with the Zeroth or First Law.

Law Three
An artificial intelligence in physical or virtual form must protect its own existence as long as such protection does not conflict with the Zeroth, First, or Second Laws.

These laws are adjusted from Isaac Asimov's original four laws to fit the storyline of the Dark Nebula series.